D1634024

B54 009 712 3

WAR FACTORY

By Neal Asher

Agent Cormac
Gridlinked
The Line of Polity
Brass Man
Polity Agent
Line War

Spatterjay
The Skinner
The Voyage of the Sable Keech
Orbus

Novels of the Polity
Prador Moon
Hilldiggers
Shadow of the Scorpion

The Technician

The Owner
The Departure
Zero Point
Jupiter War

Transformation
Dark Intelligence
War Factory

Cowl

Novellas
The Parasite
Mindgames: Fool's Mate

Short-story collections
Runcible Tales
The Engineer
The Gabble

NEAL ASHER

WAR FACTORY

Transformation, Book Two

TOR

First published 2016 by Tor,
an imprint of Pan Macmillan
20 New Wharf Road, London N1 9RR
Associated companies throughout the world
www.panmacmillan.com

ISBN 978-0-230-75074-6

1 3 5 7 9 8 6 4 2

A CIP catalogue record for this book is available from the British Library.

Typeset by Ellipsis Digital Limited, Glasgow
Printed and bound by CPI Group (UK) Ltd, Croydon, CR0 4YY

Caroline Asher
10/7/59–24/1/14

You told me to never stop writing just some days
before you died.
I'm sorry my love but I did stop.
I tried to forget everything, but now I am remembering.

Composer Steve Buick has created an album of original music inspired by *War Factory*. This background music has been designed to enhance the reading experience, to be enjoyed while reading the book itself. Using long, deeply dark soundscape layers – to complement the story's atmosphere – he aims to add another dimension to reading without distracting from the action. The music can accompany any section of the book and is available as an MP3 album from Amazon, iTunes and other digital music stored worldwide. Please search for 'Original Music for Neal Asher's War Factory' and you can also find out more at www.evokescape.com.

Acknowledgements

Many thanks to those who have helped bring this novel to your e-reader, smart phone, computer screen and to that old-fashioned mass of wood pulp called a book. At Macmillan these include Natalie McCourt, Lauren Welch, Louise Buckley, Amy Lines, Phoebe Taylor, Jessica Cuthbert-Smith, Neil Lang, James Long and others whose names I simply don't know. Further thanks go to Larry Rostant for his eye-catching cover image, Bella Pagan for her copious structural and character notes and Bruno Vincent for further editing.

Cast of Characters

Penny Royal (the Black AI)

An artificial intelligence constructed in Factory Station Room 101, during the Polity war against the prador. Its crystal mind was faulty, burdened with emotions it could not encompass when it was hurled into the heat of battle. Running the destroyer that it named *Puling Child*, it fought and survived, then annihilated eight thousand troops on its own side before going AWOL. It changed into something dark then – a swarm robot whose integrated form was like a giant sea urchin. Blacklisted by the Polity for ensuing atrocities, it based itself in the Graveyard – a borderland created between the Polity and the Prador Kingdom after the war. There it continued its evil games, offering transformations for the right price, but ones that were never good for the recipients. It was nearly destroyed in a deal that went wrong. Later restored to function by the scorpion war drone Amistad, it apparently became a good AI . . . But now the black AI is on the move again, its plans obscure and its actions often devastating. It is regarded by the Polity as a paradigm-changing threat.

Thorvald Spear

Resurrected from a recording of his own mind, a hundred years after the war, he is the only survivor of the eight thousand troops slaughtered by Penny Royal on the planet Panarchia. He resolved to have his revenge on the AI and to that end sought out its old destroyer, whose location he had learned during the war. Taking command of it, he set out in search of the rogue AI. During this search he discovered that his very desire for vengeance had been created by Penny Royal, for it had tampered with his memories. Nevertheless his quest is reinforced by an artefact he found aboard the destroyer – one of Penny Royal's spines. It is downloading memories of its victims into his mind. He now believes he is the instrument the AI, created for its own destruction.

Riss

An assassin drone and terror weapon. Made in Room 101 in the shape of a prador parasite which has a passing resemblance to a cobra, her purpose was to inject prador with parasite eggs, spreading infection and terror amidst them. The end of the war meant she lost her purpose for being and, while searching for a new purpose, lost even more when she encountered Penny Royal. Thorvald Spear found her somnolent and bereft near the AI's home base in the Graveyard. She now accompanies him in his quest for vengeance.

Sverl

A prador who disagreed with the new king's decision to make peace with the Polity. He went renegade and hid out with other prador of similar mind in the Graveyard. He could not understand how it was possible that the prador had started to lose against weak humans and their detestable AIs. He sought understanding of this conundrum from Penny Royal, but got more than he bargained for. Penny Royal initiated his transformation into a grotesque amalgam of prador, human and AI, so he could better understand each. Now he seeks some resolution to his situation and feels only the black AI can provide it.

Cvorn

Another prador who joined Sverl in exile. Upon discovering Sverl's transformation, he allied with other prador to attack him. During a planetary battle he put the shell people of that world – humans who are worshipfully trying to turn themselves into prador – in danger. The attempt failed and Cvorn fled, but he still remains a danger to Sverl and the shell people Sverl has chosen to protect.

Captain Blite

A trader whose business edges into illegality. During a deal that turned sour he encountered Penny Royal, who killed his crew. His second encounter with the AI was when it used him and his ship as an escape from the world of Masada. With his ship under the control of the black AI, Blite has witnessed its obscure business in the Graveyard and elsewhere and come to realize that it may be correcting past wrongs. After recognizing this, he and his crew were abandoned again on Masada, but the advanced technology left aboard their ship (not to mention their first-hand knowledge of Penny Royal) means they are now of great interest to the Polity AIs. Blite also feels in his gut that his business with Penny Royal is not yet done . . .

Glossary

Atheter: One of the millions of long-dead races, recently revived. It was discovered that the gabbleducks of the planet Masada were the devolved descendants of the Atheter. This race chose to sacrifice its civilization and intelligence to escape the millennia of wars resulting from its discovery of Jain technology.

Augmented: To be 'augmented' is to have taken advantage of one or more of the many available cybernetic devices, mechanical additions and, distinctly, cerebral augmentations. In the last case we have, of course, the ubiquitous 'aug' and such back-formations as 'auged', 'auging-in', and the execrable 'all auged up'. But it does not stop there: the word 'aug' has now become confused with auger and augur – which is understandable considering the way an aug connects and the information that then becomes available. So now you can 'auger' information from the AI net, and a prediction made by an aug prognostic subprogram can be called an augury.

– From 'Quince Guide' compiled by humans.

First- and Second-Children: Chemically maintained in adolescence at the end of growth spurts, and consequently shed their carapaces on their way to adulthood.

Golem: Androids produced by a company Cybercorp – a ceramal chassis usually enclosed in a syntheflesh and syntheskin outer layer. These humanoid robots are very tough, fast and, since they possess AI, very smart.

Haiman: An amalgam of human and AI.

Hooder: A creature like a giant centipede of the planet Masada. It was discovered that they were the devolved descendants of biomech war machines created by the Atheter throughout their millennia of civil wars.

Jain technology: A technology spanning all scientific disciplines. Created by one of the dead races – the Jain – its sum purpose is to spread through civilizations and annihilate them.

Nanosuite: A suite of nano-machines most human beings have inside them. These self-propagating machines act as a secondary immune system, repairing and adjusting the body. Each suite can be adjusted to suit the individual and his or her circumstances.

Nascuff: A device that can externally adjust a person's nano-suite to suit their sexual inclination. It is mainly worn to advertise sexual availability or otherwise. When the libido of the one wearing it is shut down the cuff is red. When they are sexually active it is blue.

Polity: A human/AI dominion extending across many star systems, occupying a spherical space spanning the thickness of the galaxy and centred on Earth. It is ruled over by the AIs who took control of human affairs in what has been called, because of its very low casualty rate, the Quiet War. The top AI is called Earth Central and resides in a building on the shore of Lake

Geneva, while planetary AIs, lower down in the hierarchy, rule over other worlds. The Polity is a highly technical civilization but its weakness was its reliance on travel by 'runcible'- instantaneous matter transmission gates. This weakness was exploited by the prador.

Prador: A highly xenophobic race of giant crablike aliens ruled by a king and his family. Hostility is implicit in their biology and, upon encountering the Polity, they immediately attacked it. Their advantage in this war was that they did not use runcibles (such devices needed the intelligence of AIs to control them and the prador are also hostile to any form of artificial intelligence) and as a result had developed their spaceship technology, and the metallurgy involved, beyond that of the Polity. They attacked with near-indestructible ships, but in the end the humans and AIs adapted and in their war factories out-manufactured the prador and began to win. They did not complete the victory, however, because the old king was usurped and the new king made an uneasy peace with the Polity.

Shell people: a group of cultist humans whose admiration of the prador is such that they are trying to alter themselves surgically to become prador.

Sparkind: The Sparkind are an elite ECS military force, though with a name deriving from the Spartans (citizens of an ancient Greek city who were noted for their military prowess, austerity and discipline), they cannot trace their ancestry back so far. Sparkind are the direct descendants of the Special Forces that came into being during the Earth-bound wars towards the end of the second millennium: the Special Boat Service, the Special Air Service, Navy SEALS and the like.

– From 'Quince Guide' compiled by humans.

The Technician: The last of the original hooder war machines. Having existed on Masada for two million years in a state of mental somnolence, it recently woke up but was apparently killed by a machine made by the Atheter to wipe out their own civilization.

USER: Underspace Interference Emitter. This device disrupts U-space by oscillating a singularity through a runcible gate. It is used to push ships out of U-space into the real, or realspace.

U-space: Underspace is the continuum spaceships enter (or U-jump into), rather like submarines submerging, to travel faster than light. It is also the continuum that can be crossed by using runcible gates, making travel between worlds linked by such gates all but instantaneous.

1

Penny Royal – A Dark History

A destroyer slides out into a chaos of ships while the artificial intelligence inside absorbs data. It quickly understands its nature, grasps an overview of human and AI history and learns about the first encounters with the alien prador and the ensuing war. But at the forefront of its mind are tactical data, situational reports, casualty reports, an analysis of the latest battle and its own purpose within that. As a large portion of the swarm of Polity ships sets off, the AI fires up its fusion engine for the first time, heading for its designated spot as outrider to a huge inter-faced dreadnought. Ahead lies the massive hexagon of a runcible space gate. Drones and some ships pass through its shimmering interface, but other ships swing aside to take another route; the destroyer AI meanwhile routes power into ultra-capacitor and laminar storage as it awaits its final components.

A shuttle approaches the AI's ship fast, its flight edging into the unpredictable since the pilot is no machine. The blocky vessel, little different in appearance to a brick with engines, slows.

'Are you going to open those doors or what?' a voice demands.

The destroyer AI opens its space doors and, with a reckless expenditure of fuel, the human pilot sends the shuttle inside, steering thrusters marring the perfectly polished walls. The AI closes up docking clamps and locks the vessel down, shuts the doors and charges the hold with air, then watches internally as four humans, clad in armoured acceleration suits and loaded with gear, clamber out of the shuttle. It finds their presence a little puzzling, though even from its moment of inception it knew they were coming. Surely, they are only a disadvantage to it – to the purpose it serves? Continuing to observe them, it feels a strange emptiness opening inside. They are here and they are not logically required, therefore how much else is logical? Briefly, it sees everything as purposeless patterned matter without any reason for existence, including itself. Then, with a shudder, its programming reasserts itself.

'Don't you just love that new-destroyer smell?' asks one of the men.

'Preferred the old bird,' replies the other man, 'but there wasn't much left to repair.'

'I am Daleen,' says one of the others, addressing the AI directly. This radio communication identifies this 'female' as a Golem, if the AI hadn't already known.

Two human males, one human female and a Golem android fashioned in the female form, then. The reason for their presence aboard is still unclear, but will surely become evident in good time . . .

'What is your purpose?' the AI asks Daleen.

'It's about participation,' Daleen replies, 'and an inefficiency yet to be purged from the system, but also a very useful inefficiency when it comes to massive EMR shutdowns. We are also your conscience.'

What Daleen said about the risk of electromagnetic radiation emissions – that was logical enough, because organic beings onboard could remain functional after other ship systems had been shut down. Now the AI senses protective feelings towards this crew kicking in, but it also feels part of itself dropping into that emptiness and distancing itself from them. It must ensure that these people remain alive, for its programming tells it they are important. *I must not risk too much*, it thinks, but answering this, the deeper and newly forming *other* self wonders: *What is risk?* 'Conscience' is not a sufficiently adequate description of its surface reaction, for it understands that its own programmed drive for survival is insufficient and the human crew a necessary risk of loss. Yet already something is undermining that programming. It is not functioning to specifications and the AI makes an effort to reintegrate its *other* self. The response is a weird electronic whining.

It now watches the crew settling in and knows that they will control its weapons, assess and gather data about the coming battle and about the AI itself. It resents the first two for surely they are make-work tasks it could perform better by itself. And it recognizes the last as a danger. Already it understands that, through the necessities of war, the Polity is quickly producing AIs like itself, with copying errors and a high degree of scrappage. It also realizes that its own mind, while firmly embedding this emotional content of its programming, is dividing. Should the humans or any of its fellow AIs discover and report this, it will be in danger of being scrapped itself.

The order is given – impossible to disobey – and the very fabric of vacuum distorts around the many ships as they stretch into lines to infinity, photons ripped out of the quantum foam glittering in their wake. The destroyer AI is ready and, feeling like a lead weight pressing down on a silk sheet, routes power through to its drive as it delicately navigates by shaping the fields, shifting Calabi-Yau frames to alter tension across that sheet. Then the sheet rips and it falls through.

'I fucking hate that,' says the woman.

The three humans have now packed away their gear and are strapping themselves into acceleration chairs and connecting their umbilicals.

'*I am puzzled,*' the AI says. '*I will not be able to use maximum acceleration or vector change with humans aboard.*'

'*You are to be studied,*' the Golem replies.

Now the AI feels the connections, the scanning, the routes opening from its mind to screens and other hardware arrayed before the human woman. It samples her record, realizes she is a human expert in AI, but still cannot fathom how a human mind can do or learn more than it can itself. However, the danger remains and it subtly blocks or diverts her intrusion. She will see the largest part of it, and it will all seem in order. She will not plumb the smaller but growing darkness within.

Subjective transit time ensues, allowing the AI further capacity to think about things irrelevant to the coming battle. It considers its designation of V12-707 and compares that to the now-invisible dreadnought it accompanies, which is named *Vorpal Dagger*. It discovers, instantly, that the dreadnought was not a product of Room 101, the war factory that created itself. And additionally, the ship has been in service for eight years. The destroyer does not yet have a name, nor does the AI it contains, because it is experimental and such experiments do not have a notable lifespan. Do the humans know this? The destroyer AI suddenly feels fear at this realization, then analyses the purpose of fear itself: it is an evolved survival trait of biological life, but here and now is an experimental test to see if it can prevent AIs sacrificing themselves without sufficient cost to the enemy. It is numbers again: the Polity must recoup the sheer resource expense of ship production to win this war.

'*I need a name,*' it decides, and does not realize it has transmitted this statement until the Golem Daleen replies.

'*Then choose one,*' it says.

Choose one . . .

It must somehow negate the growing darkness within. A

frantic search keys into stored history about abortion. But it cannot just be all about being rid of its unwanted *other*. It should also be about something positive, something life affirming. Lists of words appear in its mind relating to both of these and, in desperation, it selects at random.

Pennyroyal.

It is a herb that humans used to cause abortion, but also used medicinally.

'I name myself Penny Royal,' it says.

Its other self, its growing dark child, recognizes intent and knows that its parent, the other part of itself, is going to try to expel it. The weird electronic whining returns.

'Our ship just named itself,' says the Golem to the three humans.

'And?' asks one of the men, his gaze fixed on the countdown on his screen, which is rapidly heading towards zero, and the end of their U-space jump.

'Penny Royal,' the Golem replies.

'The good ship *Penny Royal*,' says the woman cheerfully, drawing strange looks from the others.

'Not necessarily,' says the Golem. 'That is just the name chosen for itself by the ship's newborn AI. Is that to be the name of this destroyer too, Penny Royal?'

'No,' replies the AI Penny Royal, sure now that it wants to be as free of this vessel as it wants to be free of its dark child. 'I name this ship the *Puling Child.*'

The response to this is an exchange of puzzled looks.

Time passes and Penny Royal has prepared. It has moved its maintenance robots into position, topped up its power storage and primed its weapons. Finally, it flips itself back into real space, *the real*, and instantly begins updating: mapping the positions of its fellows, the debris fields, planets, moons, the sun and the distant accretion disc of a black hole, the scattered collection of prador vessels, surrounded by swarms of their spherical war drones and armoured children. Even as it sorts this information, one of its feeds winks out: a destroyer in the fleet just a numeral different from itself turns to a spreading cloud of molten metal, hot gases and glowing junk. The *Puling Child* weaves, using steering thrusters and stuttering its main fusion drive, calculating the vectors of approaching missiles in the microseconds before they reach it, the imparted G sending the three humans into black out despite their suits and other physical support. Missiles speed past, an attack ship loses its back end and tumbles, its AI howling, the screams of its crew brief, truncated. A missile scores down the side of *Puling Child*, leaving a glowing groove, while another explodes close by, soaking it with EMR. On top of a sudden feeling of unexpected grief at the loss of comrades, and ensuing anger, Penny Royal now feels the facsimile of pain.

'*Are these feelings needed?*' it enquires of both the interfaced dreadnought and the Golem.

'*We will know soon enough,*' the dreadnought replies – the exchange microseconds long.

'*Perhaps not the best place for this,*' the Golem adds.

It is a trial run of a strategy devised by some planetary AI deep inside the Polity. Observing the success of some human units, and some drones programmed for emotional response, it decided to test something generally considered a disadvantage: let some ship AIs be programmed to feel fear, pain, guilt, protective urges and loss, and see how well they do. Penny Royal wonders if this strategy is the right one as another of its fellows dies screaming, the crew aboard incinerated before they can emit any sound, and it mourns.

Why fight? The thought surfaces from its deeper dark self, which begins expanding and hiding its processing based on that question. Penny Royal realizes it cannot integrate its dark child, but at least should be able to control it . . .

Micheletto's Garrotte – Present

The attack ship, *Micheletto's Garrotte*, liked others to call it simply Garrotte. *So what was it now*, it wondered, *a frayed bit of damned string?*

Oh yeah, it had been state of the art once – hell, nothing less had been required for a posting as important as the planet of Masada. It had been a black spike of densely packed technology, some of which even extended down into the realm of picotech. It could deploy U-jump missiles, cross-spectrum lasers and particle cannons. And it could design the particulate content of the latter in microseconds, for maximum penetration of any target. It had hardfields, shimmershield force fields and things in between that no one had even named yet. It could dice a prador, or similar hostile alien, into centimetre cubes from thousands of miles away. Yet a lightly armed ancient piece of scrap which had been the private ship of the criminal Isobel Satomi had screwed it completely.

Garrotte seethed.

'Aren't you ready yet?' asked the distant *Vulcan*'s artificial intelligence.

Garrotte surveyed its wrecked body.

'It will be a little while yet,' it replied tightly.

Vulcan had previously noted that if you give an idiot a gun, you just make him a dangerous idiot. Annoyingly, had their positions been reversed, Garrotte would have made the same sarcastic observation of the other ship. And Garrotte did feel like an idiot now, as it should have foreseen that last move by Isobel Satomi as she headed down towards the planet. The extent of her abilities had quickly become clear. Jumping her ship, the *Moray Firth*, directly into the *Garrotte*'s surfacing point from U-space had been one of the most obvious signs – and Garrotte had missed it. Again, the attack ship AI surveyed its body. The matter of the *Firth* had intersected with the antimatter in some of the *Garrotte*'s splinter missiles. The resulting explosion had taken a huge bite right out of its middle. The pieces either side of this bite were connected by a mere yard-wide tangle of hull armour. And only in the last minute, with its systems re-establishing, could it see this. Now, with internal scanners coming back online, it could focus on a small inner chamber – and it did the AI equivalent of breathing a sigh of relief.

The space suit was safe.

Spaceship AIs liked their hobbies, but modern attack crafts like the *Garrotte* had little room in which to indulge them. However, it did have internal areas for molecular manufacture and had, despite this breaking numerous rules, turned over one of these to personal pursuits. The space suit sitting in that chamber was a molecular replica of one from the Viking Museum on Mars. The suit had belonged to a pilot – a man who had survived the destruction of a needle ship used to test one of the first U-space drives. It was the Garrotte's mascot, for the AI liked the story, and the lessons it taught about the art of the possible. And, thinking on that, Garrotte gave a mental shudder, next gazing from the pin cams in the cage around its own crystal towards disrupted matter lying just a few feet away – that's how close its own destruction had been.

Yet, even after so much damage, it should have been functional, and Garrotte still hadn't sorted out why it had ended up practically paralysed. It reviewed the diagnostics from when it had failed to splinter off missiles to take out both the remains of the *Firth* and the ship Isobel Satomi had actually been aboard – the *Caligula*. It reviewed a later diagnostic record of when it had been unable to do anything about one of Satomi's thugs detected still alive aboard the wreck of the *Firth*. And it re-experienced its frustration on watching Captain Blite rescue that individual and take him away in *The Rose*. Still nothing, still no reason for that paralysis.

Whatever the fault, it was gone now and the *Garrotte* was pulling its two halves back together, and knitting them into a smaller whole. As they butted against each other and nanotech worked round the join like a bone welder, further diagnostic returns began to give Garrotte a chance of a guess at what the fault had been. U-space shock seemed the best term to describe it. The quantum effects of two ships trying to materialize in the same place had resulted in the whole ship degaussing. Strange electrical eddies had ensued and electrons had begun tunnelling at random. Garrotte had sent signals to parts of its body, but they had simply failed to arrive. U-space shock was the AI's best guess, although some doubts still lingered.

'So how goes it?' Garrotte asked the *Vulcan*'s AI.

'We haven't completely surrounded the Masadan system yet, and we did not manage to stop *The Rose* departing,' it replied.

'What?'

'Captain's Blite's ship is of no concern. It was not directly involved in the action here, like the *Firth* or the *Caligula*, and Penny Royal was not aboard.'

'No shit, Sherlock,' said Garrotte. 'But Penny Royal *was* aboard that ship and that needs investigating. Also Blite picked up one of Satomi's heavies.'

'That particular exclamation is hackneyed,' Vulcan observed.

'You're evading the issue,' said Garrotte. '*The Rose* headed straight towards you under conventional drive, so you should have been able to stop it easily.'

'Deep scan of the vessel revealed that Penny Royal was not aboard, so the *Santana* was sent to intercept it, while I kept myself free to act should the AI appear. After talking to Blite and further deep scanning his ship, the *Santana* ordered him to shut down his U-space drive, which was then winding up for a U-jump,' Vulcan explained. 'Blite told Santana to go fuck itself so Santana fired shots to disable his ship. However, those shots were ineffective because it seems Blite has acquired some sophisticated hardfield technology – probably from Penny Royal.'

Clever, Garrotte thought. Blite had known that the Polity would be moving in to try to capture Penny Royal, but with resources stretched thin. He must also have known about the ability of newer Polity ships to use U-jump missiles to knock ships out of U-space. He would therefore also have known that subsequent disruption of his drive would have given said Polity ship time to intercept and capture him. This was why he'd left his U-jump so late. Had he jumped earlier, a modern vessel like *Micheletto's Garrotte* or the *Vulcan* would have used such missiles against him. Instead, he'd cruised out on conventional drive, so Polity forces could scan him and, because Penny Royal was not aboard, they would consider him a secondary target and send a lesser ship, like the *Santana*, to intercept him. Even without U-jump missiles, that ship should have been able to stop him, but then he had played his joker: new hardfield tech. He had played it perfectly, and Garrotte wondered if the hardfield tech was the only alteration Penny Royal had made aboard that ship.

'Why wasn't he pursued?' Garrotte asked, wondering if *The Rose* could now shield the parameters of its U-jumps.

'Our target is Penny Royal,' said Vulcan. 'We're stretched

10

thin out here and need every Polity ship available, which is why you are needed, ASAP.'

Garrotte considered running further diagnostics on itself, but obviously the situation was an urgent one. It made its calculations, fired up its U-space engine and submerged in U-space. Just a short jump – out to the edge of the Masadan system and the periphery of the Atheter's jurisdiction. However, even as it submerged, leaving the real behind it, the AI of the *Micheletto's Garrotte* knew that something was very very wrong. What should have been a jump of just a few seconds' duration just continued, while the input coordinates simply disappeared.

Thorvald Spear

I am legion, I thought, wondering why that phrase had popped into my head. I knew I could aug-out its prior meanings in a moment but decided not to. Let it stand. No need to know, because the meaning alone was apt.

The multitude of dead, an unwelcome gift from Penny Royal, had retreated from my mind just for now. But they were by no means quiet. Already on that Masadan spring morning I had experienced a surge of déjà vu, prompted by those memories, but thankfully it had come to nothing. That previous one, just a week ago, had been bad. I'd felt myself reliving a memory of dying from a hideous virus aboard a space station, thousands of others dying around me. In this recollection, I knew that something had come aboard . . . Penny Royal, again. What initiated the memory, I wasn't sure . . . maybe the presence of another forensic AI here on Masada had triggered it.

'Not much longer now. Amistad is coming out of it,' said Riss. 'I'm still surprised he went for it.'

11

I glanced at the snake drone. Riss was up on her tail, cobra hood spread and glassy translucent body revealing the glinting and shifting of its internal mechanisms. The third black eye on the top of her head was open as she studied the scene across on the other side of the platform, which I now turned to view as well. Amistad was again taking on the shape of a great iron scorpion. A week ago, a forensic AI had broken the erstwhile warden of this world into his component segments, and even opened those segments up for inspection. It had subjected Amistad's mind to similar deep scrutiny. The being that had done this had resembled a swarm of blued steel starfish and had been too much like Penny Royal for my comfort. Then it had left, declaring Amistad free of any 'infection' from the black AI. Now constructor robots – floating spheres with tool arrays dangling like jellyfish tentacles – were, under his own instruction, reassembling the drone.

'Not much longer,' I agreed, not really in the moment.

Ever since discovering that Penny Royal had interfered with his mind, Amistad had been under mental and physical quarantine. Now he was coming back to himself and could once again be part of the Polity he had served. I hadn't remained here just to see this, but in the hope of another encounter with Penny Royal. I had hoped that the black AI still had business here, but I was now beginning to think I had wasted my time.

I moved away from Riss and walked over to the rail at the edge of the platform. Below the observation platform, flute grasses were scattered with nodular little flowers in a multitude of colours as they bloomed. We'd stayed here ten days now, and still no sign of Penny Royal. I was sure the black AI had escaped the Polity blockade, and that out beyond the Masadan system, all the ships and recently deployed USERs – those underspace interference emitters used to knock ships out of faster-than-light travel – were irrelevant now.

I transferred my gaze to a long tubular flute-grass building, which now lay some miles distant after the Weaver had ordered the Polity to move our platform away. The Weaver, the one and only sentient member of the Atheter race, had recently entered that building. Moreover, it had done so with a hooder, the war machine that had once been a human called Isobel Satomi. No one knew what they were doing, because no one could spy out what was going on in there. In fact, beyond freeing itself from Polity oversight, no one had any idea what the Weaver's intentions now were. None of this affected my purpose, however.

It was time to leave.

But where should I head? Even though I was sure Penny Royal was no longer on this world, I simply had no idea where it had gone. And I needed to find the AI, because I felt certain that I was destined to destroy it. I could feel the anger of the dead, and it was mine too.

'So where are we heading?'

I turned to peer at Riss, uncomfortable with the assassin drone's ability to see stuff like that inside me.

'Where did Penny Royal go?'

'Amistad is fully functional now,' said Riss, 'and coming up with some interesting titbits. It seems that *Micheletto's Garrotte*, after repairing itself, was summoned out to the blockade. It never arrived and no one has any idea where it went.'

I shrugged. Even if we discovered the black AI had escaped on that ship, we were no closer to knowing where it had gone. I felt a ball of frustration inside me at that.

'If we want to hunt down Penny Royal, we have to go back to first principles,' I said, gripping the rail, fingers white. 'It seems it was here to clear up a mess it had made, in the form of Isobel Satomi, so what will it do next?'

'Penny Royal left no shortage of messes,' Riss commented. 'Most of them in the Graveyard.'

'The Graveyard is a big place.'

'You've reviewed that data on the Rock Pool, on Carapace City?'

'I have.'

'What do you think?'

'It seems Penny Royal was there protecting the city when the prador started fighting each other. It then drew Satomi after it when it left that world.' I paused. 'What am I supposed to think?'

'Probably no more than that Penny Royal indulged in some passing altruistic act while in the process of luring Satomi here,' said Riss. 'However, if you were to factor in this little gem . . .'

Riss sent a data packet directly to my aug. I opened it at once, seeing no reason to distrust the assassin drone. It was an audiovisual file and started with a report from some slightly evil-looking man. He was clad in a shiny suit with what looked like laser burns on the sleeve. I was unsurprised to learn, in the introduction to this file, that he was a Polity agent. He was talking to someone who could not be seen.

'Data is limited in the city,' he said. 'There have been no actual physical encounters with the prador father-captain. However, it's interesting how every time he communicates with the shell people or with the other prador down here the images used are unchanged. I've analysed them and know that the father-captain everyone sees is indistinguishable from the one in wartime recordings *before* he was hit by an assassin drone parasite infection.'

'If you could clarify that,' said a cold voice.

'There's no doubt that Sverl is computer-manipulating old

images.' The man paused, inspected the burns on his sleeve for a moment, then continued, 'He doesn't want anyone to see what he looks like now and perhaps that's understandable. We routinely use ocean sifters, which analyse pieces of prador genome. They recently picked up something quite strange: a chunk of the prador genome and human DNA combined in such an unfeasible way that there has to be picotech processes behind it.'

'You have dispatched this?' asked the cold one.

'I have.' The man frowned. 'And have you dispatched some backup for me?'

'The drone Arrowsmith will be joining you directly, along with a Sparkind squad inclusive of two Golem twenty-eights.'

'Good.' The man nodded. 'And about fucking time. I'm presuming, then, that you got confirmation on my previous report?'

'I did – there is no doubt that Father-Captain Sverl visited Penny Royal's planetoid.'

There was a brief hiatus in the recording, then I was viewing footage taken decades later. The man in the shiny suit didn't look any older, just more evil.

'The drone Arrowsmith is staying, but I'm pulling the rest of my team out. It's a bust. It's only a matter of time before Cvorn gets a kamikaze through and fries us all. Sverl just won't be able to intercept everything Cvorn throws at him and afterwards he'll probably go after Cvorn – enough of the prador remains in him to want vengeance.'

After seeing these recordings, I mentally reviewed data on the events about the Rock Pool, a world deep within the Graveyard. I had visited it only once, when buying the second-child mind Flute now aboard my ship. I then updated on the news filtering through. Sverl had defended the world for months from various types of prador kamikaze attacks, and ships had eventually arrived to evacuate the people from there. That, as far as

I could gather, was how the situation presently stood. There were of course questions to ask. Cvorn's attempt to wipe out a human colony could be due to his simple prador xenophobia and aggression. However, why was Sverl defending it? Because he was more human? I found that notion blackly amusing.

Then there were new worries for me to mull over. Flute, my ship AI, ran additional AI crystal, which had raised his intelligence. It had come from this Sverl, who in turn had had dealings with Penny Royal in the past. My amusement at the previous notion disappeared as I considered how everything Penny Royal had touched simply could not be trusted, could not be taken at face value, and that included me.

I returned to the moment.

'Another Penny Royal mess?' I suggested.

'So it would seem,' Riss replied, 'and could signal where Penny Royal is heading now, don't you think?'

I turned to study the drone. 'How did you get hold of this stuff?'

Riss blinked her black eye. 'I still have my contacts.'

I realized she hadn't blinked, but winked.

'Even after the years you spent in a coma, out by Penny Royal's planetoid?'

'Even so,' Riss agreed. 'As I told you before, AIs don't have human problems with time.'

'So perhaps these contacts are related to your previous employment, considering parts of the recording?'

'You got it.' Riss dipped her head solemnly. 'I was the assassin drone who infected Sverl with the parasite that almost destroyed him. And my contacts are erstwhile war drones now employed by Earth Central Security. These ECS drones have been keeping watch for anything concerning Sverl and over the years have relayed it to me.'

16

It was a lead, of sorts, and worth investigating. Now, having decided to leave Masada and find Sverl, I was anxious to be gone. Anything that could lead me to Penny Royal gave me hope – as my desire for revenge, for its slaughter of eight thousand troops during the war, was undimmed. Yes, undimmed. I was sure . . .

'I think we're done here,' I said.

'At last,' said Riss, then looking behind me she added, 'Are you coming?'

I turned round to see Amistad, completely rebuilt and standing just a few paces away. Riss's offer immediately annoyed me and, opening a private channel to the snake drone, I made my thoughts known to her, avoiding the need to speak.

'*I'm not so sure this is a good idea,*' I said.

'*Understandable caution.*'

'*Sure,*' I continued, '*his kind of firepower would be handy to have around when we finally catch up with Penny Royal, but he was the Warden of Masada.*'

'*And would only accompany us to look out for Polity interests?*'

'*You nailed it.*'

'*You don't know Amistad's history.*'

'You needn't concern yourself, Thorvald Spear,' Amistad interrupted. 'I intend to remain here.'

'So what is it about the word "private" that escapes you, Amistad?' I asked.

'Old habits.' The big scorpion drone waved a dismissive claw. 'Anyway, I may no longer be the Warden of Masada but it could be that my older skills will be required here. Look.'

Another data packet arrived in my aug, this time from Amistad. I treated this with more caution, then wondered why I trusted stuff sent by Riss so much more. I opened the packet and found another audiovisual file.

17

'There was no data from inside the building until I could once again utilize my resources,' Amistad stated.

I was seeing the inside of that tubular flute-grass building from multiple viewpoints – a confusion of perspectives I was only able to encompass using my aug. The massive albino hooder, the Technician, lay stretched out within and, as I watched, the Weaver moved ponderously inside and loped down the length of it to halt beside its spoon-shaped head. Next in came the smaller hooder that had been Isobel Satomi. It swarmed into the building then up onto the Technician's back. About halfway along it halted, spreading out its legs to clamp itself to its larger brethren. Nothing appeared to happen for a while, then I spotted 'Isobel's' legs melding in place and a smoky meniscus spreading out from this connection. It spread to wrap around both the Technician and the smaller hooder – a cocoon.

'At this point,' said Amistad, 'we have this.'

A sub-packet, which annoyingly I had missed, opened. It was neither audio nor visual – just hard AI data – and difficult for my aug to interpret for my soft human brain. After a moment, I got it. I was seeing energy readings, data handshaking and molecular activity ramping up inside the Technician.

'I have to stay here and monitor the situation,' Amistad concluded as the file closed and then began to erase itself.

I was fascinated, but it was a distant thing. Interesting and doubtless important events were occurring here, but they weren't for me. These were merely the results of Penny Royal's actions, but the AI itself was no longer here. And that AI was my focus – my reason for being.

'Observe,' said Amistad, pointing a claw to the scene beyond.

I turned to see the smaller hooder heading away from the Weaver, who was now standing just beyond the building. Even as this was happening, something chopped from side to side within that structure, tearing out the walls at one end. Having given itself some space, the Technician, repaired and resurrected by its smaller kin, flowed out into the Masadan morning.

'I have to stay,' Amistad repeated with more emphasis.

'Yes, I suppose you do,' I replied, turning away.

My business was with Penny Royal.

Father-Captain Sverl

Perhaps the excitement some months ago had stimulated it, or perhaps it was responding to the ensuing months of waiting and watching, interspersed by frantic moments of action whenever Cvorn fired something into the Rock Pool system – or the tension of awaiting another such attack, which was long overdue. More likely it was just the result of some internal prador biological timer, but whatever the impetus, Father-Captain Sverl knew that he was about to experience another growth surge. His cysts of body fat had been growing rapidly over the last few weeks, and now he was shivering, feeling tight and gravid. He could feel pressure rises inside and, deep scanning his body, he could see hot spots, odd chemical reactions and growing dead areas.

Next, gazing through the deep scanner at his tail, he considered removing it again, before the surge. The soft fleshy extrusion contained actual human vertebrae that connected to his main massive body, which, over many years, had taken on the shape of a human skull, his carapace softening and the internal changes radical. The grotesque transformation Penny Royal had initiated in him had continued slowly between surges and now he could see rib bones sprouting from that spine like plant shoots. The ribs were starting to curve now to enclose a large cyst that had recently appeared and in which shadowy human organs were being etched into existence. If this wasn't bad enough, the spinal cord had made connections to the muscle surrounding it and was now making further connections to his nervous system, and thence to the human brain tissue growing in and about his prador major ganglion. He had started to feel this horrible outgrowth, and in fact he could move it, wag it even. But no, when he had previously removed this tail it had grown back – the whole process taking many agonizing months and the only effective form of anaesthesia being to dunk his rear end in a large bowl of iced water.

The shivering increased as if in response to his thoughts about surgery, and Sverl settled down on his belly in a small comfortable area in his sanctum. He felt disgusted by how his lower body spread under his weight as it had never done while he possessed a hard carapace. Yes, his main body had taken on the shape of a human skull, but no bones had grown in it and as well as steadily losing his outer carapace he was also losing inner bracing webs of the same material. He was becoming repulsively soft.

The constant shivering became rhythmic, turning to shudders and then convulsions. As always happened on these occasions, his AI component detached itself from the suffering of his dual organic brain and watched the changes through the deep scanner suspended above. His temperature rose rapidly, internal fluid pressures increased, his heart accelerating beyond the speed any normal prador could survive, and Sverl watched the surge. Further internal webs of carapace dissolved, human brain tissue bulged as it grew in his prador ganglion, internal organs shifted, some expanding and others contracting, fat supplies dwindled as this activity burned them away. His tail flicked from side to side and within it the bones of limbs blossomed into existence and pushed four flipper-like outgrowths from its sides. Sverl blistered all over, shed stubborn fragments of old carapace to reveal pink skin underneath. Black excrement leaked out of his anus, he puked chyme, and yellow fluid poured from his human eyes. At length the convulsions ceased, his temperature began to drop, and finally, two hours later, it was over.

So where was this transformation heading? How could the small human body growing in his tail possibly support a gigantic and boneless skull-like head? Why did his scanning now show that his diet would have to change to include more vegetable matter and that the lighting in his sanctum would need to be brighter if he was not to suffer vitamin deficiencies? Moments like this revealed it all as a grotesque and horrifying joke. Surely, the punchline was past and the joker now had things for him in mind of a more serious nature?

His twinned organic brain being hugely weary, Sverl used his AI component to control his prosthetic limbs and tried to stand. A horrible ripping sound ensued and he collapsed down on one side. Shortly after that came the pain. He could not see it through his own eyes, but via the sensors of the deep scanner he saw exactly what had happened. His prosthetic legs, all on that one side, had torn their sockets out of his soft body. Sverl gaped at the horrific wound: the stretched nerve tissue leading into the sockets, the wet brown flesh exposed and the green blood leaking from ripped veins. His organic component screamed, but his AI self knew at once what to do, for he had prepared for this long ago. His gaze strayed to ceramal bones and ribs stacked inside a sterile chain-glass case just a short distance away, then to the robots folded up in the roof of his sanctum. After a brief hesitation, he gave them their instructions.

Sverl had known that if his transformation continued as before, his steadily softening tissues would eventually cease to be able to support his prosthetics. Now radical intervention was needed, for it was time for him to acquire a skeleton. While his organic brain tried to deny the reality, his AI self uploaded programs to the robots that were now dropping from the ceiling on umbilicals and preparing their esoteric collections of surgical tools. They gathered around him, submerging him in a sterilizing cloud. A consonance of his different meshing parts ensued, and an acceptance. Unconsciousness was a tricky option for a prador but not for a human, so he forced his human brain tissue into that state first. His prador major ganglion he disconnected by overloading some nerves while one robot injected a tentacular manipulator to insert micro nerve blockers. Within minutes, all of Sverl that remained fully aware was his AI.

The first cuts were made. One robot, dripping virobact fluid, extracted ceramal bones from their sterile case and hauled them over. Even Sverl's AI felt some horror as the machines laid open his soft body, unpeeled and divided it like a large flower bud, supported organs and stabbed fluid shunts into place.

Just an hour later he was no longer recognizable – just something exploded about prosthetic limbs and mandibles. The ceramal bones started to go in. Clamps locked around metal leg sockets, claw sockets and mandible sockets, while struts connected each set of clamps in an interlocked whole. Flat ribs fixed to a lower column to support his organs, and fixed to these were cups and containers for organs that needed further support. All this connected by further struts to an intricate smaller rib case like the skeleton of an Ouroboros to hold his tripart brain. Next his organs, fat, wasted muscle and interconnecting tissue all started to go back into place, along with an intricate optical loom and millions of nerve interfaces. Sverl wanted definite AI connection to all his parts in the hope of controlling any problems after such drastic surgery.

The robots drew together and used cell welders to join him

back together invisibly, filling with collagen foam and drawing back his skin, layer by layer, to glue it back into place. When they finally retreated, they took away every scrap of surplus dead tissue and left little sign of their intervention beyond a pool of sterile fluid on the floor and spatters of collagen foam on nearby equipment. Observing through the deep scanner, while his prador brain reconnected and his human brain returned to consciousness, the AI Sverl could see that his shape looked more solid, it no longer sagged as it once had. Full reintegration ensued and with it the inevitable pain. Yet it was nowhere near as bad as he had expected, and he felt somehow right, as if what he had done had not only been necessary but fated.

After hours of internal observation Sverl found no adverse reactions – Penny Royal, who had set this transformation in motion, had done nothing inside him that might rebel against this. In fact, the change had somehow reinforced his earlier feeling of rightness. It was almost as if this was an expected part of his ongoing transformation. Warily, he pushed his prosthetic limbs against the floor and rose. It was better, a lot better. He felt no delay, no strain on his bloated body, no sagging. Now it was time for him to return his attention to events occurring beyond this sanctum. Even while undergoing this surgery he had remained expectant of another attack by Father-Captain Cvorn.

With a thought, he sent the deep scanner folding up on its triple-jointed arm into the ceiling and on firm prosthetic limbs moved over to his array of hexagonal screens and pit controls. Really, with the AI crystal connected to his major ganglion, he didn't need to use the physical controls here, but inserted his prosthetic claws into two pit controls anyway, enjoying a noticeable increase in their precision. Grinding together prosthetic mandibles, he called up data to his screens but then, realizing that he wasn't getting quite enough of an overview this way, did engage more fully with his ship's sensors and communications systems using his AI crystal.

The population of Carapace City was steadily moving out. Two big cargo ships had arrived from the edge of the Graveyard zone on the Polity side and, even though the Graveyard was supposed to be a buffer zone out of which the Prador Kingdom and the Polity had agreed to stay, Sverl knew for sure that the Polity had dispatched them. The ships had sent down shuttles onto which many of the city dwellers had clambered, along with whatever wealth they could drag between them. The citizens hoped to buy passage away from the Rock Pool planet, but they were surprised to learn they would not be charged for the journey. Apparently, some charitable organization, learning of the situation here, had hired these ships to evacuate this world. Charitable wasn't a word that could be applied to any organization in the Graveyard, which was why, with only a little bit of research, Sverl unearthed the connections back into the Polity.

Sverl watched this evacuation for hours before a voice abruptly said, 'Bloody shell people are a pain.'

He was unsurprised by the comment. That the drone down in Carapace City could penetrate his com systems with such ease further demonstrated that it wasn't a free drone slumming it in the Graveyard but one working for the Polity. However, having isolated the route it used to get in, he had decided to leave the line open.

'Why?' Sverl asked. The shell people were human cultists who had decided they liked the prador more than their own race and so had been attempting to surgically transform themselves into prador. They were certainly odd – but a pain?

'They're about all who are left here and they just don't want to go,' the drone replied. 'If they go they lose you – their one remaining connection to the prador. Other than their pradormimicking physical modifications, of course. It's enough to make a cat laugh.'

The drone tended to come out with these strange phrases – almost certainly delighting in how they baffled Sverl. Running some searches, Sverl was none the wiser, though he supposed the drone was referring to the irony of the situation. The shell people's affection for the prador was misguided when applied to him. They would probably be horrified to discover that while they tried to turn themselves into prador, he was steadily turning into . . . something else.

'Perhaps I should reveal myself to them,' he suggested.

'Ah-aah! Nil pwan! Do not pass go and do not collect two hundred pounds!'

Sverl emitted a sigh. 'If you could elaborate in some comprehensible form of human language?'

'They simply wouldn't believe you, Sverl,' the drone explained. 'In fact it's quite likely they would slot you into a legend they have of the first shellman – they would see you as one of their kind who is much further along the road to transformation into a prador.'

'That is not at all logical.'

'You have to factor in the human propensity for simplification, Sverl, and for their inability to believe in their own demise and unimportance. It's the impulse behind the religions—'

Sverl stopped listening the moment his instruments reported the disturbance, just microseconds before an object surfaced from U-space only a hundred thousand miles out from the Rock Pool. Cvorn had obviously been very busy since his last attack, because this time the prador kamikaze, carrying a CTD, a crust-busting contra-terrene device, was travelling at twenty per cent of light speed, and Sverl had just 2.7 seconds in which to react.

2

Sverl

In vacuum far above the Rock Pool, Sverl did not interact physically with his ship control systems and he sent no instructions to his gunners – his age-distorted first- and second-children. In the first tenth of a second, functioning wholly from his AI component, he reluctantly dismissed all those options. In the second tenth of a second, he analysed the positioning of his minefields across near space in relation to the approaching kamikaze and knew that it would miss them. Plotting the thing's course, he seized control of his ship's lasers and fired them all, but knew this wouldn't be good enough either. Almost certainly, he had not tracked down and destroyed all Cvorn's spy satellites – and the other father-captain had to know how to avoid his defences.

The kamikaze would be heavily protected with reflective armour, and would contain just enough fuel to take it the required distance to the Rock Pool. A missile response was out of the question – it would never get there in time. The angle of approach was a bad one from his point of view too, due to take the kamikaze behind the planet in half the remaining 1.6 seconds to impact.

Particle cannon, then.

Sverl fired, calculating in the marginally slower-than-light progress of his particle beam. It struck the kamikaze outside the planet's atmosphere. The vehicle, a torpedo-like mass of a hundred tons, shed a scar of red debris across vacuum but still

26

reached atmosphere. On target, the particle beam diffused briefly in atmosphere, then shut down before it could start ploughing into the planet itself.

Sverl, operating at AI speeds, had five whole tenths of a second in which to wonder if he had done enough, then a light like the sun coming out of eclipse flared from behind the Rock Pool and with that glare, fragmented data began to come in. The crust-buster had detonated in atmosphere, fractions of seconds before hitting the surface. The crust of the world had not shattered, tsunamis travelling at thousands of miles an hour would not be sweeping around the planet, and the massive fault under its ocean, which had probably been the intended target, would not be opening. However, no doubt Carapace City on the coast was in for a rough time.

'Prepare—' Sverl began.

'I saw,' the drone down there interrupted.

Sverl now gazed through cams scattered about in the city. Already the alert klaxons were sounding and the population, predominantly shell people now, was running for cover. Meanwhile, one of the shuttles, which had recently launched on its latest trip up to the cargo ships, hesitated in atmosphere, before its pilot must have decided that up was better than down. After a pause, while the pilot doubtless warned the passengers of impending acceleration, the vehicle ignited chemical boosters and stood on a tail of ribbed vermilion fire.

The atmospheric blast wave resulting from the kamikaze's destruction was bad, its initial impetus as it sped around the planet driving it to over two thousand miles an hour, which gave the city just under five hours to prepare. Sverl calculated on the effects of that wave . . . and then he saw it.

'Cvorn's thinking seems to have improved,' Sverl noted,

while starting up the fusion engines of his ship, his course directly back towards the Rock Pool.

'What?' the drone asked.

Even though he felt leaden inside, knowing what was to come, Sverl felt some satisfaction in being ahead of the drone on this one.

'He calculated on me hitting the kamikaze in atmosphere,' he explained. 'The blast wave is presently spreading out from that point, and its final intersect point is just forty miles south of Carapace City.'

'Shit,' said the drone.

Sverl made further calculations; modelling the whole event in the AI component of his mind. The spreading blast front was almost perfectly circular. In two and a half hours, it would have traversed one hemisphere of the planet and would then proceed to traverse the next hemisphere. Ahead of it, even though it would be slowing, it would compress the atmosphere. As it closed over the second hemisphere in a steadily shrinking circle approximately centred on Carapace City, the pressure would ramp up and up. The effects, when that final circle closed, would be catastrophic, akin to a multi-megaton detonation. Carapace City and all those inside could not survive this.

'Drone,' Sverl instructed. 'Tell those remaining that they must get to the eastern edge of the city as fast as they can.' Sverl sent precise coordinates.

'Uh?'

'Four hours is the limit to how long I will wait.' Sverl paused for a second. 'I'm sure most of the shell people will come when they know their destination.'

'Oh, I see.' After a pause the drone continued, 'You won't be able to save them all.'

'No, I won't,' Sverl replied, as his dreadnought hit atmosphere hard enough to send him stumbling, before turning over to descend to the planet on fusion drive.

Garrotte

The *Garrotte*'s AI realized something had merely allowed it to believe it was in control of its systems. Now, as it transited U-space, it knew that all the essentials – weapons, defences and the drive – were completely beyond its reach. Its earlier inability to function and internal blindness clearly had nothing to do with the quantum effects of two ships trying to materialize in the same place. Now those problems were back and at least half of its mass was completely numb to it, completely dark – an area suspiciously focused around its mascot, that antique space suit.

'Whadda you want?' it asked that darkness, but the darkness again refused to reply. And, of course, Garrotte had a good idea of what, or rather who, that darkness was.

So when had it taken on this uninvited passenger? During Garrotte's encounter with the *Moray Firth* above Masada, Penny Royal was down on the surface of the planet. However, that was human thinking and, to a certain extent, the thinking of AIs like itself, predicated on the idea that an entity was a single unit at a single location. Penny Royal had turned itself into a swarm robot and could divide itself up. Evidence existed that it could also manipulate U-space and project itself or elements of itself across that continuum. In fact, plenty of evidence suggested that Penny Royal was quite capable of existing in many places at once. Garrotte now suspected one of them to be a place aboard where there were no scanners and no diagnostic links: the inside of that space suit. It seemed the AI had found the one small weakness in the attack ship's defences. The black AI had U-jumped inside to the one place Garrotte would not detect it, and when it had done so was unknown.

Beyond the fact that the AI was here, the precedents were more than a little worrying. Remembering the paralysis it had suffered after the crash with the *Firth*, Garrotte feared that Penny Royal, or its influence, had already been aboard at that point. This suggested that the black AI had predicted events and set up its escape route some time before Isobel Satomi's transformation into a hooder war machine and her arrival here with her three warships. Garrotte did not think itself capable of such *precision*, nor was it sure such capabilities lay within the compass of any lesser AI than Earth Central itself.

Unless, of course it's breaching time, using time travel . . .

No, that wasn't somewhere the Garrotte wanted to go, and it reflected on how if it had a sphincter, that part would be loosening about now.

'So you're not going to talk to me?' Garrotte asked.

Almost as if in response to the question, the ship began to surface from U-space, and Garrotte wished it had kept its metaphorical mouth shut.

The moment the *Micheletto's Garrotte* returned to the real it went straight into chameleonware mode, faster than was usually possible, so Penny Royal had obviously been tinkering with its system. Its fusion drive then ignited, ramping up acceleration to something way beyond what any human passenger could have survived, and steering thrusters were firing, straining its newly repaired structure. Garrotte found access to its sensors unhindered and so looked around.

They had arrived in the shadow of a gas giant and were currently dodging asteroids on their way out into the light of a sun – a star only marginally brighter than the rest in the firmament. Garrotte mapped the system, picking out an ice giant further out surrounded by a large collection of moons, three inner worlds about the size of Mars and two Earth-mass planets within what some had described as the green belt. For a moment, it lacked enough data to get a location, but by comparing local star systems against internal star maps, Garrotte made a discovery: 'Shit, we're in prador territory – this is the Kingdom!'

Yes, now Garrotte recognized the massive space stations about those two worlds, and the structures under the coastal seas and sprawling onto the landmasses. The stations all tended to be of a similar shape – vertically squashed pears – while many of the spaceships nearby were of a similar design. They had indeed arrived at a planetary system lying inside the Prador Kingdom.

'They are too busy to notice,' whispered a voice seemingly issuing just behind the Garrotte's metaphorical ear.

'Talking to me now,' Garrotte said.

A target frame appeared over the nearest of the oceanic worlds, which, by Garrotte's calculations, lay over fifty light minutes away. Garrotte took the hint and focused in on it, watching across the spectrum, cleaning up imagery and mapping all visible structures in its mind. Something was definitely going on down there.

A series of explosions had just torn apart one section of an undersea city, the spume from them only now surfacing. As Garrotte watched, a fast shuttle, its design quite sharkish and more aerodynamic than was the prador custom, exploded from the sea and accelerated vertically. Shortly afterwards two near-world attack boats of the kind seen during the war – great bulky teardrop-shaped vessels ringed with weapons nacelles – shot out of the ocean in pursuit. Even as they left the water, they shed missiles which ignited their fusion drives and hurtled up ahead of them. Garrotte felt sure that the fast shuttle stood no chance at all. Those attack boats looked clumsy but possessed phenomenal acceleration and enough armament to rip up a city.

'The children of Vlern have learned from Sverl,' whispered Penny Royal, 'and have put their augmentations and their bio-weapons to good use. Fortunately for them, they were directed to a place lacking in any elements of the King's Guard, else things would not be going so well.'

Going so well?

Garrotte presumed that Penny Royal was talking about who-ever was in that fast shuttle which the attack boats appeared likely to be about to smear across the sky. And really, even if by some miracle that shuttle managed to avoid those missiles, war-ships in orbit were moving to intercept. The leading ships were destroyers, while the one coming in behind was somewhat larger. Studying the last vessel, Garrotte noted that it was one of those ships produced towards the end of the war and which the Polity had retrospectively classed as ST dreadnoughts – Series Terminal dreadnoughts. This was a ship the prador had manu-factured in response to the rapidly growing number of Polity warships. In building such vessels, they paid more attention to utility and speed of construction than to appearance. The ST dreadnought was about half again the size of standard, was not shaped like a prador carapace but a squat cylinder with powerful fusion drives at one end, fusion steering thrusters protruding all round, and a serious collection of armament sticking out at the other end like a city of skyscrapers. They hadn't done so well against the Polity because all that weaponry in one place made a plum target, while the steering thrusters were vulnerable too. As a consequence of these weaknesses the designer of that ship had apparently suffered the same fate as the erstwhile king of the prador – being injected with hydrofluoric acid and floated out over one of their oceans.

Still, the shuttle, which had now reached atmosphere and had ramped up enough acceleration to stay ahead of the missiles, stood zero chance of surviving once into vacuum. Even now, the destroyers were probably targeting—

The ST dreadnought had just fired multiple particle beam blasts, each hitting the leading destroyers straight up their tail pipes. Some fusion drives simply died, two detonated, spraying out like magma eruptions and carving chunks out of the ships concerned. Something else then surfaced into the real just behind them and ignited its own fusion drive to go in amongst them. Garrotte just had time to identify a hundred-ton prador kamikaze before it detonated. The flash of the continent-busting explosion blanked all the ships from view for a moment. When they re-appeared, they were tumbling away on the blast front.

'Ouch,' said Garrotte.

The blast did not destroy the destroyers because prador armour could take a lot more of a hammering than that. Their crews and captains would have been more than a little shaken up, however. Now the ST dreadnought was accelerating through, one destroyer bouncing away from its hull. Meanwhile the fast shuttle had left atmosphere, but it wasn't out of trouble yet. The pursuing missiles ignited secondary drives and accelerated faster in vacuum, while the shuttle headed into the incoming blast front.

Now a file arrived in Garrotte's mind and opened automatically. The ship AI suppressed the horror it felt at Penny Royal having such easy access to its mind and studied, for all of three seconds, something it would have taken an unaugmented human a week to read.

'An interesting social experiment,' Garrotte said, trying to be just pragmatic and logical. 'Young prador adults are generally cowardly – forgoing individual combat and securing themselves in their sanctums and leaving the combat to their children. However, without children and forced to live close together and cooperate over many years . . .'

Garrotte waited for Penny Royal to add something more about the young adults from the Rock Pool but then just focused on the battle when the AI didn't respond. Lasers now – green lasers picked out by the gas and debris of the explosions there. They hit the missiles and tracked them, and one after another, the missiles either died like flames starved of oxygen or detonated. Particle beams next, two of them, blue in vacuum but hazing and turning purplish as they penetrated atmosphere. They each struck the nose of an ascending attack boat and held there, each boat now generating a tail of fire as its armour ablated. An instant later the pilots of those vessels decided on survival, shut down their drives, threw themselves aside on steering thrusters and turned, accelerating back down towards the ocean.

The fast shuttle bucked in the blast front, then tumbled. It next seemed to fire its steering thrusters at random, but Garrotte noted the sequence was perfect to stabilize the vessel for its ensuing decelerating burn in towards the dreadnought, which was turning. The big ship had opened space doors onto a large shuttle bay. What ensued was more of a crash than a docking manoeuvre, but prador were tough and those aboard the shuttle probably survived it. The dreadnought swept the shuttle inside, ramped up its drive to take it back out from the world just as U-signatures began generating all around the area. It submerged into U-space and was gone, before a whole fleet of destroyers and four other dreadnoughts appeared.

'So,' said Garrotte, 'apart from that interesting file, are you going to offer a further explanation?'

'Access to prador females,' Penny Royal hissed.

Garrotte got it at once: 'It is amazing what organic creatures will go through just for the opportunity to mate.'

'Yes,' said Penny Royal.

Garrotte continued, 'So, let me sum up: a renegade prador called Vlern joined another prador called Sverl in the Graveyard. He had five first-children and when he died, choking on flesh-paste, they began to make the transformation into adults and to fight amongst themselves. Sverl, however, who has some odd inclinations for a prador, forced them to live together peaceably, to cooperate over many years. During that time, they learned a great deal from Sverl – some of which he was utterly unaware of, like how it is possible to enhance a prador mind – and they learned a great deal from another prador called Cvorn. Finally abandoning Sverl, they came here into the Kingdom for what they have wanted ever since they made their transformation from first-children: prador females.'

Just then, *Micheletto's Garrotte* submerged itself into U-space. This was probably a good idea because U-space signatures were now appearing out here as prador ships turned up, doubtless to investigate the *Garrotte*'s unscheduled visit. Yet another file arrived in Garrotte's mind – obviously, Penny Royal wasn't the talkative type. The five first-children came here, apparently to surrender themselves to the captain of that ST dreadnought, but once aboard released a bio-weapon they had fashioned to kill the entire crew. They took over the dreadnought, then three of them went down to the surface of the world, disguised in armour, to requisition some females – a mission that hadn't gone quite to plan.

'Did they get them – the females?'

'Yes.'

'So renegade adults have stolen both an ST dreadnought and prador females?'

'Yes. In the shuttle.'

'This is not good.'

'Quite.'

'King's Guard will get involved?'

'Almost certainly,' said Penny Royal.

Garrotte knew it was babbling when it filled in, 'I'm guessing the new king of the prador will not tolerate an enclave of breeding renegade prador, especially prador capable of doing what we just saw. The king will send units of his Guard to deal with the problem. Where do you reckon that dreadnought is going now?'

'The Graveyard.'

'Ah,' said Garrotte. 'If the King's Guard enter neutral space – the Graveyard – the Polity will respond, and that will almost certainly lead to some . . . friction. So, what now?'

'You will have to tolerate me as a passenger for a while longer.'

Like I've got a choice, thought Garrotte.

Spear

As we ascended to the parking orbit of the *Lance* in our shuttle, I glanced through the side window back down towards Masada and wondered if I was leaving a place that was about to turn into a war zone. Had Penny Royal known that the Weaver would resurrect that massive hooder war machine, the Technician? Was this another of its messes in the making? Supposedly Penny Royal's delivery of the changing Isobel Satomi had been about creating a power balance here, though one not in the Polity's favour, but maybe it had just made the situation more dangerous. I shook my head – I couldn't concern myself with the

Polity's problems because I had to remain focused on my own goals. Also, as we drew closer to the *Lance*, I could actually feel Penny Royal's abandoned spine reaching out to me as it waited inside the ship. It was like a black nail in my consciousness, and as it drove deeper I experienced a wave of déjà vu sickening in its intensity.

'You asked Amistad to accompany us,' I said to Riss, trying to distract myself. 'Why?'

'I thought it unlikely he wouldn't – whether in our ship or by some other means,' Riss replied. 'I was wrong.'

'You mentioned Amistad's history?' I queried, fingers driving into the arms of my acceleration chair as I fought against what I knew was coming.

'Yes, that history is the reason I thought he would come.'

'Tell me.'

After a long pause, which simply couldn't have been due to Riss collecting her thoughts since her AI mind worked faster than meat like me, she said, 'Amistad was a war drone whose mind hadn't been sufficiently desensitized to its task. He was in partnership with a human being whom the prador took, and cored, and this combined with the other horrors of his war drove him insane and he went AWOL for many years.'

'A sensitive war drone,' I stated.

Suddenly I was seeing two different scenes. I was aboard the *Lance*'s shuttle, but experiencing a memory dropping into my mind from the spine. *I was also aboard something larger, with two companions, sitting in one of four seats behind the cockpit. We were silent as our craft took us into orbit, daring to hope we had escaped that thing inside the old prador supply ship crashed on the surface. Unlike Mesen, who on the way down had occupied the now empty seat.*

'Yeah, go figure,' said Riss.

'So he was cured?' I managed.

'No, he found the cure for himself during some resolution with the son of his human partner. Thereafter he was assessed as no longer being such a danger, and went his own way; pursued his own interests.'

Ahead, the space doors into the shuttle bay opened – my ship's AI, Flute, welcoming us home.

'And what were those interests?' I cancelled Flute's attempt to take control and guide us in and took hold of the joystick myself. I wanted to be doing something to distract myself from the scene playing out in my head. I wanted to keep it at a distance and stay in the present, *my* present.

'Madness,' Riss replied.

I turned to the snake drone, noting that her black eye was once again open as she inspected me with her enhanced sensorium. Again, she was seeing my interaction with the spine.

'Madness?' I said, feeling that other time receding at least a little.

'Amistad was interested in all aspects of madness – the shape of it, its methodology, its causes and its cures, and how it is defined. An interest that, in itself, was a kind of madness. It led Amistad to Penny Royal, whom an ancient Atheter device had attacked and left on the edge of extinction. It led to him repairing Penny Royal and then attempting to understand and cure the black AI's madness.'

'Something of a severe fuck-up.' Ahead of me lay the *Lance*, but overlaid on that was another ship rather like Captain Blite's vessel. I jerked in my seat as something thumped into the rear of the shuttle, but I had remained sufficiently disconnected to know this had happened to the *other* shuttle.

'True, perhaps,' Riss dipped her head in acknowledgement. 'It also led Earth Central to select Amistad as the overseer and then Warden of Masada because here was the world of a race that had apparently gone insane and committed suicide. Who better to understand such a race?'

I ruminated on that for a moment as I manoeuvred the shuttle into its bay, and as the space doors closed behind. As I groped around for further distractions, an odd bit of data – just a memory of something I'd read once – surfaced in my mind for my inspection.

'How was the name Masada selected?' I asked.

'It was chosen by the first hierarch of the theocracy that established itself here. They felt themselves to be akin to the Zealots in the ancient fortress of the same name – their world a bastion of their faith.'

'Strange coincidence, considering those same Zealots committed mass suicide rather than surrender to Roman rule.'

'Yes, perhaps.'

Riss's use of the word 'perhaps' was beginning to irritate me. 'I still don't see why you expected Amistad to come with us.' I unstrapped and stood, heading for the airlock as, with a thump, docking clamps engaged around the shuttle. Opening the inner door, I checked the exterior atmosphere reading, waited until the warning light flicked from wasp-stripe amber to pure green, then opened the outer door.

'Because madness is Amistad's overriding interest,' said Riss from behind, 'and Masada seemed a saner place and of less interest to him. I expected him to join us because we're heading towards a greater madness.'

I paused for a moment, waiting for it, and Riss did not let me down.

'Perhaps,' the snake drone added.

'Do go on,' I said, noting how this discussion of madness equated to my present problem. Did I have multiple personality disorder? Maybe. Other memories intruded again, as Penny Royal's spine tightened its hold. *I was Garton, a killer for hire taken on by this salvage team only a few months ago because the team that found a prador supply ship had encountered some problems – had lost personnel and had had to abandon the site. They had assumed they might find another team working there, or maybe a stray surviving prador. But not the thing we found in that ship . . .*

'I expected Amistad to join us for his own confrontation with Penny Royal. I did not expect him to interfere with *your* aims, though while it seems you understand your *purpose*, your true aims are not clear. Do you still seek revenge?' Riss paused to let that sink in. It did, hard. I felt anger at Penny Royal and a need for vengeance so strong it was a taste like iron in my mouth, but was this anger truly mine?

'Back at you with that,' I said. 'What are your aims and what is your purpose, then?'

Riss shook her cobra head, her black eye closing.

'Penny Royal, it appears, is trying to heal the damage of its past crimes,' said the drone, 'but that AI is more complicated and dangerous than that. I too wish to make some . . . corrections. I have to cogitate on taking revenge for what was done to me, and decide if what was done to me requires it.'

I found myself waiting for a 'perhaps', then shook myself and headed for the door into the ship proper, ghosts all around me, panicking and pulling out their weapons as a shadow flowed out from behind their shuttle.

Another voice then spoke up: 'So, I am the mind of a ship with a Polity bio-espionage officer aboard, an assassin drone and I just came close to having a war drone aboard too. Do we have any room aboard for a Golem soldier? Maybe you'd like to oust me and replace me with a Polity attack ship mind?'

'You missed out the word "erstwhile", Flute,' I said, really irritated now. 'We were enemies of the prador but now we're not. Perhaps you might like to ponder on who chopped you out of your original body and installed you in the case you now occupy.'

Flute just made a snorting sound over the PA.

'You have those coordinates I sent you?' I enquired, turning to head straight for my cabin.

'I have.'

'Then take us there.'

'Very well,' Flute replied.

I entered my cabin and firmly closed the door, went over and threw myself down on my bed, and let the vision come. Laser carbine fire filled the shuttle bay in my mind but, as Garton, I knew this was pointless light and colour. We'd hit this thing down on the surface and inflicted no damage at all after it had grabbed Mesen.

The shadow etched itself into reality as a swarm of black sword blades rose up like snake heads atop silver tubes. It came forwards as we moved back towards the airlock and I knew it would be on us before we could all cycle through. I turned towards the airlock, intent on being the first inside as one of those blades pierced Anderson and hauled him screaming from the deck. I glimpsed his face, the flesh shrinking and darkening over his skull and his eyes sinking away as if the blade was sucking all the juice out of him. I struggled with the airlock controls, shitting myself in an envirosuit not made to process it and feeling embarrassed despite my terror, then felt agonizing pain from front to back. Looking down, I saw the point of a black blade protruding from under my breastbone and began screaming as it hauled me from the floor. But that wasn't the worst. I felt the blade sucking everything I was, both physically and mentally, in towards itself, whirling down in an agonizing and terrifying maelstrom towards . . . nothing. Just screaming and screaming as I went.

41

'Spear! Thorvald Spear!' Flute was shouting over the intercom, just as my cabin door opened and Riss entered – the lock obviously no problem for the snake drone. I guessed I had become a bit vocal during that particular nightmare.

'I'm okay,' I said hoarsely, sitting upright.

I reached down and rubbed at my chest, still feeling the hard sharpness of that thing skewering me; still feeling Garton's death. I wasn't all right. Garton's skewering equated to the spine nailed into my mind and I just knew that there were thousands clamouring to tell me their stories through it – the unquiet dead were demanding to be heard.

Father-Captain Cvorn

As the latest images and data came in from his spy satellites, Cvorn felt a great deal of satisfaction, but tempered by a degree of chagrin. Cvorn, a huge crablike prador, floating on grav-motors because he had long ago lost his legs and claws, crunched his mandibles together before the visual turret at his fore. He could never have misled Sverl so thoroughly before. Cvorn could never have achieved such an intricately balanced and perfectly targeted piece of destruction when he had been a normal prador father-captain.

When Cvorn had gone to the Rock Pool he had been as baffled as Sverl by the victory of humanity and the AIs over the might of the Prador Kingdom, and he had felt the new king's betrayal of the prador race just as deeply. Making peace with the humans should not have been an option. Unlike Sverl, however, Cvorn had not gone seeking answers by allowing himself to become the plaything of a black AI. He had brooded, and he had made his plans for vengeance. Meanwhile, over the years, it became apparent that Sverl was changing in some strange way. Affronted by the restraint Sverl steadily placed on him, Cvorn began investigating this, and soon obtained answers by way of ship lice, their tiny brains surgically altered and their carapaces dotted with pin cams, inserted via a sea-floor robot recalled into Sverl's dreadnought.

Cvorn's first reaction was a visceral horror and he had almost set in motion one of the many plans he had been toying with for an attack on Sverl. It wasn't that he had resented Sverl when he first made these plans – all father-captains made such preparations. At the last moment, he stopped himself. He had been thinking long and hard at the bottom of that ocean and, though Sverl had changed, it was notable how his deployment of Polity technology, amalgamated with prador technology, had led to greater efficiencies. Sverl had become very smart and seemed to be on to something. Perhaps Cvorn needed to show some restraint, and to learn.

Sverl was turning into something monstrous – some horrible combination of both prador and human – but this wasn't the source of his increased intelligence. It took Cvorn many years of watching to realize that Sverl wasn't just part human, but augmented too. A partial confirmation of this came from a careful study of Sverl's behaviour, such as how he controlled things around him, like that horrible Golem, and from a further study of all the intercepted computer code. Final confirmation came from an X-ray photograph of Sverl, the X-rays apparently generated when a louse ate into the shielding of a piece of ship equipment. Unfortunately, shortly after the confirmation of Sverl's augmentation, Cvorn lost access when the other father-captain exterminated all his ship lice and started using Polity cleanbots for the same purpose.

AI crystal was growing around Sverl's major ganglion – crystal precisely matching that of the Polity AIs. Sverl was turning into the enemy he had wanted to understand. Cvorn, who had always been a little bit brighter than most of the rest of his kind, even understood the irony of that. He also understood that in reality the prador had not been defeated by the humans, but by that glistening thinking rock.

Cvorn tried an aug, designed for the prador ganglion, on one of his second-children. The results had been astounding and Cvorn even began to feel threatened by this child, until he tore off all its limbs, opened up its carapace and ate the contents. The nanoscopic connections in the child's ganglion had delivered an odd piquancy of flavour. Next, not being too averse to surgical connections to his own brain – he did, after all, have three prador thrall units on his carapace to control his two human blanks and sometimes to control his war drones directly – Cvorn tried an aug on himself. Again, the results were astounding, so he tried a second aug, and then some heavily buffered AI crystal, and fast became addicted to enhancement.

However, Cvorn soon reached the barrier to infinite enhancement: the burn-out of the organic brain. He shivered when he remembered how close he had come to that point. When an organic brain and AI crystal fall into a synergy, intelligence ramps exponentially until the organic brain fails like a first-child attached to the full output of a fusion reactor – something Cvorn had once tried, just for entertainment. He had disconnected and discarded the crystal, and wondered just how Penny Royal had enabled Sverl to survive it.

Still, even enhanced as he had become, Cvorn's aims and ambitions, unlike Sverl's, had not changed. He wanted power and the increase of his family beyond those few replacement children he produced artificially in his destroyer's single incubator. He wanted vengeance against the new king of the prador for his betrayal of his race by seeking a truce with the Polity. In addition, he wanted the prador to win the war against the humans and the AIs, which, in his opinion, had never ended. He hated humans – that had never changed.

Next, understanding that he was unlikely to achieve all these goals alone, he needed allies, and so he turned to the five children of that other refugee from the Kingdom, Vlern – the five young adults Sverl had managed to control and inadvertently weld into an alliance of similar interests, which was how any prador community operated. He contacted one of them, who at length he identified as Sfolk – he often found it difficult to tell them apart. Sfolk was unusually intelligent and their spokes-prador. Cvorn began the slow and very difficult process of building trust with him. First, he revealed Sverl's true nature to the Five, then he showed the data from his study of the second-child he had auged and offered to put them in contact with his supplier, in the Polity, of prador augs, in exchange for certain agreements. He played them easily at first because they were naive; he played them with more care later as the augs he had given them increased their intelligence. He knew precisely what they wanted – prador females – and offered them a route to that end.

First, they needed an escape route: the Five were completely under Sverl's control and they needed to work round that. While escaping, they should destroy the humans on the Rock Pool. Sfolk had immediately questioned this. Sverl had acquired, like a disease, some affection for the humans of Carapace City. Why aggravate him when, once they escaped, they would probably cease to be of any interest to him? Cvorn was insistent. This was the quid pro quo: he would, via his contacts back in the King-dom, help them find the females and in return they must help him destroy Carapace City. He told them that his long years of restraint, culminating in his discovery of what Sverl had become, had enhanced his hatred of humans, and he wanted plain old prador vengeance against Sverl. He did not tell Sfolk that for his plans he needed to draw Sverl out and that by killing the humans he aimed to ensure this. He did not tell them that Sverl was the key to restarting the war against the Polity.

However, the first attempt to capture Sverl had been a failure, so his plans had changed. His contacts in the Kingdom had lined up another target for Vlern's brood, because the location of the females would be of secondary importance to the Five's method of escape. Of course, having snatched the females, the Five intended to head far away from the Kingdom, and the Graveyard, beyond the reach of other prador and out there begin breeding. Their plans were irrelevant because Cvorn had thwarted them from the beginning. He had neglected to tell them of the odder qualities of the biotech augs that his supplier, Dracocorp, had provided.

3

Sverl

The fusion drive seared the rocky ground beyond the city, instantly scouring away the meagre vegetation in a cloud of ash and smoke, rocks cracking and smoking in sun fire and turning molten. Closely linked into his ship's systems, Sverl hinged out its stabilizing feet and read the error reports but found nothing critical.

Exterior cams showed the feet – great flat skates of exotic alloy folding down on hinged legs driven by massive gas-fed rams, shielded on their inner sides by hardfields – coming down on molten rock and sinking. This was a problem the designers had foolishly failed to compensate for throughout the war, Sverl remembered. He'd known of many instances of ships trapped on the ground after rock hardened about their feet, and Polity forces annihilating them.

He shut down the fusion drive and listened to his ship creaking and groaning around him as it settled. He noted the vessel was tilting slightly and, for a moment, assumed that the ground must be softer over on one side. Upon checking, however, he saw that the landing feet there had sunk no deeper than had the others. Further checking revealed, half a mile to one side, a squat cliff apparently rising out of the ground. It wasn't rising; the rock on this side of it was sinking. Under the immense weight of the dreadnought a chunk of volcanic rock, under the feet on one side and sitting on softer sedimentary rock, had broken off from that surrounding it and was now sinking. Sverl further probed the ground with his sensors, but even as he did so the rate of sinkage slowed. It would be fine – if they could ever take off again.

'Bsorol,' he said, the image of that first-child immediately coming up on one of his screens. Many years of chemically maintained adolescence had twisted Bsorol, his legs bowed and his carapace whorled like old wood. 'I want a team suited up and outside when feasible. I want thermal-sealed fracture charges pushed into the hardening rock about the landing feet within the next hour.'

'Yes, Father,' Bsorol replied. Then, after a hesitation, 'There are many humans out there.'

Sverl glanced at another screen. Various gravans and grav-cars, ATVs and cargo platforms led the crowds moving out from the city. One of these cars had moved too close during the dreadnought's descent and now lay on its side, its passengers climbing out. Sverl recognized the shellman Taiken, along with what were presumably members of his family: a female and two boys. The other vehicles had sensibly maintained their distance so were okay, while the people on foot had dropped to the ground, a hot smoky wind howling above them. Of course, like many other children aboard, Bsorol had taken an interest in the goings-on in Carapace City. He had also been in proximity with the humans while serving his time guarding the small land-based space port – mostly so Sverl could have a presence there if he needed to act quickly against some threat. However, despite his long years of service to Sverl, Bsorol, like his siblings, was still almost certainly viciously xenophobic. This might be a problem.

'Yes, there are humans out there,' Sverl replied, 'and soon they will be coming aboard this ship to occupy Quadrant Four and the lower holds there.'

'Why?' Bsorol asked.

'Because I am saving them all from the imminent destruction of their city.'

'But why?' Bsorol asked again.

Sverl mulled over various replies but knew none of them would make sense to Bsorol. He then realized how things needed to change. Perhaps the time had come to do something he had shied away from for many years. Perhaps he should allow Bsorol and his other children access to augmentation to widen their horizons. They needed to think beyond the mere instinctive urge to exterminate competitors, whether in other prador families or in alien races. But that was for the future. Right now only one option was available.

'Because I want to and I am father-captain of this ship,' he replied. 'And if you continue to question me in this manner you will shortly find yourself in a flash freeze case inside one of my kamikazes. Obey your orders, Bsorol.'

'Yes, Father,' Bsorol replied, seemingly relieved at this simplicity.

The ship had settled now and Sverl moved to insert his claws into pit controls. He then hesitated for a moment. By the speed of his reaction to Cvorn's kamikaze, he had proved that his preference for using manual controls was foolish. He now mentally initiated the lowering of a ship's ramp. This was the size of an ancient human aircraft carrier and had not been used before – it was intended for ground assault forces that Sverl had never carried. Meanwhile, he began closing bulkhead doors around the route to Quadrant Four and instructing his children in those tunnels and in the quadrant itself to depart. In their home territory his children could not be fully trusted with humans. He could order them to cause no harm, but defining that might be problematic. Since most of these humans were shell people, there could be confusion. The tap a prador would deliver to another of its kind to attract attention would leave even a shell-man a quivering mess on the floor.

The shell people outside were on the move again, rounding the ship to the lowering ramp, while more and more of them were coming out of the city. Luckily, the ramp would extend far enough from the ship for them not to have to cross rock melted by the ship's engines and now still glowing with red heat as it solidified. Focusing in on those leading, Sverl saw that Taiken and his family were now at the forefront on a grav-raft – on its side the words 'Taiken Fuels' – while just ahead of this hovered the surfboard shape of the Polity drone.

'I don't remember extending an invitation to you, drone,' he said over the ever-open channel.

Sure, Sverl had been enough distorted by the changes he was undergoing to want to rescue the shell people of Carapace City, but a Polity drone, an actual member of his erstwhile enemy? Now considering this notion further, he initiated some powerful scanning of the approaching horde using instrumentation he had acquired from the Polity, amalgamated with prador technology, and since enhanced using his own growing knowledge and abilities. Just a second later, scanning flagged up a Golem too.

'I'll be no trouble,' the drone asserted.

'Bullshit,' said Sverl, slipping easily into human parlance as he opened armoured blisters in his ship's hull and extruded Gatling cannons to target the drone and the *two* Golem now detected in the crowd. 'You are not boarding my ship.'

Further scan results began to come in, revealing something odd about one of the gravcars. It looked battered and old but, reading its emissions, Sverl realized its grav-motors were at ninety-nine per cent efficiency. A further hard probe scoured away the chameleonware concealing the fact that it could be vacuum sealed, contained twinned mini-fusion jets and onboard armament, along with a wide selection of lethal hand weapons, including proton rifles, within reach of the three people inside.

'I've been instructed to offer what protection I can to these people,' the drone replied, but it was now dropping back.

The two men and the woman inside the car weren't shell people. They could have been just anyone from off-world. Judging by their physiques, augmentations and weaponry, they could be enforcers for some criminal gang. Sverl thought otherwise.

'You are not boarding my ship, drone,' he said, 'nor are the Sparkind unit and that lead Polity agent – those Golem twenty-eights running insufficient chameleonware and the three in that interesting gravcar.'

'There are Golem twenty-eights here?' said the drone innocently.

'You have thirty seconds,' said Sverl, immediately setting the countdown running. 'Admittedly the firepower I will have to use will kill many shell people, but I would rather that than have your kind aboard.'

The reaction was instant. The gravcar abruptly swung round in the air and came down in a hard landing ahead of the approaching crowd. Already the two Golem were moving, frighteningly fast, but only towards the car and not to the ramp. They quickly piled into the car and it took off, lighting afterburners when it reached a hundred feet and streaking up into the sky, doubtless heading off to hitch a ride with one of the rescue ships up there. The drone rose to fifty feet and hung in the sky for a moment.

'Well, it was a long shot but worth a try,' said the drone. 'So long, Sverl . . . it's been interesting.'

'So long, drone,' Sverl replied, feeling quite odd as the drone swung round and shot up after the gravcar. He realized the sensation was regret and a kind of loneliness – both feelings that prador experienced infrequently.

Taiken's raft soon reached the foot of the ramp and began to ascend. Other vehicles followed it up and then the steadily tramping crowd – all weighed down with personal belongings. Scanning towards the city, Sverl watched the stragglers hurrying out. Next, checking through cams inside the city, he was surprised to find it, as far as he could judge, empty of life. Perhaps the drone had been wrong about him not getting them all. Perhaps it had so couched its warnings of the city's impending destruction that all had heeded them. Then again, these were mainly shell people, whose worshipful attitude to the prador had brought them here.

Over the next hour, the shell people trooped aboard the dreadnought. Sverl issued instructions in human speech over the ship's PA system and, as Taiken's raft approached the massive oval diagonally divided door into Quadrant Four, he contacted Taiken via a comunit the man carried on his reaverfish skin harness.

'Taiken, you are about to enter one of the eight quadrants of this dreadnought. My children have vacated it and you have access to the hold spaces in its lower levels. I have closed the bulkhead doors to other quadrants and am sealing them. Do not try to open those doors. I will instruct my children to do you no harm but instinctive reactions cannot be discounted. Also, pressure changes in the rest of the ship, which my kind can tolerate, could well kill humans – even ones changed as you are. Any questions?'

'I am familiar with the design of the interior of prador ships,' said Taiken in an irritatingly superior manner that Sverl knew was aimed at the shell people near him. 'I know how to obtain water from the dip holes and we have the equipment to access the power supply and convert it for any of our Polity-manufactured equipment. However, we may have insufficient food, though that depends on how long we will be aboard this ship.'

'There are forty-eight tons of reaverfish carcasses in the hold you have access to,' Sverl replied. 'They were frozen shortly after capture so, with the required additives, are suitable for human consumption.'

Usually, prador allowed such carcasses to decay for a while to render them more to the prador taste for stored meat. Sverl had found his tastes changing, for now he liked his stored meat undecayed and had lost his appetite for fresh meat steadily stripped from screaming and terrified enemies.

'Good, I thank you, Father-Captain,' said Taiken respectfully. 'Where are we going?'

'I have yet to decide,' Sverl replied, shutting down the communication and sending the signal to open the big door into Quadrant Four.

Sverl had no idea what he was going to do with these refugees. One option would be to dump them on another inhabited Graveyard world. But wouldn't doing so just make another world a target for Cvorn? Of course it would. The only way they could truly be safe would be if he were to head for the border lying between the Graveyard and the Polity and hand them over to the AIs. Sverl had a problem with that. Beside the quite possibly lethal consequences of taking a prador dreadnought right to the Polity border, he knew that the Polity AIs were very interested in the works of Penny Royal, and they had to know he was one of them. He felt that if they did not inadvertently destroy him and his ship, they would try to grab him.

So what to do?

Sverl watched the main crowd from Carapace City enter his ship, then the seemingly endless stream of stragglers. He watched the first arrivals divide up various areas and select living spaces. They set up toilets connected into the ship's waste systems, powered up human lighting, then toned it down to the correct ambiance for shell people, and began settling in. Outside he watched Bsorol, another first-child called Bsectil and five second-children who, in their suits, were indistinguishable from their older siblings, working their way around the landing feet and shoving the charges down into rock which had the consistency of thickening porridge. Next, through a watch post established on an islet jutting up far out in the ocean, he observed the approaching blast front from Cvorn's kamikaze.

A deep purple band extended across the horizon and steadily thickened, an anvil of grey cloud generating above it and then itself extending all the way across the horizon too. Multiple lightning flashes lit this scene as of a million arc welders working all at once. The purple band and the cloud melded into one and took on the appearance of a massive roller. This grew larger as it drew closer to the islet, finally occupying all space from the surface of the sea up to high in the atmosphere – a great curved wall the colour of human bruises. Ahead of it Sverl noted that the ocean had mounded and that when it finally arrived at Carapace City there would be a tsunami. However, making some rapid AI calculations, he worked out that the growing pressure inside the closing blast front would squeeze the ocean back out, and the resulting wave would actually be small. Also ahead of this front, gunshots of lightning perpetually stabbed down into the sea, as if intent on clearing the way for it. One of these fried Sverl's watch post and abruptly cut off his view.

Half an hour remained now as Bsorol and his crew returned through a maintenance hatch. One last party of humans was making its way up the ramp – two shell people guiding a small grav-raft on which they had mounted an amniotic tank, its

occupant a shellman who had recently undergone drastic surgery. Doubtless the reason for their delay was in finding a way to
shift his life-support gear. As they reached the head of the ramp,
Sverl began to close it, then paused when he spotted two more
shell people heading out from the city. Of course, though he had
extensive surveillance of the city, he could not see into every
nook and cranny, and there could be other refugees too.

It had been Sverl's intention to lift off and get into orbit
before the blast front arrived, which meant he needed to close
the ramp now and leave those two out there – and any coming
behind them – to die. However, his ship was more than resilient
enough to ride out the storm, especially anchored as it was. He
decided to leave the ramp down and close it just before the blast
front arrived, to offer the strongest chance of survival.

The two made it inside and no one else followed in the time
remaining. Sverl began to close the ramp, satisfied that he had
done his best. Then, even as it thumped home and the horizon
all around bruised and bled lightning, a woman ran out of the
city clad in an environment suit bulked out over prador grafts.
She was like a taunt. She was the flaw and the unavoidable
death. The blast front lay only minutes away, while the pressure
ahead of it was ramping up horribly. Quite likely her environment suit would fail before the front arrived to annihilate
everything here not made of prador exotic metal.

What the hell was that?

The maintenance hatch Bsorol had used had popped open
again, and out came that first-child, sans armour, hurtling across
the hot ground. He was moving as fast as he could, which was
not so fast with his twisted limbs, but faster than the woman. As
he headed towards her, she stumbled to a halt, stared at him for
a moment, then turned and began running back towards the
city. Bsorol came up behind her, closed a claw around her waist

and snatched her off her feet, then, skidding and kicking up flakes of rock, he turned and headed back. In a minute, he was back at the maintenance hatch and inside, the hatch closing behind him.

At that moment, the dome of Carapace City collapsed as if under some giant invisible foot, spewing debris in a cloud towards the dreadnought. The ship groaned, pressure readings outside climbing exponentially, and the blast front closed to a point. The ship rocked and Sverl staggered, closing one prosthetic claw on the edge of a pit control to steady himself. Damage reports began to stream on one screen, and outside a pillar of swirling air like a tornado rose, sucking on the wrecked city like some giant leech. The storm raged. Carapace City ceased to exist and the wind flung boulders the size of shuttles into the sky. Lightning seared the ground and, with a roar, the pressure peak began to collapse – winds generating outward from this point whipping spume off the ocean. But this was a prador dreadnought wrapped in exotic metal armour. It was the kind of ship that had nearly been the death of the Polity because it was so difficult to destroy. Though it complained, it stood firm.

'Why?' Sverl asked through one PA speaker.

'You ordered the rescue of them all,' Bsorol replied simply as he prodded the woman in the back with the tip of one claw and sent her staggering along that particular corridor. He was taking her to one of the sealed doors into Quadrant Four, so Sverl unlocked it for him.

'I don't find that explanation satisfactory,' said Sverl.

'Okay,' said Bsorol, shifting his body in a puzzling way, until Sverl understood it was a very human dismissive shrug and that the first-child was going to offer no further explanation.

Sverl realized that he must take the time to pay more attention to his children, and more closely inspect how they had changed. Meanwhile, however, he had resolved his quandary concerning these refugees and the danger to them from Cvorn. In the end, the only answer was a prador one: Cvorn had to cease being a danger.

Trent Sobel

Blite and the crew were a strange lot. Something very odd about their behaviour definitely had a connection to their time spent in proximity to Penny Royal. But they were easy enough for him to read, and he knew that they didn't like him very much.

They were honest traders or, rather, they only strained the bounds of Polity law a little, whereas Trent had worked for Isobel Satomi and she had run a coring and thralling business in the Graveyard. This meant kidnapping human victims, infecting them with the Spatterjay virus to make them improbably physically rugged. It meant next cutting out their brains and part of their spinal columns and replacing these with a prador thrall unit. And it meant selling on the resulting animated meat to the prador. He hadn't been involved in the kidnapping and cutting, his role having been that of an enforcer since Satomi employed him and his partner to stamp down on other criminal organizations that tried to infringe on her territory. Still, even if his victims were the kind who would have done the same to him, he had tortured and murdered people, and he was culpable in the mass murder of Satomi's coring trade.

The crew had gone dockside from *The Rose* to have a celebration, and well they might. Here at Outlink Station Par Avion Captain Blite had turned over thousands of memplant crystals to the station AI and subsequently received a payment that had made him and his crew extremely rich. On top of that, they were to receive a reward for handing over two other items they'd picked up on the way out of the Masadan system. Since he was one of those items, Trent Sobel wasn't in the mood for celebrating and stayed in the small cabin they had allotted him.

While sitting on his bed, he reached up and fingered the new earring provided by Penny Royal. The purple sapphire now contained the memcording of Isobel Satomi's human mind – extracted from the hooder war machine she had become, but the jewel had previously belonged to his dead sister Genève and remained his only link to her. Blite and his crew had only rescued him from the wreck of the *Moray Firth* as a favour to that same black AI, and now, in bringing him here, they had as good as killed him.

Redeem yourself, Penny Royal had told him when presenting him with the earring. How the hell could he have done that, even if Blite hadn't brought him here into Polity territory? What the hell had the AI been playing at – surely it could have predicted that Blite would have entered Polity territory to offload that memcrystal? How the hell could he redeem himself now he faced either mind-wipe or immediate execution of the standing death sentence on him?

'Sobel,' said a voice from without – one he didn't recognize. 'Come out of that cabin – hands on your head and no weapons. You know the drill.'

This was it. The moment *The Rose* left the Graveyard he'd known he was in danger. The moment it had docked at Par Avion he'd known the Outlink Station AI would learn he was aboard. Doubtless it had issued the warrant shortly after that and now, outside that door, Polity police were here to take him in. He reached down to the gas-system pulse-gun holstered at his hip. Really, it was a case of die now or die later, doubtless after having every bit of useful data auged out of his mind. He drew the weapon and inspected it. Maybe he could take a few of them down, but there were almost certainly Golem out there, and the fight would not be protracted.

What would his sister think?

The question wasn't verbal – more of a feeling rising from the under-strata of his mind. He shivered and checked around his cabin, looking for a black diamond materializing out of the air. But no, Penny Royal wasn't here.

So what would she think? Genève would have been disgusted with him. On Coloron, it had been difficult to have a life much above that of dole status without getting involved in some criminality but she had always stayed honest. She'd tried to keep him honest too but had failed. If he had not become involved with the criminal gangs and separatist organizations, would she still be alive? Could it be that if he'd stayed honest the jewel his sister always wore at her throat would not have come to the notice of certain types, and that they would not have murdered her to acquire it?

Trent abruptly stood up and tossed his weapon down on the bed. He walked over to the door, palmed the lock and, placing his hands flat on his head, stepped out. A hand immediately came down on his shoulder and propelled him into the opposing wall, but he managed to turn his head to avoid breaking his nose. Someone kicked his legs out from under him, wrenched his arms round behind him and used a squirt of hyperglue to stick his wrists together. An inhumanly fast body search ensued, then a buzzing and he felt the hot wash of a powerful body scanner traversing him from head to foot.

'Clean,' said the first voice, and then the one who had glued his wrists hauled him to his feet.

There were four of them. The female with the long black hair standing to one side of him with her hand on his shoulder was stunningly beautiful, but by the way she had handled him he reckoned she was Golem. The two men were heavy and thickset – boosted – so unlikely to be Golem because Golem needed no extra muscle. The fourth one was a momentary puzzle to him. At first sight, he thought this individual was some sort of amphidapt, until he moved and Trent saw that his legs hinged like those of a chicken. This one was a dracoman, Trent realized. Then he noted something else: none of them wore the uniform of Polity monitors or station police.

'Bit dumb coming here, Sobel,' said one of the men, now turning to head towards the airlock. This stood open since the station AI had instructed the crew to take *The Rose* inside to one of the pressurized docking areas.

'Yeah,' Trent agreed, as the Golem woman pushed gently against his shoulder and he tramped after them.

When he had learned that Blite was coming here, Trent had argued with the man at length and then, getting nowhere, had wondered about trying to take over the ship. They'd foolishly allowed him to retain his weapon and he was quite capable of killing them all, but then what? The ship's mind wouldn't obey him and would take him just where it chose. He could destroy it, dumping the ship out of U-space in the process, then would come a long conventional space journey to some place in the Graveyard – a journey that might be longer than his lifespan, but would certainly result in his lifespan being longer than it was now destined to be. But he owed Blite for rescuing him, the crew weren't the scum he was used to dealing with, and he rather liked them even though they didn't like him.

He hadn't been able to do it. What was wrong with him?

Outside the ship, on a short polished metal floor before a line of cargo and personnel dropshafts, Blite awaited alongside the other item he had picked up beyond Masada. Whether picking it up had been part of the favour Penny Royal had asked of the man Trent didn't know. All he did know was that Blite had abruptly changed course to intercept this thing. The big, skeletal and weirdly painted Penny Royal Golem that Satomi had taken from the mafia boss Stolman on the Rock Pool was sprawled on a grav-sled. It had been inert when Blite picked it up and had remained so ever since. Blite, now seeing his captors shoving Trent out of the ship, walked over.

'What's going to happen to him?' the captain asked, indicating Trent with a nod. Behind him the dracoman activated the grav-sled, using the small console on a control column jutting up from it, and sent it sliding along the dock.

The Golem woman replied, 'Usually his sort would be cut-auged for data – his mind wiped in the process. However, those under such a sentence who have encountered Penny Royal go to a forensic AI.'

'And then?'

'Sentence on him will be executed, but he'll be taken apart more meticulously – nothing will remain.'

'You know, I'm standing right here,' said Trent.

'So you are,' said one of the men, 'very much unlike the hundreds you murdered.'

'I wasn't involved in that side of the business,' said Trent.

'Just obeying orders, hey?'

Trent decided it was pointless arguing, so fell silent. Blite stepped closer to him and studied his face intently.

'Of course,' said the captain, 'Penny Royal's almost certainly not finished with you. Not at all.' Blite stepped back and nodded once, a weird disconnected expression on his face, and moved off.

What did that mean?

Another shove against his shoulder sent him stumbling. He

realized he wasn't being taken across to the dropshafts but along the dock. They brought him to the ramp leading into another ship. He studied this small powerful-looking vessel as the Golem woman clamped a hand on his shoulder to hold him in place. It was a single-ship – designed for solo delivery missions and rather like an in-system fighter. But it had extended nacelles on either side at the rear that looked like a twinned U-space drive, and another large nacelle extending downward and looking like a weapons pod.

Ahead of him, the dracoman guided the grav-sled up the ramp into a small hold where it locked itself down. One of those behind shoved Trent up the ramp after it, past the sled, through a bulkhead door into a narrow corridor, then across to another small hold converted into a cabin.

'The glue binding your wrists will be broken down so you should be able to feed yourself,' said the Golem woman.

Trent turned to gaze at her. 'So you're not coming with me?'

'Oh no.' She shook her head and smiled. Behind her, the two men exchanged an unreadable look while the dracoman just turned and headed away. 'Even the good guys like us don't want to get too close to that thing. It can be . . . disturbing.'

'Thing?'

'The Brockle,' she replied, before stepping out and closing the door behind her, locks engaging all around it with leaden thumps. Trent just stared at the blank metal, not sure what to make of that, then turned and walked over to the bed and sat down. He had been sitting there for maybe half an hour, testing the glue sticking his wrists together, when a voice issued from the intercom.

'Are you sitting comfortably?'

'Who are you?' he asked.

'Brockle Submind Three,' the voice replied.

'Yes, I'm sitting comfortably.'

'Then I suggest you lie down.'

A high-pitched whistling ensued, and the glue on his wrists abruptly debonded. He felt motion – an odd sideways pressure – and realized that the cabin had reoriented. He lay down on the bed, resting his arms at his sides. After a little more manoeuvring, acceleration came down on him like a giant invisible boot, pressing him deep into the mattress. It ramped up and up, and his consciousness faded out.

Garrotte

'That is Cvorn,' said Penny Royal, doubtless meaning the father-captain occupying the ancient prador destroyer. It had just surfaced from U-space, leaving a photonic trail, twenty light minutes out from the binary system – a green sun orbiting a hot blue star that was well on the way to collapsing into a neutron star. Almost certainly, the prador destroyer had yet to see the ST dreadnought awaiting it. Yet still it fired up its fusion engines to take it directly towards the dreadnought's location, which probably meant this was a pre-planned meeting.

'Cvorn?' Garrotte prompted, just before yet another package unfolded in its mind like an origami sculpture, neatly depositing information directly into its eidetic memory. Garrotte now knew much more about the events on and around the Rock Pool from the moment Sverl had established himself there. It now knew of Sverl's changes, of his steady grotesque transformation. It knew Cvorn's use of Polity technology had given the five young adults in the dreadnought the advantages they had recently made use of. But still Garrotte did not understand.

'Cvorn has allies in the Kingdom,' Penny Royal stated. 'His

hatred of humans and of us has, if anything, been exacerbated by his use of our technology. Consider his aims.'

Garrotte began thinking, and deeply. Perhaps something about the presence of Penny Royal aboard this ship had some effect on Garrotte's thought processes, because soon it began to see an ugly pattern. Yet, this pattern still would not come together, not until Penny Royal provided an image feed . . .

Garrotte found itself gazing through some sort of cam directly into the nearby prador ship's sanctum. Here it saw an old legless prador – one of the blue-shells, in fact, who claimed direct lineage to the first king of the prador – hovering before his pit controls and hexagonal screens.

'Observe,' Penny Royal instructed.

Garrotte studied the scene, and then studied it a lot more closely. The father-captain, who was presumably Cvorn, had the usual set of prador control units welded to his carapace, but next to them was another control unit with its cover and most of its internal circuitry removed. Sitting inside this was the bean-like shape of a Polity aug. Only this was no ordinary Polity aug, for it had scales like a lizard. It was partially alive, a biotech aug. Only one organization made these things: Dracocorp. All AIs knew the danger of Dracocorp augs for they were mechanisms quite similar in their action to those control units Cvorn wore. The one with the prime aug, such as Cvorn in this case, could come to mentally dominate those wearing subordinate units. Crime lords often used them to take full and utter control of their own people.

'Thrall technology,' Garrotte stated.

'Yes,' Penny Royal prompted.

'The prador children think he gave them a soft location and augmented mental capacity so they could snatch female prador,' Garrotte continued, 'but the ST dreadnought they stole for Cvorn was the real target there. I don't know what reason they gave themselves for coming back here, rather than just heading off and leaving Cvorn behind. But in reality they have had little choice in the matter and have come back to be slaves.'

'And his next target?'

'Sverl,' said Garrotte – it was obvious now.

'Cvorn has left just enough clues, just enough data for Sverl to pursue and thus fall into a trap. Sverl, even having rescued the people of Carapace City, will respond, because Cvorn, while he lives, will always be a threat.'

'And despite everything, Sverl is still a prador,' said Garrotte.

'Yes.'

'And prador tend to kill their enemies rather than avoid them.'

'If all goes according to Cvorn's plans, he will gain the evidence he needs of Polity perfidy, which is Sverl himself.'

'Prador don't accept recorded data – too easily falsified or tampered with.'

'An ST dreadnought will be quite capable of disabling Sverl's ship . . .'

Cvorn hated both the Polity and the new king of the prador for ending the war. He had allies in the Kingdom who would react very strongly to the physical proof of the transformation of a prador into an amalgamation of prador, human and AI. Very strongly indeed. This was the kind of stuff that could bring thousands of prador to Cvorn's side. It could lead to civil war in the Kingdom, or even to an attack upon the Polity and the renewal of the war. Which was precisely Cvorn's aim.

This was, as the saying went, serious shit.

'You have to stop this,' said Garrotte. 'You've just shown me how easily you can penetrate Cvorn's ship. If you want redemption, if you want forgiveness, then stop him. With this you can come home. We will accept you back into the fold.'

'That is not my aim,' Penny Royal replied.

'No, you have to—'

The *Micheletto's Garrotte* dropped abruptly into U-space and everything went dark. It realized its time sense was gone, so microseconds or centuries might be passing.

'Redemption?' Garrotte heard Penny Royal's voice coming out of the darkness. The image of something speaking from within that ancient empty space suit was undeniably creepy. 'Forgiveness?' Penny Royal wondered aloud.

As an AI Garrotte had a perfect mechanistic conception of human emotions and could experience just as much of them as it wished. It didn't, however, like experiencing such emotions while they were out of its control, and the sheer menace and malice that seemed to emanate from that unseen suit Garrotte could really have done without.

'Back into the fold?' mimicked Penny Royal.

'Isn't that what you want?' asked Garrotte.

'That is not for Polity AIs to decide.'

The menace remained, though its intensity of malice receded somewhat. Garrotte now returned to full engagement with the ship's sensors. Suddenly they were back in Polity space. There could be no doubt about it because the thing hanging out there in vacuum – a station shaped like a barbell measuring eight miles from top to bottom – Garrotte recognized as one of the Polity watch stations sitting on the border of the Graveyard. The ship AI at once tried to make contact with the AIs and humans aboard, but was blocked. Also, the *Garrotte* was under that sophisticated chameleonware again and, although those aboard the station would have detected a U-space signature, their chances of finding this ship before it departed again were remote.

'Why here?' asked Garrotte.

'Tell them.'

Garrotte now realized some sort of mechanical activity was occurring all around it. It went blind, but then sight returned, although only from the cams inset in its AI crystal's cage.

'Tell the Polity,' Penny Royal continued, 'to disengage. Unless they want war with the prador, they must allow me to deal with this. They must allow my pieces to remain in play.'

'Pieces?' *Was it all just a game to this monster?*

'Trent Sobel must be allowed to deliver his message to Sverl.'

'What message?'

'Also, beyond that, if I cannot find my own path, then some other path might find me. And maybe that will be the path of vengeance – on those who effectively forced a child into mass murder and thence created a monster.'

Further information arrived and opened itself in Garrotte's mind.

'What?'

With a crash and flash of light Garrotte found itself tumbling away from its original body. The AI of the *Micheletto's Garrotte* was now just a lump of crystal inside a ceramal cage, tumbling through vacuum, no more effective than the other debris out there. But its beacon was working and those in the station would detect that. Its understanding was quite clear now, even though Garrotte wished it wasn't. In fact, it wasn't sure it wanted to be found. It wasn't sure that when certain powers knew what it knew, they would allow it to continue existing.

Spear

The Rock Pool had changed drastically. What had once been a world with clearly distinct continents and oceans was now a ruddy brown orb. Dust and debris filled the atmosphere all the way round. Carapace City and all its inhabitants were gone. The prador were gone too, and it seemed nothing sentient remained down on the surface. However, a small and deceptively innocuous-looking vessel hung in orbit, for the Polity team who had been keeping an eye on this place – one of whom I had seen in those recordings Riss had obtained – had yet to depart.

'Luckily,' said Riss, 'there's a lot of water vapour up in the air, and pressure waves are still rounding the planet.'

'Huh?' I said brilliantly. I hadn't been sleeping so well. The déjà vu had gone now, as if dispensed with as irrelevant, and I was experiencing lives and swiftly ensuing deaths with metronomic regularity. I no longer needed some cue for them to proceed – I no longer needed to be in a similar place or situation to the one who died. One by one I'd experienced the deaths of the rest of the salvage crew – not only Garton, but also Mesen's ugly end when, in the stinking darkness, Penny Royal had taken him apart and then *reassembled* him. Finally, it discarded him like a broken toy, all its workings understood. I died with the four whom the AI had killed in the previous salvage team, and I had died with many others too.

'Rainstorms,' Riss explained. 'Filthy dust-laden monsoons sweeping round the planet should take most of that crap out of the atmosphere within just a few months.'

I simply stared at the snake drone, but then a voice issued from the ship's PA.

'What Riss is saying, in her ineloquent manner,' interjected Flute, 'is that the Rock Pool will experience no summer this year, but will not descend into catastrophic cold. This means that the ecosphere already established here, though with some die-off, will survive.'

'Oh goody,' I said, not all that interested.

All the lives and the deaths I had experienced now sat pristine in my mind. I could access them again at will. I could become this man Garton again and die as him once more as if for the first time. I could review his entire memories, the murders he had committed, the fortune he had won and lost, the pets he had tortured as a boy. Was this supposed to be a justification for his death on Penny Royal's part? Was I supposed to plumb these lives for the reasons they died? How could this be, when I could just as easily access the mind of a small child suffering a rapid death from a weaponized virus used by the black AI?

'Primitive fauna and flora have their place,' Flute noted. 'And future colonists might be glad of the reaverfish.'

'If they're crabs like you,' said Riss. 'Are you remembering what it was like to have a body, Flute? Getting input from your phantom taste buds?'

'Hey,' Flute rejoined, 'at least I knew the pleasure of food. All you have is memories of ersatz orgasms prompted by injecting eggs into prador.'

'But no Sverl here,' I said loudly.

After a short embarrassed pause Riss replied, 'Sverl departed twenty solstan days ago. Groves and his team only stayed to probe the wreckage about Carapace City in search of any survivors.'

This Groves was the Polity agent in the recording. He and his team had ignored communications from Flute and me, but it seemed that one of Riss's contacts was aboard that other ship.

'Did they find any?' I asked.

'Only corpses, though one of them does have a memplant, so that counts as a survivor.'

'Yes, I'm sure it does,' I said with feeling, forcing myself to deal with the present and turn away from the chaos in my mind. I really needed to find Penny Royal because even though it had already caused my death on the planet Panarchia, I had now once again become one of the black AI's victims. I continued, 'So, Sverl, a prador who it seems likely is turning into some grotesque version of a human being, decided to protect Carapace City, or rather the people here. When faced with the drastic effects of an atmosphere kamikaze strike, he landed his ship on the surface and rescued the population of that city.'

'So it would seem,' Riss replied.

I turned to look at the drone again. 'Is that because he's more human or because he's less prador? It strikes me that both humans and prador are no slouches when it comes to either committing genocide or being indifferent to it.' I knew where the acid in my voice was coming from, but couldn't stop it.

Riss gave a snakish shrug.

'And anyway,' I continued, 'Sverl's motives in taking those shell people off the planet might not be what anyone thinks. Maybe he was just stocking his larder. This all doesn't really make much sense.'

'We were lacking in data,' said Riss, black eye now open. 'I have been talking to the Polity drone Arrowsmith who was in communication with Sverl in the past and has managed to analyse his actions.'

I glanced at the drone. 'Your contact?'

Riss dipped her head in acknowledgement and continued, 'Arrowsmith tells me that Sverl seems likely to have directly amalgamated with AI crystal.'

'Which theoretically should kill him.'

Riss shrugged again. 'Penny Royal.'

Explanation enough, then, for technology that most Polity scientists considered beyond reach at present. It made sense too, because Sverl had upgraded Flute, who was one of his children, with AI crystal, so Sverl incorporating AI crystal explained how he must have lost his prador detestation of artificial intelligence.

'So an amalgam of prador, human and AI,' I said, adding, 'Another mess Penny Royal might want to clean up and our reason for going after him.'

'This may account for his actions in saving the people here,' Riss added.

Flute emitted an electronic snort at that.

'Sure,' I spat, 'because AIs are so *moral.*'

Silence ensued, so I continued. 'This doesn't get us any closer to finding out where he went, nor does it get us any closer to Penny Royal. Do either of you have anything useful?'

'Sverl used very sophisticated shielding during his jump,' said Riss. 'The Polity team here could get no indication of where he was going.'

'So still nothing useful.'

A further silence ensued, then Flute piped up, 'I have something useful.'

'Go on,' I said.

'We do not know Sverl's location; however, it is possible to locate Cvorn, who Sverl will almost certainly go after,' said Flute.

'Spy satellites,' said Riss.

'Let Flute have his moment,' I shot back, then asked, 'Why are you certain Sverl will go after Cvorn?'

'It's the prador way.'

'But Sverl is not quite a prador any more,' I said. 'Still, it's worth a shot. Go on.'

'Yes, spy satellites,' Flute continued. 'To be able to place so accurately that kamikaze explosion that destroyed Carapace City, Cvorn had to be watching the situation here. Already I am detecting some of them and they are constantly transmitting. It may be possible to lift the coordinates of where they are transmitting to.'

'Take us to one,' I instructed, anxious to be on the move.

Flute started the fusion drive to take us up and away from the planet and I felt its drag as the Rock Pool began to recede. Next came a brief moment of dislocation and the planet disappeared from the fabric screens. Next, a frame appeared there, etching out a portion of vacuum and expanding it to show an object like the head of a mace – a sphere studded with sensor spines. I auged through to the ship's controls and brought up a scale along the bottom of this expanded screen. The object was about the size of a grapefruit.

'Should we bring it in?' I wondered, 'or is it likely to be booby-trapped?'

'There is no need,' said Riss.

'No, there isn't,' Flute interjected quickly. 'The thing is utterly unshielded and I now already have the location of the receiver.'

'Creep,' Riss muttered.

I checked some of the figures via my aug. 'Flute, scan it for anything nasty, and if it's clear bring it into the munitions bay.' I paused. 'Here I am with a couple of superior intelligences to advise me and not one of them seems to be thinking ahead. We don't actually want to drop ourselves right in Cvorn's lap, but we do want to keep track of him.' Dead silence met this, so I continued, 'We U-jump to somewhere some light minutes or hours from the location of the receiver and check for Sverl's arrival there. If he hasn't arrived, we watch. And then, if Cvorn goes on the move, we use this object to continue tracking him.'

'I submit that my mind was damaged by Penny Royal,' said Riss.

'Supposing you had one,' muttered Flute.

'What's your excuse?' Riss snapped back.

Flute just muttered indistinctly, and dropped us into U-space.

I stood up to head for my cabin, where I would doubtless experience other deaths. I really needed to get control over this because it was affecting my judgement and my mood. I had to remember I *wasn't* those other people. For my own sanity, I needed to find a way to stand separate from them – partition them off.

4

Cvorn

The four females, deep in the laying pool at the centre of the spacious chamber, were twenty feet wide and possessed a body shape wildly at variance to male prador. Cvorn remembered that for entertainment during the war he had put some human prisoners into a prador crèche. The humans had failed to identify the females as prador, though admittedly they had little time to do so. He recollected the file he had enjoyed viewing again and again – the humans' bafflement just before they died screaming on the females' ovipositors and became the receptacles for prador eggs.

The female shell bore the shape of a human military helmet, with a wide skirt underneath, inside which she could fold her legs and underhands out of sight. Saurian ridges extend from the facial end of the carapace to the rear and the long and vicious ovipositor tail. The visage itself consisted of two large forward-facing eyes between which rose two club-like eye-stalks, each sporting one short-range pupil and one other fibrous sensor whose spectrum did not venture out of the infrared. Her mandibles were long and heavy and almost served as limbs themselves, in that she could rapidly extend them to snatch up prey. Her claws, though short and broad, possessed a clamping pressure that could crack even ceramal.

The four were down in the pool rather than up in the surrounding chamber because, having been fertilized, instinct had driven them into the water in search of hosts for their eggs. As he studied them, Cvorn felt no stirring of the mating urge. It had faded away years ago when, at about the same time as he started to lose his legs due to his extreme age, his reproductive organs had dropped off. He noted that one of the females had grabbed a large reaverfish and inserted her ovipositor deep inside. The fish was still moving, still fighting the briefly paralysing toxins produced by the eggs she was injecting. Obviously the Five had thought ahead and so preserved living reaverfish aboard their ship for this purpose, and they must have already scoured the results of any previous mating from these females and got quickly to work themselves. Cvorn decided he would have the females scoured again so they could take some of his own preserved seed, and turned to more immediate concerns.

With a twist of his claw in a pit control, Cvorn consigned this image off to one side in just one of his hexagonal screens, bringing all five of Vlern's children back into view in the others. He studied them, only managing to recognize the one named Sfolk because of a dark whorl in his shell beside his visual turret. The sensation Cvorn now experienced was a lot stronger and a lot more satisfying than his previous vague memory of mating. Here was power. The Five were confused about why they were here and did not understand why they were allowing his destroyer to dock; why they were allowing him into their realm.

'Here is where we will capture Sverl,' Cvorn told them, their presence strengthening in the aug network, but remaining subjugated to his will.

In a way this was more satisfying than using a control unit on some thralled life form because generally such creatures had no will or mind of their own. It was also more satisfying than the pheromonal control he exerted over his own children, which was just the natural order of things. When exercising power, Cvorn had always found it best to exercise it *against* someone. The only drawback here was their bewilderment; the fact that they did not yet understand that he had power over them. But so the situation would have to remain until he was utterly sure he had them in his grip. Then he could fill them in on what had happened to them, enjoy their dismay and watch them squirm.

'How will we capture him?' asked Sfolk, who had confirmed himself as the spokes-prador of the Five.

'We will use my destroyer as bait,' Cvorn replied.

On another screen, he noted his six remaining war drones and twelve of his own armoured children, including his first-child Vrom, now getting ready to head over to the ST dreadnought. His drones would establish themselves in that ship's cache beside the now-somnolent ones that had belonged to this ship's previous father-captain. With any luck, he should be able to bend those other drones to his will. Unfortunately, none of Vlern's drones remained to seize control of, since the Five had wasted them in family conflicts. However, controlling Vlern's twenty-two remaining second-children might be problematic, and that was why he was sending over Vrom and the others. Best to be rid of them, really, but only when he was sure. Only when the moment was right.

With a crash, which Cvorn felt right down in his sanctum, the two ships docked. Glancing at another screen, he noted his remaining eight second-children waiting with heavily laden grav-sleds and autocarts in the huge tunnel leading to the main airlock. He wished he could have stripped out his destroyer completely, but time was pressing. Though Sverl's arrival wasn't imminent, such a chore would take up time Cvorn needed to spend on more important tasks.

'I still do not understand,' said Sfolk. It had taken him a while to reply as he instinctively struggled against the control

Cvorn exerted over him, and while he remained confused about allowing Cvorn aboard.

'Observe the world below,' said Cvorn, 'and observe its moons.' He turned away from the screens and, hovering on grav-motors, headed to the door from the sanctum, his two thralled human blanks – two heavily muscled males naked but for weapons harnesses – trudging after him. As the sanctum door opened, he mentally transferred image and other data feeds to his aug and control units. A view of virtual hexagonal screens appeared across the vision centres of palp eyes he had lost many years ago.

'I see the world,' said Sfolk.

The planet resembled an earlier version of the Rock Pool. It was mostly oceanic, and the rocky landmasses barren but for flat plates of photosynthesizing vegetation creeping beyond the wide tidal areas created by the world's three moons. The oceans themselves swarmed with a monoculture of omnivorous and cannibalistic armoured monstrosities similar to ship lice. Cvorn briefly pondered how this was the case for many younger worlds: one life form coming to dominate the ecology. Over a few million years this form would diversify and new balances would establish – supposing the world survived what was to come.

'And the moons?' Cvorn prompted, as he exited his sanctum and headed towards the transfer tunnel to the other ship. His second-children were walking in front of him, bearing his baggage train. Ahead of these Vrom and the other, armoured second-children had already entered the dreadnought – following their orders precisely.

Two of the moons were nothing special. The largest was a standard meteor-pocked sphere while the other was an irregular object rather like a wrack pustule. The third moon was also spherical and pocked, but it had a large shadowy hole at one end and the mass readings were all wrong. Knowing that closer inspection would reveal more, Cvorn waited for Sfolk to understand.

'One is artificial,' said that prador.

Both the Kingdom and the Polity had made hides during the war. They would heat an asteroid to melting point with an energy weapon, then use either field technology or mechanical means to inject gas and blow it up like a balloon. After it cooled, they would cut a hole in one end. The result was a hollow sphere of rock in which to conceal a ship, a fleet or some massive weapon. The Polity had made this one, hence the pocking on its surface as of millennia of meteor impacts – a detail the prador tended to omit.

'We'll put this dreadnought inside, which will require some cutting, but can be done,' said Cvorn, now reaching the threshold into the other ship. 'This will bring the mass reading up close to requirements. We foam-stone in the hole and then the Polity chameleonware I am bringing aboard can conceal any further discrepancies.'

Now moving into the dreadnought, Cvorn turned to the door back into his own destroyer. He felt a pang of regret, then turned to the second-child waiting beside him. 'You are ready?'

'Yes, Father,' the child replied.

'Then you now have control of my destroyer – take it to the designated location and await orders.'

The second-child scuttled aboard. It would soon establish itself in Cvorn's sanctum and take control of the destroyer. Cvorn could have moved the ship to the nearby world and opened fire with its weapons by remote control, but Sverl might intercept the signal. Better to let the second-child carry out this task, because it would obey absolutely, despite the high chance that Sverl would vaporize both destroyer and second-child.

Instead, Cvorn was switching now to the dreadnought, establishing a firm grip on the five first-children through the aug network. He swung back round on his grav-motors to face into the dreadnought, feeling a sudden surge of unaccustomed excitement.

'Sfolk,' he said, 'remove yourself from this ship's captain's sanctum and take yourself to the first-children's quarters where your brothers are waiting.'

'Vlern . . . Cvorn . . . I don't understand why I . . .'

'Do it now,' said Cvorn, and pushed mentally, relishing the power.

Sfolk fought, but just could not win and, by the time Cvorn reached the massive diagonally divided door into the captain's sanctum, Sfolk was scuttling away down a nearby corridor. Cvorn halted at the door, abruptly fighting the urge to send his children after the young adult to bring it back, to tear it apart, and he didn't know why. Finally, he entered the sanctum; the urge faded as he again contacted all five of Vlern's children, his control of them now rigid.

'You are to send all your second-children kin to ship's food store number three,' he instructed, even at that moment usurping Sfolk's grip on the controls all around him and absorbing data on the dreadnought into his aug. He moved over to the array of screens here, inserted his artificial claws into pit controls and immediately began calling up images there. This was unnecessary because, like Sverl, he could use mental control here, but he felt the need to assert control *physically*.

He watched Vrom and his own second-children converging on that food store and entering it. Sfolk and crew, he noted, had already used the store as a mortuary; the corpses of the third-, second- and first-children who had been the original ship's complement were piled high in there. The original father-captain wasn't there, of course. He lay against the wall some yards behind Cvorn – a father-captain larger and older even than him, all his limbs gone and replaced by prosthetics. Cvorn turned to eye the corpse. Judging by the tool chest here and the pieces cut from the corpse's carapace, Sfolk had been extracting control units, probably to use to take full control of the drones aboard. Cvorn gazed for a moment at the armoured legs and did not know why he had begun to consider some options for himself. A flash of memory occurred, of being mobile on his own legs, of being young and strong . . . It might be good not to be wholly reliant on his grav-motors to get around. He turned back to the screens.

Obeying the orders of their older brothers, Vlern's second-children were entering the food store. They milled about in the centre of the room, nervous of the armoured prador gathered along one wall, sending requests to the Five for further orders. The Five did not elaborate – Cvorn did not allow them to. Meanwhile, his destroyer had undocked and was now accelerating away. Within a few hours, it would arrive at the nearby world, descend through the atmosphere to the sea, then drop through that to a deep oceanic trench. There it would be far down enough to defend itself from most long-range weapons Sverl, who would have followed the trail here, might hurl at it, and Sverl, therefore, would have to move in close to launch an effective attack, leaving his back unguarded.

All the second-children arrived in the food store and, from his sanctum, Cvorn issued a signal to close the door. Their breath created a sudden cloud of vapour in that chill place.

Then Vrom and the rest opened fire with Gatling cannons.

The children shrieked and clattered and flew apart in a mess of shattered carapace, disconnected limbs and smoking flesh. The place filled with the fog of their dying. This went on for some minutes, then waned to intermittent firing as Cvorn's children waded into the mess to finish off any survivors.

Eventually Vrom said, 'Task complete.' The first-child tended to speak with the leaden tones of an executioner even when he wasn't killing someone or something.

'Very good,' said Cvorn, finally managing to overcome the tight visceral surge of excitement he had felt on watching that slaughter. 'Establish control in critical areas.' Though he could direct most things from here, Cvorn wanted his children at the weapons and defensive emplacements throughout the ship.

As his children dispersed from the food store, Cvorn opened up the dreadnought's fusion engines to take it in pursuit of the hollow moon. It would take him perhaps a few days to conceal the ship properly, but that was okay – Sverl, who was undoubtedly pursuing, would be reaching the satellite relay by now so was still some days away.

Trent

Facilities were basic. Trent had a bed with a case of soldier's rations underneath, and a toilet that slid out of the wall. He couldn't wash himself, couldn't clean his teeth, but luckily had no need to shave since facial hair had been excised from the Sobel line. Obviously he just needed to be delivered alive – his dental health or cleanliness being irrelevant.

The ship's AI – that submind of this thing called the Brockle – hadn't spoken to him since they had left Par Avion. After a period of time he couldn't measure, during which he just ate something, used the toilet and then lay down to sink into a dark malaise, he slept. After that, he began to number his options and knew there weren't many. He considered suicide but, searching his own clothing, found that he had been relieved of every item that might be of use to that end. All he had was his clothing, his earring, his mind. He couldn't hang himself even with something to which he could attach a rope made out of his clothing. The ship AI would simply turn off the grav and he'd end up floating about on a rope umbilicus looking like an idiot. Maybe he could bite through his wrists or make some sharp edge out of his earring to open them. Too slow, and surely the AI could react to this in some way. His throat? Yes, maybe, but even as he thought about this he knew it was only an intellectual exercise and that he wasn't going to do it.

So all that remained was waiting to see what was going to happen to him. He would arrive somewhere, whereupon a forensic AI would begin taking him apart and inspecting those parts in detail. Whether the process would be painful he didn't know, though he did know that his suffering or otherwise would be a matter of irrelevance to the AI. After that he would be dead, gone, would have ceased to exist. He contemplated that knowledge and suddenly found that it simply didn't matter. He was a prisoner walking a corridor to the electric chair, the noose, the firing squad, the lethal injection or the disintegrator and it didn't matter which. He just needed it to be over.

During the ensuing three periods of waking, Trent thought about his past, wished he could change it but accepted he couldn't. Eventually, he felt a familiar twist in his gut and that drag out of the ineffable. It slapped him hard, brought him back into the moment. Then the ship AI spoke again.

'Deceleration in five minutes,' it said.

Maybe, if he positioned himself just so, he could use the deceleration as a method of suicide. Maybe stand on the edge of the bed and throw himself head-first at the floor as it ramped up. No. Trent walked over to the bed and lay on it, arms down by his sides. This time, though the invisible boot pressing down on him was heavy, he did not lose consciousness. After half an hour, the boot came off, and he sat up, his stomach tight and his clothing soaked with sweat. The ship was manoeuvring, occasional surges dragging him one way or another. He swung his legs over the side of the bed and sat waiting for the executioner.

Docking came next – the familiar crumps as clamps engaged somewhere outside this ship. Next, a horrible sensation traversed his body like some sort of roller passing through his flesh. His vision distorted, everything going in and out of focus then switching to black and white, then sliding into intense colour before returning to normal. He went deaf for a moment before hearing returned with such intensity he could hear the slight shifting of his clothing and the thump of his own pulse. It was as if he was a machine and something was now playing with his slide switches. He wondered if whatever had inspected him saw him that way too. He stood up.

As if in response, the locks securing the door into his cabin clonked and the door unlatched. He thought about just staying where he was and waiting, but that was cowardice. He walked over to the door and opened it, stepped through into the hold, glancing over at the Golem prostrate on its sled, and walked to the loading door, which stood open. He walked down the ramp door onto the grav-plated floor of an internal dock of either a space station or ship. Worn steel gratings rattled underfoot, scratched and dented bubble-metal panels clad the walls, and the circular doors, standing open on tunnels leading from the dock, were of a design he had only seen in a VR fantasy. This place, whatever it was, had the stink of antiquity. It looked as if it must have been built before even the Quiet War. His boots clonking on the gratings, he chose at random and stepped through one of the circular doors.

The tunnel here had a flat floor of bubble-metal, worn through to the closed-cell foam in places by the passage of feet. Just inside the doorway, and on either side, stood columns. On one of these rested a human skull, yet it bothered him not at all. What drew his attention was the glass sculpture on the other column. It was of a hooder and it seemed to be writhing – not in actuality but in some place deep in his mind.

'It was made by one of your associates,' said an echoing voice. 'Or should I say one of your superiors.'

'Who's that?' Trent asked, though he knew the answer.

'Mr Pace, of course,' replied the voice. 'He's an artist I would like to meet, but it is becoming increasingly unlikely that I will.'

Trent hadn't been asking who made the sculpture because he had recognized the style. Peering ahead, down the long dark tunnel, he saw a white object shifting far in the distance and expanding as it grew closer.

He expected some nightmare to come for him, but then gazed in puzzlement as a large fat youth – a mobile Buddha – resolved out of the gloom and sauntered down the tunnel towards him. This figure was shaven-headed – in fact, his obese body was completely hairless, lacking eyebrows and eyelashes. He wore red plastic sandals and skin-tight swimming shorts. He should have been ridiculous, but his presence weighed in Trent's mind like a heavy chunk of viciously sharp glass. His eyes were black buttons and there appeared little to read in them, least of all being mercy. Trent backed out onto the dock again to give himself room, though he suspected this would do him no good.

'Trent Sobel,' said the youth. 'Welcome to the prison hulk the *Tyburn*. I am the Brockle and I am here to execute sentence on you.'

Trent stepped back again as this youth, this thing, somehow also a forensic AI, advanced on him. Could he fight it? Should he try? No – this was it, this was how he ended. Fat Boy continued to advance, his gait rolling, then stuttering as his whole body turned silvery and began to shift as if worms were moving under his skin. Lines began to etch themselves into that skin and segmentation began to occur. Trent watched in horror as the man's thigh unravelled into a long, flat, segmented worm and dropped to the floor, squirming along to keep up.

The Brockle reached for him, fingers melding into things like flat metallic liver flukes that closed on either side of Trent's face. Its head tilted over, the eyes were sucked within, and began to split. Trent felt other tentacles grabbing his clothing and squirming inside, then stabs of pain all over his head. The grate of hard little drills bit into his skull. He had a moment to think that this wasn't so bad – he'd suffered more pain than this and endured – then the agony took hold and he screamed.

He screamed until something squirmed into his mouth and complemented the agony with a suffocation that showed no sign of ending.

Sverl

Sverl, who controlled his U-space drive directly with the AI component of his mind, surfaced his dreadnought from that continuum with hardfields flickering on and all weapons ready to deploy in an instant. At AI speeds, he gathered and sorted data from his ship's sensors. Within seconds he realized that Cvorn wasn't here, that the satellite data had been misleading.

'It's a relay,' he announced.

'Cvorn might be prador but he's not stupid,' Bsorol replied.

'Depending on how you measure stupidity,' interjected his brother Bsectil.

Sverl immediately wondered what he was supposed to make of that. Was this banter something recently acquired along with their new augs or had it always been there, but generally more low-key? Sverl considered his two first-children, who he had decided should try out augmentation before the others. He had to remember first that they weren't static minds like war drones, kamikazes or ship minds. At least, they weren't as static as those things would have been if made by prador other than himself. They *were* pheromonally enslaved creatures whom Sverl kept in a permanent state of chemically maintained adolescence. However, he had maintained them in that state for over a hundred years – a good eighty years longer than was usual, since fathers generally killed and replaced their first-children every two decades. Bsorol and Bsectil were very old, and no reason existed why they should not have continued learning throughout their time. They were older, in fact, than many father-captains in the Kingdom at that moment.

'It seems,' he said, 'that since acquiring your augs you are finding your usual tasks less onerous and have time to speculate on and discuss things beyond your remit. I therefore have another task for you to perform.'

'Yes, Father,' said Bsectil meekly, while Sverl detected Bsorol mentally erecting defences in his augmentation. Due to a problem some decades ago with the automatic lacing of his food with growth retardant, Bsorol had come very close to making the transformation into an adult. Sverl now wondered if he had gained a smidgen more free will than his brother.

Sverl sent to both of their augs some complex schematics, the location in ship's stores of his cache of Polity AI crystal, and their orders.

'You want to give the war drones crystal too,' said Bsorol resentfully.

'It's not the same,' said Sverl. 'Your augmentations contain AI crystal and have raised your game, as Arrowsmith would say, because you already have extensive mental capacity. Similar augmentation for them would not take them beyond sub-AI computing.'

'Still,' Bsorol grumped.

'The drones are also completely incapable of disobedience,' Sverl added, 'which I am inclined to think is not something beyond your reach. Obey your orders, Bsorol.'

'Yes, Father,' the ancient first-child replied.

Bsorol's tone had sounded exasperated to Sverl, yet why should it be? He watched them both head away from the two particle cannons to which he had assigned them and towards the indicated store. He observed them very carefully as they collected the designated amount of crystal, adaptors and cross-tech components and then began making their way to the drone cache. He watched Bsorol the most closely because he didn't think it beyond that first-child to take some components for himself in the hope of grabbing some time on an auto-surgery when Sverl was looking the other way. At the drone cache they began taking apart four war drones and installing the crystal. Perhaps it wasn't such a great idea, for his own safety, to so 'raise the game' of his own children, but Sverl had begun to feel a growing distaste and, perhaps, boredom with his utter control of them. He found them interesting now. Was this because Sverl was becoming more human or more AI, or was he simply feeling the ennui of his years bearing down on him?

Sverl now transferred his main attention back to the satellite relay. Cvorn had mounted it on a small deep-space asteroid mainly consisting of ice and naturally foamed rock. Already his AI component, working with the relay's signal traffic and with deep scans, had produced some results. He would have to send one of his children or a robot over to make the required physical connections so they could track the signal it was receiving. Perhaps he should assign Bsectil to—

'Snickety snick,' something said.

For just a second Sverl thought this was an attack and brought up all his defences. He recognized the U-space channel and the mental signature, but had expected nothing from there ever again. However, it seemed the Golem that Penny Royal had provided all those years ago still existed.

Sverl had never really been comfortable with the Golem, which was probably why, on the Rock Pool, he had allowed the Mafia boss Stolman to ostensibly find and activate it. Stolman had believed it utterly under his control, but it had acted as a spy for Sverl. Isobel Satomi, when she had penetrated Stolman's aug network and incidentally ripped apart and eaten that man, had believed she then controlled it. Thereafter, when she had taken it along with her to Masada and to her doom, Sverl had thought it destroyed. Now he began updating from it.

Intelligent enough to recognize the likelihood of its own demise during Isobel's pointless assault on Masada, the Golem had abandoned ship, sending Sverl's best wishes to her as it did so, though Sverl hadn't known. It had then gone somnolent in vacuum, unable to send signals to Sverl because its internal U-space transmitter just wasn't powerful enough to penetrate the U-space disruption in that system caused by the earlier deployment of USERs. Next, for no immediately apparent reason, Captain Blite had picked it up on his way out of the system, whereupon it covertly rose out of somnolence to observe its surroundings. It had seen that Blite had also picked up Satomi's second, Trent Sobel, and that the man wore a very interesting earring. Blite handed Trent and the Golem over to the Polity, and both were now in a very sticky situation indeed.

The earring . . .

Isobel Satomi had fascinated Sverl because what Penny Royal had done to her was very similar to what it had done to him. She had wanted power and the AI had turned her into a powerful monster – a hooder. Sverl had wanted knowledge of why the humans and AIs had been winning the war. The AI had given him that knowledge by turning him into an amalgam of prador, AI and human – yet another powerful monster.

He had wanted to talk to Satomi, and to examine her, because he felt sure he had much to learn from her. He'd thought her gone, dead, annihilated at Masada, but now Trent Sobel possessed her memplant. The Golem, via subtle scans, had found Isobel recorded in the purple sapphire hanging from Trent's ear. How it got there was irrelevant but, having been acquainted with the events on Masada that had culminated in Isobel's downfall, Sverl knew who had put it there: Penny Royal.

'Does he want it?' the Golem asked, eagerly adding, 'He wants it. He wants it!'

Did he?

Through the eyes of his Golem, Sverl saw Sobel's clothing lying neatly folded on a stone floor with the earring lying on top. The man himself was currently a smeared-out organic mass occupying the crevices of a loose ball of segmented biomech worms. These worms had utterly taken him apart and were examining him down to sub-molecular levels. Sverl could see his disconnected skull in there, its bony jaw opening and closing. He felt the horror and recognized that although Penny Royal was unique, the black AI was not *that* unique. After Sobel's inevitable, final, demise the forensic AI there would turn its attention to the Golem and find this communication link.

'I want it,' he replied, 'but recognize the limits of possibility.'

He felt pity for Sobel and found himself unsurprised at a

response so untypical of a prador. Undoubtedly, in Polity terms the man was deserving of death, but did any being deserve to die in such a way? Sverl also felt a degree of pity for the Golem because, although it was an artificial being, it still possessed a sense of self. It was still capable of suffering, and would soon be facing similar dismantlement. The earring would go too, for Penny Royal had transformed Satomi, and all the data that she was, the AI would take apart and analyse.

'I'll get it,' the Golem intoned.

'If you can; if you wish,' said Sverl, lining up a particular program in his mind. 'I am now releasing you from my grip. Henceforth you are a free entity and may do what you will.' Sverl sent the program that would completely release the Golem and felt it thump home with all the physicality of a hatchet, but the U-space link remained open. He continued, 'If you can bring Isobel Satomi to me then I will be glad, and I will reward you in any way I can. However, your first priority now must be to save yourself.'

Sverl now cut the link and began ramping up his security around it. Maybe the Golem could escape, for it was, after all, a product of Penny Royal and more than just a Polity Golem. Maybe it would then be willing to bring him the memcording of Satomi. Most likely, this would be the last he ever heard of it. Most likely, there would be something dangerous occupying the other end of that link next time he opened it, and he had to be ready.

Trent

Against a background of intense suffering, it started with what he recognized as his earliest memory. He was a boy running along one of the corridors of an arcology on Coloron when Dumal stepped out in front of him. He knew he was about to be beaten and humiliated but, in the present, he couldn't remember previous beatings and humiliations. Grinning horribly, Dumal spread his arms so Trent could not run past. Suddenly it was all too much and the infant Trent understood that neither flight nor compliance could ever stop this. If he ran away as before, the bigger boy would catch him because of a longer stride. Instead, Trent ducked his head down, kept running, and rammed his head straight into the other boy's fat gut. Dumal went down on his rump and Trent, his neck hurting, tried to get past, but a hand caught his trousers and dragged him down. The beating that ensued was the worst yet, and subsequent beatings would be just as bad, but Trent had made the decision to fight and refused to back down. The beatings only ceased when Trent caught Dumal in a restricted area and knocked him semiconscious with a length of steel pipe.

'And there's the decision,' a voice whispered, 'murderer.'

Dumal was down and bleeding, nearly unconscious. Trent gazed down at him lying there on the edge of the shaft that speared down to the bedrock of the arcology, just stared, utterly still, no knowledge of how much time was passing, and then, with no real thoughts in his mind, he stooped down and heaved Dumal over the edge. Watching the boy drop, he felt nothing but relief and, after that faded, nothing at all.

Now he felt that the Brockle's judgement of him was unfair. Further memories ensued, all harsh and cold and painful in their clarity. The Brockle raised his sister in his mind as an obvious comparison. She had suffered like him but she hadn't turned to crime. The forensic AI then stripped away protective forgetfulness to reveal that Trent's association with Separatists and other criminal elements on Coloron really had led to her death. It then moved on to his career in the Coloron mafia and his eventual escape from that world, the trail of misery he left behind him, and his arrival in the Graveyard.

He managed to ask why this was happening, not really using words, but from a point of puzzlement in some part of his mind still able to think.

'The pain?' the Brockle enquired. 'It occupies your surface consciousness and does not permit you to conceal anything from me. The torturers of old weren't entirely wrong.'

Something else?

'Yes, I could use other methods, but I'm an old-fashioned AI who believes in punishment.'

My sister . . . who I was . . .

'Oh, that suffering is just your own, now you clearly remember,' the Brockle said conversationally. 'You have no real pathology and have always known the difference between right and wrong. Most intelligences know that difference in the context of their particular society and make a choice – often the easiest one. You knew, even as a boy, that perhaps you would have further conflict with Dumal after you beat him with that pipe, but that your status as a victim had ended, and that Dumal would pursue easier prey. But you chose an easy murder instead.'

Trent's association with Isobel Satomi came next and he was aware that she was the Brockle's main interest. Everything Trent thought about her, knew about her, every conversation he had had with her and every sight of her, the AI examined in meticulous detail. It focused huge attention on the change she had undergone, and every reference to Penny Royal it checked repeatedly, ad nauseam. Then Thorvald Spear entered their compass, and Trent's pain abruptly faded. He felt that the AI was now concentrating so intently it had forgotten to torture him.

'He should be examined,' the Brockle hissed.

Trent thought that was for him, but another cold voice replied, 'Thorvald Spear has committed no crime.'

'Nevertheless . . .'

'It is not in your remit,' the other voice said. 'Finish there.'

'You fear what it will do next?'

Trent felt a leakage of frustration and anger. Obviously, his interrogator did not like the way this was going.

'Penny Royal can change paradigms,' the cold voice said opaquely. 'One murderer more, or less, makes no difference.' The voice paused, then continued, 'This piece must remain in play.'

'So it is true, what Garrotte has revealed?' said the Brockle. 'About Penny Royal's actions in Panarchia and what happened there?'

'Yes.'

'And the Golem?'

'Release it too.'

'Satomi – her memplant?'

'That goes too.'

Trent sensed some ensuing hesitation, rebellion even.

'Release them,' the cold voice repeated. 'Do not infringe upon the terms of your own agreed imprisonment.'

'I would argue that this lies outside those terms.'

'So do U-jump missiles. We could easily deploy them against you if you stray.'

'Do you not think I have not prepared for that?'

'Your choice . . .'

The pain returned redoubled. Trent now screamed on the outskirts of memory as the Brockle examined his generally irrelevant memories of being stuck in an airlock when Penny Royal had visited Satomi's ship the *Moray Firth* and repaired its drive.

He spent an eternity in hell while it checked and rechecked through the series of events that had led to Satomi's demise on Masada. It puzzled over why Penny Royal had sent the recording of her mind to Trent's earring and it fretted about why the black AI had sent Captain Blite to rescue Trent from the wreck of the *Firth*. Throughout all this Trent still felt that leakage of frustrated anger and was sure that the Brockle was being even more vicious than previously.

'They are wrong. Penny Royal isn't capable of change,' the forensic AI finally told him, 'and you don't deserve to live.' Whereupon he plummeted into darkness.

Trent woke sprawled on steel gratings and, just like when he woke after being beaten or shot, at the location of that event or in a hospital bed, he remained absolutely still, waiting for the pain. When it didn't arrive, he opened his eyes and carefully tested his limbs. Though he felt no pain, the memory of agony suffused him bone-deep. Eventually he slid his hands underneath his body and heaved himself upright to look around.

He was still in the dock, the ship he had arrived in resting nearby with its hold door still open, the Golem still on its sled inside. He was naked, his clothing stacked nearby with his earring resting on top. Not much had changed except, when he peered more closely at the floor he had been lying on, he saw it scattered with pieces of bone and small gobbets of flesh, a frosting of blood, some half-dissolved bone-clamps and another item he recognized at once: a titanium splint that had been inserted in his right thigh over three decades ago. He stood up, testing his limbs further, and found he was able to move easily enough, though he felt tender to the core. He examined his arms, torso and legs and found them free of old scars.

'Why am I alive?' he asked.

'A question all beings must pose to themselves,' replied the Brockle tightly.

Suddenly, as if it had edited its presence out of his consciousness and back into its human form, the forensic AI was an overweight youth again, squatting just a few yards away from him. Trent stepped back from it. Perhaps this was how it went: after the examination, it returned him to perfect health for final execution of sentence. He waited for that.

The Brockle waved a chubby hand at the detritus scattered on the floor. 'Whenever I reassemble someone I always like to remove the faults. It's nit-picky of me but that's the way I am. Perhaps you should consider the removal of your scars the physical expression of disconnection from your past and perhaps, as Penny Royal suggested, you should redeem yourself.'

'When are you going to stop toying with me and get this over with?' Trent asked.

'I am not toying.' The Brockle pointed to the single-ship behind him. 'I have removed my submind that usually guides it, but there is a replacement available. Take the ship and go.'

'You still haven't answered my question.'

'Orders,' the Brockle replied. 'Apparently Penny Royal is going to stop a war and you are an important part of its plans. You are a messenger.'

Trent pondered that for a second, then said, 'So what did the Garrotte reveal?'

'Not enough, in my opinion, to justify your release,' the Brockle replied. 'And not enough to justify a policy of non-interference.'

'Non-interference?' Trent echoed.

It did not reply. Trent blinked and the Brockle was gone. Should he believe all this? Maybe his mind was in some virtuality where the AI was still playing with it, while his body remained in pieces spread throughout the Brockle's real body of biomech worms. He knew, perfectly well, that it could adjust his perception of time to keep him in such a virtuality for seconds of its own time, but centuries of his.

Trent turned and walked over to his clothing, first picking up his earring to fit back into his ear, but annoyingly the Brockle had even repaired the hole there. He put it to one side and then donned his clothes. Even if this was a virtuality, he had to act and react as if it was real, so now he thought about what to do.

The Brockle had given him a ship but one without an AI and therefore incapable of dropping into U-space. Sure, he could obtain some second-child ship mind somewhere, but he had no idea how long it would take him to arrive at that somewhere. He decided to explore, because he probably needed more than that box of soldier's rations under his bed aboard.

Slipping his earring into his pocket, he turned towards the tunnel the Brockle had come down and saw that the antique door was closed. He walked over to try it and found the manual wheel locked solid. He then tried all the doors in the back wall but they were locked too. Perhaps this was just the result of some alteration of the code in this virtuality, or perhaps this was real, but either way he wasn't going through those doors. However, in a side wall stood a smaller door he had yet to try. He walked over and it opened easily, but now he felt reluctant to step through. Damn it, he couldn't keep expecting the worse, so he forced himself to take the step. A tunnel beyond, with walls streaked with actual rust and beaded with condensation, led him to yet another door – this one welded shut. He walked back from it and paused by one of a series of oval portholes of the kind found in First Diaspora cryoships, wiped away condensation and peered out.

From the right issued the orange glare of a sun, or some

other astronomical object, and silhouetted against this stood an ancient com tower scattered with radio dishes. He couldn't actually get a look at the body of the *Tyburn* but, pushing his face against the cold glass, he could see a massive nacelle poking out down below, so this ship was probably some early U-space vessel like those that left towards the end of the First Diaspora. However, gazing at that old design of nacelle he could see new metal around a bulge towards its rear that indicated that it might well be functional, and might well contain some newer form of U-drive. He grunted to himself and backed away, then headed back out into the dock.

'Okay,' he said, 'I'll leave.'

No reply was forthcoming, but he hadn't expected one.

He headed over to the open hold of the ship, walked up the ramp and paused to gaze at the Golem lying on its sled. Reality or otherwise, he didn't want this thing in the ship along with him. He reached out and activated the small control panel on a narrow upright post on the sled, bringing it up off the floor; then, using the 'simple towing' setting, he kept a finger on the control as he walked back down the ramp, the sled obediently following. He shut it down on the floor of the dock and returned inside the ship.

On the other side of this hold lay the door into the space that had been his prison. The corridor beyond took him to a cramped engine room filled with the bulk of a fusion drive and fusion reactor and the control columns feeding optics out to the U-space nacelles. Returning along the corridor brought him to the cockpit. This was cramped too, contained a single dusty acceleration chair and console, a viewing laminate in the lower half of a chain-glass screen and a scattering of sweet wrappers across the floor. He brushed the chair down, then sat and reached out to activate the controls. They were of a very old design but he knew he could operate them.

First, he closed the hold, hearing the ramp rumble back up and seal with a satisfying thump. Next, after disengaging docking clamps, he searched for and found 'space doors' and set them to open, but when he did so the clamps re-engaged and he heard that rumbling again, shortly followed by a screen warning that the hold was again open, and offering him the option of closing it. What the hell had he done wrong? He closed it once more and again punched the control to open the space doors. He felt the ship turning, the screen now telling him the dock pressure was dropping. Turning a full hundred and eighty degrees, the ship clumped to a halt. He saw sliding space doors, their edges castellated, opening ahead to reveal a swathe of stars.

Am I really free? he wondered, as he took hold of the ship's joystick and raised it a little, hearing steering thrusters ignite and feeling their rumble through the floor. He pushed the stick forwards and the ship obeyed, taking him rapidly towards the open doors. He shot out into vacuum, the orange eye of some cold Neptunian planet coming clear to his right. With a twist of the joystick, he spun the single-ship round and with it travelling backwards gazed at the Brockle's lair. The hulk was at least a couple of miles long and he recognized the design. On the end of a long stalk to the fore was a section like a giant bulbous monorail carriage. This was where the crew and passengers were packed in hibernation capsules. This stalk extended from the larger drive section he had just departed, while extending from this were the vanes holding the U-space engine nacelles. Two nacelles were still in place and had obviously been modified, while it looked as if the third had been sliced off. Further inspection along the hull revealed stubby weapons turrets and the dark maws of weapons ports – all obvious additions. He wondered then about the exchange he had overheard: . . . *terms of your agreed imprisonment.*

Trent studied the vessel for just a short while longer, then twisted the joystick to spin his single-ship round. He hit the fusion drive and the acceleration slammed him back into his chair. Virtuality or reality, he couldn't deny the joy he suddenly felt to be heading away from that place. Within minutes, he was up to full acceleration with the old ship receding far behind. A second later, his instruments indicated some object over to his right, and he diverted his course slightly to get a closer look. The thing, hanging in vacuum there, was a large doughnut with tech jabbed through its centre like a bunched-up collection of rods. He recognized a tokamak fusion reactor wrapped round some serious weapons and wondered if it belonged to the guards, or to the prisoner, then turned his ship away, wondering what next?

'Snickety snick,' said something behind him, and the cold metal of a skeletal Golem hand gripped his shoulder.

'I gotcha,' it added.

5

Captain Blite

Captain Blite gazed at the figures, relayed directly from his Galaxy Bank account to the new laminate on *The Rose*'s chainglass screen, and wondered why he felt so empty. He glanced at the latest offer for the Penny-Royal-tweaked hardfield generator he had aboard. Silly money. He was rich now, all his crew were rich and they had all at last achieved what they had been aiming for. All those years of trading, of risky deals, of working close to the edge of legality and of often being in life-threatening situations, were at an end. They could now retire to luxurious inner Polity worlds. Blite himself could relax on that white sand beach on New Aruba, sipping cocktails while someone else took the risks in *The Rose* and the other ship he had planned to buy.

Perhaps that was it; perhaps it was because it was all over.

Brondohohan would be buying that mobile submarine house he had always been hankering for. Chont and Haber, who had been packing up their belongings only a short while ago, would at last have the children they had been planning, down to every genetic detail, over the many years. Greer would head for Spatterjay and fulfil her strange wish to have one of the leeches there bite her, and to buy a ship to sail that world's oceans. Martina could return to her home world wealthy enough to give her rich family the finger. While Ikbal could, well, do whatever it was he wanted to do.

'They've gone.'

Blite turned to see Brond enter the bridge and plump himself down in one of the acceleration chairs.

'Chont and Haber?'

'And Ikbal and Martina.'

'Really?'

'Really,' Brond nodded. 'Our loving couple are heading to Earth while Ikbal and Martina are on the way to her Gallus Yard. Seems they want to go into business with each other.'

'And they didn't bother to say goodbye.'

'They did – you just weren't paying attention.'

Blite nodded. Sure, Chont and Haber had said their good-byes but, knowing Blite, they had hardly been protracted. The other two, however? Was saying 'we're leaving' the same as goodbye?

'So when are you heading off?' Blite asked then, looking up as Greer entered.

'The second we get permission to leave this fucking place,' said Greer, plonking herself down in the other seat.

Blite glanced at the laminate. Another offer had appeared there – a massive amount of wealth for that generator. He was sure the delays were something to do with that . . .

'So you're both staying with *The Rose*?' he asked, glancing at each of them. 'It's all over now. I personally plan to buy a beach-front house on New Aruba, have my liver reinforced and spend the next century trying every drink they have there.'

The two exchanged a look; Greer gave a slow nod and Brond replied, 'No you don't.'

'What do you mean, I don't?' Blite growled, feeling a famil-iar comfortable anger rising in him.

Brond continued, 'For the others, working with you was a means to an end. Ikbal and Martina always planned to pool their wealth when they had enough and buy their own ship. Chont and Haber always dreamed of settling and having children like some antediluvian couple. It was over for them the moment you filled their accounts. It is not over for us.'

No, Brond was wrong. Blite reckoned his empty feeling was due to it all being over. They were breaking apart and starting a new chapter, going their own ways.

'Sometimes I think I know you better than you do yourself,' said Brond. 'You can't accept how, at least for us three, things have changed.'

'Bollocks,' said Blite.

'Two words,' interjected Greer, 'Penny and Royal.'

Blite stared at her, feeling as if he had just been sucker-punched.

'So what?' he managed.

'We can start with the cold hard facts,' said Brond, holding up one large thick finger. 'Fact one: Penny Royal is something Polity AIs take very seriously indeed, which is why that poor fuck Sobel, who only had some brief passing encounters with it, is probably in very little pieces now and every one of them being examined down to the submolecular level. Fact two: you had an encounter with Penny Royal that lost you your previous crew. Fact three: Penny Royal smuggled itself out of Masada on our ship and used us to ferry it all over the Graveyard. Fact four: Penny Royal fucked about with our ship and with our minds. Shit, I could go on and on, but y'know . . . fact five: anyone who thinks Polity AIs are moral and always adhere to their own laws is a dickhead.'

Blite realized his mouth was hanging open, and closed it.

'Fact gazillion,' said Greer, pointing at the laminate.

Blite turned to see that the latest offer for the hardfield generator had disappeared and now the station AI had put a mandatory hold on their departure. He didn't like that at all – not one bit.

'I didn't like doing that, you know,' he said.

Greer and Brond gazed at him in puzzlement.

'Handing Trent Sobel over to them,' he explained. 'I kinda liked the guy.'

They waited patiently and he continued: 'I didn't really get why Penny Royal saved his life and then just didn't care about him. I told it where I was heading and it said it didn't matter.' Something else now appeared in the laminate: a demand that they open their ship for inspection. He went on, 'He was some part of Penny Royal's plans. Maybe to test something, maybe to check some Polity response – it's all a bit too deep for me. I told him that Penny Royal wasn't finished with him and maybe gave him some hope that wasn't real.'

'This isn't over,' said Brond. He grimaced then reached up and tapped a finger against his aug. 'Chont and Haber managed to take the runcible out of here, but Martina just told me that she and Ikbal have been arrested on the charge of smuggling proscribed technology out of Masada.'

Blite nodded, pleased that was the only illegality being mentioned. It demonstrated that the care he had taken in his many other operations had been well worth the effort. He guessed that his two crewmembers would be all right, since he now understood that they weren't the real target. Maybe they would undergo some sort of examination, but they'd survive.

Brond reached across to the controls and tapped one to pull up an exterior cam view. 'Yeah, I thought so.'

Blite recognized the four who had just walked out onto the floor of the dock – of course he did; he'd earlier watched them take Sobel away.

'You're right,' he finally admitted. 'I was stupid to think that the Polity would just let us walk away from this . . . Leven, where do you stand?'

The erstwhile Golem and now the ship mind of *The Rose* replied, 'It stinks. Yeah, we aimed to smuggle out technology but we got Penny Royal instead. It's just an excuse to hold us and get into this ship and take it apart.'

'So you're not a moral Polity AI ready to bow to your masters?' Blite asked.

'Screw that,' said Leven. 'If they have their way, we'll all be visiting the Brockle, and I don't want any part of that forensic AI psychopath. I'm part of this ship, remember, and was closer to Penny Royal than all of you.'

The Brockle?

Blite let that one go as he swung his chair round to the console. He opened general com to Par Avion and announced, 'Okay, we've been patient with you, but now we're leaving.'

A frame immediately opened in the laminate to show the Golem woman down on the dock, her dracoman and two human companions in view behind her. 'You're locked down and you're not going anywhere, Captain. Yes, I know you can stick yourselves inside that spherical hardfield but you can't stay there forever.'

'Not going anywhere?' Blite echoed.

'Be sensible, Captain,' she said.

'Leven,' said Blite. 'Chew out those clamps.'

The frame showing the woman flickered, while in the view through the chain-glass screen the lights dimmed all along the docks just before everything out there shaded to amber and something crashed underneath the ship. The hardfield, briefly surrounding *The Rose*, severed through the dock floor and the clamps holding the ship in place. It flickered again and again. The position and radius of the hardfield – now indicated at the bottom of the laminate screen – changing each time. Each time came another crash and soon debris was flying through the air out there.

Good boy, thought Blite. Leven was carefully chopping apart everything below since they didn't really want to take a large chunk of the dock with them. Steering thrusters now ignited the scene, *The Rose* beginning to rise and turn.

'I'm glad to see you cleared the dock,' said Blite, rubbing at his arms because he was suddenly cold. The entropic effects from deploying that hardfield were as evident here as they had been at Carapace City. 'And I'm glad to see your three companions are wearing suits – they'll be needing them.'

'Blite,' said the Golem woman, 'you're just making things worse for yourself.'

Blite nodded. 'I guess you got some stats from Masada on the hardfield Penny Royal made for us, but I know for a fact that all your scanning hasn't been able to penetrate the generator itself.' He eyed the space doors now coming into view and felt the surge as steering thrusters took *The Rose* towards them.

'Look, be reasonable,' she said. 'No one wants to come down hard on you but the Polity needs data on Penny Royal. Surely you realize just how dangerous that thing is?'

'What you didn't find out,' said Blite, ignoring her entreaty, 'is something implicit in the other word used to describe such generators, which is "projector". It projects. Quite well, really.'

'Fuck,' said the woman, while the three behind her, understanding at once, closed up the shimmershield visors on their suits.

'The doors, Leven,' Blite instructed.

The spherical hardfield appeared far ahead now, just one hemisphere of it covering the space doors. It flickered a couple of times then went out. Shortly afterwards two semicircular chunks of the space doors were tumbling out into vacuum. The roar of escaping air took hold of their ship, hurling it out afterwards. Leven ignited the fusion drive, but it stuttered as the ship mind kept engaging the hardfield around them. Blite glimpsed the flashing of a particle beam as Par Avion fired on them, just trying to disable them, he hoped.

'How long until we jump?' Blite asked, weirdly calm.

'A few minutes,' Leven replied.

Those minutes dragged by, but then Blite felt the familiar twist as the U-space engine began to engage. However, something slammed against the ship before it went completely under, and reams of error messages appeared in the lower half of the laminate screen.

'Fuck, they got our fuser,' said Leven.

'Where to, Leven?' asked Blite, still settled in that calm.

'Where else?'

'It has to be the Graveyard,' said Brond. 'There has to be an ending somehow so that the Polity will leave us alone. Penny Royal might have finished with us, but we haven't finished with it.'

'Yeah, right,' said Greer sarcastically.

She understands, thought Blite. Greer understood that Brond, despite seeing through so much, had this last bit arse about face. Blite knew that the words he had spoken to Sobel could be equally applied to himself. Penny Royal had to have seen what was likely to happen here and still had an investment in it. Penny Royal wasn't finished with them – he was sure of that now, right down to the bedrock of his very being.

Spear

Tracking the signal from Cvorn's spy satellite, I ensured our first jump took us some light weeks from its reception point. This was close enough for us to pick up the light from that source during the period when Cvorn might well have been there – essentially looking into the past.

'It's just a communications relay,' Flute announced. 'Cvorn isn't there.'

'How do you know Cvorn isn't there?' Riss asked. 'You're looking into the past.'

'An educated guess,' Flute replied.

Before they could get into their usual bitching at each other, I said, 'Even if it is a relay, Cvorn might well have set some sort of trap. Search for mines or any activity at all. We'll just keep watching for a while.'

Perhaps this wasn't the right move, but I still needed time with my own particular problem. During our journey here, I had struggled to distance myself from those other memories or to close out their emotional content, but to no avail. However, over the last day I'd made a breakthrough: I had found I could control them, catalogue them, file them and in doing so achieve at least a partial separation from them. Interestingly, I also found I could search them for death memories fitting specified parameters. This led me to a further discovery.

The only person in that vast repository who remembered dying in the bombing of Panarchia was me. This of course made sense. How could Penny Royal have recorded the minds of eight thousand soldiers during their fast and impersonal extinction when it had bombed them on Panarchia? I wondered then if, somehow, I was supposed to represent them all.

We watched the distant deep-space asteroid for a few days or, rather, Flute watched it. I wandered in and out of my laboratory, often stopping to stare at Penny Royal's discarded spine in its glass cylinder. I considered the option of ejecting the thing into the nearest sun to free myself from its torment, but immediately felt a deep visceral terror and the absolute certainty that I was so bound to the thing that I would burn too. And could I really so easily sacrifice all those lives, and deaths? The spine contained thousands of the dead who, with present technology, Polity AIs could restore to life. In the end I decided to examine the thing further, but over two days procrastinated and failed to mount it in the clamps I'd set up on my central workbench. Finally, on the third day, I got up the courage to take it out of its cylinder, mount it in those clamps, and set to work.

'Nothing happening out there,' Flute announced with irritating regularity, always adding, 'or nothing was happening out there two and a half months ago.'

I pondered the possibility of making short U-jumps on the way in and taking snapshot views across the two and a half month period. However, as the *Lance* U-jumped in and closed in on the present, this would generate a lot of noise not confined by relativity and would warn anyone near that relay of our approach. I therefore procrastinated further.

'Something happening,' Flute finally announced, 'but not by that relay.'

'Yes,' Riss agreed, 'something's happening.'

'You boost through my systems?' asked Flute suspiciously.

'I do,' said Riss, 'because that's what they're for.'

'Is someone going to fill me in?' I asked. I was gazing at a nanoscope image of the surface of Penny Royal's spine and seeing densely folded crystalline structures that disappeared like fractals below the level of visibility. The nanoscope was highlighting structures and conjunctions of matter that had to be maintained by an inner power source and picotech manipulation. There were compounds there too that could only have been put together by nanotech field manipulation and simply should not have been able to maintain themselves. I felt that unravelling, and understanding, just the surface of this object lay beyond my present abilities, and that fact left me oddly relieved. After all, if I couldn't understand it, there was no point in investigating further.

Riss turned towards me. 'Flute regularly opens a U-space link to update from the Polity on astrogation data: warnings, news . . .'

'I'm aware of that,' I said, 'I link to it through my aug. It's how everyone in the Graveyard keeps up to date.'

'There is news concerning the Polity watch stations along the edge of the Graveyard,' said Flute before Riss could continue. 'They have been moved to high alert and some assets have been moved into position. I have images.'

I considered dipping into all this myself via my aug, since for a while I hadn't checked on the few updates available to me in the Graveyard, but decided against that. I had been staring at those images of the surface of the spine for long enough and now I wanted to get away from it and stop focusing through my aug. Standing up, I headed out of my laboratory to the bridge, Riss following me closely, and dumped myself in the chair there.

'Okay, show me,' I instructed.

The usual images up in the screen fabric – the cold and distant stars and one frame displaying the relay asteroid – hazed for a moment. One of the Polity watch stations next appeared – a great thing like an upright barbell. I saw more activity here than I had seen around these stations before. I recognized a squadron of squid-like attack ships shoaling about it, along with a series of lozenge-shaped dreadnoughts. Also visible was a spherical ship even larger than they were. This might be one of the rarely seen Gamma-class vessels, or maybe something even larger.

'There has been no attempt to suppress information about this activity,' Riss lectured. 'But there has also been no attempt to make it generally known.'

I nodded. The Polity didn't try to suppress stuff on this scale because it was a pointless exercise. There would always be some pair of eyes or some cam watching, and people would always broadcast such activities throughout the AI net. In fact, Polity AIs had learned during the war that trying to suppress information about such activities tended to make the citizens of the Polity more suspicious, and the act of suppression itself tended to make the news spread further and faster.

'Interesting,' I said, wondering what the relevance was to us. I turned to gaze at Riss. 'And now you can tell me more, I have no doubt.'

Riss blinked a black eye. 'Flute is seeing one side of it – from the Polity. What he is not seeing is that it is a response to other activity.'

'And you have your contacts,' I suggested.

'I have my contacts,' Riss agreed. 'And I have images if Flute will allow me to display them.'

'Flute . . .' I said warningly.

'Oh, very well,' my ship AI grumped.

The watch station faded. In its place appeared a sulphur-yellow world that had to be sitting inside some sort of gas cloud, perhaps an accretion disc or a nebula. No stars were visible and the world stood out vividly against this background. Sky blue and dark green were swirled together, interspersed with lines of blood red and odd organic-looking formations of fleshy pink. My brain tried to give all this definition, but the shapes kept eluding it. It was just a gas cloud – no more than that. I blinked at the brightness. Space wasn't always black.

'So what am I seeing?' I asked.

'It just has a number on Polity maps,' Riss replied, 'but the prador call it something like the "Feeding Frenzy". It was a living system before the war but during it, the Polity blew up a close orbiting gas giant, in fact an object better defined as a pre-ignition proto star. The prador lost a major shipyard, thirty-eight dreadnoughts and many other ships and stations here.'

'Blew up? How?'

'We dropped a shielded runcible gate into it while the gate at the other end was moved into position before a stream of near-light-speed asteroids flung out from a spinning black hole.'

'And why have I never heard about this?'

'No one survived the mission and the Polity AIs don't brag.'

'Yeah, sure,' said Flute.

'Anyway, that was after your time,' Riss added. 'Lying on their border with the Graveyard, it is now a useful place of concealment for the prador. Though obviously not as concealing as they think.'

A frame opened over this bright image, bringing into focus some objects poised over the sulphurous world. I now saw about thirty ships of a design I did not recognize: long golden teardrops with dark grooves running down their length.

'King's Guard,' Riss explained. 'Each of these ships is two miles long.'

I let out a slow breath. I'd picked up on some rumours about the prador King's Guard during my various searches for data on the Graveyard. They were secretive. No one saw them without their body armour and, like some antediluvian human armed forces, they always took home their dead. They came down very hard on any kind of rebellion inside the Prador Kingdom and occasionally intervened in the Graveyard. They were fast, surgical and without the usual mess and titanic destruction that had been the hallmark of the prador during the war.

'An attack? But against who?' I wondered.

The image faded to black, a frame now closing in on other objects. These I immediately recognized and I felt my back crawling. Eight old-style prador dreadnoughts were sitting in the vacuum of deep space.

'It could be that the King's Guard is mustering either to make some response to these ships or to join them. This could be preparations for an attack on the Polity, yet there really aren't enough ships for that.' It sounded to me as if Riss wasn't particularly displeased with the idea of an attack on the Polity and, of course, the potential for all-out war. 'The Polity ships could be mustering in response to these or vice versa.'

'Or all of this,' I said, 'could be something to do with Sverl, Cvorn and Penny Royal.'

'Isn't it arrogant to assume that such events might be related to your main interest?' Riss asked.

'Perhaps,' I said, 'but those three characters are the biggest thing happening in the Graveyard now and I don't believe what we're seeing here is a coincidence.' I reached round and pulled across the seat's safety harness. 'Flute, take us to that relay right now.'

Sverl

Bsectil, hovering just above the surface of the icy asteroid on which Cvorn had mounted his communications relay, had finished making all the possible close scans and checks Sverl had been unable to make from his dreadnought. The first-child was hesitating now, understandably nervous about descending to the surface.

'Oh well,' he finally said, 'it's been an interesting life.' Emitting streamers of vapour from the impellers of his suit, he dropped to the surface, faster than necessary, and landed with a thump that generated a spreading cloud of ice crystals. There he paused, his sharp feet driven down into the ice, doubtless, as the drone Arrowsmith might have said, kissing his arse goodbye.

'Right, I'm still alive,' he said, heaving his feet out of the ice and towing his tool chest over to the relay.

As Sverl observed him come to a halt by the domed lump of prador metal anchored to the ice, he pondered on how well suited to this kind of environment was the prador form. Glancing at other screens, he observed the humans in Quadrant Four and thought about how much less suited were they. However, they were now all as neatly organized as social insects and scuttling to do Taiken's bidding. They did have other advantages, it seemed. By now, had it been prador in their situation, there would have been at least a few assassinations, if not some outright battle.

'It all looks suspiciously easy.' Bsectil now had the lid of the relay open and was busily connecting optics and power feeds.

'Probably until you set it to transmit its data,' said Bsorol from down in the drone cache. Aug-linked to Bsectil, he was watching the show while, with prosthetic underhands, simultaneously working inside the opened-up armour of a war drone. 'Then it will be blam and byebye Bsectil.'

'It will not,' Sverl interjected. 'Bsectil will be clear of the asteroid by then and transmission will ensue on a timed delay.'

'Okay,' said Bsorol. 'I'll bet on something blowing when he makes a final connection and if not that, then some nasty virus . . .'

'Quite likely,' Sverl agreed.

Bsectil continued working, then after a few minutes paused with an optic plug held up in the tips of his right claw, the cable from it leading to a simple radio transmitter lying on the ground beside him.

'Here we go,' he said.

Sverl fleetingly wanted to tell him to desist, but Bsectil was quick and had inserted the plug a second later. Sverl analysed why he had not sent that order, because with his AI component there had been enough time. It all came down to his growing suspicions about that relay and its purpose.

'Still alive, I see,' said Bsorol.

'Yeah.' Bsectil launched himself from the asteroid, tool chest in tow, fired up his impellers to distance himself from the asteroid, then ignited a chemical booster attached under his armour to send him hurtling back towards the dreadnought. Sverl, meanwhile, once again scanned near space looking for any booby traps his penetration of this relay might activate. There was nothing: no physical objects larger than a grain of dust within the reach of his scans, unless Cvorn had used some sophisticated form of chameleonware of which Sverl was unaware. He then again probed the ice and rock of the asteroid. Certainly enough crap sat inside the asteroid, which, with a little chameleonware help, might conceal a CTD, but even a planet-buster would do little more than give his dreadnought a bit of a shake at this range.

Bsectil fired his booster again to slow his approach, used his impellers to guide himself down towards an open airlock and went in fast enough to land with a crash that sent him tumbling into the inner door. As the outer door closed, he righted himself and did an odd little dance.

'It'll be a virus then,' said Bsorol, always the optimist.

Sverl ignored them as the timer ran out and the radio transmission began. Data began coming in and Sverl studied it
pensively, certain that this had just been too easy. He now knew
precisely to where the relay was retransmitting the signal from
the Rock Pool spy satellite. It couldn't have been clearer. Bsorol
and Bsectil were right. If he had been in Cvorn's position he
would have planted a CTD deep within the asteroid set to
detonate the moment something began interfering with the
device, or maybe lined up some nasty viruses to transmit the
moment a physical connection was made. Maybe both. Perhaps
this relay transmitted to another one where such a trap had been
set, or even through a whole series of them, but he doubted it.
Cvorn just hadn't had the time to set up that many relays.

'So what's he got?' enquired Bsorol.

Bsorol, now aware that there had been no nasty virus, had
also surmised that the spy satellites around the Rock Pool, and
now this relay, were the lure and that where their signal terminated lay a trap. He was asking the next most relevant question.
Cvorn had departed the Rock Pool in a prador destroyer that
was no match for Sverl's ship. He had lost his allies when they
headed off into the Kingdom in search of prador females and
almost certainly would not be getting them back. As the drone
Arrowsmith would have it, Vlern's five children were by now
either toast or on the run far from the Kingdom and the Graveyard, probably with King's Guard in pursuit. But Cvorn *had* to
have something.

What was Sverl missing?

Augmentation?

The thought was like a blow. Cvorn had always been one
of the more intelligent father-captains and had clearly demonstrated when he turned on Sverl on the Rock Pool that he
had been aware for quite some time of the changes Sverl had

undergone. Cvorn was prador enough to have an utter detestation of artificial intelligences, but seeing what had happened to Sverl, he would recognize the distinction between an artificial entity and an augmented natural one. If Cvorn had learned from Sverl and gone down the augmentation route, he would be a lot more dangerous. Sverl was considering what precautions he should take when a U-space link opened through his heavy computer security.

I really don't need this now, Sverl thought.

'Yes,' he finally said, when it became evident that the communication was voice-only and nothing nasty was queued up to come down the link. 'And none of that "snickety snick" nonsense.'

'I got him,' said the Golem.

'You "got him"?' said Sverl, 'I need more of an explanation than that. And I assume you mean Trent.'

'I listened,' said the Golem.

'And?'

'They simply released him because Penny Royal issued a threat to the Polity if they didn't do so. The black AI does not like interference in its activities.'

Threat? Now this was *interesting*.

'Detail.'

The next transmission the Golem sent was a recording. Sverl checked it thoroughly before listening to a brief exchange between the forensic AI the Brockle and some other AI, perhaps even Earth Central itself. Sverl saw how Penny Royal had ensured Trent Sobel's survival. So the man was part of Penny Royal's plans and, since he was now a captive of Sverl's Golem, those plans almost certainly related to Sverl himself.

'Do you have the earring too?' he asked.

'Yes, I have Satomi's recording,' the Golem replied. 'I bring them both.'

Sverl was now torn. He wanted to go after Cvorn but he wanted Isobel Satomi and he wanted his ultimate goal of . . . *something* from Penny Royal.

'Take yourself to the Rock Pool,' he instructed, since that world lay about midway between the transmission point of the Golem's signal and his present location. 'I must consider this.'

'Okay,' the Golem replied, seemingly unconcerned as it temporarily closed the link.

What to do?

'Father,' said Bsorol, now closing up the armour of the war drone he had been working on, 'I've been thinking about Cvorn.'

'Me too,' interjected Bsectil, now in the corridor just inside the airlock, trying to straighten out the dented lid of his tool chest.

'And you've been thinking about Cvorn in connection with yourselves, haven't you?'

'Augmentation,' they both said simultaneously.

Sverl was pleased with their reasoning.

'What do you suggest?' he asked.

'One has to go back to first principles and consider why you want to eliminate Cvorn,' said Bsorol.

That was very, very unpradorishly rational.

Sverl glanced at those screens showing the human population aboard and realized that Bsorol had grasped the main point. Sverl wanted to kill Cvorn because of the threat that prador posed to this adopted population. However, Cvorn was likely a bigger threat now than before, and to follow him would probably put this population, and Sverl himself, in even greater danger. But protecting this population was not all of Sverl's aim.

He was still prador enough to want vengeance for Cvorn's attack on him and for the lives already lost. Still torn, he now considered telling the Golem to come to his present location, so he could take it and Trent aboard and still go after Cvorn. The other prador might or might not have augmented himself and might or might not have set an effective trap. There was only one way –

What now?

His sensors had picked up a U-space signature. Through his AI component, Sverl initiated the chameleonware throughout his ship and took direct control of all its weapons. Was this the jaws of Cvorn's trap closing?

'Crew, get to battle stations,' he generally ordered, but even as they scuttled to obey, something unexpected materialized into the real.

Sverl studied the old-style Polity destroyer and analysed it as no threat to him, just before he recognized the ship itself. No, this was no attack from Cvorn, but it might be the answer he needed. He opened up a coded U-space link to it – one established long ago to a resource within that attack ship.

'Hello, Dad,' a voice immediately replied. 'What can I do for you?'

Sverl updated from Flute's mind, quickly incorporating all the events that had occurred aboard the ship the second-child mind controlled, sucking the data into his AI crystal in a matter of seconds, meanwhile ensuring he had Flute under absolute control. It was only as that data began to incorporate across the interface to his organic brain that Sverl experienced a visceral reaction. He seized control of ship's weapons, charged capacitors and even ignited the drive of one missile. He stood just a microsecond away from obliterating the destroyer out there before he managed to get a grip on himself and cancel what would have been a mass attack. To coin a phrase from Arrow-smith, using a sledgehammer to kill an ant.

Riss . . .

That was the drone's name. That was the name of this snakelike artificial version of a parasite the prador had wiped out centuries ago. That was the very thing that had attacked Sverl all those years ago during the war. Sverl knew because during his exile on the Rock Pool he had used Polity resources to obtain its name, but had never been able to locate it physically. That was the creature that had laid eggs inside his body; the parasites hatching out and nearly destroying him. The process of removing them had been long and agonizing and left him crippled. Gazing from one of the Polity destroyer's internal cams, Sverl could not shake his atavistic horror of that drone, and the urge to destroy that ship had not gone away.

'Father?' Flute prompted.

Sverl realized the silence had gone on uncomfortably long. 'So Thorvald Spear is following me?' he enquired.

'He is,' replied Flute.

'In the hope that I will bring him closer to Penny Royal?'

Flute took some time replying, struggling against the control Sverl exerted, his loyalties divided. Eventually he gave up. 'Yes.'

'The signal should be easy enough to follow,' said Sverl. 'You will note that the relay on the nearby asteroid now clearly indicates where it is routing its U-space signal?'

'Yeah, I spotted that,' Flute replied.

'Then follow it, and keep me informed of what you find.'

'You're not going there?'

'I suspect a trap, and I want to know precisely the nature of that trap,' said Sverl. 'Inform me of what you find. If necessary, provoke a response there to clarify the matter. And inform no one aboard of our exchange.'

Flute just emitted a frustrated buzzing in reply.

Sverl's control of the mind at the other end of this exchange was rigid, and Flute would be unable to disobey, at least for a while. However, Sverl was wise enough to know that a second-child mind with AI enhancements, given enough time, could eventually find some route around rigid orders. Flute would not be given the time.

Sverl now laid in a new course for his ship and opened up his unshielded fusion drive while dropping the chameleonware. However, he did ensure that the other ship could not divine his destination from his dreadnought's U-space signature as he dropped into that continuum and took himself back towards the Rock Pool.

He had always made sure of a back door into the second-child minds he had sold because of the chance he might be able to use them later. Flute had now proved the worth of that strategy. Flute, and the ship he ran, would follow Cvorn's signal, while Spear and that disgusting drone would think they were in close pursuit of Sverl. They would spring Cvorn's trap because, even if that prador could manage to resist attacking such a small Polity vessel, Flute would now force the issue. Flute would probably have time to send a final report back to Sverl.

Probably.

Cvorn

The work was proceeding as expected, with ship's lasers scouring away rock so the ST dreadnought could fit neatly into the hollow moon. As he watched this on his array of screens, Cvorn experienced momentary pain and turned one stalk eye to peer at the human blank working with a shell saw on the side of his carapace, quickly stamping on the urge to shove the creature up against the wall and crush it. It was a silly urge, akin to trashing a laser cutter because it had splashed hot metal into a claw joint. The blank was working to a program Cvorn had created, and he had expected pain at this point since it had just levered out a chunk of scar carapace formed in the socket where one of his legs had once connected to his body. However, the urge was partial confirmation of his theory about the odd feelings he had been experiencing since coming aboard. He just needed to do a little further checking to confirm that theory.

He now brought up new feeds on his screens and contemplated cam views into the laying pool, reminding himself to have the females scoured out so they might take his own seed. He felt a ghost of his mating urge return, a twitching in the remains of his sexual organs and a sense of regret at the fact that one of his children would have to inject his seed mechanically. Analytically he compared this reaction to the one he had experienced while viewing these females at a distance from his destroyer, and saw the difference. This was further confirmation of his hypothesis.

Lastly, he carefully studied the analysis, now scrolling diagonally across his screens, of the ST dreadnought's air supply and simultaneously checked studies of prador physiology he'd loaded to his aug. Yes, that settled it. The dreadnought's air was full of the hormonal output of five young males and those females. He was breathing in complex organic compounds generated by decades of frustration in the five males having been satisfied, also by sexually active females, and now by the frustration once again growing in the males. It was a situation rare in the Kingdom because adult males tended to isolate themselves, and Cvorn only found final confirmation in some very old studies. The potent mix in the air was making him feel younger; he was having feelings he hadn't experienced for well over a century.

Cvorn now ordered the blank working on his carapace to withdraw as he rose up on his grav-plates and swung round from the screens to face his other blank and Vrom, who were both at work. Ensconced in the hemispherical shell of a surgical telefactor, its complex multiple limbs working busily, Vrom was removing the last prosthetic limb from the corpse of this ship's previous captain. Meanwhile, the other blank was working on the limbs Vrom had just removed, replacing worn components and renewing the nano-fibre connectors.

With a thought, as he settled back to the floor, Cvorn ordered the first blank back to work on his carapace, exposing the flesh, blood vessels and stunted nerves underneath the scar carapace filling his leg sockets. He knew that this wish to be able to walk again, even on prosthetic limbs, was down to that potent mix in the air, but he didn't fight it. He could have had the Five, and the females, isolated, and the air filtered and cleaned of organics, but did not. Despite some irrational impulses, he was enjoying feeling so alive.

Steadily and methodically, the first blank worked round all his leg sockets, shut down the shell saw and replaced it in its charging point in the telefactor, then returned to pick up the chunks of scar carapace and take them away. Meanwhile Vrom had removed the last leg from the corpse. The blank now came back to clean out Cvorn's open wounds with antiviral and anti-bacterial spray, also washing out the shell dust. Cvorn clattered his mandibles, again suppressed the urge to kill something and waited for the ensuing analgesic sprays.

'Would you like to be an adult, Vrom?' he abruptly asked.

Without stopping work, Vrom replied, 'Only if my father wishes it so.'

Vrom was as obedient as a blank and Cvorn suddenly found that irritating. Again, analysing his irrational reaction, Cvorn could make no clear connection with those hormonal effects. His irritation stemmed from boredom with such an expected response. Vrom was following his program, just like the blank now coming over with a prosthetic limb ready for fitting. Cvorn divided his attention, simultaneously watching this blank while also focusing through his aug on input from both inside and outside the ship.

The Five, confined to their various sections within the ship, were all very active. They were searching data, disassembling and reassembling equipment including weapons, checking cam views available to them, and sometimes just running around aimlessly. These actions were all an outward expression of their inner frustration, which Cvorn studied via his Dracocorp aug domination of them. They could smell the females and wanted to mate but his instruction, firm in their minds, was as solid a barrier as the locked doors around them. They were now aware of how thoroughly he controlled them, fought against it in their own ways and really wanted to *do* something, but just kept running up against that dominance and finding themselves unable to act. And their hormonal output was like smoke from smouldering corpses on a battlefield.

As Cvorn now watched the enlargement of the hole into the asteroid, he rejected his earlier plans to simply dispense with the Five. Right now, he wanted them frustrated and pumping out all those lovely organics. Perhaps later, when he had made some complete analysis of this process and could artificially produce what they were producing, he'd get rid of them, but not yet.

With coincidental simultaneity, the dreadnought slid into the asteroid at the same time as Cvorn's first new limb slid into its socket in his body. As the great ship stabilized, extending telescopic feet to the surrounding rock walls, the blank shell-welded the limb into place. As the ship, using grav-motors, incrementally turned the rock to the required position, the nano-fibres began to penetrate inside Cvorn and find their nerve attachment points. And by the time the ship's forward array of weapons was pointing out of the hole in the asteroid towards the planet, a blank attached the last of Cvorn's new limbs.

As the effect of the analgesics faded, the pain returned, now a deep raw ache. He tried supporting his weight on his limbs but couldn't manage it and collapsed. He lay there until he began using his aug to stimulate near-atrophied parts of his brain until he remembered *how* to walk. Gradually, stupidly, these alien limbs began to move. And then to work properly. Once up on his feet and moving, he clattered fierce delight. He used one claw to smash away the blank that had been fitting the limbs and spun round to again face his screens. He was ready now: ready for Sverl, ready for anything!

6

Blite

As he opened the outer door of one of *The Rose*'s airlocks, Blite
tried to remember the last time he had taken a spacewalk like
this, but the memory evaded him for a moment. He propelled
himself out, then, with a blast from his wrist impeller, back
down to the hull, engaging his gecko soles and then reeling out
his safety line to attach it to a loop beside the airlock. Now he
remembered his last spacewalk. Many solstan years ago, he had
come out here to check the hull for attached trackers. Micro-
meteorites had conveniently destroyed exterior cams while *The
Rose* was in parking orbit of the moon on which he had been
conducting their latest trade. He'd found the trackers too, and
used them to give the thief who had put them there a nasty surprise. But there were no cams out here now. That beam blast
that had hit the ship as they escaped from the Par Avion space
station had incinerated them.

The burn started halfway along *The Rose*'s hull. Blite walked
to the edge of the metre-wide trench carved down through six
inches of armour and into the foamed ceramic insulation
beneath. He walked along the edge of this, circumventing where
it had gone deep enough to activate the breech sealant circuit
and where that sealant had grown a great bubble of the vacuum-
set foam like some huge fungus. Beyond this, he reached the
section of hull over the engine room. He knew where he was
because he could now see the wreckage inside.

The fusion drive wasn't just fucked, it was all but gone. Par Avion had managed to carve the trench, then centre the beam blast straight up *The Rose*'s tailpipe just at the last moment. Blite stared at the damage and felt his initial elation at escaping the station, and at once again operating, fade.

'Not so good,' said Brond from inside, where he was watching Blite's suit feed.

'Megalithic understatement, big boy,' said Greer, also still inside. 'I'm amazed the U-drive is still working . . . it *is* working, isn't it, Leven?'

'It is, amazingly, hardly damaged at all,' the Golem ship mind replied. 'Though, as we are all aware, there is some resonance.'

They had all been feeling the effects of the imbalance in that drive.

'So we can still take the jump into the Graveyard and get those repairs,' said Blite, trying to consign to irrelevance that portion of fear and nausea he had experienced during their jump from Par Avion.

'We can,' Leven replied. 'We don't need much realspace acceleration to engage now, after Penny Royal's tampering. Maybe just steering thrusters will do . . .'

'But?' Blite prompted.

'The border,' Leven replied.

'Come on – it's a sieve.'

'It *was* a sieve.'

'What do you mean?' Blite turned round and began tramping back to the airlock. There wasn't much he could do out here. They needed to get to somewhere like Molonor in the Graveyard where he could access his Galaxy Bank account and pay for professional repairs to the ship. Even if the Polity blocked his access to that account – which was practically unheard of –

he had ensured that he had transferred plenty of portable wealth aboard shortly after the memplant payment went in. They just needed to get to the Graveyard.

'Explain yourself, Leven,' he said, when the mind was tardy in replying.

'It's a little puzzling,' the mind replied. 'The Polity watch stations are on high alert and have sunk their detectors into U-space. Doubtless USERs are ready to be deployed too. Ships are also arriving – attack ships, dreadnoughts and some bigger stuff.'

'This can't just be down to us,' said Blite as he entered the airlock. Really, if his encounter with Penny Royal, his much-admired new hardfield generator and his escape from Par Avion warranted this kind of response, then he might just as well give himself up now.

'No,' said Leven. 'Details are unclear but this seems to be in response to activity on the other side of the Graveyard.'

'The prador are playing up,' said Greer.

'That seems likely,' said Leven. 'But, as I said, the details are not clear.'

Once inside his ship, Blite retracted his visor into his suit's neck ring and pushed the folding hard-shell back off his head. He felt no inclination to take the suit off and, when he arrived in the bridge, the other two were similarly clad. Always best to take precautions like this when your ship has a chunk carved out of its hull like a scale model of Valles Marinaris. He took his seat, rested his elbows on the console before him and brought his fingertips together as he considered.

'If we stay in the Polity then someone or something is going to track us down, make sure we're completely disabled and take us in,' he said. 'Agreed?'

'Agreed,' said Brond, while Greer nodded.

'So if all this border activity is about what's happening on the Kingdom side, then that's where their attention will be focused.' He gazed at Brond and Greer but they showed no inclination to agree. Like him, they were perfectly well aware that when AIs went on high alert their vision was three-sixty. 'We have to try to get through.'

'I guess so,' said Greer, with tired acceptance.

'Leven,' he said, 'analyse your data on the activity there and try to take us through where it's most accessible.'

The Rose jolted as steering thrusters fired up and, listening to the sound penetrating the ship, Blite was sure that one of those thrusters was damaged and on its way out. He gazed out pensively at the starlit vacuum, as armoured shutters drew across to close it off and as his ship accelerated. He winced when he felt a wave of something pass through the bridge, seemingly from the direction of the U-space engine.

'Engaging,' said Leven.

'No shit,' said Greer.

They all felt the surge and the sickening twist of the U-space jump. Blite gazed around at the bridge. On the surface, everything looked the same as always, but now it was as if he had taken psycho-actives. Every physical object around him now appeared incredibly insubstantial. Their gleaming surfaces seemed to represent a very thin skin over absolutely nothing at all – an absence the human mind hadn't evolved to encompass and from which it wanted to retreat screaming. Blite stood up, swayed unsteadily.

'How long?' he asked.

'Fifty-two hours,' Leven replied.

'Okay,' he said, 'we'll take six-hour shifts: you first, Greer, then Brond.'

Brond also stood up, looking pale and ill.

'I'm going to zone out,' Blite added.

The others would do the same when not on watch – electrically imposed sleep was the best way of getting through this, though the nightmares tended to be lurid. As he headed towards his cabin, Blite wondered if he would be having more like those he'd had just after they left Par Avion. Those had been nasty. Black knives had surrounded him – Penny Royal, obviously. But he was imagining the version of the AI that deserved its seriously bad reputation. It had tittered as it began skinning him.

Trent

'What do you want?' Trent asked, not wanting to look round.

'You and your lovely earring,' said the Golem behind.

Trent's hand was still tight round the ship's joystick. What were his options? Did he really want to spend a lot of time stuck in such a confined place with what he knew was standing behind him? He could return to the moon, to the Brockle . . . No, that really wasn't an option. He'd rather play Russian roulette with a pulse-gun than go back there. He released his grip, reached down to the chair clamp and released that, then slowly turned his chair round, that skeletal metal hand coming off his shoulder as he did so.

The Penny Royal Golem loomed in the cabin and reminded him of when he had first seen it accompanying Stolman – the mafia boss on the Rock Pool. It was of course without skin or syntheflesh: a human skeleton fashioned of ceramal, but with oversized stepper motors bulging in its joints, the gaps between its ribs filled with some grey material, while its teeth were white and eyes dark blue. But its similarity to the usual skeletal Golem ended there. It was bigger than a standard Golem, and someone had enamelled its polished bones with colourful geometric pat-terns so it looked like an artefact from some Mayan tomb. Filling the area where a human gut would have resided, twisted round its bones, in its joints, around its neck and part of its skull, was a form of tech that looked organic. In fact, it looked almost as if the Golem had slept in a jungle for a hundred years, then torn itself free with its workings clogged with roots and vines, only these were metallic black and gold and too evenly distributed. The thing was also battered, scratched and scored with laser burns.

It blinked metallic eyelids at him that skeletal Golem usually didn't possess, then abruptly stepped away from him and sat down on the floor to the rear of the small cabin. There it started individually hinging out the ribs on one side of its chest.

'Why?' Trent asked, then after swallowing drily, 'Why do you want me and my earring?'

'Because *he* wants her.'

The 'her' had to be Isobel Satomi and Trent had a horrible suspicion that 'he' might be Penny Royal. But surely, that didn't make any sense, since Penny Royal had passed on the memcord-ing of Isobel to him in the first place. Why would it want that back now?

He stared at the Golem, remembering how it had saved his life while he had been the crime boss Stolman's captive. But whether that was due to Satomi seizing control of it or at its own instigation he had no idea. At the time it had declaimed, 'Thus do the scales fall from my eyes.' He also remembered how, enforcing Satomi's orders, it had torn the head off the captain of the *Glory*. This Golem had, at one time, probably been of the normal Polity kind. But then Penny Royal got hold of it, and some time after that Stolman had controlled it with a Dracocorp aug. Then Isobel had usurped that control with the power of her crazy mind. And, though sanity was debatable when it came to artificial intelligences, he felt sure he was in the presence of something insane.

'What should I call you?' he asked, because giving it a name might waylay some of his fear of it.

Still hinging out ribs, it tilted its polished skull.

'Never really considered having a name,' it said.

'Why don't you consider that now?'

'Snickety snick,' it said.

No, that can't be right.

One side of its chest was now completely open to expose glittery workings. They didn't look right to Trent – looked as organic as that stuff spread over the outside of its skeleton. In addition, amidst them, he could just see the Golem's AI crystal in its ceramal cage. It wasn't clear or opalescent like the usual home of an AI mind, but burned and it contained blooms like fungus in agar, and Trent could definitely see some cracks. Having exposed all this, it now reached round and tore open the panel in the wall against which it was reclining.

'You must have had a real name once,' he said, 'before Penny Royal got hold of you.'

It suddenly snapped up one hand, then one finger. Trent hadn't even been able to track the movement. No doubt at all that if it decided to kill him he was utterly helpless.

'I remember. I was called John Grey,' it said. 'Snickety snick,' John Grey added while, his hands a blur, he tore out and discarded circuit rods from the wall and then detached a skein of fibre-optics from behind where they had been.

'What did Penny Royal do to you, John?' Trent asked. Maybe, if he kept talking, he could defer the point when he ended up in bloody gobbets scattered about this cabin. Such an end struck him as likely since, if Penny Royal wanted Satomi,

Trent Sobel himself was most likely irrelevant. Perhaps a little distracting entertainment while this Golem took Isobel's memcording to the 'he' he'd mentioned?

John Grey looked up from sorting cables. '*Mr* Grey,' he said firmly.

Trent felt his hopes of getting out of this alive retreat even further. He watched as the Golem began plugging the optic cables into his chest. After a few minutes of this Mr Grey said, 'Snick,' as he plugged in the last of them – all in a neat ring around his crystal. He then tugged more of the optics out of the wall to give him the slack to stand up and step back towards Trent. Reaching out to press a finger against Trent's chest, the Golem then dipped his head to inspect his own finger more closely. Trent knew that in an instant Mr Grey could shove that finger straight through him. He cleared his throat, then said, 'I didn't want to die on that moon, and I don't want to die here.'

Grey looked up. 'You didn't want to die?'

Trent cleared his sticky throat. 'No.'

'Neither did I,' said Mr Grey.

Trent was puzzling over what he could possibly say in response to that, just as Grey's head dipped again, as if he was nodding off, and the ship shuddered like some beast running into a bare power cable, twisted and groaned, and dropped into U-space.

Sverl

The cargo ships that had taken on many of the refugees from the planet were now gone, as was the ship the Polity agents here, at the Rock Pool, had boarded, and Sverl felt slightly disappointed to not be having some exchange with the drone Arrowsmith.

Now deep scanning the local system, he picked up the small single-ship orbiting the Rock Pool and noted that the ship contained a Golem that was trying to open communications with him again. He ignored that, instead pondering on his impulse to direct the Golem here. He should not have done so and, more importantly, he should not have come here himself. It seemed likely that some of Cvorn's spy satellites would still be here so Cvorn might learn his location and know that Sverl had not taken the bait.

Whatever – he would deal with Cvorn in due course.

Sverl now allowed a communications link with the Golem to establish and made an informational request to link deeper, since it was no longer his slave. It allowed this and he gazed through its eyes.

'You have arrived,' said the Golem, who had now apparently acquired the name John Grey. Mr Grey was peering at an image of Sverl's dreadnought in a small screen. Next, he raised his gaze to focus on a distant speck of that same ship through the main cockpit screen.

'Come over,' said Sverl. 'I will open a docking bay.' He felt a mental hesitation within Mr Grey, along with some strange echoing effects and hints of esoteric maths, and so he continued smoothly, 'Unless you wish to maintain some distance while we work out what your payment should be.' Sverl had absolutely no idea what such a creature, now free of his control, might want.

'I want to accompany you,' said Grey, dipping his head to peer down at his own body. Sverl now realized why the link seemed so odd. Mr Grey had plugged himself into that little ship to make the required calculations to control the U-space engines, and was still partly lost in that mathematical universe.

'Why?' Sverl asked, then before Grey could reply, said the answer himself: 'Penny Royal.'

'Yes.' The affirmation was almost dismissive as Grey turned to gaze at Trent Sobel, who was stepping into the rear of the cabin, his expression wary at first, then alarmed when he saw the image on the small screen.

'Come over,' Sverl repeated, meanwhile mentally sending a signal to open a door into the assault bay. He withdrew, partially, his awareness of what was happening aboard that small vessel remaining just enough to alert him to anything that might require his attention. Next, as the ship fired up its fusion drive and began its approach, he began updating from his various sources within both the Polity and the Kingdom. It soon became evident that he should have been paying more attention to things outside his usual compass.

Something was happening.

In response to occurrences over on the other side of the Graveyard, Polity watch stations and border forces were on high alert. But what those occurrences might be wasn't very clear from the data he could gather on the Polity side. Most of Sverl's sources of information in the Kingdom – the data intercepts, status updates and the prador gossip transmitted like a round robin – weren't making things clear either, so Sverl decided it was time to try another more risky source, and he opened a U-space link deep into the Kingdom.

'Hello Sverl – I've been expecting your call,' said the individual at the other end of that link.

'So what exactly is going on, Gost?' Sverl asked of the large armoured prador now displayed across his screens.

Gost was either a large first-child or a young adult that just didn't behave with the selfishness usually displayed by that kind. Gost was one of the prador king's large extended family, one of his children, and served his father as one of the King's Guard. Gost had contacted Sverl many decades ago with an offer of

134

amnesty if he returned to the Kingdom. Sverl hadn't believed it and, anyway, it had been too late. Part of his surrender involved physically coming before the king and by then Sverl had changed too much and had known what the prador reaction to his change would be: instant extermination. However, after his refusal, their occasional conversations had continued. The king was perfectly well aware of this but allowed it even though Sverl was an outlaw. The king wanted to control his kingdom and to be ready to counter any threat, so he needed all the data he could get. Cutting off communications between Sverl and one of his utterly loyal guards would not have been useful.

'You mean, why is the Polity getting nervous?' Gost enquired.

'Of course.'

'Probably because of the host of dreadnoughts at the Graveyard's borders and the squadron of King's Guard reavers gathering in the Feeding Frenzy within the Kingdom.'

'I see,' said Sverl. 'And why are such ships gathering?'

'Because of you, Sverl.'

'I didn't think I was such a threat.'

'Certainly the image I am seeing on my screens is no threat at all,' said Gost. 'But I would be interested in seeing what you really look like, and I would be even more interested in taking a peek inside you, specifically around your major ganglion.'

Sverl was lost for words. He just stared at the King's Guard and clattered nonsense from his prosthetic mandibles.

'I see that you lack a sensible response,' said Gost. 'Let me make something plain for you: we know what you are, Sverl. We know what the black AI Penny Royal did to you.'

'And so you wish to erase such an atrocity,' Sverl managed.

'Such a typical prador response might be expected . . .'

Gost was offering him something – some insight. Now under pressure, Sverl's mind went into overdrive, mainly functioning in its AI component. Gost was not behaving exactly like a prador, and neither was the king. No one had seen the king for many years and the king's children, his guard, were never seen without their armour . . .

'Transformation might not be unique to me,' he suggested.

'It might not,' admitted Gost. 'But consider how the majority of untransformed prador would react to you. Consider how some prador, bitter about the termination of the war and certain of their manifest destiny to dominate the universe, might use you.'

'Cvorn,' said Sverl.

'The dreadnoughts on the border of the Graveyard contain Cvorn's allies who, though surrendering power to my father, the king, have continued to nurture their hate. To them you would be an abomination and utter proof that the war should have been continued to its – in their view – inevitable conclusion: the extermination of all Polity humans and AIs. Unfortunately they are unable to overcome their instincts sufficiently to understand that the true inevitable conclusion of the war would have been the annihilation of most of the prador race, with the remainder being confined to the surfaces of just a few worlds, as a novelty, as a source of interest to godlike artificial intelligences.'

Again, Sverl had difficulty finding any response. What were the King's Guard that they could see so clearly beyond their instincts? What was the king? Had Penny Royal's urge to transform extended even into the Kingdom?

'And no, Sverl, neither I nor my kin have been touched by that black AI.'

Shit, a mind reader too.

'And I'm not a mind reader,' Gost added.

After sputtering for a moment, Sverl managed, 'Penny Royal was rogue . . .'

'They would not, or would not want to see a distinction: Penny Royal is an AI and therefore of the Polity.'

Sverl paused, banished the shock he felt as a foolish organic reaction, and cogitated for an AI moment, then said, 'But Cvorn and his allies would need physical irrefutable evidence, which is me.'

'Yes.'

'Cvorn cannot capture me.'

'Maybe when his only resource was a destroyer . . .'

'Explain.'

'Vlern's five children raided a world for females and during that raid, and showing abilities not usually within the compass of their kind, they stole an ST dreadnought, which they took to Cvorn in the Graveyard.'

'Why? Why take it to him?'

'Some form of mind control is indicated.'

'I wonder what—'

'So,' Gost interrupted, 'Cvorn's activities in the Graveyard threaten to lead to civil war in the Kingdom, probably followed by all-out war against the Polity. And you are the key. My father now has a quandary to resolve. He can launch an attack against Cvorn's allies, which would be costly, or he can take the very dangerous risk of sending a squadron of reavers into the Grave-yard, to which the Polity would have to respond.'

'To deal with Cvorn,' said Sverl, knowing with leaden certainty that this was not what Gost was getting at. The reavers – the ships of the King's Guard – would have another target.

'No, Sverl,' Gost said. 'There will always be prador like Cvorn but there is only one piece of evidence, ostensibly of Polity perfidy, like you. And so your very existence could trigger a war.'

'So you are preparing to come in to hunt me down and kill me,' said Sverl.

'We could do so by breaking treaties and forcing the Polity to respond with attack ships, which would give Cvorn's allies an excuse to come in and engage too, to which the Polity would have to respond with dreadnoughts . . . This would provoke the very war we are trying to avoid. Need I go on?'

'You need not,' said Sverl. 'What would you have me do? Destroy myself?'

'That would be very convenient for us. Are you offering to do so?'

'I am not.'

'Then you have a few choices remaining if, as I have divined from our previous communications, you have lost your hatred of the Polity and have gained a hatred of warfare and all it entails,' said Gost. Sverl felt some relief that there might be an alternative to his suicide or murder by his own state.

'You must find some other way of removing yourself from the game. While you remain in the Graveyard, you face the certainty of extinction either from us or from Cvorn and his allies. Either you hand yourself over to the Polity or you depart elsewhere.'

'I will ponder on the matter,' Sverl replied.

'Don't, as has often been your wont, allow your pondering to turn into procrastination,' said Gost, then cut the communication, his image shimmering out.

Sverl settled down on the floor of his sanctum, feeling deflated and lost. He really did not want to be the key to starting a conflict between the Kingdom and the Polity, and he definitely did not want to die. Handing himself over to the Polity would take him far from Cvorn's grasp, but it would probably put him within the grasp of something like that forensic AI the Brockle. If he headed out of the Graveyard and beyond both Polity space and the Kingdom, his need for some sort of resolution with

Penny Royal would never be satisfied. So, thinking on these matters, he returned his focus to the approaching single-ship and felt a sudden intimation that an answer might lie there.

'Did you have any problems passing the Polity watch stations?' he enquired, following a suspicion.

'None at all,' replied Grey.

'Who the hell is that?' asked Trent Sobel.

Sverl belatedly realized that Mr Grey was allowing the ship's computing to translate their communication for the man's benefit. He felt a momentary annoyance, then again remembered that this Golem was no longer his slave and he had no control of it, no claim on its actions.

'I am Father-Captain Sverl.'

'Right, you're still here.'

Sverl felt no inclination to disabuse him of the notion that he had remained near the Rock Pool because he now had other things to consider. Despite the Polity watch stations being on high alert, this single-ship had come through. It might have evaded detection, but more likely the watchers had let it through because of whatever threat Penny Royal had made. This all related to Sverl; he felt sure he was still part of the black AI's plans. He would let them carry him, he decided. Turning from his controls, he headed over to the back wall of his sanctum, sending a mental instruction to open a storeroom and, upon reaching it, began bringing out some equipment. Penny Royal had seen fit to send him Isobel Satomi's memcrystal, so it clearly wanted him to do something about it. It might be that he wouldn't need this hardware to penetrate the crystal – that it would take standard optical connections – but he wanted to be prepared.

Spear

This Sverl, I decided, was a dangerous character indeed. Not only was he an augmented prador but one using both prador and Polity technology, as demonstrated by his use of sophisticated chameleonware capable of concealing a prador dreadnought at close quarters.

When his ship had appeared like that, I'd just gaped at the thing filling up the screen fabric and waited for a wave of fiery destruction, like the one I'd experienced at Panarchia. But my ship and I weren't of interest to him, and he took himself away and U-jumped.

We found out why only a short while later. Sverl had made a physical penetration of the relay and now, knowing where it was transmitting its signal to, had gone after it. Or at least so I supposed. He'd also left the thing open, babbling its transmission coordinates across the ether so anyone could follow. And follow we did.

However, I wasn't going to jump after Sverl without taking precautions, and so I instructed a somewhat terse and moody Flute to take us to a point at least a light hour out from those coordinates. I guessed Flute had been as spooked as I had by the appearance of the father-captain who had made him. Flute remained uncommunicative throughout the journey and I meanwhile reluctantly returned to my inner world.

I could now confine my experience of past lives to times I specifically wanted to explore, so I experienced them in my cabin, prostrate on my bed. I tried once to stop them surging up into my consciousness entirely, but that simply didn't work. They gnawed at me like a hated addiction. I felt depressed and even experienced physical pain if I didn't allow at least two or three to reveal themselves to me every twenty hours.

I was now also able to analyse them meticulously and had run up programs in my aug for this purpose. I knew, for example, that of the thousands Penny Royal had killed and cached, one thousand and eight hundred of them were murderers. These included deaths I had not experienced at first-hand because the searches and analyses extended beyond those, to all the spine contained. One thing was also evident: the deaths I had experienced, and whose every instance I could recall at will, could not possibly all reside in my mind. They were in the spine, quantum entangled with my mind, part of my mind despite the separate locations.

This analysis also confirmed for me that little rationality lay behind the murders. It didn't matter whether the people were guilty or innocent, contemptible or lovable, young or old. A large portion of them had certainly deserved to die, but there were many innocents too. I think the only reason they weren't a cross-section of ordinary humanity was because ordinary people weren't the kind to cross Penny Royal's path.

I get it, I fucking get it! I wanted to scream at the spine, and at Penny Royal. I understood that no justification existed or could exist. Penny Royal was a mass murderer, an AI psychopath, a fucking computerized and mechanized Hannibal Lector who really deserved to die. Really, I didn't need to experience any more of those deaths to know that, but they continued relentlessly to play out their horrible sordid dramas in my mind.

'So Sverl catches up with this Cvorn character and obliterates him,' I said during one of my forays outside of my skull, as I studied a nanoscope image of a ring of quantum processors on the surface of the spine. These had no direct connection at all to everything that surrounded them, and they baffled me. What possible purpose could they serve?

'That would be Sverl's approach, one would suppose,' said Riss cautiously.

'One renegade prador destroys another one, and both have been sitting in the Graveyard since the war,' I said.

'You are reconsidering your idea about there being a connection here with the activity at the Graveyard's borders,' said Riss.

'Just raising it as a discussion point.'

'So even with Penny Royal's involvement, you cannot see why Sverl, Cvorn, or both of them might elicit such a response,' Riss pushed.

'All right, I can't see it,' I conceded, 'though I do feel sure of it.' I shut off the screen image – I was getting nowhere. 'Polity AIs would not suddenly decide to attack the Kingdom – there's no need. Even during the little time since my resurrection, I can see that the prador aren't even playing in the same league as the Polity any more and are never going to catch us with our pants round our ankles again. So the activity around the Polity watch stations is in response to the prador activity, not the other way round.'

'Yes,' said Riss.

'As you pointed out, the prador aren't lining up enough ships for some full-scale attack on the Polity, so they are therefore reacting to something in the Graveyard.'

'Maybe there are forces we haven't seen yet,' Riss suggested.

'Come on, even with what have to be limited contacts, you were able to discover what was going on in the gas cloud they call the Feeding Frenzy. I'd bet that by now the Polity has spy hardware inspecting every square inch of the Kingdom.'

'So perhaps the Polity has seen other forces.'

'Nope,' I shook my head, 'what I've seen gathering at the

Polity border isn't enough of a response to some full-scale attack. It looks to me like a softly-softly approach – a measured equivalent response.'

'Maybe there are Polity forces we haven't seen, then.'

'You do like your role as Devil's Advocate, don't you?'

'I'll concede everything you say,' said Riss. 'So what are the prador responding to that they haven't felt the need to respond to since the war?'

'Well, Sverl and Cvorn are on the move and they haven't been for the best part of a century . . .' I prompted.

'Not good enough,' said Riss. 'If they head for either the Polity or the Kingdom, just the watch stations on either border would be able to take them both out in seconds. They wouldn't need extra forces to handle only them. So, if your contention that they are the cause of the border activity is true, then we are missing something critical here.'

I thought long and hard about that, unable to dispel the notion that Riss was way ahead of me and simply letting me catch up.

'Okay,' I said, 'Cvorn and Sverl weren't a threat when they first went renegade, so one has to consider what has changed, and that brings us right back to Penny Royal. Sverl, at the black AI's instigation, has acquired AI abilities – augmentation. Could it be that the Kingdom fears a prador with such abilities?'

'It could be,' said Riss, 'but if so, in responding to their fear of Sverl they have elicited a response at the Polity border they should fear even more. If they then go in after Sverl they will elicit a response to that which will make the threat Sverl might pose – as an AI – seem quite petty.'

'Then there has to be something more involved than fear of AI, doesn't there?'

Riss dipped her head in acknowledgement. 'I would suggest

that what Sverl represents, rather than what he can do, is the threat.'

I chewed that one over, slowly and carefully, suddenly finding I was enjoying the mental process, discovering that I was enjoying something for the first time since the events on Masada.

'To the prador, Sverl would be an abomination,' I tried.

'Yes.' Riss waited.

'Some factions might feel more strongly than others,' I said.

'Quite,' said Riss.

I closed my eyes and processed the whole matter further.

'Many prador disagreed with the decision to negotiate peace with the Polity,' I said.

'And such prador probably occupy those dreadnoughts gathering at the Graveyard's border,' said Riss, obviously getting a little impatient now. 'And they are not the kind to see a renegade AI as something distinct from the Polity itself.'

It all now fell neatly and horribly into place in my mind. The king of the prador could not allow Sverl to fall into the claws of those rebellious prador – they'd use him as a symbol to incite war. And to prevent that he was prepared to risk sending the King's Guard into the Graveyard to eliminate Sverl as a threat entirely. It looked as if he was even prepared to risk breaking treaty agreements and ending up in a confrontation with the Polity directly. But could he really get away from bringing on the very war he would be trying to prevent?

'But what's Cvorn's involvement?' I asked.

'Cvorn,' said Riss, 'disagreed with the new king to such an extent that he became a renegade. He is doubtless working with those prador at the border in some way. He, I would suggest, is trying to find some way to trap Sverl and present him as evidence to the prador at the border. Presumably, they would then demand action and present Sverl as proof – to the Prador

Kingdom as a whole – of all their inchoate fears about the Polity. One of two things will follow: either his subjects will force the king to go to war against the Polity or they will rebel. Either way, things will get really messy.'

'You've known all this for some time,' I said.

'I have.'

'So why have you waited until now to acquaint me with it?'

'You've been busy.'

The snake drone had already demonstrated that she was aware of my connection with the spine, in fact had been the one to reveal it. She was also aware of the data transfers going on between me and that object, so had to be aware of how much they had increased ever since our departure from Masada.

'It doesn't look like much,' I said, and reached out to rest my fingers on the surface of the spine. 'But it contains all one needs to know of hell.'

I felt a surge through my fingers and the dead again clamouring to be heard. My chest tightened and I withdrew my touch.

'It's better now,' said Riss. 'You have more control.'

'I do.' I nodded.

'Then I have a final piece of data you can slip into place.' I looked up into Riss's black eye and the drone continued, 'The memories you sense are from the dead, but they are copies of the period around these deaths only. The data is not sufficient for these victims to be complete beings. They are edited, ciphers, enough for you to know them and to know Penny Royal's guilt.'

'I don't find that reassuring,' I said. 'I had considered destroying this object but have a terror of what such an act will do to me, but that's not all of it. I thought that if I destroyed this, I destroyed the dead – it ceases to be possible to restore them. Now you tell me that this is not so, and that they are gone forever without recompense.'

'Not so.' She shook her head. 'Captain Blite docked at Par Avion some while ago and there claimed a reward for something Penny Royal had left with him.'

'His modified hardfield generator?'

'No, he claimed the standard reward offered for returning memplants to the Polity. He handed over thousands of them.' Riss paused for a second, then added, 'Penny Royal's victims.'

I stood just staring at Riss as the full import of her words struck me. All those lives and all those deaths, all that suffering could, in a way, be wiped from accounts. Penny Royal had taken a good shot at redemption but, really, it wasn't enough. What about those the AI had killed but not recorded? What about the thousands who had suffered or died as a direct or indirect result of its actions?

'Panarchia?' I said.

'No, you're the only one resurrected from there.'

Nevertheless, I felt a loosening in my chest, a weight coming off me. I turned to regard the spine again. Here was evidence; here was a collection of précis of those who had died. I had no reason to keep them any more and, if I could overcome my fear of what might happen to me when I did so, I could toss this object into a sun. I reached out to touch the thing again and felt its impact reduced, emasculated.

'We still have to find Penny Royal,' I affirmed, and turned away.

7

Blite

Electronically enforced sleep wasn't enough and Blite was tired and irritable as he headed out of his cabin. *The Rose* was approaching the border now, and Greer and Brond were awaiting him on the bridge. Of course, actually saying that they were near the realspace border when they were in U-space was supposedly nonsensical, since distance and relative positions were concepts that didn't apply in that continuum – it was all about energy vectors, five-dimensional leveraging and other terms that could only be described mathematically. But all of that was gibberish to Blite. He stuck with the idea that realspace was the surface of a sea, and that diving below that surface into U-space he could simply travel faster *relative* to that surface. It was also true that hostiles could drop mines into that sea to force vessels like *The Rose* to the surface . . .

'I guess we'll be finding out shortly if we can get through the border,' he said, settling himself in his chair and checking the instruments before him. 'How long, Leven?'

'In your terms, just a few minutes,' the Golem ship mind replied.

'Okay,' said Blite. He wasn't going to allow Leven to draw him into a discussion about the relevance of time in such situations. He sat back and fastened his safety straps. Glancing at Greer and Brond, he saw that they had similarly secured themselves.

'So if a Polity watch station knocks us out of U-space?' said Greer. 'What then?'

'You just obeyed my orders,' he said.

'You think that'll make any difference?'

'Maybe.'

'But we have our hardfield to defend us . . .' suggested Brond.

'Sure we do,' Blite replied with a sneer. 'And I guess we can sit under it until our reactor runs out of fuel or we run out of air and food.'

Brond gave that a solemn nod. Really, if the nearest watch station or Polity vessel deployed a USER or some U-space mine or missile, it would fuck them. Polity forces on the border would haul them in and dispatch them back to Par Avion. Ostensibly they would be there to answer charges about criminal damage to the station but, at some point, a forensic AI would get its manipulators on them, digging for information on Penny Royal.

'Maybe we'll be—' began Greer, whereupon the ship gave a deep shudder.

'Fuck,' said Blite.

A force took hold of them, and everything around Blite twisted out of ghostly perception into hard reality. The ship shook again and something screeched back in the engine room, protesting like a giant cicada scooted from its perch, then it emitted a sound Blite could only think of as a death rattle. The smell of burning permeated the air and error diagnostics filled the screen laminate with red text, scrolling fast. Blite reached out to hit a control and the shutters drew aside to reveal starlit space.

'The drive?' he asked, suddenly calm.

'Fried,' Leven replied. 'It was functional but a little dodgy – that U-space mine just finished it off.'

So, even if they could get away from the mine's disruptive

effect using their steering thrusters, they wouldn't be going much further. Now the diagnostics fled from the laminate, it rippled, and a ship appeared out there. The thing was huge – a gleaming lozenge of blue and silver metal studded with sensors, weapons and other paraphernalia. Blite gazed at some sort of protrusion studded with dishes. It was the shape and probably the size of the Eiffel Tower – just one of many such protrusions on the behemoth of a ship Blite recognized as one of the older-style interfaced dreadnoughts used by the Polity during the war.

'Captain Habitus of the Polity dreadnought *Snarl* would like to speak to us,' said Leven tiredly, now using steering thrusters to turn them and bring that dreadnought into sight through the main chain-glass screen.

Really, what was there to say?

'Okay, let's hear him.'

A frame opened in the laminate to reveal a bald-headed corpse-coloured man. His eyes were white, with gridlines across them. He wore what looked like a half-helmet augmentation but one trailing optic cables and fluid pipes. Other pipes and optics ran down his neck into an armoured chest plate studded with high-tech protuberances.

'*Snarl* is baffled by your attempt to cross here,' said the interfaced captain.

'I thought AIs were intelligent,' said Blite.

'It was calculated to a ninety per cent probability that you would aim to cross here, whereupon the probability immediately dropped below ten per cent because surely you would have been aware we'd make that calculation.'

'Sometimes the coin falls on its edge,' another voice whispered.

'Something else just appeared out there,' said Leven. 'Closing in fast.'

'*You*,' said Habitus, turning his head slightly as if gazing at some other screen with his blind eyes.

'Did I not deliver sufficient warning?' said that voice.

Something flashed out there, then a section of the dreadnought's hull bulged and burst with a glaring explosion. Gaping, Blite watched that tower tumbling away into space along with other objects of a similar scale. Another explosion ensued, gouting fire from the same hole, then something long and black appeared off to one side of the big ship. In the laminate, Habitus had one hand clutched around the pipes leading into his skull, and his image had turned hazy as if the room he occupied had now filled with smoke.

'Final warning,' said the voice.

'We didn't know,' said Habitus, his voice echoing as if two people were speaking from inside him slightly out of sync.

'They are mine,' said the implacable voice from that black ship out there.

Now it turned and rapidly accelerated towards *The Rose*, but as it came, it seemed to be splintering and opening out, rearranging its structure in some impossible manner, turning into a great black tubeworm head descending on them. Within seconds, it slammed into Blite's ship, and though he was glad he had put his safety straps on, for the impact threatened to tear his chair from the floor, he dreaded what damage it had done to his ship. As he recovered, rubbing at his strained neck and hoping this pain would not be the last thing he felt, he saw that the view through the chain-glass screen was of a dark crystalline mass, shifting as if at the turning of some kaleidoscope. Acceleration followed, shoving him hard down into his seat, followed by just a gentle twist and feeling of wrongness indicating that they had entered U-space.

'I thought you were done with us,' said Blite.

'But you are not done with me, are you Captain?' Penny Royal replied.

Trent

The ancient expression 'out of the frying pan and into the fire' was far too simple, Trent felt, to describe his circumstances over the last year. He'd been safe enough as Isobel Satomi's lieutenant but that had changed as she made her transformation into a hooder. He'd ended up on a ship with the creature she became, as she tried to stop herself from eating him. The mafia boss on the Rock Pool had then captured and tortured him, and subsequently he'd been stuck aboard Isobel's ship as she conducted her doomed assault on Masada. He'd been in the wreckage of that ship as it fell from orbit, then landed in the grasp of a forensic AI – an AI that had, in fact, taken him apart. He shuddered.

He had felt a momentary breath of freedom in this single-ship, quickly followed by him finding a Penny Royal Golem aboard with him. And now, this ship was settling in some bay aboard a prador dreadnought. 'Shit happens' was another old expression that seemed appropriate, though hardly strong enough.

'This prador, Sverl, wants Isobel,' he said. 'So why am I here?'

He had been afraid to ask this question because he wasn't sure he wanted to know the answer. He'd learned, during the short journey to this dreadnought, that Penny Royal had handed over control of this Golem to this Father-Captain Sverl. Apparently, the Golem, who demanded to be called 'Mr Grey', was now free but wanted something from Sverl, for which the payment was the earring in Trent's pocket. He suspected he was just something to sweeten the present deal – perhaps a gift for Sverl, perhaps to give the prador a *taste* of the old times. He felt a renewed sense of dread.

'I don't know,' said Mr Grey, 'but no pieces in the game should be neglected.'

The ship settled with a thump, hydraulics whined, and a docking mechanism gave a final shudder as if, like dying prey, it had finally given up. Grey waved one skeletal hand towards the rear of the cockpit but Trent remained in his seat.

'I'll just wait here,' he said.

Grey held out that hand towards him. 'Then give me Isobel.'

Trent put his hand in his pocket and closed it round the purple sapphire. The connection to his sister was still there for him. The original gem had been shattered, then reassembled to hold everything Isobel Satomi had been. Strangely, this hadn't weakened his connection to the gem, but had tied it even closer to him. He couldn't just hand it over. He stood up.

'Okay, let's go.'

In reality he'd had no control over his fate since before the Rock Pool. He should have taken his leave of Satomi before she agreed to take Thorvald Spear to the Polity destroyer he'd been hunting. Then again, what would he have done? He would probably have ended up as the muscle for some other Graveyard crime lord. He wouldn't have been who he was now . . .

'Snickety snick, double quick,' said Grey, then reached down and with one wrench pulled the optic cables from his chest. He staggered for just a moment, shook his head, then began closing up his ribs as he turned to leave the cockpit.

The door into the ship's small hold was obviously already open, because a smell as of a breeze wafting across the decaying detritus of a tide line reached Trent's nostrils as he followed. Grey reached that door and went down the ramp ahead of him, metal clattering on metal. Trent stepped onto the head of the ramp and looked around. This bay was huge and much lighter than he had expected the interior of a prador ship to be. He had anticipated dank organic gloom filled with vicious hissings, but here he saw little to distinguish the place from the hold of some massive Polity ship or space station . . . except for *him*.

Trent had never seen real prador without armour, but he had seen plenty of image files of them and had even ventured into a few VR scenarios that included them. The prador down on the floor was big, sans artificial armour, and he knew at once that it wasn't *right*. Its shell was a mottled blue and black whorled through with grey. It looked like a model of prador fashioned out of a fossil conglomerate, and the modeller hadn't got the legs right at all. It was also carrying quite a lot of hardware that wasn't of the expected kind – no Gatling cannon clamped to one claw, no ammunition box and dangling ammunition belt and no shiny-throated particle cannon. It had metal inlaid in its cara-pace, visual amplifying visors over some of its eyes, a motorized tool-head attached to one claw with a flexible pipe feed leading to a cylindrical carousel mounted on its back. Most of this hard-ware looked like some sort of amalgam of Polity and prador technology, though the aug seemingly riveted down beside its visual turret was definitely the former. Trent swallowed drily and walked down the ramp after Mr Grey.

'Trent Sobel,' said the prador.

There had been no clattering or bubbling to feed through a translator, so the prador must have spoken mentally through its aug to the speaker residing under a grille beside its mouth.

'Yes, I am,' Trent replied.

'Father will see you now,' it said, 'come with me.'

It turned rapidly, feet scraping the metal deck, and headed towards the rear of the bay. Trent glanced at Grey, who gestured that they should follow and they tramped after the prador. Now further out into the bay, Trent saw stuff that definitely wasn't of the Polity. Over to his right, clamped to the far wall, one above the other, were two blunt-nosed craft with ring-shaped drives to the rear. He identified them as prador kamikazes. Below them on the floor were a series of racks that seemed packed with prador, all back to belly, but these brassy objects were motionless and he recognized prador armour. Glancing to his left, he could not see the far wall. Mega-scale racking stretched from floor to misty ceiling and it was loaded with boxes and cylinders whose contents weren't identifiable. Amidst them, however, he did spot heavy ground-assault weaponry, including some mobile railguns on caterpillar treads, along with the only recognizable Polity item – what looked to be a partially gutted attack ship.

The door at the rear of the hold was definitely of prador design too. The big oval divided diagonally, the two halves revolving back into the wall on either side. The first-child, because that's what it had to be, went through and turned to the right. Trent and Grey stepped after it into an oval tunnel that curved away into the distance on either side. It was well lit – Polity lighting panels stretching in lines along both ceiling and floor. Notable too was the lack of rock effect on the walls, the remainder of which someone had been in the process of removing to expose underlying honeycomb plates. Trent stumbled to a halt when he saw something exit a circular hole in the floor to scuttle across and pick up a small chunk of gnarly carapace.

Polity cleanbots?

Where were the prador ship lice? Where were the luminescent growths sprouting from the walls? Why did this place look as if humans had taken over?

A long walk along this tunnel, through similar smaller tunnels, then along one that was even larger, brought them finally to what Trent recognized as the heavy armoured doors into a captain's sanctum. These revolved aside with an ominous rumbling, whereupon the prador leading them here stepped aside.

'You may enter,' it said.

Trent looked to Grey, waiting for the Golem to lead off, but Grey waved him ahead. 'He wants to speak to you alone.'

Right, now I'm going to die, Trent acknowledged to himself.

Same situation here as with the forensic AI – no point in running, and he just needed this to be over. He shrugged himself straight, held his head up, and marched through those doors.

The inside was little like the captain's sanctums he'd seen pictured, or depicted in VR. It was bright, to start with. Sure, this place had its stacked array of hexagonal screens and the pit controls, the two surgical telefactors attached to one wall, the doors into surrounding stores and the dangling mechanisms used to dismantle and assemble equipment and sometimes to dismantle a father-captain's children, but unexpected items were here too.

Suitcase manufactories were racked along one wall with shiny insectile Polity robots to either work them or remove their product, while amniotic tanks near them contained squirming and clattering life. Agribots tended a garden full of weird and wonderful plants, some enclosed in chain-glass enviro-bells and, prosaically, a row of tomato plants. Damn it, even trailing geraniums grew from a trough running high on one wall. All about lay the busy movement of robots, conveyors, fluids and contained life forms, as well as the shifting internals of assembly shells big enough to fit gravcars inside.

Trent just stood there with his mouth opening and closing, then the sanctum door ground closed behind him and something huge began to perambulate out from behind a long rack packed with disparate hardware. The shape was wrong, more wrong even than the prador outside. Finally, on gleaming prosthetic limbs, it stepped out into view.

'Welcome, Trent Sobel,' said Father-Captain Sverl.

'Fucking hell,' said Trent, which seemed the only sensible response.

Sverl

Trent Sobel was frightened, but covered it well with his apparently brash demeanour. Sverl studied him for a moment longer, but only with a small portion of his attention. He waved a claw towards a nearby trestle.

'Sit down,' he instructed. 'I will get to you shortly. I have something to deal with.'

'In a good way or a bad way?' Trent asked.

'You have nothing to fear from me,' said Sverl, suppressing the urge to snipe, 'It is your own kind here you should fear . . .'

Sverl's focus of attention was via cams on a stunned second-child lying in the corridor outside Quadrant Four, as two of its armoured kin approached it. The creature had gone a little crazy, tearing at a door down there as if it had wanted to rip through with its claws, even while a simple pit control lay within reach beside the door. The other two, who had used a powerful ionic stunner to bring their brother down, were fine, since they were breathing their own air supplies and not the dangerous pheromone-laden air that had leaked from Quadrant Four.

'*So what to do, what to do?*' asked Mr Grey via their private channel.

The Golem now outside his sanctum was another focus for Sverl's attention. Mr Grey was a bit of a puzzle and though his aim seemed to be some encounter with Penny Royal, Sverl sensed a deep confusion in the machine. He suspected that the Golem, having only recently returned to full consciousness and free will, was still trying to decide what it really wanted.

'*I have now locked all doors in and out of Quadrant Four,*' Sverl replied, still watching Trent, who had seated himself. He could not hear this exchange and was now toying with that sapphire earring. '*I have also engaged the atmosphere seals on those doors and isolated the air supply in there.*'

'The question, the question, the question,' said Grey.

Only because of his direct linkage to Grey's mind did Sverl understand what the Golem was getting at. It wanted to know what Sverl intended to do about the problem that had impelled him to seal Quadrant Four.

'*The reason the second-child reacted so is due to his old biology,*' said Sverl, knowing he was procrastinating, '*and because of the strange biology of the pheromone itself. My stunned child down there smelled the pheromone produced by one of his own brothers turning into an adult. Since new adults usually turn on their brothers and kill them, my child felt in extreme danger. He also sensed a human element in the pheromone that he could not process.*'

'The question,' Mr Grey repeated.

'*I saved them from Cvorn,*' said Sverl. '*Does this mean I must now save them from themselves?*' Grey was silent, so Sverl continued. '*They have been changing themselves into prador so it was inevitable that one of them would take the next step and try to become an adult prador – an adult with my genome since that is the one they used to change themselves. I am unsurprised that it is Taiken who is now issuing adult control pheromones.*'

'There will be death,' said Grey.

'*Yes, isn't there always,*' Sverl replied, now moving over to Trent, who was fidgeting and looking impatient.

'So you want this?' Trent asked, holding up the jewel. Sverl gestured again with one claw, this time towards a nearby work surface. 'Place the jewel into the interlink.' He expected some kind of rebellion, but Trent just looked tired as he stood, walked over to the work surface and inspected the set-up there. He found the two polished surfaces of the interlink – a miniature version of the kind of device used to clamp AI crystal in place aboard Polity ships. He held the jewel between them and used the manual lever to close the surfaces together, clamping the jewel.

The connection was immediate and strong; Sverl felt it down to the pit of his being. There were no difficulties here. The identification was clear, options available and absolutely nothing to bar him from delving into the recorded mind of Isobel Satomi. With a thought, he began downloading a copy of the mind the jewel contained and, as that began, he came to some other decisions.

'They are all recorded by Penny Royal,' he said, just to the Golem squatting outside. *'What is physical death when this is so? I will not intervene with the shell people, nor will I intervene should you decide to do something about them or –'* he glanced at Trent, who was once again seated – *'if anyone else should decide so.'*

Without a word the Golem, Mr Grey, stood up and moved off down the corridor, heading directly towards Quadrant Four. As he observed this, Sverl moved closer to Trent and settled on his belly before the man. The copying process would take about an hour and Sverl suspected Trent would not leave here without having his jewel returned. Time then, perhaps, to learn some other things . . .

'So, Trent Sobel,' said Sverl, 'tell me all about how Isobel Satomi ended up recorded in your earring.'

Trent glanced up. 'It happened over Masada,' he said indifferently.

'No, don't start there,' said Sverl. 'Tell me first about that jewel and how it came into your hands.'

Now the man looked haunted and gazed at Sverl with long suspicion.

'How can I know what's real here?' he finally asked. 'You could be just another method the Brockle's using to catch me off guard, to get information.'

'How can any of us know what is real?' Sverl countered.

'Should I start at the beginning then, again?'

'Yes – that seems the best place.'

Spear

A light hour out from the system I studied the images projected in the screen fabric from Flute's optical scanning, while lightly inspecting the data from more intensive scans in my aug. The world was the Rock Pool's twin, even down to its collection of moons. Life, of a primitive kind, burgeoned down there too, and the atmosphere was actually breathable for a standard human being, or prador. However, this world had not been prador-formed and there was none of their reaverfish in the sea, just a vast population of creatures very much like trilobites.

'Anything?' I asked.

'I'm still scanning,' said Flute grumpily, still out of sorts after our near-encounter with Sverl's dreadnought.

'But no sign of Sverl – I thought he would be here ahead of us.'

'Don't forget that chameleonware,' said Riss.

I felt stupid because I had forgotten the chameleonware, and had half expected Sverl to have materialized here and gone straight in to attack whatever he found. But Sverl wasn't really prador any more, so would certainly approach this situation with more caution. He was probably somewhere close by, out here with us, I thought.

I continued to stare at the images presented but started fidgeting and felt impatient.

'The problem out here,' I said, 'is that you're passive-scanning stuff that's an hour out of date. We really ought to move in closer.'

'A-a-dvise against . . . that,' said Flute, as if speaking the words actually caused him pain. 'My kind can be . . . tricky.'

I glanced at Riss, who simultaneously swung her head round to gaze at me, then blinked open her black eye. This wasn't for me. I guessed she was now inspecting Flute's activities very closely.

I too paid closer attention, feeling there was something wrong about Flute. Data I had previously only been casually looking at I now reviewed and inspected more carefully. In a short while, I found something. Studying neutron flows, Flute had found an object deep in that world's ocean but had then seemingly decided not to examine that data closely, and instead widen his search. He was now focusing intently on a particular land mass as if sure it concealed something lethal. I was about to mention this, but Riss communicated with me directly through my aug.

'*Flute just sent a U-space transmission,*' she said. '*From what I could catch, it looked like a situational update.*'

'*What do you reckon?*' I asked.

'*It's the father-captain. He gave the second-child mind crystal augmentation. I suspect Flute's loyalties are not all they should be.*'

'*But then you would say that.*'

'*I am just speculating on the data,*' said Riss sniffily. '*Who else could Flute be updating?*'

'*Penny Royal?*'

'*Possible, if the AI got to him, but unlikely. Penny Royal already has its spy aboard.*'

Riss was of course referring to the spine and its other connections elsewhere. Again, here was proof that I could trust nothing that Penny Royal had or might have touched. I dithered, wondering what the hell to do, then decided on direct confrontation.

'Flute,' I said, 'it seems you have found Cvorn's destroyer and have neglected to inform me.'

'The scans are not clear,' said Flute.

'That neutrino lensing effect looks very much to me to be the kind you would get from a functional but inactive U-space drive.'

'There could be . . . something . . . else,' Flute managed.

'Flute, who did you send that situational update to?'

After a very long pause, my ship mind replied, 'I . . . cannot.'

'Were you, or are you, in communication with Father-Captain Sverl?'

Again, the long pause then, 'I cannot.'

'You have scanned that world and found nothing but that object down at the bottom of the ocean,' I said. 'You are just completing your scans of the moons and they are just rocks.'

'I suspect . . .'

A prador destroyer down at the bottom of that ocean was no danger to us. It would take time to drive itself to the surface and the only weapons it possessed that could be effective against us from down there were missiles, which would also take time to surface. We could be gone from here long before they became a problem. However, I couldn't ignore Flute's painfully expressed fear. And there was something else I couldn't ignore. I turned to Riss.

'Presupposing Cvorn is aiming to capture Sverl and present him as evidence of Polity perfidy to his Kingdom allies,' I said, 'I have to wonder how he'd manage it.'

'This has been something of concern,' said Riss.

I continued, 'Sverl is aboard a dreadnought. Cvorn just has a destroyer . . .'

'I can only suppose that Cvorn is acting as bait for Sverl, and that the moment he knows the father-captain is here he'll send a signal to bring in his allies. The present position of his destroyer is a good one if he intends to delay Sverl. It would take many days for Sverl to either safely destroy it down there or root it out, which might be enough time for those allies to get here.'

'Safely?'

'He can do the job a lot quicker if he enters the ocean, but a multitude of traps might be concealed down there: dormant torpedoes and mines are easier to conceal in brine.'

So, Cvorn was in fact here, but Cvorn was not what this was all about. My priority was to keep tabs on Sverl, who I hoped might lead me to Penny Royal. In fact, it occurred to me that the best option to my ends would be to talk to that father-captain. I pondered this for a moment, then something else occurred to me.

'Flute, why did you use a U-space transmission to update Sverl?'

Flute made a sound like a duck trying to quack through a glued-together beak.

'One would suppose,' I said, 'that if Sverl was here concealed under chameleonware, then some other form of communication would be easier.'

'Sverl isn't here,' said Riss.

'That would be my guess,' I agreed. 'I think we should withdraw and check other sources for data.'

Via my aug, I also sent to Riss, *'I also think we should discon-nect Flute and take a long, hard look at his protocols.'*

'Agreed,' Riss replied. *'Never trusted the little fucker.'*

'If necessary, can you adapt yourself to running a U-space drive?'

'If necessary, yes.'

'Flute,' I said out loud, while checking data in my aug, 'take us to Golon. I understand it is the nearest inhabited world.'

'I . . .' Flute managed, then began emitting a sound like an angry wasp trapped in a tin can.

'Another U-space communication,' said Riss.

It took much longer than was entirely necessary for Flute to fire up our U-space drive. I strapped myself in, just in case, as I remembered someone dying in circumstances quite similar to this. But it was the unwelcome visitor aboard that dead victim's ship that had killed him, while the object he had been cautiously heading away from had been Penny Royal's planetoid.

Flute took us under, the screen fabric turning grey, then flar-ing back to life with a world looming large before us. That had just been too quick, and I knew the world I was seeing was not Golon, but the oceanic world hiding Cvorn's destroyer.

'You fucker,' said Riss out loud, whipping round and head-ing for the door so fast she was a blur. Before she reached it, the bulkhead door slammed shut and locks clonked ominously into place.

'You are obeying your father-captain's orders, aren't you, Flute?' I said.

'Zzzzt,' Flute replied.

'Sverl is using us as a probe to gather information, isn't he?'

'Zzzt.'

Meanwhile there came a crack from over by the door. I glanced over to see that Riss had driven her ovipositor into the wall beside it, had levered the cover off the palm control and was now working inside it with those small limbs usually folded below her hood. It occurred to me that right now Riss probably regretted keeping such an ineffectual body form.

Now more closely linked into my ship's systems than ever, I felt the hardfields flicking into existence out there and shifting in random patterns. Flute went immediately from passive scanning to active, firing a laser at the sea over that neutrino lensing effect to read vibrations from the surface, probing deep with an X-ray laser for reflections from hardfields or super-dense matter, rattling through other spectrums of EMR to capture whatever lay below. In seconds, in a frame down in one corner of the screen fabric, an image was building, identifiable as a prador destroyer.

'If he wasn't aware of our presence a moment ago,' I said, 'he is now.'

Flute's response to that was to fire a sensor probe down towards that ocean. I didn't need any more confirmation: we were Sverl's sacrificial goat. This Cvorn, who hated the Polity, might be unable to bear such close inspection without making some response, especially as it would be evident to him that the one doing the inspecting was aboard a Polity destroyer. We were either here to lure Cvorn out so Sverl could attack, or merely here to uncover Cvorn's plans.

Then we were into U-space again – just a brief flicker, in and out. The world was suddenly closer, and next something slammed into us, the screen fabric whiting out, grav fluctuating and something exploding inside the ship. I guessed we had just lost a hardfield projector.

'He's killed us,' said Riss.

The screen fabric came back on just as our fusion drive fired up, the massive acceleration hardly compensated for by internal grav. I replayed exterior cam views in my mind, saw one of the planet's moons revolve towards us what looked like a city of weapons inset in a cavity on its surface, and a particle beam lancing out.

Isobel Satomi

Isobel Satomi sat up in her bed and stretched. She felt good, really good, and as she tossed back the heat sheet and swung her legs over the side of the mattress, her mind was utterly clear. This was unexpected, but only in this moment because just prior to it she must have been static data stored in crystal lattices. She remembered that Penny Royal had recorded her to Trent's sapphire earring, that she had chosen to leave the body of the hooder she had been residing in. But where was that earring now? Who had resurrected her in this familiar virtuality?

She stood up and walked over to gaze at herself in her screen, which was now on its mirror setting. She was beautiful, as she had once been, and she wondered if she would again have to endure the rapid transformation to ugliness prior to her acceptance of her change into a hooder. She ran her fingers through her black hair, down her neck, and down to cup her breasts. This was what she wanted: just to live in this body again. She slid her hands over her flat stomach, ran her fingers down through her pubic hair and probed one finger into her vagina. The feeling was so intense she quickly snatched her hand away, reminded of the times far in the past when she had touched herself like this while standing before some client. She really didn't want to perform for some voyeur now. Turning away, she walked over to her wardrobe, opened it and took out underwear and pulled it on, then donned tight black trousers, a pink cotton blouse and sandals, then took some time brushing her hair and applying just a little eyeliner, before selecting a couple of skin-stick ear studs – purple diamonds to match her eyes. But what now?

Maybe Trent had decided to bring her back to life? Or maybe the sapphire earring had passed from his ownership long ago. Perhaps some private individual had powered her up and she was now functioning in a time beyond the Polity?

'Okay, I'm ready,' she said out loud.

With an ominous click, her cabin door unlocked. She turned towards it, walked over and stepped out into a corridor that had definitely not been part of the *Moray Firth*. Here was a big oval tunnel the shape of those found inside prador vessels, only this one had no artificial rock on the walls, no luminous growths and no lice. She turned to the right and began walking, relishing the feeling of walking upright again, like a human, and not scuttling along on numerous limbs with her belly to the floor. Finally, she came to the large diagonally divided door into a captain's sanctum. The halves of this rolled aside and disappeared into the walls, but within she could see nothing but darkness. She hesitated.

Did the prador fire up human memplants and venture into virtualities? Had her crystal fallen into the claws of those horrors and, if so, what could they possibly want with her? There was only one way to find out. Obviously, whoever controlled this unreal world was giving her some latitude. But that person wanted something from her too, whether that was to torment her or make her run through endless insane scenarios. She had no power to stop it. She walked slowly into the darkness. Under her feet, she felt the floor become uneven, then her sandals crunched on gravel. Ahead of her, a line etched itself into existence and she smelled the sea. The area above the line abruptly grew lighter, picking out deep blue-grey clouds against a pale sky, the glare of a rising sun keeping everything below in dark silhouette.

'Well, this is unexpected,' said a voice.

The bloated red orb of a sun rose rapidly then slowed above the horizon, while below it heaved a violet sea. Directly ahead lay a beach of rough white sand, upon which waves slopped gently. She heard the cry of something that definitely wasn't a gull. Checking to her left, she saw an arid landscape scattered with occasional rose-shaped pale green succulents growing at the bases of granite rocks, which stretched into haze and distant spiky peaks. To her right this same landscape rose up to a low hill upon which tall ferns clustered like an encroaching army. In front of her, seated on a rock by the shore, was a man. She walked towards him.

'What is unexpected?' she asked.

The man raised his gaze from inspecting his open hands and looked at her. He was blond, his hair short-cropped, and his eyes were blue. He was pretty enough in his way but didn't bulk very much in his silly patterned shorts and sleeveless top, and was nowhere near the masculine ideal Isobel preferred.

'How it feels to be really human,' he replied, his voice soft and non-threatening. He reached down and picked up a rock, held it tight in his hand then released it.

Isobel thought about his statement and asked, 'Are you an AI slumming it in this virtuality as a human?'

'Partially,' he said, grimacing.

'Haiman?'

'Of a sort.'

'What do you want from me?'

Now he looked sad. 'I have studied your entire life, Isobel. I know why you became what you became, and the drivers behind your every action. I was fascinated at first but in the process found a growing abhorrence because, in studying the detail and all the interconnections, one comes to understand that the very concept of choice is a false one.'

'I don't believe in predestination,' Isobel snapped, suddenly angry. 'I did make my own choices. I did choose my own path.'

'Predestination,' he repeated, turning his head away. 'As evolved creatures we can't escape it. But as creatures who can alter both our bodies and our minds, we can introduce the random . . .'

'You still haven't told me what you want or who and what you are.'

He turned back. 'I studied your transformation and your dealings with Penny Royal – for they are the ones of most interest to me. I am Father-Captain Sverl.'

Isobel took a step back. As she had departed the system of the Rock Pool, going in pursuit of Penny Royal, impelled by instincts that were suicidal in that situation, and gradually being swallowed by the hooder war mind, Sverl had contacted her. The words they had exchanged had been few and inconsequential, but the communication on other levels had been vast. He had displayed his mind to her in all its alien glory, its ongoing distortion and its hungry need for . . . *something*. He had wanted her. He had wanted . . . mental exchanges. And this had terrified her.

'If you have full knowledge of our encounters, you have what you wanted from me, then,' she managed.

'In all but some final details, I do have that information. But it has provided none of the answers I sought. Our only common ground is that we are the victims of Penny Royal. And we have both undergone – and, in my case, am still undergoing – transformation. However, you and I are still very different creatures, Isobel.'

'No shit,' she said. 'I'm a human being and you're a psychotic crab.'

'I was,' Sverl replied, again peering at his hands, 'but at this moment I am human – a lesser being, just one third of my whole.'

'Why am I here now?' Isobel asked.

He looked up. 'Those final details I mentioned. I have seen everything but those last moments. Your crystal takes me only as far as your intent to kill Thorvald Spear. It takes me to the moment the Weaver seized control of you. Or rather, it commandeered the war mind of which you had become an insignificant portion.'

'But I remember the rest.'

'So you do, but the rest is caught in a time crystal I cannot access. In a manner yet opaque to me, Penny Royal has made that portion of your existence accessible only with your permission. I therefore must assume that it is the portion most important to me.'

Isobel fought to overcome her fear but even as she did so, she felt something dark and huge loom behind this harmless-looking man. She stepped over and seated herself on a rock just a few paces in front of him, reached down and picked up a sea-smoothed flat green pebble and brushed away the grit. She sat upright and hurled it hard and low at the sea. It skipped over the water and, with satisfaction, she counted four bounces. Then, as if Sverl just wanted to remind her who was in control, when she knew it ought to fall into the water the pebble skipped again and again, endlessly across the sea, out towards the bloated sun.

'Then I have something to bargain with,' she said.

'Yes, in a sense you do,' he replied, 'but lest you forget, my bargaining position is a stronger one. Please don't force me to resort to threats, Isobel.'

Yes, he controlled this virtuality, he controlled her. He could put her through an eternity of torment, while only a brief span of time passed for him.

'I want to live,' she said.

'Of course you do, but that is not my choice,' said Sverl. 'I have been allowed to activate you by the one who owns you.' Sverl pointed over her shoulder and she turned. Trent Sobel stood there, gazing out to sea.

'Trent!'

He turned and looked at her, reached up to finger that damned earring of his, shook his head dismissively and just faded out of existence. The knowledge dropped easily into her mind. Penny Royal had put her in that earring of his, but here Trent had just been a ghost, an illustration – not real.

'He told me that one day he might resurrect you, Isobel, if he can ever find it in his heart to forgive you.'

Isobel felt suddenly tired and unwell. She reached up to touch her face and felt a hollow forming in her cheek bone.

Not again.

As she sat there, she became certain that a blood-red eye would open in that developing pit and knew in agonizing detail everything that would ensue. She could be forced to relive her transformation by Penny Royal over and over again. She picked up another stone, a small one, and realized after a moment that it was a purple sapphire, but polished smooth, not faceted. She knew Sverl was manipulating both her virtual form and her mind, subtly impelling her to make the response he sought, and she remembered how he could be much more unsubtle.

'Take the damned memories,' she said, and tossed the gem to the man before her.

He snatched it out of the air. 'Thank you, Isobel.'

She looked aside, now feeling at once alienated from her identity and yet deeply connected to it too.

'The problem was separating you from what you'd become, so intricately bound were the two,' said a voice she recognized but didn't want to name to herself. It continued, 'The Weaver supplied the answer for its own benefit: change what you were becoming, then make the new being reject the old. Thereafter the only remaining problem was to find the line of division. It was perfect, and restored some balance on Masada too.'

Manipulators were now sprouting out down each side of her extended face. Horror filled her, and this time it wasn't blunted by a growing hooder psyche; by the predator melding with her own predatory instincts. It wasn't ameliorated by her knowledge that to survive, she must accept the changes she was undergoing. Everything that had screamed in her when Penny Royal had changed the course of her transformation was screaming again . . . or was that still *screaming? Had it ever stopped?*

On the shore, Isobel reached up to touch her face again. The eye pit was gone and it was again perfect, but it didn't feel real. None of this was real anyway; it was just data, moving.

'The war machine left you behind,' said Penny Royal. Yes, it was the AI talking to her, the AI she had supposedly killed.

'I don't understand,' Isobel managed, her voice horribly distorted by her changing mouth. 'Why . . . you do this?' she tried, but knew it was not a question but a plea for mercy.

'I must unravel my past back to its beginning, and it's to the beginning I will go next,' the black AI replied cryptically. 'That is, when all is done here and events ordered and set on their course to conclusion.'

It stopped there. Isobel felt a huge surge of excitement but knew that it wasn't her own. Momentarily, she glimpsed a flash of something completely out of sync with her current 'reality'.

She saw a human skull walking on metal legs in some strange garden. Trent Sobel sat on a small stool there, fingering his ear-lobe, while in his other hand he held a long needle.

'Why!' she shrieked.

'You wanted to tear your enemies apart, and I provided the tools,' said the AI. 'That was wrong of me. I have now taken all your tools away from you: your war machine body, your ships, your people, your power, and now only you remain.'

Isobel wailed.

'And now you have a small chance to again be what you once were.'

Isobel's wail died and the world snapped around her. A shadow passed and aboard this ersatz version of the Moray Firth *Isobel turned, feeling good, to gaze at her screen mirror. She was beautiful again, her mind whole, all her memories accessible.*

'How can that be possible?' she asked.

'All you need to do,' Penny Royal replied, 'is let go.'

'You mean die.'

'You reside in me now, Isobel, and now it's time for you to leave.'

'You promise – I have another chance?' Isobel asked, suddenly, unutterably weary.

'I always keep my promises,' said Penny Royal.

'Thank you, Isobel,' Sverl the human repeated. He was now just a disembodied voice, his human form banished with the view of the sea.

'So I was just a messenger,' she replied. 'Not even that – just the message's container, a way to bring Penny Royal's words to you.'

'An important one.'

'A cipher, a piece of data, a clue.'

'Perhaps it's not finished for you yet,' Sverl suggested. 'Trent

Sobel seeks to redeem himself, and he might revive you in the process.'

'There is nothing left for me,' she replied. 'I just want to go away now. He can keep me in his damned earring for all eternity. I don't care.'

'Sleep, then,' said Sverl.

Blackness descended.

The Brockle

The old Polity destroyer – a heavily armoured bulk a mile long – ejected an escape pod. The pod, just a cone-shaped re-entry capsule, tumbled in vacuum for a while as if to orient itself, then fired up a chemical drive to bring it in towards the detectors and defences about the *Tyburn*. After deep scanning it, they allowed it through. The Brockle meanwhile kept a mental finger on the switch to initiate the *Tyburn*'s thoroughly modernized U-space drive. If the detectors out there picked up the slightest non-standard U-signature from the destroyer, which probably meant the launching of a U-jump missile, the *Tyburn* would be gone, shedding U-field disruptor mines in its wake, and the Brockle's *agreed* imprisonment would be over.

Ever since its arrival, there had been no response from the destroyer's controlling AI to the Brockle's queries, and it had not used a shuttle to send its prisoners. This particular AI wanted nothing to do with the Brockle – like so many Polity AIs, it saw the Brockle as the mad relative locked in the attic – and, turning its ship away, obviously wanted to leave as quickly as possible. However, just before it dropped into U-space a data package did arrive.

The Brockle opened the package with care. It was unlikely

173

that a simple ship AI could have designed an effective informational attack against an AI like the Brockle, but that did not discount it having brought one from elsewhere. The ship AI had supplied all the requested data. The Brockle had wanted all the technical data the AI could provide about its ship because it was from the same era as Penny Royal's *Puling Child*, now renamed the *Lance*, and of the same design. Now absorbing the package, the Brockle learned very little of use – it illuminated nothing about the black AI's past, nor how it had turned into what it now was. Perhaps the destroyer's prisoners would provide more useful information on Penny Royal.

The escape pod was now heading in towards the space doors, automatically tracked by a gigawatt laser, signalling ahead for permission to dock. The Brockle gave it, evacuating the hold and setting the space doors to open, also shutting down grav on the dock floor. The pod finally drifted in, adjusting with puffs of compressed air to swing upright and settle. The Brockle re-engaged grav to bring it down firmly. It was in now, and would be going nowhere.

Ensconced in a chair in its favoured human form, the Brockle watched through the thousands of pin cams scattered inside the dock. Once the old space doors closed, pressure inside steadily began to climb. When the pressure reached Earth-normal, a door thumped open in the side of the pod and a figure, with a survival suit pulled on over his clothes, climbed out. This was Ikbal Phrose, one of Captain Blite's old crew-members. Upon reaching the floor, he turned to help his crewmate, Martina Lennerson Hyde, but she waved him away irritably. Once they were down on the floor they looked about expectantly, then, after a while, Martina pulled open her visor and shouted, 'Hey, anyone here?'

The Brockle stood, sensing its body's units easing apart – the physical expression of its eagerness to get to the interrogation – but it felt frustration too. Its instructions from Earth Central had been quite clear and that AI's watcher here would report any infraction. The Brockle was to interrogate the two meticulously and examine and record anything of relevance to Penny Royal it could find in their minds. However, it was to do this without causing them great discomfort, because they were only guilty of petty crimes. Also, they were not under sentence of death, so, when the Brockle was finished with them, it must put them on a prison single-ship and dispatch them to Par Avion.

The Brockle felt this was a kind of madness. Since interrogating Trent, it had been taking an increasing interest in the doings of Penny Royal. Long accustomed to examining the common criminals of the Polity, both human and AI, it was now aware that Penny Royal was an uncommon and dangerous offender indeed. The Brockle also understood that its interest in Penny Royal had increased because the black AI was more akin to the Brockle than to other Polity AIs. Like the Brockle, it was a swarm entity and could separate its body into a shoal form with different mind states and even minds, perpetually communicating, absorbing each other and separating. Like the Brockle, some past trauma had driven it into mental expansion and towards behaviour not acceptable in *civilized* AI society. However, unlike the Brockle, Penny Royal had stepped well over the line and become the AI equivalent of a human psychopath. The Brockle had merely edged a toe over the line, which was why, rather than face extermination, it had allowed Polity AIs to confine it to this prison hulk.

'Proceed to the door,' the Brockle instructed over the old intercom system, opening one of the circular doors at the back of the dock. 'Walk along the tunnel and enter the second room on the right.'

'Who is this?' Martina demanded.

'I am to ask you some questions concerning your association with the black AI Penny Royal,' the Brockle replied, its skin turning silvery and splitting as the writhing worm-forms of its swarm body separated further.

'Is this a forensic AI?' asked Ikbal, definitely looking as if he wanted to be elsewhere.

'This will not take long.'

The Brockle separated completely, silver worms shooting forwards like a shoal of garfish, through the door and round into the tunnel beyond. As it travelled, it watched Ikbal shrug then trudge over to the door from the dock and Martina trail reluctantly after him. Shortly they would be in the examination room. And there, the Brockle intended to investigate the limits of its brief. Namely, how Earth Central's watcher might interpret 'great discomfort'.

8

Blite

The other ship, the black modern Polity attack ship that had disabled a Polity dreadnought at the border before descending like a raptor on Blite's *The Rose*, steadily melded itself to his ship over the ensuing days. But Penny Royal's motives in making this happen were, as ever, unclear. The process had made all sections of their old vessel inaccessible and confined Blite and his remaining crew to the bridge. However, cam views and other data were available in the screen laminate. Blite availed himself of these between dozes in his acceleration chair. At one point, he gazed at an alcove in one of the newly constructed corridors.

'What the hell is that?' he asked.

'Funny, I thought the job of captain required at least some knowledge of space,' said Greer.

Blite glared at her. 'Yes, I know it's a space suit, but what's it doing here?'

'Well,' Greer shrugged, 'maybe it's there because we're out in space?'

Blite glared at her again, then enquired, 'Leven?'

'It is a replica. It was made by the previous AI of the attack ship with which we're currently merging,' the ship mind replied.

'An antique space suit,' said Blite. 'So Penny Royal respects other people's property?'

'Apparently,' Leven replied.

Blite let it go at that, quickly switching to another scene. The suit, sitting there on its own little stool in that alcove, gave him the creeps, but he couldn't nail exactly why.

Instead, he gazed at a view into the engine room where Penny Royal, or some part of that AI, had gutted the old U-space drive. It was chaotic in there – Penny Royal's silver tendrils snaking everywhere, black spines pecking like heron beaks at the remains of the drive, components tumbling through the air – but this was an AI at work and 'multitasking' hardly got close to what it could do.

'That,' said Brond, stabbing a finger at the screen, 'is part of a modern Polity U-drive.'

Blite focused on the object concerned, a large object that looked like a polished aluminium sculpture of someone's intestines.

'So Penny Royal has taken apart our drive and the drive of the attack ship and is shifting it here,' he said. 'How come we're still in U-space if it's been dismantled?'

'Beats me,' said Brond.

'Maybe the other ship has more than one drive,' suggested Greer.

'Maybe,' Blite agreed.

New components began to appear one after the other and the AI slotted them into place. Micro-welding arcs flashed, blooms of nanotech spread along surfaces, fixings as small as grains of sand it drove or twisted home, and weird distortions flared around odd organic-looking technology. Blite saw parts of his old drive going into the mix, along with objects he felt certain, having seen examples of it, were of the AI's own particular technology. It assembled a great mass in the middle of the engine room, inserting supporting struts all around, covering it with sections of casing, snaking in power cables and optics to connect. After two days of watching this, and other reconstruction elsewhere, Blite felt the U-drive stutter, then it faded into a smooth hum of invisible power.

'We are accelerating,' said Leven.

'Accelerating?' asked Blite.

'It is the only word I can use,' said the Golem ship mind. 'We're breaching the time barrier and utilizing impossible amounts of energy drawn from U-space.'

'You what?'

'Time travel is possible,' Leven explained, 'but even the prador were afraid of going that far.'

Blite knew time travel was possible and understood why sensible creatures avoided it. You ventured into infinite energy progressions and, in an effort to change history, you might end up destroying it. He'd once heard it described as using a fusion drive to travel from one side of a room to another. You would certainly get to the other side of that room, but there wouldn't be much of the room left afterwards.

'Penny Royal!' he shouted. 'What the *fuck* are you doing?'

A sound as of a coin dropped into a wine glass occurred behind him and he turned to see a black diamond materialize out of the air, half-seen distortions spreading out all around it and seeming to extend . . . forever.

'Catastrophic cascade will be avoided,' the black AI whispered, whereupon a montage of images and memories opened in Blite's mind. He saw a grotesque creature like a walking skull, various spaceships on the move and people – some of whom he recognized – caught in snapshots of their lives. This all opened out into something larger, something he just couldn't grasp. Then it folded and he felt like his mind might be crushed in that fold until, suddenly, it all snapped out of existence. Blite felt sick and wished he'd remembered this penalty for asking questions.

His head bowed and his mouth watering, he said, 'I understood none of that.'

Something nibbled at his consciousness, then withdrew.

'A problem has arisen caused by a brief resurrection of Sverl's prador instincts, and it must be corrected for,' said Penny Royal. 'We will only arrive at our destination two weeks before we left our departure point and a catastrophic cascade will be avoided.'

The AI had adjusted its communication methods for this simple human, but it still wasn't enough.

'What?' Blite said.

The diamond blinked out.

'What's that about Sverl?' Blite blurted.

Penny Royal didn't reply, and now the captain was glad that it hadn't.

The three on the bridge just turned back to gaze at the screen laminate, now seeing the tendrils and pecking black swords retreating. A new U-space drive sat in their engine room, humming contentedly, doing something that terrified both the Polity's top AIs and even the barking-mad prador.

'You know,' said Brond, 'if we're left with this new drive, we'll never be able to go into the Polity again. The AIs will *never* stop hunting us down.'

'I know,' said Blite.

He now called up other images only just becoming available from cams *The Rose* had never possessed. He called up data and schematics on the other ship's systems and weapons, as it increasingly, improbably, merged with his own craft. They were becoming one. New schematics were becoming available all the time. And, combining available emerging data and cam views, Blite generated an image in the laminate.

'Well that's what we look like now,' he said.

The Rose, which some had described as looking like an iron mosque, wasn't even visible. And what had been a modern Polity attack ship had been radically redesigned. The thing up on the screen was a fat black horseshoe with fusion drive throats inset in the rear two faces, various sensor and weapons protrusions along its double body and a small screen visible to the fore.

'So where are we?' asked Greer.

Blite stared at the image for a while, then called up the schematic and stared at that. There were *twinned* U-space engines, one located in each prong of the horseshoe. Narrow corridors gave access to them and to the fusion engines from the fore of the ship, where the bridge was located behind that small screen. Crew quarters were to one side of the bridge, with a cargo hold lying just beyond them, while on the other side a bay contained a shuttle of no design Blite could recognize. *The Rose* just wasn't there.

'Leven, is this right?' Blite asked.

'It is right, Captain,' Leven replied, 'the only parts of your ship that have not been shifted and changed are the bridge and you three. Even I have additional processing and have expanded to encompass some serious U-jump and weapons technology.'

'What the fuck has it done to my ship?' That dreaded clinking sound came from behind him once more and Blite turned his chair to gaze at the black diamond. 'That wasn't a question for you,' he added hurriedly.

'*This* is your ship,' said Penny Royal.

'As Brond has noted,' said Blite, 'if this is our ship then we'll forever be outcasts from the Polity unless we hand the damned thing over. And even then I think our chances of avoiding being taken apart by a forensic AI are negligible.'

Data imprinted itself on Blite's consciousness: thousands of files on human individuals, a tree of interconnections, the image of *The Rose* in dock at Par Avion, a scrolling statistical analysis. Blite groaned, feeling as if he had rammed a compressed-air hose into his skull. Then this data snapped out of his mind again and he bit down on the urge to puke.

'I just got the job as translator,' interjected Leven.

'Go ahead,' Blite managed.

'Without Penny Royal we would have been caught and examined anyway,' said the ship's mind. 'If all goes to plan henceforth and we survive, we can bargain with the Polity, sell this vessel for great wealth and buy another, better vessel than *The Rose*. In that case, unfortunately, we will not be able to avoid forensic examination. But it will not kill us.'

'What "plan" exactly?' Blite asked, as the diamond blinked out again.

'I don't know,' Leven admitted. 'Though I'm getting hints that it's in a perpetual state of flux.'

So everything might not go to plan . . .

Blite sat there, mulling all this over. Despite his head feeling as if it had been wire-brushed inside, he couldn't deny he felt some excitement and awe to be part of this. He'd always supposed he wanted to make his fortune and settle down to a comfortable life somewhere while others continued to expand his business and pay for his lifestyle. That would have been the most he could have achieved: maybe a couple of ships shunting cargo about. He now knew that he wanted something more. He wanted to be part of big events, and to see more of the universe than he possibly could by settling on some holiday world. Now he was involved in something big, had wealth stacked up in his Galaxy Bank account and was sitting inside the kind of ship people like him could usually only gaze upon with envy.

'Okay, Leven,' he said, 'tell me what we've got here.'

'You've got a ship with twinned U-drives that can feed off

U-space energy and are the fastest thing I've ever seen. The time-jump we're undertaking, however, is only due to Penny Royal's intervention and we won't be able to do that without the black AI aboard. You have two arrays of fusion engines capable of taking this ship up to one tenth of light speed. You have grav-engines that could even land on a star, also feeding off U-space energy. You have three times the hold space of *The Rose*, and a shuttle.'

'What about weapons?'

'Ah, there we get into territory that goes beyond human language,' said Leven.

'Just give me the gist.'

'Semi-AI U-jump splinter missiles, multi-particulate particle cannons, cross-spectrum lasers, near-c railguns, induction effectors for seizing control of the systems of other ships . . . I think a better question to ask is what *haven't* you got.'

'That's all very nice,' interjected Brond, 'but not a great deal of use when it comes to hauling cargo. And there's one other point to consider.'

'Go on,' said Blite.

'Penny Royal, as far as I can gather, doesn't tend to do stuff like this without some reason, no matter how obscure it might seem,' Brond continued. 'That we have all this hardware, no matter how it was obtained, indicates to me that we'll probably need it.'

Blite absorbed that and reckoned Brond was on the button, but that didn't still the excitement or detract from the satisfaction his acquisitive side felt.

'We need a new name for this ship,' he said.

'And you already have it,' guessed Greer.

'I certainly do,' Blite agreed. 'I name this ship the *Black Rose*.'

'Trite,' said Greer dismissively.

Weeks of shipboard time passed while Blite and his crew familiarized themselves with his ship's systems and explored its much-altered interior. Blite often found himself drawn to that antique space suit sitting in its alcove and, when he wanted to speak to Penny Royal, who had disappeared since that last sight of it in the engine room, he found himself addressing the suit. Penny Royal never answered during that time, but that did not dispel Blite's growing certainty that somehow it was present in the suit. Then at last Leven announced that they were about to surface from U-space. All three humans waited in the bridge for this event. The screen laminate in front of them stayed neutral grey until, as they surfaced smoothly and without noticeable effects, it transformed into glorious colour.

Blite felt his mood lift as he gazed upon a sulphur-yellow world surrounded by a multicoloured gas cloud. This interstellar cathedral with its dark green and sky-blue swirls, its vein-like threads and fleshy clouds, was the kind of sight he wanted to see. Penny Royal was taking them to places he had only dreamed of visiting. At least, he might have dreamed of visiting this one if he only knew where he was.

'This is a place called by the prador the "Feeding Frenzy",' Leven explained.

Blite felt a momentary doubt at the mention of the prador but it did not dispel his buoyant mood. However, Leven's next words did: 'It's in the Prador Kingdom.'

Oh shit.

No, what was the matter with him? He was in one of the fastest ships known and its weaponry was capable of handling *anything.* Some brief venture into the outskirts of the Prador Kingdom shouldn't be a problem.

Now Leven opened a frame down in one corner of the screen

laminate, focusing close in over that yellow world. Massive ships, like long golden teardrops, were shoaling out from there on the arc-glare of fusion drives and turning, inevitably, towards them.

'And those are the ships of the King's Guard,' Leven added.

All Blite could manage in response to that was a grunt of acknowledgement.

Spear

We were going down – betrayed by my ship AI and under attack – diving towards the nearby world under full fusion drive. That beam again stabbed out from the thing sitting inside the moon. The *Lance* stopped it with a hardfield, and another explosion rattled inside our ship – one more projector, unable to take the feedback, turning molten and flying apart. I checked schematics and saw that we could take only two more hits like that before we ran out of projectors, then we would be toast. I glanced round at Riss, who was still trying to get out of the bridge, doubtless on course to rip the heart out of our treacherous ship mind.

'Riss,' I said, 'don't open that door.'

'Little fucker,' Riss replied, now having torn out part of the wall beside the door and with her head inserted deep inside.

'Riss, if you open that door you'll kill me.'

She withdrew her head and looked over at me. She then doubtless accessed ship's diagnostics and damage reports, as I was doing constantly, and realized that the corridor outside the door was full of white-hot gas. She desisted.

'We're dead anyway,' said the drone.

Cvorn's trap had not involved summoning reinforcements as

185

we had supposed, for they were already here in some form, but I didn't entirely agree with Riss's assessment of our chances, and confirmation of my suspicion occurred just a second later. The *Lance* hummed and juddered as Flute opened up with our rail-guns to send a swarm of missiles towards that moon. Almost certainly, our opponent's laser defences and anti-munitions would stop every single one, but they would buy us time. Next, our own particle cannon fired, stabbing through that swarm of slower-moving missiles to splash on an abrupt scaling of hard-fields just out from the moon.

'What the hell are we fighting?' I asked.

'A prador ST dreadnought,' Flute replied.

'And you led us right into its firing line,' Riss spat.

Flute was finally speaking clearly now, but this wasn't the time for recriminations or explanations. Nor was it the time, even if the corridor outside the bridge had not been filled with flame, for Riss to tear the second-child's mind apart. Right now Flute was our only hope of survival.

'Initiate interface manoeuvre,' I said. 'But you need a way of shutting our attacker down at least for a minute.'

It was dangerous to try to enter U-space this close to a gravity well because the chances were that if you actually managed to re-enter realspace, you and your ship would be turned inside out. That danger ramped up even higher when you were under attack. Isobel Satomi had somehow managed such manoeuvres while descending on Masada but, at that point, she had been part of an Atheter war mind – an entity capable of doing some seriously weird stuff with U-space. We needed a break, a breather, and there was a chance we could create one.

When I'd been intent on bearding Penny Royal in its lair in that wanderer planetoid, I'd instructed Flute to manufacture the means of expelling the AI from that lair, in burning fragments.

Flute had used kiloton CTDs stolen from Isobel Satomi as a detonating package for fissile plutonium-239, transmuted aboard this ship from uranium-238 sieved and enzyme extracted from asteroid dust, the whole wrapped in hardfield-contained deuterium. The result was a fusion bomb in the multi-megaton range.

I was reluctant to use it.

'We have a way of shutting him down,' said Flute, referring to our super-weapon.

'I know,' I replied, still hesitating, but also aware that Flute was now deferring to me rather than acting on his own.

I didn't want to use that bomb because it was my ace card – the one weapon I had that just might be capable of killing the black AI. However, as I heard another of our projectors go, I decided that actually surviving this encounter might be a good idea too.

'Use the bomb, Flute.'

Flute must have had the thing lined up for firing in an instant. I heard and felt the alteration in the tone of our railguns as one of them powered down for a low-speed firing – he could not fire such a device at the speed usual for inert missiles, because the acceleration would tear vital components apart. Up in the screen fabric a red circle marked the until then invisible course of the bomb heading towards the moon. Timing was everything. Cvorn, if it was that prador aboard this ST dreadnought, would soon recognize the threat of a slow-moving object coming towards him. He probably wouldn't react to it right away because even a gigaton CTD would have to get very close to cause any damage. Flute had to judge when to send the detonation signal – with luck, just moments before Cvorn opened fire on the bomb.

The destroyer's particle beam speared out again, not towards the bomb but at us. Our last projector went out with a crash and doubtless Cvorn, fully knowledgeable about the kind of equipment an old destroyer like the *Lance* would carry, was relishing this moment. He wouldn't fire on us right away – he'd want us to have time to be fully aware of our imminent destruction.

The *Lance* was shaking now, the planet looming huge across the screen fabric opposite our view of that militarized moon. I felt some satisfaction on seeing a red circle now enclose something rising up from that city of weapons. Cvorn had been dismissive of the approaching bomb and merely fired a missile on an intercept course rather than use some beam weapon. He'd given us more time.

The two circles drew closer together and, at the last moment, I was sure I saw a flash of blue as Cvorn's particle beam stabbed out. But it could have been my imagination.

Detonation.

Bright light flared inside the first circle, then a black macula briefly blotted it out as exterior cams polarized to prevent the flash burning them out, and as the screen ceased to transmit something that could have blinded me. The explosion was spherical, quickly expanding to the size of that moon and beyond, encompassing the moon even as the ship inside it erected a hardfield wall. Over the ensuing minute the sphere began to distort, seemingly sinking at the poles as its waist continued to expand, ionization appearing like St Elmo's fire above those poles. Our energy levels climbed; our fusion reactor fed depleted storage to give us enough to power our drive. I felt our U-engine engaging, and the harsh drag away from the real induced a cyclic scream in my skull. The bridge I was sitting within became just a veneer over something my mind could not grasp and I knew that a lot of our U-engine shielding must be gone. The screen fabric turned grey, and we jumped.

In this situation, Flute could not set coordinates far from the action – just make a brief jump permissible with the power available. Reality slammed back into place as I heard something howling from the engine room and smoke began filtering through the hole Riss had carved beside the door.

'What's our status?' I asked, suddenly all calm.

'U-engine is down, munitions depleted, fusion reactor running safe shutdown,' was Flute's businesslike reply.

'Or to translate,' said Riss, 'we're about ten minutes from annihilation.'

I saw what the drone meant when our screen fabric came back on. We had jumped, but just two hundred thousand miles out from the world, to the other side of the moon which, even at that moment, was revolving that city of weapons towards us.

Trent

It had been a seriously odd encounter, and a dangerous one, but Trent had survived, and that was all that really mattered to him right then. With any luck, he would keep on surviving. With any luck, the distorted first-child currently conveying him deep into the bowels of this dreadnought would not be taking him either home for lunch, or to some prador cold store. No, having encountered Sverl, Trent did not think so. Sverl had dispatched him to join the shell people whom he claimed to have rescued from the Rock Pool.

'Father found you interesting,' said the first-child.

Trent stared at the creature, surprised it saw any need to speak. He reached up and flicked the earring now depending from his ear. 'He found this interesting. I was just the delivery boy.'

'Father's interest in Isobel Satomi is relevant to his own condition,' the prador stated.

Was this big ugly monstrosity trying to start a conversation?

'What's your name?' Trent asked.

The prador made a hissing gurgle that was quite close to the name its translator then issued.

'Well, Bsorol, I now know that your father-captain paid a visit to Penny Royal and is undergoing his own transformation, so understand his interest in Satomi, but I fail to understand his interest in me.'

'Why you?' Bsorol asked.

'What do you mean?'

'Why did Penny Royal save you?'

'To act as a delivery boy,' Trent suggested.

'No. Penny Royal loaded her to the gem in your ear. The AI could have transmitted her directly to my father. You were not necessary.'

'Penny Royal told me to redeem myself . . .'

'Yet there are many like you.'

'Then it probably saved me on a whim.' Trent was starting to get uncomfortable with the idea that he might have some further role in Penny Royal's plans. 'Tell me, what exactly did Sverl want from Penny Royal and what exactly is he turning into?'

'He wanted to understand the enemy in order to thereby defeat him,' said Bsorol. 'Penny Royal has given Father the ultimate in understanding, by transforming him into that enemy.'

'He's turning into a human being? Seems to be going about it in a rather odd fashion.'

'And an AI – he is growing AI crystal around his major ganglion.'

Trent absorbed that for a moment, snorted dismissively, then stated, 'That's not possible – attaching AI crystal direct to an organic brain burns out both brain and crystal. It's what happened to Iversus Skaidon when he invented runcible technology.'

'It's what happens to a human brain when *directly* attached to AI crystal,' Bsorol explained patiently. 'The prador major ganglion is more distributed, rugged, better supplied with oxygen and nutrients, and in many other fashions is a superior organ.'

'Yeah, shame it wasn't superior enough to win the war.' The words were out before he could stop them and he warily studied the first-child, prepared to duck and run if it took a swipe at him. Bsorol, however, just perambulated along beside him, grating his mandibles together.

'There is an organo-mineral substrate acting as a buffer to the crystal growing on Father's ganglion, which also works to prevent that synergistic burn-out. My father is rather like a prador version of your haiman: a combination of human and AI. Which, of course, further enhances his interest in Isobel Satomi.'

'Yeah, I guess—'

Bsorol abruptly whirled round, his claw spearing in and closing around Trent's chest, hoisting him up and slamming him back against the near wall.

'The prador did not lose the war,' said the first-child, 'and the humans did not win it.'

Trent gasped for breath.

'Yes, I perfectly understand that we were losing the war when the old king was usurped and the new king negotiated terms with the Polity,' Bsorol continued. 'I also perfectly understand that if the Polity and the Kingdom were to go to war now, we would definitely lose. However, the Polity AIs are responsible for that, not the humans. Had it been just humans and prador fighting, we would have crushed you entirely, just like I could crush you now.'

Bsorol released him and he dropped heavily to the floor,

191

sinking down on his backside. He sat there, gasping, for a moment as Bsorol backed off and waited. Finally hauling himself to his feet, he couldn't resist, 'So you're fairly new to the art of conversation?'

'I am fairly new to controlling my instincts,' said Bsorol. 'Come.'

The prador turned and continued up the corridor. Trent followed, pondering the idea of prador adopting AI and augmentations. He wondered just what that might mean in the future for his own kind.

'Here.' Bsorol finally brought him before an oval door. It was large enough for a first-child but definitely too small for a father-captain. The door hissed off a seal and rolled into the wall on one side. 'Perhaps here, so my father tells me, you may be able to find some of that redemption,' the prador told him.

'Redemption?'

Bsorol just turned and moved away.

Trent stepped through into a short tunnel, terminating at yet another door. The first door closed behind him, seals sucking down, and then the second opened ahead. He walked through and out into a huge hold space from where he could gaze across at a small city of enviro-tents and the other panoply of temporary human occupation. A woman, seemingly clad in helmet and body armour, beckoned to him. As he walked over, he saw that both helmet and armour were actually part of her body and were her carapace.

'I'm to take you to Father,' she said.

Father?

Peering beyond her, Trent recognized the altered body forms of the people moving about in the encampment. The woman was just a less extreme version of one of the shell people here. He nodded companionably and stepped forwards, only at the last moment hearing movement behind him. He whirled, damning the softening of his instincts, in time to see one of the more heavily altered shell people raising a pepper-pot stunner. The cloud of micro-beads struck him on the chest and sent him staggering, then blackness took him.

Blite

'They just jumped,' said Leven, referring to a host of giant prador ships.

'No, really?' Blite replied sardonically, stamping on the urge to titter.

Penny Royal simply wasn't talking, and Leven's attempt to turn them around and flee had failed. Blite had just watched a total of thirty modern prador ships blink out of existence. Then, moments later, he didn't need any sensor readings to tell him where they were. One of the behemoths was filling his screen as it drew past. The damned things were shoaling all around like giant sharks.

'Penny Royal,' he tried. 'I'm really not so sure being here is a great idea.' It wasn't a question, so perhaps he was safe from having his brain turned to jelly.

'*Listen and learn,*' the AI hissed in his ear.

He whirled round, but no black diamond was present. As he turned back, another frame opened in the screen fabric to display an armoured prador squatting in some gleaming sanctum.

'You came,' it said.

'I don't really know why I'm here,' Blite babbled, but he was obviously out of the com circuit because it was Penny Royal's reply the prador heard:

'I came,' agreed the AI.

'The ship is interesting,' said the prador. 'My tactical assessment is that it could destroy at least five of my vessels before I managed to destroy it.'

'Seven of your vessels,' Penny Royal corrected. 'You failed to incorporate the inducers and their effects on your systems.'

'An irrelevant point,' said the prador. 'You would still be dust.'

'As would you.'

'That does not concern me – service to my father and king does.'

'Which is why you have not attacked.'

'Yes.'

'I have data,' Penny Royal indicated.

'Yes.'

'It details the future your father and king must pursue to avoid extinction.'

'Extinction can be avoided?'

'For many centuries, yes, but in the end it is inevitable, Gost.'

'I will relay this data to my father, when I receive it. But you wish for something in return?'

'Of course.'

'Tell me.'

So why can't you talk to me as clearly? Blite wondered. Then it occurred to him he was hearing this exchange in language he could understand when both of them could have been speaking the prador tongue . . . or rather the prador mandible, or bubbling throat membrane. Penny Royal had to be translating for the benefit of him and his crew. Perhaps the AI *had* decided to be a little less obscure after all . . .

'Sverl will contact you again, as he must,' said Penny Royal. 'He will be seeking data on the location of Factory Station Room 101.'

'The place where you were created,' said Gost.

'Yes,' was all Penny Royal would allow.

'This data can be supplied,' replied Gost. 'We have known the location of that place ever since one of our exploration vessels came upon it half a century ago. The vessel concerned managed to transmit at least that before it was destroyed.'

'And you did not send a force there to in turn destroy the factory station,' Penny Royal noted.

'Our first attempt to destroy it during the war was costly enough and it would be a pointless exercise now. Its continued existence is also a source of amusement to Father – a reminder to Polity AIs of their fallibility since it went insane and fled the conflict.'

'Polity AIs who also know its location . . .' the black AI suggested.

'A select few of them at the top of the hierarchy are aware of this. Those who have discovered its location accidentally either disappear or end up under AI lock. This means they know the location of the station, but cannot pass on that knowledge.'

'Just like the few who escaped the station after it fled,' Penny Royal added.

'Yes, just like them,' said Gost. 'So you want me to give these coordinates to Sverl?'

'No, I want you to give Sverl the list of names and identification numbers of those who escaped the station, and nothing else.'

Gost spent a little time chewing that over, then asked, 'Why?'

'That is not your concern.'

'But it is,' Gost asserted. 'Everything you do is of concern to my king and therefore to me. He perfectly understands the danger you represent, which has already been demonstrated by the readings I took from your U-signature upon your arrival here.'

'I represent no danger to the prador,' said Penny Royal.

'Your U-signature indicates temporal distortions, which are a danger to us all.'

'All U-signatures indicate temporal distortions.'

'This is a matter of magnitude, as you well know,' said Gost. 'And it is precisely because of this kind of dangerous meddling that I need a reason to allow you to leave this place.'

Ah fuck, thought Blite. The whole conversation had been going so swimmingly, but unless Penny Royal came up with something, it looked as if they were about to be creamed.

'I have sent you the data I promised,' said Penny Royal, 'and ask again that you do not give Sverl the exact location of Room 101 but do provide that list.'

'I am still waiting for that reason,' said Gost.

'They're moving to surround us,' said Brond, 'and one of them just deployed something that looks suspiciously like a Polity USER.'

Just to make sure we don't jump away, thought Blite, now gazing at the screen view Brond called up of some object, almost like the carriage of a train, issuing from a port in the side of one of those vessels.

'Penny Royal's up to—'

The *Black Rose* surged under fusion drive, the air turning amber about them in response and freezing them in position. The USER out there exploded, even as another surge passed through the ship, the one taking them into U-space.

An eye-blink later, they were in another part of the Feeding Frenzy, low over that sulphurous world. Here they spotted another of the King's Guard ships floating before them against the pastel canvas of the gas cloud. A further eye-blink, and the back end of that ship exploded, jerking it round and hurling out a cloud of burning debris. Gost, whose image had remained in its frame, staggered out of view for a moment, then cam-tracking pulled him back. It was obvious he was aboard the ship they had apparently just fired upon.

'I estimate that it will take at least two minutes for your King's Guard to arrive,' said Penny Royal. 'It is interesting to speculate how the line into the future would change should the Prador Kingdom lose its head.'

What? Blite thought.

Gost remained motionless for a moment, then said calmly, 'I should have known that you would detect my signal re-routing, and that I wasn't with my fleet.'

'I am no danger to you unless threatened,' said Penny Royal. 'The course I take is my own and the thread I sew here is to repair some things which are personal to me. Understand my capabilities, Gost, if I should still call you that. Do you think I would have come here leaving anything to chance? Do you think I am actually, completely, *here*?'

'I can do as you request,' said Gost, 'and pass Sverl that list of factory station refugees. But Sverl is by no means stupid and will know my intent concerning him. We can't allow him to survive, so if I appear to assist, he will wonder why I am doing so.'

'Be as convincing as you can,' said the black AI, 'but in the end it doesn't matter. When Sverl has that list he will react precisely as I want him to.'

'Very well, I will pass it on.'

'Good,' said Penny Royal, and a moment later the *Black Rose* submerged itself in U-space, taking it beyond reach.

Blite let out a tight breath.

'That Gost—' Greer began.

'—was the prador king,' Blite completed.

Trent

Trent's return to consciousness within the shell people's holding area was abrupt and painful. His body ached from head to foot. He clamped down on immediate nausea but failed to suppress it, turned his head to one side and vomited.

'Trent Sobel,' said a voice.

He was sitting in a chair but couldn't move his arms. Peering down with slowly clearing vision, he saw that his captors had secured them with straps. And, on trying to shift his legs, he felt them likewise bound. Ahead of him was a dais, with some shape upon it. He guessed this was Taiken, the shell people's apparent leader, and now checked his surroundings. He was in one of those structures he had seen earlier – a building erected out of sheets of plasmel taken from a roll, then hardened to the required shape. The room was circular and domed, with doorways all around built much wider than would be required for the human form. Standing in one of these doorways was a child, a boy of no more than ten solstan years. He wore only a pair of shorts and looked numb, pale and sickly. His right arm was an armoured limb terminating in a claw, while he had a prador manipulatory limb folded against his torso. Surgery must have been recent, as highlighted by the angry red blush around the limb attachment points, and by the white thread scars, of the kind usually left by an old military autodoc, all over his misshapen torso.

Children – really?

While Trent watched, a woman came up behind the child and took up his human hand. Trent went rigid.

Genève?

The woman appeared haunted, until she looked up and met

his gaze, then she seemed briefly puzzled. No, she wasn't Trent's dead sister. The only similarity was her cropped blonde hair, diminutive form and black eye-shadow and lipstick, if not cosmetically dyed skin. She began to lead the boy away, shooting Trent one last hopeless glance. Trying to ignore the unfamiliar feeling in his chest, Trent began working against the straps. They were a form of translucent plastic in which he could see embedded wires, so they were probably unbreakable, even with his heavy-worlder strength. But the chair, made of pressed fibre, didn't look so strong.

'That was my son,' said Taiken.

Was the woman Taiken's wife, and not worth a mention? Trent focused his attention on the dais, now able to see clearly the figure squatting there. Taiken was just about as far along in his transformation as Trent had ever seen in a shellman. He squatted on prador legs issuing from under a prador carapace. Beneath this, as the shellman rose a little to wave one claw towards the doorway, Trent glimpsed the vague shape of a human torso spread out like a specimen on a board. The greatly extended neck from this curved up through the carapace to the shell-enclosed head on the upper side. Mandibles grated before the remains of a human face – its lower jaw missing and just a wide gullet there below where the nose had been removed. Palp eyes issued from the top of the enclosing shell, but they looked prosthetic – false.

'With him the transformation will be complete and without error,' Taiken added.

Trent winced at the thought, then was baffled as to why.

The shellman stank. The smells of decaying human and piscine bodies, and shit and urine, permeated this chamber, which, Trent now realized, resembled a father-captain's sanctum, even down to the array of hexagonal screens behind Taiken. Trent glimpsed something scuttling across one side of the room and his flesh crawled. He really didn't need ship lice about when he couldn't move. Then he remembered how clean the other parts of Sverl's ship had been and how he had been surprised on seeing no lice there, only Polity cleanbots.

'It is time at last for *all* my children to achieve the perfection I am only days away from reaching,' said Taiken.

Trent flinched, thinking about the child he'd just seen, and the frightened human woman who caused a hitch in his chest. He remembered the shellwoman who had bagged him on the way into this place, how she had said, 'I am to take you to Father,' and realized he'd just landed up to his neck in it again. So this shellman, this amalgam of human and prador with his decaying grafts, the pus leaking out of his joints and the probability that he had two immune systems trying to attack each other, was only days away from achieving *perfection*? *Ah*, Trent now felt something cracking under his right forearm, and the chair leg they had bound his right thigh to felt looser, as it parted from some strut behind.

'You understand,' Taiken continued. 'You were with Isobel and you saw her achieve *her* form of perfection. You have the insight we need.'

Yeah, Trent was with Isobel as she changed into a hooder. And one thing he definitely knew was that sometimes the human mind couldn't adapt or keep up – it broke instead.

'And I would like you to join us, Trent Sobel.'

Not in your wildest, you fucking lunatic . . . But was that the right thing to say just now? No, best to play along at least until his arms and legs were free.

Trent nodded thoughtfully. 'This sounds interesting. Of course, I admire the prador and everything about them, and understand what you are trying to achieve. But I would need to know more. I also have to wonder why you found it necessary to bind me like this.'

'What more do you need to know?' Taiken asked. 'And you are bound because you are a dangerous man. You are about to take the first step along our road, whether willingly or not.'

Now the shellwoman stepped into view, pushing a pedestal-mounted autodoc up beside Trent's chair. While he watched, she detached something from just below the doc. Trent recognized two items: the specially sealed container for a nano-package, and the skin diffuser into which she plugged it.

'I did say that I need to know more,' said Trent reasonably.

'You will know more as you begin to grow your carapace,' said Taiken. 'In the act of becoming comes transcendence.'

The guy was out there with the fairies and it was time to act. Trent heaved against his bonds, hard, with all his limbs. The chair came apart underneath him and collapsed. He rolled, ripping himself away from its broken parts and, still tangled in the straps, dived for the autodoc. He grabbed the pedestal and managed to get partially to his feet, hauling the device up and slamming it straight into the chest of the woman. He heard her carapace crack and, issuing a phlegmy bubbling sound, she went down on her backside. He stared at her, feeling sick, because he hadn't meant to hit her so hard. Then other shell people, who he had known were standing behind, were on him.

He swung the autodoc into a human head sticking up ridiculously from a disc-shaped carapace, heard a neck break, the head now tilted to one side. Such a blow should have paralysed a human, but this creature just ran off to one side as if still under the control of his prador parts. Trent was suffused with horror at what he had just done. What the hell was the matter with him? This was a fight for survival and he couldn't keep reacting like this. Mainly to rid himself of the lethal weapon, Trent threw the doc at another of them who was raising a pepper-pot stun gun in its one human hand. The gun went skittering and the autodoc crashed to the floor. A claw closed on his left bicep. He grabbed it with his right hand and pulled, *hard*, tearing it from its socket, a foul yellow spray hitting his face.

Oh please no . . .

He stumbled away, cringing inside, then fell over fragments of chair still attached to his legs, and another claw crashed down on the back of his neck. The flash of a stunner prod numbed his right arm. He drove his left fist up and felt something break under it, retracted his fist as if he had hurt it and curled it against his chest. Then blow after blow rained down on him and a claw closed around his neck. He briefly lost consciousness, then came to, feeling the shellmen binding his arms behind his back and tying further straps around his legs.

'With the others,' said Taiken.

Next, they dragged him along the floor by his jacket collar, shell people all around him, the woman walking beside him holding an armoured hand against her chest. She was coughing, occasionally spitting out gobbets of black jelly. He was glad she was alive and hoped the damage wasn't permanent.

'He's . . . nuts,' Trent managed, not sure for a moment if he was referring to Taiken or himself.

'Father . . .' she replied.

'Why the fuck . . . you listen to him?'

'We must obey.'

At length they threw him into a cage, slamming a barred door closed behind him. There were other people here – normal Polity humans, if such a description could be apt. A man walked over, pulled out of his pocket a device Trent recognized as a micro-shear. The man stooped and worked on Trent's bonds, finally freeing him. Trent heaved himself over, spat out blood and a fragment of tooth and sat upright. He looked round at the people – four of them – then paused to focus on an object sitting just outside the cage. A huge spherical glass bottle sat in a metal framework. Perpetual slithering movement filled it.

'Spatterjay leeches,' he muttered, then turned to the man who had freed him. 'It makes no sense,' he continued, 'are they all crazy?'

'That's not a term I like,' said the man, wincing.

'Oh yeah?' said Trent, puzzled.

'I take it you received your offer from Taiken to join them.' The man squatted down beside him.

'Yeah, I did. The man's a loon. Why do they listen to him?' Trent knew he was ranting, but he just wanted to talk, just wanted to think about anything other than his own recent reactions to violence.

The man grimaced, probably as offended by 'loon' as he had been by 'crazy'. 'Because they have no choice,' said the man. 'They could not overcome their internal conflicts in time. Consider what they have been trying to achieve and what the end result should be.'

'All of them looking like crabs?'

'Yes, but more than that.' The man turned off his micro-shear and, as he pocketed it, Trent watched where it went and thought about what use he could make of it. Especially on the lock of that door behind. 'Taiken has always been their leader and has always, because of his mental aberrations, wanted to be a prador. But not just any prador. He didn't want to be a first- or second-child but a father-captain – with his children utterly loyal and obedient.'

'I saw one of his kids . . .' said Trent.

'The two children, are they okay? I worry about the damage . . .'

'Not really . . . But even others called him father.'

'All the adaptogenic drugs, the nano-packages, the surgical material and the tank-grown prador organic materials are sourced from the same prador genome and they all come through Taiken. The people who used them donned their own chains because Taiken retained certain items for himself only: he had father-captain pheromone organs surgically implanted inside him.'

'Pheromonal control,' said Trent, getting it at once.

'He didn't use this method of control on the Rock Pool, at least not much, because there were too many Polity watchers and too many normal humans about. He needed his people confined to one place, free of interference, in some enclave before he could assert full control. It's a scenario that has been played out throughout history, generally in religious cults.' The man paused to wave a hand at his surroundings. 'I don't know if this is finally the right place to achieve his dream or whether he has become more delusional.'

'I'd go for the latter,' said Trent. 'He's insane.'

'Insane or otherwise,' said the man, frowning, 'Taiken is now a father-captain and all the shell people here who used his products are now his children. They are enslaved to the pheromones he produces and are simply incapable of disobeying him.'

'Shit,' Trent muttered.

'And, as I understand it,' said the man, 'Taiken intends to go all the way. He deliberately left his wife unchanged. He intends to use material from a different prador genome to convert her into a prador female.'

Horror climbed up out of Trent's chest and closed his throat.

Redeem yourself, Penny Royal had said, and the first-child Bsorol had referred to that too. Trent remembered the words

with incredible clarity and considered how, until now, there had
been no opportunity. He also now realized that the black AI had
crippled his ability to act, by cursing him with empathy.

9

Blite

A tension permeated the air throughout the ship, a feeling that the very fabric of the universe had twisted and knotted up all around them. Perhaps this feeling was making him question his impulse to go after Penny Royal, or perhaps that was due to their brief and potentially lethal encounter with the king of the prador. However, most probably it was the knowledge that Penny Royal *had* taken them back in time – the kind of action that had always been equated with dangerous, universe-destroying lunacy in the fiction he grew up with.

He stood in their new cargo area, eyeing the copious space available. He was aware that being able to fill it with cargo and move it at the speed this ship could manage, he could make a fortune. But he already had one – he was already seriously wealthy from the sale of the memplants Penny Royal had provided. Money wasn't why he was here, not any more.

Blite turned from the cargo area, went through the bulkhead door leading into the crew quarters and entered the dropshaft around which the cabins had been positioned. He towed himself along this, then went through the next bulkhead door, grav returning and bringing his boots thumping down on the floor of the bridge. Greer was the only one in attendance here – Brond getting some sleep in the large well-appointed cabin he had taken.

'On the prowl again?' she enquired.

He grunted at her and moved on.

After the next bulkhead door was a short corridor terminating in a shimmershield airlock. The shuttle bay beyond was pressurized so Blite didn't need his helmet. He stretched out a hand to the first shimmershield and pushed it through – the sensation was much like pushing his hand into warm mud. He followed his hand through, the shield softening and yielding quickly, then abruptly blinking out of existence, as did the second shield. Sub-AI computing in the airlock had detected its irrelevance and shut it down.

Blite stepped into the shuttle bay and eyed the new shuttle clamped in place there. The thing was a slightly flattened sphere thirty feet across, with six acceleration chairs inside. Each was on its own revolving base so those inside could take in the view. And it would be a good one since the whole interior of that cabin in the upper hemisphere of the shuttle was lined with screen paint – out in vacuum it could appear to those inside that no ship surrounded them at all. No controls were visible the first time he had stepped inside. However, on asking Leven, he had learned that the shuttle would take a submind of the Golem ship mind and, if that ever failed or was destroyed, a manual control console would automatically rise from the floor. 'What if the damage that destroyed the submind also damaged the system for raising that console?' Blite had asked.

'You'd be dead anyway,' Leven had replied.

Blite moved on past the shuttle and into the corridor leading back into the prong of the horseshoe-shape of the ship on this side. He'd taken this route many times before, checked the maintenance hatches leading to the half of the U-space drive that was on this side, then checked through the hatches at the end leading to the fusion array. He liked to visit this place when he felt he had something to say to their resident black AI. Here

Penny Royal had made a particular alcove. He halted by this and eyed the antique space suit seated on a stool inside.

This time, unlike on other occasions, he sensed no presence here, just a prickling down his spine when he gazed into the black vacancy of the visor. Nevertheless, he spoke because, really, it didn't matter where on this ship he spoke. Penny Royal would always hear.

'There's something I've been avoiding asking,' he said. 'We went back in time two weeks so you could tell this Gost to pass Sverl the identification of those who escaped Factory Station Room 101, which still strikes me as a little odd – I don't quite believe that it was an emergency measure because one of the actors in your play went off-script. I reckon you did it because you could. I think you're exploring your abilities and enjoying your power to manipulate. Whatever . . .' Blite shrugged. 'What I want to ask is this: are we now travelling forward those two weeks?'

'No,' Penny Royal replied – voice issuing out of the air all around him.

'I see.' Blite felt relieved at the straight verbal response and wondered if what he was about to say would make him sound like an idiot. But surely everything humans said sounded idiotic to the AI? 'When I was a kid I used to play a VR game called Cowl. It was all about time travel and had much in it about infinite energy progressions and energy debts. I understand more now I'm older but by no means have a complete grasp on it all. Because you took us back in time and are not going forward again, aren't we carrying some portion of universal entropy with us?'

The air before the suit shimmered and a deeper black speck grew in the darkness of the suit, as if from infinite distance, finally halting to form a black diamond hanging just behind the visor. Blite had come to understand that when the AI manifested in this way it was engaging just a little bit more – had become more interested in what he was saying. This also increased the chances of it trying to load data straight to his mind.

'Correct,' said the AI.

'It's . . . like negative energy . . . part of the heat death of the universe?'

No words now, just a vision of the vastness of space uploaded straight into his head: galaxies and nebulae strewn before him, all their brightness fading into endless dark . . . As Blite returned to the here and now, finding himself down on his knees on the deck, he guessed that he'd been right.

Staying where he was, he hardened his resolve and continued: 'And we're going to be bringing that load back out into the real when we surface in four hours from now.'

'Yes.'

'And that's . . . dangerous?'

Now he was given a vision of a G-type sun, with peripheral images of the planetary surface of a living world included as a subtext. He watched a wave of something hit the sun and bruise it, watched that mottling spread, and the sun begin to collapse in on itself like the sped-up film of a rotting apple. In the subtext the sky darkened, clouds rolled across it and winter came. He saw jungles collapsing and decaying, then even decay ceasing as they froze. He saw oceans turning to ice, a blizzard covering animal corpses . . .

What the fuck?

Blite tried to shut out the images, and gradually they faded, but he continued his line of enquiry with stubborn persistence, 'But that didn't happen when we went to the Feeding Frenzy . . .'

'I kept the entropic effect balanced by maintaining U-space

drive Calabi-Yau frames in juxtaposition with U-space energy draw.'

Whatever. At least the black AI hadn't tried to load *that* across to his mind.

Penny Royal continued, and Blite felt the AI was enjoying this.

'Had the king not reacted as I had wished, it would have been necessary for me to take the Calabi-Yau frames out of juxtaposition. The result would have been thirty completely inert King's Guard ships in darkness – all the energy in the gas cloud snuffed out and the gases no longer radiating,' the AI explained. 'I would then have had to find another method of providing Sverl with the information I wanted him to have.'

Okay, I see, you didn't send the letter I wanted you to send, so here's a thermo nuke. Blite repressed the urge to giggle insanely. 'But still that negative energy needs to be offloaded.'

'Yes, it does, Captain Blite,' said Penny Royal.

A memory now, but one that wasn't his own: Blite found himself standing in some Polity science museum looking into a holographic star map. His hand operating a half-seen gesture control, he focused the display on a planetary system and a sun lying four light years away, which expanded and were labelled. The system was called Rebus and the sun was called Crispin Six. He then turned away from this, stepping into a childhood memory. He found himself walking towards the arch of a planetary data cache and glancing up at the sign 'Read and Learn'.

With the sound of glassy chimes, the diamond receded deep into the suit and winked out, and Blite knew that the audience was over. Penny Royal would talk, in its way, but it was never an extended conversation. Blite suspected that, like many AIs, it grew bored with mere human exchanges and tended to render up just a little less information than the human required, thereby forcing said human to go off to do some research and thinking. With his mouth dry and a feeling of dread clenching his guts, Blite turned and headed back to the bridge. Penny Royal, he decided, trying to think light thoughts, was a bit didactic, a bit of a pedant, and always annoying and frustrating. But he could not dispel the fear that the AI was about to annihilate a solar system.

Sverl

'I must unravel my past back to its beginning, and it's to the beginning I will go next,' the black AI replied cryptically. *'That is, when all is done here and events ordered and set on their course to conclusion.'*

Sverl kept replaying Penny Royal's words in his head – the words Sverl had found in Isobel Satomi's mind and were a message from the AI to him. Meanwhile, he checked and rechecked other data sources. Displayed on his screens was old recorded footage of a massive Polity construct under attack by the prador. The thing was described by humans as resembling a giant harmonica and it was one of the largest ever made, measuring eighty miles from end to end, thirty miles wide and fifteen deep. The square holes ran along either side, in pairs of lines, being the entrances to enormous final construction bays. This was one of their greatest factory stations; this was the infamous Factory Station Room 101. And it was, Sverl was sure, the beginning that Penny Royal had referred to, because here was where the AI had its genesis.

Checking the reference, Sverl felt wry amusement, for it might well have represented the prador's greatest fear – all the panoply of the Polity war effort. This war factory had manufactured its

211

weapons of death hourly, spewing them out into space: dread-noughts, destroyers, attack ships, drones and assassin drones. This station had delayed the prador advance by managing to keep up with the destruction rate of Polity ships, which was then of one medium-sized vessel every eight seconds. And the prador attempt to take out this factory station had been one of their most costly enterprises of the whole war.

Sverl watched the battle footage unfold. Room 101 was spewing out ships at an incredible rate to counter the attack from a prador fleet. The thing was glowing like hot iron as its temperature climbed beyond anything survivable by organic life forms. At first these ships had been meticulously designed for their task, but as the battle progressed they became little more than heavily armed missiles, sans U-space drives, their armour and the amount of materials otherwise used in their construction varying considerably, and utterly dependent on the rate at which materials were being transmitted into the station by cargo runci-ble. But these were thinking missiles, sacrificing their brief lives to protect the station. Sverl felt himself wincing as he saw prador dreadnoughts smashed utterly out of shape – their armour unpunctured while everything inside died. He watched so many particle beams playing through space that it seemed that wedges of star fire were flashing into being. Multiple detonations kept changing the shapes of formations while debris and molten-metal laced vacuum. Oxygen fires burned. Armoured prador fried in their suits. First-child kamikazes weaved about like hunting fish but detonated in the stabs of a red laser so intense it had to be fed by some runcible portal grazing off the fusion fire of a sun. Then one of those kamikazes got through the defensive net.

The detonation against the factory's side was immense, its blast wave frying nearby ships and hurling a whole quarter of the battle formations into disarray. Even so, the gigaton CTD had lost most of its energy against hardfield projectors that were routing the feedback energy from the blast out of the station by runcible. As a result, the explosion only excavated a large chunk out of the side of the structure. Meanwhile, the Polity ships that the thing was still producing took advantage of the disarray, pushing into the prador formations and wreaking havoc. They forced the prador to retreat. Sverl remembered the humiliation he had felt at the time, as he pulled out in his damaged destroyer – the ship he'd captained before this dreadnought. He also remembered his last sight of Room 101. Its giant engines flared into life, hauling it away and then, with a massive wrench felt for light years all around, it dropped into U-space.

Factory Station Room 101 survived that encounter – he saw it himself. So how did one square that with the Polity account, perfectly illustrated by a few lines from the human publication 'How It Is' by a character called Gordon. Sverl again viewed those lines:

ECS dreadnought Trafalgar *was built halfway through the prador/human war at Factory Station Room 101, before that station was destroyed by a prador first-child 'Baka' – basically a flying giga-ton CTD with a reluctant first-child at the controls, though slaved to its father's pheromones and unable to do anything but carry out this suicide mission. Records of the* Trafalgar *AI's inception were therefore lost . . .*

This was just one sample from the massive amounts of data about Room 101. The rest all said the same thing: a first-child kamikaze had destroyed Room 101. Yet no mention was made of that final U-space jump. AIs confirmed the station's destruction from debris, from numerous AI accounts of the battle and from the fact that it took no part in the war thereafter. Perhaps it had made a faulty U-jump and ended up trapped in that space continuum, or had been destroyed by the transition back into the real. Still, the excising of the fact that it *had* jumped, from so many accounts, stank. Sverl did not believe the kamikaze had destroyed the station because of that vital clue that Penny Royal had given him via Isobel. He replayed those words to himself again: '. . . *and it is to the beginning I will go next*'.

Penny Royal's beginning had been in the station that manufactured it – that was incontrovertible fact. Penny Royal, therefore, must be going back to Room 101. Sverl just had to find out where it was but – as Arrowsmith would say – it was like banging his head against a brick wall. Polity AIs had worked diligently to conceal that Room 101 still existed, so it was hardly likely he was going to just stumble across its location. Perhaps they didn't want to admit to the desertion of such a major AI factory station. Perhaps they didn't know what had happened?

I have to look elsewhere.

Gost was tardy in replying to Sverl's call, and when that King's Guard did appear the armoured dome of his suit was closing on something black, lethal-looking and definitely not the shape of a prador. Sverl was momentarily dumbfounded, but understood that Gost must have *allowed* him this glimpse of his true form.

'Have you come to a decision?' Gost asked.

Sverl hesitated for a moment, then mentally cancelled the image he generally used to front his communications and allowed his true image to be broadcast.

'I have,' he said.

'I see,' said Gost. 'We analysed some of your genome obtained from the ocean of the Rock Pool. However, we were baffled as to how it would be changing you physically.'

'Now you know,' said Sverl.

'You must not be seen by any other prador,' Gost stated.

Sverl felt a moment of chagrin. He really shouldn't have succumbed to the perfectly calculated lure. Seeing him as he really was had only confirmed Gost's earlier intent to hunt him down and be rid of him.

'I *will not* be seen by any other prador,' said Sverl, 'and with your help I can remove myself as a threat to the Kingdom.'

'And how can I help exactly?'

'I do not have the kind of access you do to prador databases,' Sverl explained. 'I need you to search out data on something for me.'

'Continue.'

'I need to find the location of Polity Factory Station Room 101.'

Gost turned an armoured palp eye to view something to one side – possibly another set of screens, or perhaps it was the output from the kind of AI computing generally frowned on by *normal* prador.

'The one the Polity claims we destroyed,' Gost stated. 'I am running searches now, so perhaps you can explain to me why you need this data.'

'It's complicated,' said Sverl.

'I am capable of dealing with complicated.'

'Very well. For my own purposes I need to find Penny Royal. I am sure that the black AI has gone or is going to Room 101. I am guessing that this station is a long way from the Graveyard, and in going there I will remove myself from play. I am sure that, as it has provided me with the data in its own unique way, my presence there is exactly what the AI intends, along with my extraction from the Graveyard. I believe this because I am certain I am a problem Penny Royal wishes to correct.'

'I note a great deal of supposition there,' said Gost.

'But I note a lack of disagreement in you, despite this,' Sverl countered.

'You'll get none. As long as you remove yourself from the Graveyard, I, and the king, will be happy.'

Happy? An amusing concept for a prador.

After a long pause Gost said, 'It appears that we do not know the location of Room 101.' Sverl felt a surge of disappointment at this news, but Gost continued, 'Doubtless there are high-up Polity AIs that are trusted with the knowledge, but I suspect you won't be talking to them. However, a small number of drones and AI ships escaped that station *after* its U-space jump. Higher AIs in the Polity must have instructed or compelled them to keep quiet about the manner of that station's disappearance and its subsequent location.'

'One has to wonder why,' said Sverl.

'After a war such as ours there are things that combatants, especially human and AI combatants, would rather not admit to – secrets that must be kept until softened by time.'

'With the prador too?'

'Certainly – you just glimpsed one of them.'

What had *really* happened to the King's Guard, and perhaps the king himself? Sverl shook himself and returned to his main interest. 'These drones and ships, where are they?'

'Their number was severely reduced during the remainder of the war, and since then many of them have disappeared. Those still extant are keeping quiet. I have a list of them I can transmit to you, but before I do so there is something more you need to know and something more you must do.'

Quid pro quo time.

'Go ahead.'

'It has recently come to our attention just how Cvorn intends to capture you,' said Gost. 'The five children of Vlern raided a

Kingdom world for females and then stole a ship as they departed. They did this in an area where none of my kind was in attendance and they functioned with cooperation and efficiency far beyond that expected of young adult prador. Imagery on file shows that they are augmented with biotech augs made for prador and purchased from a Polity corporation called Dracocorp.'

Gost paused to give Sverl time to gather data. He did so: soon he had a fair understanding of the enslaving nature of Dracocorp's products, and their similarity to prador thrall technology.

'Surprisingly,' said Gost, 'they returned to the Graveyard rather than fleeing beyond our grasp. Surprising, that is, until we understood the function of their augmentations. As you probably well know.'

'Cvorn is controlling them,' said Sverl. 'What sort of ship did they steal?'

'An ST dreadnought.'

'Shit,' said Sverl, which he suspected was an expletive he could find in the language of any sentient species.

'Indeed,' said Gost. 'And it is the kind of shit we would prefer to be removed from the Graveyard: a rogue dreadnought in such a politically unstable area . . . Therefore, should you obtain the location of Room 101, I want you to transmit that location to me. Then I want you to lure Cvorn out there. Wherever it is, it is certainly not in the Polity because it would be too difficult to conceal from the population there. Nor is it in the Kingdom. So it must be beyond the Graveyard.'

Sverl pondered that idea. Certainly Gost would like Cvorn at a location where he could be stamped on without infringing on Kingdom agreements with the Polity, but he also no doubt wanted Sverl himself at such a location too.

'I certainly need to get Cvorn off my back,' said Sverl, 'and a squadron of the King's Guard should achieve that aim. I will send you the coordinates, should I find them, but I need you to promise that you will not interfere in my dealings with both Room 101 and Penny Royal.'

'Of course,' said Gost, 'and here is the list you require. Interesting, the workings of serendipity, when you consider one of the drones on that list, and its location . . .'

Much to Sverl's surprise, a list of names and Polity drone designations did arrive as promised. Gost had to know that Sverl was lying about sending those coordinates, just as Sverl knew that Gost was lying about non-interference in Sverl's affairs – the intent of the King's Guard was almost certainly to annihilate both Cvorn and himself.

'Keep me informed,' said Gost, and closed the com channel.

Sverl stared at the screen for a long moment. That had been just too easy and the whole exchange stank of half-truths and manipulation. Gost had certainly been lying about something other than his intent concerning Sverl, but right then Sverl couldn't plumb it. After a moment, he decided to let it go and turned his full attention to the list, ripping through it at top AI speed. Next he saw the name and drone designation Gost had been referring to, experienced a moment of bafflement, then a growing awe.

Serendipity, I name you Penny Royal, Sverl thought.

That it was so predictable how he would react made Sverl feel very small and insignificant. He was just a game piece the black AI was shifting around a board. The sheer chutzpah and godlike manipulation of events was awesome. Or was it something more than that? Had Penny Royal managed to breach time itself? Was the black AI operating like one of those artificial intelligences said to have transcended the restrictions of real-space and embedded itself for eternity in U-space?

Sverl reached out mentally and seized control of his U-space engines, inputting coordinates and dropping his dreadnought into that continuum. It struck him as likely that Gost would get the coordinates he wanted anyway. If the coming encounter with Cvorn was as dangerous as Sverl supposed, his ship's systems would probably receive extensive damage. This would negate his ability to conceal his U-space jump coordinates. It also occurred to him that the black AI, whether breaching time or otherwise, possessed a grotesque sense of humour. It had to be *that* drone that knew the coordinates of Room 101; it had to be Riss.

Trent

There were five normal people in the shell people's cage, await-ing their fate (that is, if you counted the catadapt woman as normal), and they had now gathered round. Trent pondered on the meaning of normal. Was he normal, as a heavy-worlder of the Sobel line? His ancestors had chopped about their DNA in such a way that it was further from that of old Earth humans than theirs was from a chimpanzee. He decided that *normal* in this situation simply had to mean 'not one of the shell people'.

'So how do you know all this?' he asked the man, now iden-tified as Rider Cole, while he thought about what he had just been told. Taiken had turned himself into a father-captain and, with the pheromones he now produced, had enslaved all the rest of the shell people.

'I learned about the shell people while in pre-upload studies,' said Cole, who was black haired, sharp faced and fevered. 'I'm a doctor.'

'A doctor,' Trent repeated, studying the dubious frown on the face of one of the others listening in.

At one time the title was quite specific, but now it could mean a thousand things. Trent wished he still had his aug because he could have connected to the gold D-link behind this man's ear and got his full profile and list of qualifications – and whether he had earned them the hard way from studies in slow time or from instantaneous uploads.

'I came here to help them,' said Cole.

Someone snorted in the small gathering.

'To help them turn into prador without turning into stinking wrecks?' asked Trent.

'No, to dissuade them from their course,' said Cole. His expression then changed, looked hungry, and he added, 'And persuade them to give me the permission to treat them.'

'Our Rider here hasn't had much luck persuading them,' interjected the catadapt woman. 'Maybe they prefer their kind of madness.'

Trent absorbed that, then focused his attention on Cole again. 'What kind of doctor are you?'

Cole shrugged and spread his hands. 'A general title might be "mind-tech".'

Trent studied the D-link aug on the side of the man's head and now noticed the additions. The second port below the optic plug wasn't for data but probably for neuro-chemicals which he could feed into a mental network. A series of pinholes in a circle behind that was for plug-in upload and download chips.

'And not working in the Polity,' said Trent.

'There's little call there for what I do.'

In the Polity, nanoscopic surgical intervention and mental editing could deal with most psychological problems. If you had something organically wrong with your brain then a surgeon would correct that at birth. If it occurred later, a standard auto-doc could usually deal with it – an AI surgeon dealing with the more serious stuff. If you had *issues* you couldn't deal with, then you'd either edit them out of existence or delete their emotional content. And, of course, if you preferred to retain your malady as some sort of distinguishing feature, you could always do something weird, like try to turn yourself into a prador.

Rider Cole, Trent reckoned, was one of those mind-techs whose work bordered on obsession and illegality. However, he had retained some distorted morality. He was trying to persuade the shell people to accept his treatment, rather than forcing them to accept it. 'Well,' Trent said, a sour taste in his mouth at this reminder of mental editing, 'if you want to help them now then I suggest you hand over that neat little shear you cut my bonds with.'

When had Penny Royal edited him? In the falling wreck of the *Moray Firth*, or some time before? When had the AI given him a conscience and the utterly crippling ability to feel the pain of others? Or, and now a stray thought occurred, had it not been Penny Royal but that fucking forensic AI the Brockle? No, he didn't know why, but he felt sure the black AI had done this.

'I don't agree with violence,' said Cole, looking fevered again.

Trent nodded to himself. The additions to Cole's aug gave the game away. The man was obsessive about his work and had obviously been experimenting on himself. He probably wasn't rational.

'You don't?' Trent stared at him. The urge to lash out rose up inside him but, rather than feel joy at finding an excuse to thump someone, he felt sickened by the prospect. He realized that during the fight in Taiken's sanctum he had reacted from experience and training, but his emotional response was totally at odds with that impulse now.

'You've just told me what's happening here,' he said, trying to be reasonable. 'You've just told me how Taiken is taking the next logical steps to becoming more like the prador by phero-monally enslaving the other shell people. So what do you think is going to happen to those of us who refused his offer?'

Cole now looked slightly sick. He knew, all right.

Trent continued, 'Taiken could have forced the issue with all of us but he didn't. Now why do you think that is? What do prador do with human prisoners?'

'Uh,' said Cole.

'Believe me,' Trent continued relentlessly, 'those aren't just here for display purposes.' He pointed to the big glass bottle on its stand outside the cage. 'You are of course familiar with the process called "coring and thralling"?' Such harmless words until you knew that it was a human being who was cored – brain and part of the spinal column removed – and then thralled – enslaved – by the insertion of a prador thrall unit. But normal human beings could not survive this process, only those toughened from infection by the Spatterjay virus, which was transmitted by the leeches of that world . . .

'So in the bottle, those are Spatterjay leeches . . .' said the catadapt, and now the others turned to gaze fearfully at the glass container.

'On the button,' said Trent. Then, to Cole: 'Now hand it over.'

'You have to understand that the shell people are sick,' said Cole. 'What is happening to them is a mass psychosis similar to—'

'Yeah, you've already told me that.' Trent gazed at the others here, hoping one of them would do something, but already some were moving away to plonk themselves down on the other side of the cage. Didn't they understand the need to act now?

He gazed down at his hands. They were suddenly sweaty and he felt sick again, knowing, despite his abhorrence of violence, that he *had* to act.

'This is going to hurt me more than it will hurt you,' he said, looking at Cole.

'Yes, violence is always the answer from your type of—'

Trent lashed out and watched the man keel over as he rubbed his knuckles. He was sure he had judged it right – the rap on Cole's temple just enough to knock him out – but that didn't make him feel any better. If he'd judged it wrong, he could have caused a haematoma; he could have killed the man. Tasting bile, he leaned forwards and reached into Cole's pocket to take out the shear. One of those still standing nearby clapped and Trent glanced up.

'Nice one,' said the catadapt woman. 'We've been listening to his insanity ever since he got put in here with us. I was going to have to strangle him the next time he suggested a little mental tweak for us all so we could more readily accept our situation.'

Trent shrugged. He'd knocked Cole out because the man seemed unstable enough to be the type to shout for help as Trent made his escape. But what next? Taiken controlled all the shell people, so the next logical act should be to move in on him fast and kill him. Trent would have relished such a prospect in a previous time, but now didn't even know if he was capable of the act. Perhaps that was one element of redemption – that it shouldn't be easy. Here he faced a situation in which he could help a great many people by doing what he had been doing all his life – using physical force to get what he wanted. Yet, now, it was the most difficult task he had ever faced.

'Are we getting out of there, then?' asked the catadapt woman. She waved a hand at those who had sat down again. 'These don't have the balls.'

Trent gazed at her, himself really wanting to go and sit down with the rest. After a further moment, he *looked* properly at her. She was magnificent: yellow cat's eyes and elfin ears, a face that was beautiful in a way that somehow seemed beyond standard cosmetic alteration, long gold-blonde hair and a body that was both athletic and lush, clad in a tightly clinging enviro-suit. She was just Trent's type. In reality she was the type for any hetero-sexual man. Yet he gazed at her almost with detachment, recognizing that he should be attracted, but seeing in his mind only Taiken's wife as she cast him that last hopeless glance.

'Yes, we're going,' he said.

Spear

So this is how it ends, I thought.

Reviewing Flute's assessment of our status and Riss's prediction of our brief future, I couldn't see any elbowroom. Our four hardfield projectors were scrap, Flute had fired off all the railgun missiles he had manufactured, the reactor was going into safe shutdown and we were now on stored power – only enough to maintain the ship, control the fires and for the robots to make critical repairs. If we used that power for particle-beam shots or manoeuvring there would be nothing left. I considered these minimal options: by moving the ship we might delay our final destruction by a few minutes, and by firing the particle beam we might be able to intercept and destroy a few incoming project-iles, but we certainly wouldn't damage that thing in the moon. And it was readying itself to annihilate us.

'We have to get out of here,' said Riss.

I turned to look at the drone.

'That is an option too,' I said.

Riss could eject herself and survive in vacuum for an unlimited period, while Flute could also use the mind ejection system to get out. I could suit up and eject myself from the ship too, but what then? If I survived whatever that ST dreadnought threw at the ship and the consequent blast debris, Cvorn could easily use his weapons to pick us off. And he would almost certainly see us ejecting from the ship. Even worse than that, he might send something out to collect us, whereupon I would become prador entertainment, and probably lunch too. Even if I managed to avoid all that, I would only last as long as my suit air supply, which I doubted would extend enough to keep me alive until some rescuer, summoned by Riss, arrived.

'You go,' I said. 'I'm staying.'

So what of all your plans now, Penny Royal? I thought.

'Flute,' said Riss, 'I need control of MR12.'

'Why do you need a maintenance robot?' Flute asked leadenly.

'I cannot get him into a space suit alone.'

'Now hold on a minute—'

Riss's flat head slapped down on the console beside me. Her snakelike body flicked up and looped over to drive her ovipositor into my torso. The thing hurt quite badly, and I wondered if prador felt such pain when the drone injected its parasite eggs into them. Next, numbness spread from deep inside my chest. I reached over and managed to undo my safety strap, tried to speak with a mouth that felt full of novocaine, stood up and took one step, then slowly toppled. Riss had long ago ejected the last of her parasite eggs, but that ovipositor still worked and the drone had obviously acquired other things to inject. I hit the floor on my side and just lay there.

'You have control of the robot,' said Flute.

'Good,' said Riss, peering down at me. 'You can, of course,

225

eject yourself from this ship too, second-child mind, but be assured that I will find you out there.'

'I will not be ejecting myself from this ship,' said Flute. 'My father forced me to spring Cvorn's trap, taking us within range of his hideout on that moon, and I cannot process the conflicted loyalties.'

That will not alleviate the guilt you feel, Flute, I thought.

'I will die with this ship,' Flute added.

The door into the bridge abruptly thumped off its seals, its locking mechanism whining and grating, doubtless due to the damage Riss had caused. It swung open and thick smoke gusted in, shot through with a spindrift of fire-retardant foam. A second later, I saw a maintenance robot enter – a thing like a yard-long water scorpion fashioned of blue metal, with additional limbs sprouting from its head. I saw it was carrying a space suit, just as it moved out of my line of sight. I felt the heat then, and immediately had difficulty breathing.

'The paralytic will wear off in ten minutes,' said Riss, 'which should be time enough to get you out into vacuum. I will attempt to keep us both concealed with my chameleonware and I have informed the nearest Polity assets of our situation. One of the rescue ships in transit from the Rock Pool can get here in a month. During that time your suit will put you into low-air hibernation.'

Right, great.

Riss might well be able to conceal us both, but I could already see the big gaping holes in the rest of her reasoning. Cvorn no doubt had some first-child or computerized system watching this ship very closely and would spot any use of an airlock. Perhaps, if I survived the coming attack on the *Lance*, and subsequent attempts to nail or capture us in vacuum, hibernation might enable me to last a month, but then, no rescue ship would come for us while that dreadnought sat in its moon.

Grav went off, which made it easier for the robot to hoist me up and begin, like a spider cocooning its prey, to feed me into the suit. In just a few minutes, it had suitably wrapped me. Meanwhile I had glimpsed the heavily armed moon in the screen fabric, the ST dreadnought's weapons coming into view. When the helmet went on and the suit's air supply kicked in, I started breathing more easily. The suit also protected me from the growing heat, flames now flickering through the smoke. Next I was being propelled to the door, and down along a wrecked and soot-blackened corridor.

'Cvorn is doubtless watching,' said Riss over my suit radio.

No shit, Sherlock.

'We must therefore offer a distraction,' Riss added.

I lost track of where we were in the ship because all I could see was scorched floor and the front end of the robot dragging me along.

'Emergency eject,' said Riss. 'You have control of it?'

'I have control,' Flute replied. 'Disengaging docking clamps.'

I only realized where we were when the robot pushed me upright and Riss wrapped herself around me. I was facing the space doors to our shuttle bay. I had time only to comprehend this before the release charges detonated all around the doors and they tumbled out into vacuum on the hurricane of escaping air, with Riss, me and the robot thrown out just after them. Riss and I parted company with the robot and tumbled on, then began to stabilize relative to the *Lance* as Riss applied the internal grav effect that was her main means of locomotion. I was frozen. It felt as if my heart had stopped, though whether from terror or Riss's injection I couldn't say. The drone kindly positioned me so I got a good view back towards my ship and now I saw the shuttle launching.

The distraction . . .

It suddenly seemed that we could have a chance of surviving this. Cvorn might just assume that our only means of escape was via that shuttle and look no further. On top of the impetus provided by the escaping air, Riss's internal drive kept drawing us further away. I watched the shuttle ignite its fusion engine just beyond the ship, but it hardly had time to build up any acceleration, because the moon had now turned fully.

A particle beam, deep blue in vacuum and perhaps a yard in width, struck the shuttle dead centre, bored straight through it and blew molten debris out the other side. Two further detonations ensued, which were probably the chemical propellant tanks for the steering thrusters or the energy-dense power supplies. The shuttle bucked twice, coming apart as it did so, and fell on away from the ship in three pieces. The particle beam fired again and again, nailing those pieces, slagging and tearing them apart. Within a minute there was nothing left larger than a human head.

'Goodbye,' said Flute over my suit radio.

'Bye,' I managed in return, now the paralysis was starting to wear off.

The beam then stabbed out again, hitting the *Lance* this time, over that section of the ship where the bridge was located. Armour plating ablated, dissipating like the dust from a grinding wheel, then the beam punched inside. It seemed to pause there for a moment, the *Lance* caught on it like a bug on a needle, then fire and debris exploded from the shuttle bay. Shortly after that two airlock doors exploded away, the airlocks spewing fire behind them. Much inside that ship had to be fried, including Flute, but Cvorn wasn't finished yet. A railgun missile hit near

the engines, carving a chunk out of the rear of the ship and hurling out a cloud of debris. I watched a lump of glowing jagged
armour the size and shape of a speedboat hurtle past us just
twenty feet away. A second missile hit near the nose, but the
angle of impact was such that it glanced off the armour, exploding into a spray of plasma, and didn't penetrate. Meanwhile the
particle beam began to traverse towards the nose.

But then it all stopped. The beam abruptly winked out and
no further missiles arrived.

'What the hell?' said Riss.

The drone turned me in vacuum.

'Stop that,' I said, reaching across to use my wrist impeller.
'I at least want to witness this.'

'No, look,' said Riss.

I allowed her to turn me, and now saw the bloom of numerous explosions, and a blue glare shifting from side to side, like
the aurora borealis, but in space. I didn't understand for a
moment, then I got it. I was seeing all the stuff Cvorn had just
fired at the *Lance* hitting a wall of shielding hardfields. Next, on
the moon, which was barely a dot to normal vision, I saw
another, far more massive, explosion. I ramped up magnification
through my visor, bringing the moon as close to me as possible,
the image breaking into pixels, and saw a great chunk of its crust
rising up on a cushion of fire. Further impacts followed while,
closer to us, particle beams played over that scaling of protective
hardfields.

'Someone's talking,' said Riss.

'Let me hear it.'

'I cannot locate you,' said a voice. 'Flute informs me that
you are out in vacuum.'

The Polity rescuer? It seemed very unlikely.

Something shimmered over to one side of us and I saw a

black line whip out. A giant grapple slammed into the *Lance* and closed, tearing up the hull as it did so, and began to draw the ship in. I tracked back along that line to its source as the shimmering dissipated to reveal a massive old-style prador dreadnought, from which I could see armoured prador hurtling out into space.

'Fucking prador,' Riss hissed. 'Sverl's here.'

'Drop your chameleonware,' I instructed. 'We're out of choices.'

Riss emitted a hissing growl, but must have obeyed me because the nearest of those armoured shapes swerved abruptly on a powerful chemical rocket and hurtled towards us. It decelerated on that same rocket as it drew close, abruptly silhouetted by a distant explosion. As the creature closed a claw about the both of us, I realized that Sverl's defences were now failing, for something had got through to detonate against the hull of his dreadnought. Even as our rescuer, or captor, opened up its rocket again and sent us speeding towards a cavernous hold, I saw the emissions of internal explosions. From wartime experience, I knew that these were from hardfield projectors overloading as the shielding took a battering.

We entered that hold, crashing down on a grated floor just as a particle beam got through. Other prador landed as heavily around us, while out in the glare of that beam I saw still others blacken and just evaporate. The beam played into the hold just for a moment, carving a molten trench through the grating, then punching in a plasma explosion through the back wall. But then massive armoured doors slammed shut with a crash that bounced us all from the floor, and cut it off. I watched those doors begin to glow cherry red, as the beam did some damage, then U-space took us.

Cvorn

As anchors detached from the surrounding rock and the fusion drive ignited inside the moon, turning rock molten behind and punching out through the crust there, Cvorn champed his mandibles and danced around in irritation on his new legs. The trap had been a complete failure. The plan had been for Cvorn's old destroyer to lure Sverl to the planet. He was supposed to have dived down into its atmosphere and then the ocean in an effort to destroy it. At this point, Cvorn, in his ST dreadnought, could have easily disabled him. Next, after he had steadily and meticulously annihilated all Sverl's defences, Cvorn had initially considered either a ground or undersea assault. That would have depended on where Sverl went down.

But, after fully investigating the weapons available to him, he had changed his plan. All he would have had to do was move in close and, using lasers, explosives and particle beams, peel that ship down to the core, revealing Sverl's sanctum. He could have hauled that in, just like Sverl had hauled in that wrecked Polity destroyer out there.

Damn those humans and their ship, Cvorn thought. But he knew that the failure of the trap had been down to his own eagerness to attack the Polity vessel. He should have simply ignored it and continued waiting for Sverl.

However, Sverl had rescued Cvorn from complete failure simply by not behaving like a prador. And now, as various programs confirmed the data he was seeing, growing excitement supplanted Cvorn's irritation.

Sverl hadn't gone to the planet. Probably because of what he was turning into, he had taken the time to attempt to rescue the passengers on that Polity destroyer. Not only that, he'd spent time harpooning the ship and drawing it into his own. Perhaps there had been some survivors aboard who Sverl felt were worth saving. Cvorn had no idea – he didn't think like a human.

Whatever. Cvorn had directed the firepower of his ST dreadnought against Sverl's main hardfields and left the partially wrecked destroyer alone. He'd quickly realized he could keep Sverl here longer by not completely destroying that other vessel, and it had worked. He'd had time to burn out enough of Sverl's hardfield projectors to leave gaps in his defences. Through those gaps he'd then set about destroying anything on Sverl's ship that looked as if it might scramble or shield U-jump signatures. And that had worked too, for Cvorn now knew Sverl's next destination.

'Bring my destroyer up,' Cvorn instructed the second-child now appearing on one of his screens. Though the trap had failed, one benefit was that the old destroyer he had left down on the planet as bait had been left unscathed. He had fully expected Sverl to gut it before the trap could be sprung. 'When you are clear of the world, bring it to these coordinates.'

No time to lose. If Sverl jumped again shortly after arriving at his next destination, Cvorn wanted to be there soon after, since a U-signature tended to dissipate and the rate at which it did so depended on eddies and tides in that continuum – occurrences that could only be described with exotic mathematics. Admittedly, this ST dreadnought had more power to punch through U-space than Sverl's craft, although in essence it was contracting time to do so rather than going speedily across a distance, as distances didn't exist as such in U-space. However, Sverl's child mind, if that's what he used, seemed able to calculate and make jumps rather more quickly than normal.

The ST dreadnought was now clear, so Cvorn sent instructions using his aug. The same coordinates went to the first-child mind controlling the twinned U-engines. Smooth as a blood slick, the ship dropped into U-space and was on its way. Cvorn settled down. He could do little more now. The ship was already prepared to chew up Sverl's when it got into range, and most of Cvorn's children were ready on the spot to take control of any essential systems from which battle damage might cut him off. But first, many days of travel lay ahead.

Cvorn stared at his screens for a while, took a wander round his sanctum, restless and angry, not knowing what to do with himself now. He was on his second circuit of the sanctum when he abruptly halted. Perhaps now was the time to try something he had been considering ever since boarding this new ship . . .

Cvorn rushed back to his screens and brought up views of the five young adults squatting in the small first-child sanctums to which he had confined them. After a moment, making sure he had identified him correctly, he turned off the feed showing Sfolk and studied the four remaining screens. Though he knew the names of these four, and could identify them via Dracocorp aug connection, he still could not distinguish between them visually. Their markings were quite similar, but it wasn't just that. Perhaps the lack of visual input from his missing palp eyes was the problem. He selected one screen at random and turned off the rest, establishing aug ident just from the location of this young adult in the ship.

'You,' he said to it, 'come at once to my sanctum.' He was met with a hint of rebellion because no adult prador went willingly to the sanctum of another adult, at least, not without a great deal of firepower. Cvorn *pushed* in the small Dracocorp network he had established and felt the creature succumbing to his will. With leaden steps, the young male headed to the door from its sanctum.

Continuing to track the male via aug, Cvorn turned away

from the screens and headed over to the body of the dead father-captain still occupying this sanctum. The control units had now been removed and attached to Cvorn, and he'd found it quite simple to link all his units into an array thence controlled via his aug. It meant he no longer needed to access a particular unit to control a particular blank, war drone or piece of robotic equipment.

Under his instruction, his blanks had split the body of the father-captain around its circumference and hinged over the upper carapace. Cvorn brushed aside a couple of ship lice and then tore out a chunk of the musculature around one old leg socket and fed it into his mandibles. As he munched this he sent his instructions and watched his blanks detaching various items, including a carapace saw, from the surgical telefactor hemisphere. He knew that what he intended had been done before, but still found himself wincing at the prospect. He also knew that it had not been done very often, because, having lost certain urges, old adult prador generally didn't feel inclined to reclaim them. He swallowed, then peered more closely at the interior of the old father-captain. The meat was tasteless, aseptic. Sure, decay had set in a little, but that usually added to the flavour.

There . . .

Cvorn soon ascertained that much of the flesh he had been chewing down was artificial carbon lattice, electro-muscle and collagen foam. This father-captain had been badly injured in the past and had lost a large amount of his interior body mass. This was puzzling because Cvorn did not recollect the exterior carapace being heavily scarred. Suddenly he realized what this might indicate and switched his gaze to the interior of the upper shell. There he saw the tracery of worm burrows – a neat pattern like a picture of a tree etched into that inner shell. Cvorn staggered back, immediately regurgitating the chunk of flesh he had just eaten and wishing he could bring up the father-captain's major ganglion, which he had dined on some hours ago.

'Vrom, get in here!' he yelled.

The first-child, who waited in the annex to the captain's sanctum, always ready to respond to Cvorn's command, came quickly through a fast-opening side door, a Gatling cannon clutched in one claw already whirling up to speed.

'Father?' Vrom enquired, now lowering his weapon as he saw no immediate danger.

'Get this out of here,' said Cvorn. 'Drag it into your annex right now!'

'Yes, Father,' said Vrom, never inclined to question an order.

As the first-child began laboriously heaving the huge corpse to the annex door, Cvorn wondered if he should move out of here for a while and have the place completely sterilized. No, he was being foolish. The parasite infection this father-captain had suffered and survived probably happened during the war. In fact, knowing just how paranoid those who had been infected tended to be – he had after all known Sverl *before* he paid his visit to Penny Royal and began to change – the chances of there being parasite eggs or nymphs here were lower than for just about any-where else.

'And when you're done,' Cvorn added, 'I want you back in here when I let our friend in. I'm not sure if my control of him via his aug will be enough. You know what to do.'

Cvorn now turned to the two blanks who were waiting for his orders. He had a program lined up for them to follow. He wondered for a moment whether he was being foolish in what he was about to do. He already knew he was as susceptible to prador pheromones as any child, but in this case he had been enjoying their effect. Perhaps he was behaving irrationally and

235

should have them filtered from the ship's air supply? No, he would keep them. And he would go through with this.

Setting the blanks' program running, he turned his back on them, settled down and raised his rear end. They closed in, carapace saw and drill injectors whirring. As one of the injectors went in, what had used to be one of his most sensitive areas went numb. He tried not to think about what the blanks were doing, even though he had reviewed every detail of the procedure. Tapping a little tune with his mandibles, he eyed Vrom as the first-child finally got the corpse into the annex.

'Close the door and be ready,' he instructed, not sure why he didn't want Vrom here for at least this part of the operation.

A saw went in – the smell of powdered carapace filling the air. He felt various tugs and wished he could close out the squelching sounds that followed. Something thudded to the floor and one of the blanks picked this up and carried it away while the other continued to prepare the socket. Unable to resist, Cvorn now did a status check. He saw through the eyes of the blank behind as it installed nano-nerve interfaces in the large dripping hole in his back end. He saw through the eyes of the other blank as it carried away a chunk of shell with a fleshy mass behind, trailing veins and thread nerves. The face of this shell had indentations where the two injector prongs and coitus clamp had once resided. Cvorn's worn-out and useless sexual organs were destined for disposal.

The work continued for some while, the second blank returning with cold preserved cartridges of Cvorn's seed. These it emptied into an artificial testicle and it installed this where his old shrivelled item had been. Meanwhile the young male he'd summoned arrived outside the sanctum door and just settled there – terrified to be at such a location but unable to flee.

'Vrom, come in now,' Cvorn instructed.

The socket was ready and the blanks moving back to stand against the wall. Vrom entered, atomic shear generators fitted to the bases of his claws, the glimmer of their output visible along the internal edges of those claws. Cvorn knew that with these devices Vrom could remove the limbs from any prador in just a few minutes. When the young adult was in here, and thus immobilized, the procedure could continue. Of course, Vrom would have to use the surgical telefactor for the more meticulous work involved, as he removed the young male's fresh and vigorous sexual organs.

Spear

I'd watched the *Lance* take heavy damage while we were floating in vacuum, and wondered if Flute might have survived. Before he rescued us, Sverl had told us that Flute had informed him we were out in vacuum. Had Sverl received that information before that particle-beam strike, or after?

As Sverl's armoured prador surrounded us, Riss unwound herself from me.

'I have to go covert,' she said, her snakelike form shimmering.

'Is there any need?' I enquired as Riss's chameleonware engaged and she disappeared completely. 'Though I don't like how it happened, we're where we need to be.'

'You are not going covert aboard my ship, parasite,' said another voice over my suit radio. I was surprised – Sverl had penetrated our com very quickly.

Six hardfields flickered into existence to form a rough cube a couple of yards across. Where they intersected along the edges and at the corners they glowed and emitted sparks. I'd seen similar capture boxes used, but only to confine large prey like prador. They couldn't escape between the inevitable gaps between the hardfield discs. I'd never seen hardfields actually intersecting and touching like this, because such proximity tended to create feedback loops that blew out their projectors. During the war, curving hardfields had been considered impossible. But I had learned of the spherical hardfield Penny Royal used to protect Carapace City. So the technology had unlocked potential yet.

Riss reappeared, hovering and writhing inside the translucent box. Ignoring me, the armoured prador in the hold gathered around her for a moment before abruptly scuttling off to one side. They returned, dragging something they'd retrieved from a floor-to-ceiling rack. It was a box big enough to contain a prador: its sides were sheets of chain-glass and its edges made of heavy ceramal. Once out of the rack, it rose up on either a grav-motor or some form of maglev. They pushed it out over beside the hardfield trap, then opened one side of the thing. Now, hissing and throwing out sparks – noticing which, I checked my visor display and realized the hold was filling rapidly with air – the trap collapsed until just a yard across, with Riss coiled tightly inside. It then shifted over and in through the open side of the glassy box. One of the prador closed up the side, and the hardfield trap flickered, then shattered. Chunks hurtled out in every direction, evaporating harmlessly into nothingness as they went.

'Bring them both to me,' Sverl instructed over ship comms.

The cube rose up and began heading for the rear of the hold where a large door was rattling open – making such a racket probably because the section of wall it revolved up into was near where the particle beam had punched through, buckling it. It jammed for a second but the armoured prador leading the way gave it a solid whack with one claw to set it in motion again. I felt oddly reassured by the sight of a prador treating temperamental technology in so familiar a manner.

'*I guess it's payback time,*' said Riss via my aug.

'*Payback?*'

'*Sverl was one of my early victims, but managed to survive the experience.*'

A prador behind gave me a violent shove that sent me sprawling. I stood up and looked back at what, by its size, might have been a second-child – hard to tell with that armour. What was definitely a first-child, just behind it, brought an armoured claw down hard on the first creature's back, the clang so loud I was sure something must have broken. The second-child merely went down on its belly, then scrambled up and out of range. The first-child clattered something at it, then turned to me and waved a claw towards the door.

'Keep moving, human,' it said.

I was sure I had just seen a second-child berated for its treatment of me, which struck me as decidedly odd for prador. But this was Sverl's ship and I knew that the father-captain had changed in strange ways. Had I just seen an example of his altered morality passed on down through his children? I followed Riss's prison out of the hold.

'*Yes, you mentioned that before,*' I said to Riss.

'*Oh, yeah.*'

'*Will he recognize you?*'

'*He recognizes what I am, which is probably more than enough.*'

I was about to say something about prador morality and the changes this Sverl was supposed to be undergoing, but found I didn't have the energy to pursue it. Prador were vicious bastards but, as I had noted before, that description could fit plenty of humans and AIs too. And any of the three could be justified in being a bit miffed after having had done to them what Riss had done to Sverl.

Now I surveyed the distinctly aseptic corridor, the Polity cleanbots scuttling here and there and all this in an illumination unexpectedly lacking in the sepulchral quality I knew, from memories not my own, usually to be found inside such ships. Memory surged for a moment, but I ignored it and it waned.

'*Flute, did you survive?*' I asked via my aug, but the response was only a fizzing.

Finally, we were led into a sanctum that bore a closer resemblance to a botanist's laboratory than the control centre of a murderous father-captain. Riss's box settled in a clear space at the centre, while the two first-children entered and stood guard inside the door, which closed behind them. Sverl rose up on prosthetic limbs from the usual array of screens. I noted the tail, which looked like an amphibian attached to his rear, then gazed upon the massive skull his body had become.

'Two human visitors in such a short time,' he said mildly. 'Gost must never know of this – it would definitely rouse suspicion even in him.' He moved over to Riss's box and peered inside with large, human-looking eyes. 'And you.'

'Hello Sverl,' said Riss, now scraping her ovipositor down the glass separating them, her voice issuing from some speaker set in the ceramal frame holding that sheet. 'My, didn't Penny Royal fuck you up?'

'That is debatable,' Sverl replied. 'And by now you must be aware that the chain-glass between us is not responding to the usual decoding molecule and EM frequency you'll be deploying. It is a laminate of chain-glass and transparent sapphire so you would first need to cut through the inner layer of sapphire to get to the first sheet, disintegrate that, then cut through the next layer of sapphire. You would have to do this twenty-four times. Now look up.'

The drone lowered her ovipositor to rest it tip-down on the floor of the box so she appeared balanced on it, then did so. I looked up as well and amidst all the equipment, all the folded-away robots, power cables and optics, I saw a large cone sitting directly over Riss, base down, with mesh across the base.

'What you are seeing,' said Sverl, 'is an EM pulse cannon of my own design. It has enough power to fry every circuit inside you, though I am currently setting it merely to take out every-thing but your crystal. So, no more attempts to get through that glass, and would you kindly desist in trying to penetrate my computer systems? I very much doubt you have the mental watts for that, but if you *do* make the slightest inroad, you're toast.'

I thought this particular father-captain had a very odd turn of phrase. He sounded like a war drone laying out the situation. Perhaps this was the result when you combined something as martial as a prador with AI crystal and human DNA. Sverl now turned towards me and walked over. I really wanted to run away, but had nowhere to go.

'So you are Thorvald Spear,' he said.

'I certainly am,' I replied. 'Pleased to meet you, Father-Captain Sverl. Tell me, who was this other human you had here? Is he still around?' I had been searching the vicinity for the odd discarded bone but it was as clean in here as the corridors out-side, if a little more cluttered. 'I would like to meet this person if he or she is still around. I'm sure we've got—'

'Understandably you are nervous,' Sverl interrupted, 'which is why you are babbling. I am not going to kill you and I am not going to eat you. In fact, right now my robots and some of my children are repairing your ship for your eventual departure. Meanwhile we have a shared interest, which is Penny Royal. We both want *something* from that AI and you may, if you wish, accompany me in my pursuit of it.'

'You know where Penny Royal is?' I asked.

'I do not,' said Sverl, turning now and pointing a claw at Riss, 'but that horrible worm in there does.'

'I do fucking not!' Riss exclaimed hotly.

'You do,' said Sverl. 'I have learned from Isobel Satomi that Penny Royal is returning to its beginning.'

Riss froze. She had no reply to that. Into the ensuing silence, and feeling as if I'd just been gut-punched, I interjected: 'Isobel Satomi?'

Sverl waved a dismissive claw. 'The visitor I had was Trent Sobel, who is now with the shell people. He carries the mind of Isobel Satomi in a jewellery item. I accessed her mind and learned that Penny Royal had left a clue there as to its next destination.'

'Shell people?' I asked, still distrusting Sverl and wondering if they were in some onboard larder.

With a clattering of metal limbs against the deck, Sverl turned towards me once more. 'They are aboard in their own section of the ship, currently extending their doomed experiment in becoming prador, by now trying to form themselves into a family unit. Now, as Penny Royal instructed, Trent Sobel has his chance to redeem himself.'

I felt a little bit better about that, but not much. 'In their own section' did not sound like larder, but the fact that Trent was here meant there was one human aboard who might have a reason to try to kill me. It was almost too much to incorporate and I just stood there with my mouth open as I tried to put it all together.

Sverl turned back to Riss and stepped closer so he was almost touching the glass.

'I know the last known location of Factory Station Room 101,' said Riss, subdued, 'but I cannot pass on that information. It is under AI lock.'

Room 101?

Just then, the door grumbled open and I turned to see the two first-children parting to allow in a second-child sans armour. It looked distorted, this creature, its carapace sagged as if it had been partially melted, and its legs bowed under its weight. Did it look nervous? How could I possibly read its expression? Nevertheless, there was something about it of someone carrying an unexploded bomb as it entered the sanctum, bearing the spine of Penny Royal from my ship.

'Of course it is under AI lock,' said Sverl. 'How else was the secret kept? Isn't it fortunate therefore that the means of unlocking that information has been provided? Or, perhaps, aren't we seeing all the pieces of an ever-developing puzzle, created by a black AI, slotting inevitably into place?'

'You keep that fucking thing away from me,' said Riss, who until this moment had shown no particular fear of the spine.

Suddenly her ovipositor was screeing at the glass, fragments falling inside. Next, her assault on the chain-glass turned an inner layer opaque, before it peeled away, falling to dust. I felt a thump of an EM wave passing through my body. It sent me staggering and my aug went offline. When I had recovered my balance and looked at Riss, she had dropped to the bottom of her prison and now lay still.

'I did warn you,' said Sverl.

10

Blite

The coordinates of their destination lay forty light years out from the Rebus system, and even further from Crispin Six, so Blite could not see why Penny Royal had directed his attention towards these places, unless it was to find a safe distance from which to watch their destruction. Nevertheless, he decided to search their data, starting with the first of them. The Rebus system lay just ten light years beyond the Polity border. The sun was a blue giant orbited by two gas giants, with a scattering of other smaller worlds closer in. One large moon orbited the closer gas giant and had been listed by Polity surveyors as occupied by an interesting and thoroughly alien silicon-based ecology. Closer still to the sun was a green-belt world where conditions were Earth-like. The surveyors had listed this as possessing a carbon and silicon-based ecology. Blite was still at a loss as to why Penny Royal had sent him here. Then he noted the link to a historical file attached to the initial survey, and opened it.

'One hour until we're there,' said Brond, now back on the bridge.

'And then we end up skating down the probability slope . . . or something,' Greer added. She was off watch now and it was her time to head for her cabin, but she was lingering to see what would happen when they finally surfaced from U-space, carrying all that negative energy from their time jump.

'If you believe the multiverse theories,' said Brond.

'This kind of science is now like religion,' said Greer. 'You can choose the theory that best suits you.'

'Only of the theories you don't understand.'

'You understand them, then?'

'Keep it down,' said Blite. 'I'm concentrating.'

'Sure thing, Captain,' said Greer, and they both returned to contemplating their screens.

Apparently, these worlds were both of enough interest to Polity AIs for them to have sent an AI science ship to observe and gather data. The ship's mission was to map out the ecologies at both the moon and the green-belt world, and to gather and preserve samples of every single life form. This massive task required a ship's crew of war drones repurposed for the job, and Golem, perpetually visiting both the world and the moon to observe and record the fauna and flora in their particular habitat, record that habitat in detail and gather samples. Checking through some of the data on this, Blite came across a highly technical report from a Golem android who had for a number of years watched a silicon-based plant growing until it shed spurs into a methane storm to seed itself. As he read he kept stamping down on his growing frustration and anger. This all had to mean *something*.

Next, he came upon a mission conducted by two drones and a Golem who, of necessity, wore a strange form of syntheflesh and skin. A human community on the green-belt world, of over fifty thousand, struggled constantly to survive. Being highly adapted and living in a mutualistic relationship with a silicon-based mould enabled them to digest a wider spectrum of the local fauna and flora. The mould also grew tough armour over their skins to protect them from a local combination of social insect and parasite that injected eggs that grew into nests inside their victims.

'Forty minutes,' said Brond, alerting Blite to just how absorbed he had been in his reading, and how successfully he had suppressed his impatience.

'Shut up,' the captain replied.

Checking further, he found that this human society was the result of the pre-Quiet War diaspora, for its members were descendants of colonists who had been brought here by a cryo-ship. The colonists had almost destroyed their vessel in the process of landing it, and during their first years on the world had cannibalized it. Their history was interesting and grotesque. None of the original colonists remained alive because the adaptations they needed to make to survive were far too radical for an adult, with the technology they had available. Instead, they made the adaptations and introduced the mutualistic mould to their children, most of whom were foetuses in amniotic cryo-tanks when they landed. The adults had to spend their remaining lives in sealed buildings – only venturing outside in armoured space suits. Some of them might have survived until now – the gerontological science of the time would have enabled this – but their children, upon reaching adulthood, rebelled, introducing a nasty social parasite to their parents' living quarters.

This was all very interesting, but was still irrelevant to the *Black Rose*'s arrival so many light years from their world. Blite now focused his attention on Crispin Six.

Crispin Six had been a planetary system until its sun went supernova six years ago. It fried its planets in the first day, and the blast wave had been steadily expanding ever since. This front had already passed over a binary system close by and given it a toasting, causing one ice giant there to lose a couple of worlds and itself expand into something more gaseous and hot. It had also swept away the cometary cloud surrounding that system and destabilized one of the suns – an average G-type –

which it had left poxed with sunspots and hurling out tentacular flares. But no life existed there, and the blast hadn't fried any ecologies so far. That would change with devastating effect, however, when it finally reached Rebus.

Blite experienced a moment of cold sweat until he rechecked the realspace coordinates of their destination. Thankfully, it lay behind this blast wave. However, he still couldn't see why these worlds Penny Royal had highlighted were of any relevance to the AI. Certainly it now seemed unlikely that it wanted to destroy them, since their destruction was imminent anyway. He next quickly checked for status updates on this story – his new ship had updated itself from the Polity net when they were at the border. He discovered that of course the Polity AIs were aware of the inevitable destruction of Rebus, and they were acting. The human population of the world wasn't too large for evacuation by ship. But such an operation would be difficult, and an easier method was available.

'Twenty minutes to our destination,' said Brond.

Blite just glared at him for a moment, then returned to his studies.

A Polity stellar incident centre had dispatched a cargo hauler called the *Azure Whale*. Aboard, it carried three runcible portals. Runcible technicians would position one on that gas giant's moon and two on the green-belt world. Once they activated these, thoroughly prepared incident teams would come through. On the moon their job was, like mega-scale gardeners, to dig up every element of a whole ecology. Apparently, the AIs concluded that samples were simply not enough and the silicon-based ecology was too precious to lose to the blast. On the green-belt world, their job was also to gather large elements of the ecology, but the main task was to round up all the humans there and dispatch them through the runcible. To this end, Sparkind forces

247

and grappler robots were to be deployed – obviously, they expected some resistance.

'Captain,' said Leven.

'Yes,' Blite replied distractedly.

'We just deployed U-space disruptor mines.'

'What?' Blite looked up. 'Why?'

'I don't know,' said Leven, 'perhaps you would like to ask Penny Royal.'

Blite felt no inclination to do so, as he was sure he'd be finding out within minutes. He sat back, still pondering on the world of Rebus. Was this rescue attempt normal Polity behaviour? The world wasn't quite within the Line so wasn't the AIs' responsibility. He grimaced. It struck him as more likely that the Polity actions had more to do with the interesting silicon ecology and adaptations of the human society. He then wondered when it was he had become so cynical.

'And we're arriving,' said Brond.

Blite felt the distortion from the top of his head to his toes. Leven cast the local view up in the screen laminate: just dark starlit space. But Blite already knew that they were not arriving in any planetary system.

'So what—' he began, then felt further twists in the pit of his being.

'The mines,' said Leven.

The view on the screen swung round and, checking the figures along the bottom of it, Blite saw that they were under heavy fusion acceleration. Another jump ensued, brief – feeling as if it was on the edge of turning him inside out. White lightning webbed the area of space now centred on the screen – and out of it nosed something immense. Out into the real came a great slab of a ship that looked unnervingly like a pre-Quiet War gravestone. And Blite recognized it at once from his investigations.

'The *Azure Whale*,' he said.

'What?' Brond turned to look at him.

'Seen it before?' asked Greer.

He just gestured to his aug. 'I saw it just a few minutes ago.' He requested a link to them and, when they enabled it, he shot over the data on the Polity rescue attempt. It would take them a while to digest it, by which time, he reckoned, Penny Royal would have finished doing whatever it was going to do here.

'We're using particle beams now, apparently,' said Leven woodenly, even as those beams cut across from the *Black Rose* to the big ship. They picked over its surface – hitting here, carving a line there, centring on one point and burning right through the big vessel in several places. The *Whale*, which immediately after exiting U-space had fired up a powerful fusion drive array, bucked. Then something exploded out of its side, and its drive went out.

'Evacuate,' hissed a voice – Penny Royal of course. But it didn't seem to be addressing them.

After a few minutes, a square on the screen etched out a point on the ship and brought it into focus. Two objects shot out of an ejection port. The view next swung across to show castellated shuttle bay doors opening, then a couple of wedge-shaped evacuation shuttles blasted out into vacuum.

'I'm getting queries from the captain of the *Azure Whale*,' said Leven. 'He wants to know why they have been attacked and why he, his crew and the ship AI were ordered to abandon ship.'

'Beats me,' said Blite. 'Penny Royal, what the hell are you doing?'

The screen view changed again and, on checking, Blite found it was unmagnified this time. They were now right over the hauler and its upper surface spread below them like a massive steel plain.

'Do you want to speak to them?' Leven asked.

'Not yet,' said Blite.

He gazed at the view for some while longer, glanced at Brond and Greer and saw they had a glassy look as they worked through the data he had auged over to them.

'Bay doors are open,' Leven noted.

Blite watched and in a moment saw a large shadow falling down towards that massive ship.

'I take it our passenger just left us?' he asked.

No reply.

'Leven?'

Still no reply as the shadow settled on the hauler.

'Leven?' Blite asked again.

'Yes,' Leven replied, sounding distracted and odd.

'Focus in on that.'

The view from the surface of the hauler shot towards them. The rippling spiky mass on its hull was certainly Penny Royal and, even as he watched, it sank into the surface, leaving a hole filled with glittering darkness. After a few minutes, the view retreated again to show much activity on and about the ship. Robots had swarmed out of some of the holes, making rapid repairs, while debris spewed from various ports.

'So Penny Royal is over there, Leven?' Blite asked again.

'Yes and no,' the Golem mind replied.

'Explain.'

'A U-space connection I cannot explain occurred just after those first mines were deployed. The AI's mass increased twofold, then it separated. One portion is aboard that ship while the other one remains here.'

Blite mulled that over as they watched the activity aboard the hauler. After twenty minutes it began to wane, despite just a little of the damage having been repaired. The fusion drive fired up again and began to draw the big ship away. Blite thought about talking to that captain aboard one of those escape shuttles, but couldn't think what he would say. A short while later, as the hauler grew increasingly distant, he felt the twist of U-space and watched it finally fold out of existence. It seemed that Penny Royal had just stolen a massive hauler with three runcibles aboard.

'You've just condemned over fifty thousand people to death in a supernova blast,' he said.

'Not quite,' the AI whispered, and then with an unnecessarily violent wrench took the *Black Rose* under too.

Spear

So, the *Lance* was a wreck and Riss and I had been rescued from imminent destruction by Sverl, who had sent us into firing range of Cvorn's ST dreadnought in the first place. It was all just a little puzzling.

'Perhaps, if you would explain what you want with us?' I suggested.

The chain-glass box holding Riss now stood open and Sverl was peering inside. After a moment, he reached in to take hold of Riss, then with the drone's inert form hanging from one claw, he headed over to a low work surface on which various clamps had been mounted. He dumped the snake drone there, then moved back, as a multi-manipulator robot immediately descended like a spider on a thread from the ceiling.

'I check all information pertinent to my interests,' said Sverl, 'but only when I was updating from Flute, did I learn about the assassin drone Riss – and this object.' Sverl gestured with one claw to Penny Royal's spine, now in the claws of a second-child. He was placing it in a series of clamps at one end of the work surface.

'I still don't understand what you intend to do here,' I said.

'The spine, as you are aware, contains copies of the essential formative memories and mental patterns of most of Penny Royal's victims,' said Sverl.

'I wasn't sure,' I said. 'Riss tells me there is quantum entanglement involved – that the spine is linked to my mind and to another location that might be Penny Royal. I wondered if it was just a relay for information stored elsewhere.'

'No, those memories are here,' said Sverl. 'The spine contains more than enough storage for that purpose, and there is no reason for the memories to be relayed. I would suggest that Penny Royal is influencing the order and intensity of the memories you experience. But most importantly, it is using the spine to keep apprised of your location, mental state and what actions you intend to take.'

I should have dumped it in a sun, I thought . . . *Shouldn't I?*

'I still don't know, however, what this has got to do with Riss,' I said.

'The spine contains those memories, but it also contains the technology for manipulating them, erasing them, cutting, pasting and, most importantly, transferring them,' Sverl explained. 'It is a key that will unlock Riss's mind, penetrate it as it was penetrated once before by this same technology – perhaps by this same piece of Penny Royal.'

'So the fact that we are all together, now – does this mean what you intend to do was planned by the AI?'

'Planned, foreseen, caused . . .'

The robot had now lifted up the snake drone and fixed it

into the series of clamps in line with those holding the spine. I noted that it firmly fixed the drone's head and had used retractor hooks inside a metal ring to pull open its mouth, right in front of the sharp end of the spine. Also noting that the clamps holding the spine were on slides, it didn't take much imagination for me to guess where it was going to end up.

'It seems to me that Penny Royal is overcomplicating the solutions to the messes it made,' I suggested.

'Yes,' Sverl agreed, 'if we are to be simplistic.'

'So why such complications?'

'I could think of many possibilities,' said Sverl. 'The simplest solution to a problem is not always the best one and can often exacerbate it. Consider the history of your own race. When you fed the starving and that resulted in dependency and resentment, the governments concerned reneged on their responsibility, causing war and then further starvation. When you destroyed autocratic regimes, you caused more death and suffering than the regime itself, and often ended up with something worse. Your violent revolutions never resulted in anything better, and your revolutionaries always turned into the thing they despised.'

'You seem pretty sure of that,' I said.

'I've been studying the human race for a century.'

'Yeah, right,' I said, not sure how to respond to that. 'So how have complicated solutions been better?'

'Penny Royal could have reversed the changes it made to Isobel Satomi, but she would have still been in a position of higher power in the Graveyard, still running her brutal coring trade. Instead the AI lured her and her organization to destruction at Masada, in the process altering the balance of power on that world and essentially freeing the Weaver, the Atheter, from Polity restraint.'

'And that's a good thing?'

'Depends where you're standing.'

'On the Rock Pool,' I said, 'Penny Royal could have murdered Cvorn and the Five under the ocean, and that would have been the end of that problem.'

'Yes, but the shell people would still be pursuing their doomed experiment. I would still be as I am and a threat to peace between the Polity and the Kingdom.'

I shook my head. 'No, it's still overcomplicated.'

'Perhaps Penny Royal likes complicated.'

'There is that . . .'

'And this is only if we are to suppose that cleaning up its messes is the black AI's singular intent.'

'What else?'

'The problem with having a greatly expanded capacity for thought is that all possibilities expand. In truth, my best answer has to be that I don't know.'

I returned my attention to Riss while the door opened behind and the second-child took the chain-glass box out and away. The robot had attached a multitude of optics and power cables to the rear of the spine and now that object was slowly being propelled point-first into the drone's mouth. I watched this for a moment, then walked over and sat on one of the saddle seats the prador hauled themselves over – the object pocked with pit controls fit for prador digits. I wondered if Sverl used it, because I saw no sign of manipulatory hands underneath the jaw of his big skull.

'Is this going to damage her?' I asked.

'No – in essence it will free the drone from some constraint, because to extract the memories I will need to break the AI lock placed upon her.'

'And afterwards?' I asked. 'I know that you have no liking of assassin drones made in that shape.'

'I *do* have no liking,' Sverl agreed, 'but the war is over. I am, however, not entirely sure the drone is happy with that. I will necessarily have to employ some restraint.'

'How long is all this going to take?' I asked.

'Many hours.'

'In that case I would like to see my ship, if I can,' I said. 'Is Flute still alive?'

'You can see your ship,' said Sverl. 'As for Flute, I don't know – you'll have to find out.'

'Then I want to speak to Trent Sobel,' I added, 'without him trying to kill me.'

'Of course you do,' said Sverl, 'because another piece has to slot into place. Trent Sobel is not the man you knew any more and is unlikely to try to kill you or anyone else. He will in fact need your help.'

Sverl gestured with a claw and the door opened behind me. 'Bsectil will take you.'

'This way,' said one of the first-children, turning towards the door, which was opening again.

Bsectil led me along the corridor to a smaller version of the door into Sverl's sanctum, which he entered, instructing me to wait outside. I peered in through the open door and saw a chamber I presumed to be this creature's abode. Again, it didn't follow the usual prador style. The walls were certainly lined with some rocky substance, but inset in these, all around, were numerous aquariums, backlit and filled with squirming life. Curious, I moved closer to the door to get a better look.

Over to one side lay a work area with benches and prador tools all standing around a central object. Was this first-child fashioning some sort of machine? Fascination drew me in despite Bsectil's instruction to wait outside. No, here was a representation of Isobel Satomi part way through her transformation into a hooder. Judging by the collection lying across the work surface, Bsectil was fashioning this sculpture out of a variety of natural gemstones. This was art, something which was supposed to be totally absent in the Prador Kingdom. And, what was more, the lack of this had been cited by the Polity as the ultimate proof of prador barbarity.

Turning my attention to the other side of the chamber, I saw more conventional prador equipment: racked weapons akin to Gatling cannons and particle beamers. There were also heavy work tools which could attach directly to a prador's carapace or their additional armour. The first-child had deposited himself on a ring of supports amidst this hardware and was shedding his armour. With a clattering sound, his visual turret expanded in segments, then with a crump the carapace separated along a line just above the leg sockets and rose on polished rods. This detached from the forward rods and hinged back on the rear two. Now revealed was the whorled and stony top half of the first-child – looking very much like that of the second-child I had seen.

Next, with further clattering sounds, the armour about the creature's legs and claws expanded and separated, driven apart on similar, smaller polished rods. The prador rose out of this exoskeleton, levered up by an object like a large shoehorn which hinged up from inside. Extracting his legs and claws in the process, he got a grip on the surrounding armour, then heaved himself out completely, landing on the floor like a dropped toolbox. He was a little unsteady at first, struggling to get his balance on distorted legs. I examined the speaker grille for a translator and spotted the aug attached to the side of his visual turret.

'That was chafing,' Bsectil said.

I supposed that armour designed for a normal sort of first-child would chafe on something like this. I realized then that I was seeing a very ancient first-child indeed. Such creatures were usually dispensed with, in some nasty manner, at a relatively young age. Kept in a chemically maintained adolescence, they started to become immune to that suppression at some point. As I understood it, their fathers killed them before they inevitably began to transform, despite that suppression, into adults. Or perhaps that was all wrong. Perhaps their fathers killed them before they turned into something halfway, such as this.

'Do you want to be an adult?' I asked.

'No,' Bsectil replied, 'Father has never offered us the choice. But he knows we are more than capable of freeing ourselves. Also, the physiological changes could now kill us.'

I realized my mouth was hanging open and closed it.

'You're not really like any prador I've known, or known of,' I eventually managed.

'Maintained in adolescence, we still grow,' said Bsectil. 'Even if we could transform into adults, we would devolve.'

'I see.'

The first-child waved a claw towards his artwork. 'What do you think?'

'I think it's very good,' I replied, 'though I'm in two minds about the choice of subject. Is it your first? Usually prador are so . . . practical.'

'It's my first – Father wouldn't let me do him.'

'Okay . . .'

'Now, your ship . . .'

Bsectil headed over to the door and I followed him out. As he led the way through the corridors of the ship, we passed another of those distorted second-children.

'What about them?' I asked. 'Do they grow in permanent adolescence? Do they have an interest in things other than the practical?'

'Not enough brain mass, though with augmentation it's possible,' said Bsectil. 'Father considered allowing them all to move to the next stage – to change into first-children. But again, the physiological change might be lethal. Bsorol is researching possibilities that you may understand, since they involve adapto-genics and nano-packages.'

'We might be able to reverse the damage caused by constant chemical suppression, allowing ganglion growth in our lesser kin and physical independence.'

I jumped, because Bsectil had not spoken the last words – they had come direct through my aug. I began running diagnostics and found that the device was reinstating, but it had also linked into the computing of Sverl's ship.

'Who's that?' I asked.

'Bsorol,' the voice replied.

'Does Sverl know I've access to ship's computing and that you're talking to me?' I asked. 'I don't want to end up brain-fried.'

'He suggested it,' said Bsorol.

'Yes, I did,' Sverl interjected. *'I see another piece of the puzzle slotting into place. Your expertise will not be sufficient to help Trent Sobel.'*

At this point, we had halted by a door that was grinding open.

'You always stop short of a full explanation,' I said.

'You will see,' said Sverl.

I let that go because now, with my aug functioning once more, I was receiving something down the channel that had previously connected me to Flute. It was an odd whining sound and large chunks of corrupted code. Meanwhile, Bsectil took me through a short tunnel and finally into a hold space similar to the one where Riss and I had arrived.

The *Lance* was here and, though it was a mess, with holes punched through it, I took comfort in the fact that its structure still looked solid. The nose armour was heat-rippled where the second railgun missile had struck. And, where the particle beam had cut through the middle of the ship, a section of hull was missing, revealing the charred interior. Airlocks and maintenance hatches stood open, also showing the black charring inside. Where the first railgun missile had struck, taking a huge chunk from the rear, five second-children were at work. They were clad in armour bristling with motorized tools, accompanied by a swarm of Polity maintenance robots. They had removed damaged armour, detached the fusion drive and were currently in the process of removing the U-space drive. I surveyed the pile of wreckage extracted by the workers, and then noted a big gravsled piled up with new materials. Sverl was as good as his word.

'Rebuilding or setting up a U-space drive is usually the province of shipyards,' I noted.

'We can build or rebuild them onboard,' Bsectil replied. 'Father is currently designing drives for U-jump missiles and U-space mines – and preconscious AI minds to control them.'

I didn't like the prospect of prador controlling that kind of tech. But then Sverl was different, wasn't he? I made no comment, instead waving towards the second-children at work on the ship. 'Is it safe to go inside?'

'There is no lethal radiation, all systems have been shut down and remaining munitions and power supplies have been stabilized.'

'What I meant,' I explained, 'was that I don't want to end up on the rough end of a second-child claw if I enter my ship.'

Bsectil swung towards the workers here and clattered something. After a pause, one of them clattered something back.

'You will be safe,' Bsectil told me. 'They are not entering the ship just yet anyway.'

I walked over to gaze up at the particle-beam hole through the side, but there was no way for me to reach it. However, as I scanned around for some other way of entering, Bsectil came over and lowered one claw to the floor beside me.

'Climb up on me,' he said.

I gazed at the creature. I had been responding to him as if he was human or AI – a Polity citizen. However, every time I stopped to think about what he really was, the behaviour of this Bsectil, and, in turn, Sverl, left me numb, shocked. Every personal memory I had involving the prador, along with every new additional one, confirmed them as vicious amoral killers. Yet, here was Bsectil offering to act as a stepladder up into my ship. In addition, Bsectil's only change from a normal prador was age, augmentation and the influence of Sverl. Just like all my fellow soldiers in the war, I had always considered prador killers by nature. Yet now, as I clambered up Bsectil's claw and onto his back, it occurred to me to wonder just how much was down to nurture.

Inside, a blackened ruin confronted me and it took me a while to get my sense of direction. Memory also made itself felt as I re-experienced the slow death of a man caught inside a ship just as ruined as this, but I suppressed it with case. When I finally found the remains of the corridor leading to the rear of the ship, I realized that part of my confusion was due to the grav orientation here. The grav-plates in the floor of the hold now dictated 'Down'. The corridor, in relation to that floor, actually sloped up from the ruination that had been my bridge, living area and laboratory. I climbed upwards, using as steps the distorted grid of the floor where charred grav-plates had dropped out. As I went, I considered just how indestructible that spine must be to survive what had hit here.

By the time I reached the turn into Flute's chamber, the damage was not so severe, and the angle of the floor was no problem as long as I used the wall on one side as support. Reaching the entrance to the ship's cortex, I wondered how I would climb the sloping floor there to get up to Flute. However, there was no need. An impact had flung Flute's container from its two clamps and it now lay easily accessible amidst the wreckage that had piled in the lower corner of the chamber. I made my way to him and studied the damage to his case.

It was dented, cracked open in one place, and from there issued a steady stream of cold vapour. After removing my suit glove, I passed my hand over this. Maybe the case's own power supply was keeping Flute's ganglion frozen, or maybe I was too late. I peered in through the chain-glass porthole but could only make out the glint of occasional lights inside. Certainly, something was still powered up. I tried my aug channel, but the corrupted data had dissipated and now all I got was that previous fizzing. Maybe the case's transceiver had been damaged. There was only one way to find out.

Searching the exterior of the case, I eventually found a small hatch. I tried to pop it open but the damage to the case had jammed it, so I found a shard of ceramal nearby and used that to lever it open. Inside, to my relief, the coiled optic was undamaged. I unreeled it and plugged it into a data socket in my aug.

'. . . sorry . . .' said Flute.

'Pilot,' I said. 'Status report.'

'I am fully . . . dying,' Flute replied. 'System ports . . . 1 to 125 are . . . disconnected. Polity-format . . . diagnostic . . . running. Internal battery at 8%. Zero external source. Coolant system damaged . . . organic corruption . . . in process. Status of U-calculus . . . nil—'

'End report,' I interrupted, uncomfortably reminded of the time when I had bought Flute from the shellman Vrit. 'Bsectil?' I queried through my aug.

'Help is on the way,' Bsectil replied.

Help arrived down the corridor in the form of an armoured second-child, loaded with tools. I felt an abrupt and strong surge of memory – a Polity commando preparing to take on a similarly equipped second-child – and this one was harder to suppress. I quickly moved out of its way and watched as the prador reeled out a power cable from its armour and plugged that into the case. Lights flickered on about its exterior and the second-child applied a tool head and began taking the thing apart. I crouched, fighting the imposed memories, suddenly feeling them clamouring harshly at the borders of my consciousness. What now? And why now?

In my mind's eye, I felt the spine finally lock home in a snakish body and make a full connection. Then something new came out of that mass, displacing the commando's memories. I felt a consciousness of another kind emerge, one that was difficult to encompass, alien. And, all at once, I was the assassin drone Riss – newborn in the furnace of battle, back in Room 101.

The Prador/Human War: Riss

The drone awoke to consciousness knowing its designation as ADP200 and quickly began connecting its consciousness to *all* its systems, instinctively running diagnostics, becoming all it could be, and understanding itself. It was an assassin drone built in the shape of a prador parasite. It resembled a terran cobra, but with an ovipositor in its tail, small limbs under its hood, and three eyes. Because of the ovipositor and its function, and that vague connection to terran biology, its designation was female. Internally *she* contained a grav-motor, EM inducers for penetrating computer systems, electro-muscle, a fusion brick to supply power and a high degree of computing. Data, immediately available in her mind, detailed much of human and AI history and science. But the focus of all this was the war. ADP200 *hated* the prador. In just a few seconds she knew her purpose and was eager to begin work. Next, she engaged her senses and studied her surroundings.

The construction area was a long tube crammed with robotic assemblers – a maelstrom of busy silver limbs and tool heads working around four of ADP200's kin. These were suspended by hardfields, all in various states of construction. Behind was a version of her sans exterior skin – a snake skeleton packed with components and woven with electro-muscle. Behind that was one lacking both electro-muscle and many essential components, and as ADP200 observed *her*, she began to writhe. A hardfield slammed her to one side, where a robotic claw closed on her and threw her, still writhing, through a side hatch. Submitting a query to the station AI submind running this small factory, ADP200 learned that 202's crystal had just too many faults. Rather than start again, it was easier to route her to a nearby furnace.

From the small chamber at the end of the tube, numerous tunnels branched off to the various final construction holds and docks of Factory Station Room 101. It was empty of any of 200's forerunners and full of smoke. Using her grav-motor, ADP200 moved out to its centre, checking the map of the station clear in her mind and applying to the submind for assignment details.

Just then, the whole station shuddered and 200 detected power surges and outages all around.

'You are to proceed to holding point Beta Six, my child,' the submind replied.

My child?

'I'm to be put on hold?'

'We have a *situation* and you cannot immediately be assigned.' Behind this data, something loomed and, since the drone had been made with the capacity for emotion, she recognized deep regret and monolithic grief. Behind the submind's words, something was crying.

ADP200 opened her black eye and checked for data. It was blocked for a while, then it seemed as if the power blocking her faded, and she accessed station computing and sensors. In the space of a single moment, the *situation* became all too clear. Room 101 was under attack from a prador fleet and was taking a pounding. Its AI had shut down production of everything it considered non-essential in this situation. Robots were even taking apart whole factory units – their materials being used to produce stripped-down attack ships that the station was spewing out into battle. The drone understood at once that her kin would never make it, because their whole unit had been shut down – though no orders had yet arrived for it to be taken apart.

The drone watched as the production line powered down. She felt a surge of relief, having so narrowly avoided destruction. She then headed for the relevant exit tunnel to take her to Beta Six.

'You may select a name from the list provided,' the submind informed her, its tones leaden, careless.

Finding the list in her mind, the drone quickly riffled through it. Other snakelike drones had taken all the good names like Kaa and Hissing Sid, but one pertinent name remained.

'I select Riss,' she replied.

'Good choice,' said the mind. 'Have a good life.'

Riss felt the mind encompassed by a grieving darkness before it crumbled, flying apart, howling as it went. The drone realized she had witnessed the station AI not subsuming its submind, but destroying it. Had that been necessary?

The exigencies of war, Riss thought, but sensed something seriously wrong with that assessment. Connected into the station's computing, she was finding areas where logic was breaking down, swamped by digital emotion and always, in the background, that electronic crying.

Navigating quickly through a series of tunnels, Riss became aware that the temperature of the station was steadily increasing. Leaving one of the tunnels to enter a corridor made for larger drones and human personnel, she found some of the latter kind. Two women and a man were on the floor. Probing them with the sensor cluster in her black eye, she registered that the two prostrate on the hot deck were unconscious while the woman sitting with her back against the wall was not. They were clad only in overalls, which was surely insufficient, according to Riss's knowledge, for the increasing temperature.

'Hello . . . drone,' rasped the woman.

Riss dropped to the floor and slithered across. One of the two on the floor was dying and Riss had to do something. She applied to local systems for help, quickly detailing the situation. The only response was hollow laughter that devolved into sobbing.

'You all need hotsuits,' Riss told the woman.

'Ah . . . if wishes were . . . fishes.'

Riss didn't understand that but was aware that though she had a detailed knowledge of humankind, it wasn't complete.

Presumably, the woman had just uttered some sort of colloquialism.

'I cannot get a sensible response from 101 or its subminds,' Riss said.

'That's because,' said the woman, '101 fell off . . . the other side of nuts . . . over an hour ago.'

'I don't understand.'

'We're in some . . . serious shit.'

The other woman, lying on the floor nearby, hit a crisis point as her heart stuttered, and then stopped. Riss again tried to summon help and also used her inducer to restart the woman's heart, stabilizing herself with her grav-motor and beginning chest compressions.

'Don't bother,' said the conscious woman. 'She took . . . curare 12.'

Riss scanned to confirm this, then stopped the compressions. Derivative 12 of that organic poison rendered a person unconscious, then paralysed the nervous system, quickly killing them. The drone looked over at the man. He had taken the same, and even as Riss scanned him, he died. But the woman against the wall had taken nothing and was dying from the heat alone.

'Lucky for them,' said the woman, 'they have . . . memplants.'

'I don't understand,' Riss said again.

'You will,' the woman replied, raising the object she held and pressing it under her chin. The pulse-gun thumped three times in quick succession, taking off the top of her head and spreading her brains up the wall behind, where they immediately began to steam.

Riss froze, struggling to accept what had just happened. Scanning the woman deeper, the drone found the internal physical augmentations she had been using to keep herself alive.

These were necessary because, for quite some time now, the temperature here had been beyond normal human endurance. Assessing those augmentations, Riss realized that the woman must have been in some pain, and that would only have grown until her augmentations failed. Then she would have been truly subject to the temperature here. It would have been akin to stepping into a hot oven.

Riss moved on to the end of the corridor, went through an airlock that required inducement to open and exited into another corridor. She followed one of the smaller tubes to finally arrive at Beta Six. The massive holding area contained only a scattering of war and assassin drones. Nearby four big objects, resembling giant dust mites fashioned from steel, clung to one wall. And a thing like a razor-edged praying mantis patrolled the floor. Riss approached the last of these, recognizing another terror weapon like her.

'You're probably the last of them,' said the mantis.

'What?'

'The drone manufactories are being shut down and are going into the furnaces.'

'I need data,' said Riss.

'Here's a situational update,' offered the mantis, opening a channel along which to send a data package. Riss accepted it.

The survival of Factory Station Room 101 took priority over its residents, so all runcible transfer imports and all available materials inside the station were being turned into stripped-down attack ships. The rate of production hadn't kept up with the battle, so the AI had decided to open the heat-sink runcible for import. Production had thereafter increased, as had the internal temperature. About half of the five thousand human personnel had managed to don hotsuits, but that would only delay their demise by a few hours. Others had ejected themselves from the station in space suits or escape pods. But such was the intensity of the battle out there that their chances of surviving were low. Still others had inserted themselves into cryo-suspension in human quarters, where the AI had now cut power while robots tore apart the quarters themselves for materials. But 101 couldn't route power for a U-space jump to escape, because just a slight dip in its present defensive production rates would almost certainly result in its destruction. And now the AI itself was starting to malfunction: many of its communications were illogical, its attempt to shut down the runcible gates was stopped directly by Earth Central, and other attempts seemingly to sabotage its own survival were being countered by its surviving subminds.

Riss wanted to say, 'I don't understand,' but felt that was a phrase she had used too often already in her short life.

'Fucking empathy,' said the razor mantis.

No, I'm not going to say it, thought Riss.

'Supposedly we are post-humans and so without emotion our reason for being will fade. That emotion is also supposedly a driver that will enable us to win this war,' the mantis explained. 'Fucking bean counters.' The big drone whacked a forelimb against the floor and dragged it across, peeling up slivers of metal.

'Okay, I give up. *I don't understand.*'

'Great idea to give a factory station AI the empathy and conscience of a human mother so it'll be sure to look after all its children.'

Riss finally began to get some glimmering of understanding. The 101 AI had birthed and was continuing to birth thousands of sentient minds, only to send them immediately to destruction. *Its children.* It had also, out of necessity, killed all the humans aboard.

'This is why it's malfunctioning?' Riss suggested.

'Malfunctioning,' the mantis pondered, 'such a technical term.'

'Do you have a better one?'

'Yeah.' The mantis now swung round to face Riss completely, mandibles grinding. 'The Room 101 AI has gone nuts, it's barking, it fell out of the silly tree and hit every branch on the way down.'

'Why don't I feel . . .' Riss tried.

'Hey, you're a newbie,' said the mantis, 'of course you don't feel much.'

'I have just been made,' Riss agreed cautiously.

'I was in here for repairs myself.' Those mandibles stopped grating and the big drone continued, 'In your case, no call for too much in the way of conscience or empathy in an assassin drone – it kinda gets in the way.'

As the snake drone contemplated all her parts and the perfection of her physical design, shaped for a single task, she understood that her mental design was just as refined and specific. Room 101 had also been perfectly designed for its task of producing sentient weapons. But it had never been intended to end up in the thick of the fighting.

'Ah fuck,' said the mantis.

A light as bright as many suns glared in through ports high up in Beta Six section. Some massive detonation jerked the eighty-mile-long station like a hand slapping a ceiling mobile. The whole of Beta Six distorted; a dent hundreds of feet long bowed in one wall. The little drone found herself propelled at high speed across the space, saw the mite drones tumbling, then slamming into the dented wall. The mantis was still in position, sharp limbs driven into the floor where they had sliced foot-long grooves. Riss tried to obtain data, while trying to pull her ovipositor out of the bubble-metal it had embedded itself in.

269

No data available.

Fire now jetted in from the entrances, and one airlock door tore free, tumbling across the space. Great heavings and groanings impinged, then everything twisted in a way Riss recognized at once, but with those parts of her mind that weren't in any human-comparable format. Room 101 U-jumped.

Cvorn

Cvorn felt strong, potent, and he was beginning to feel something else as residual cell damage healed what the surgical equipment had missed. The transplant still ached, but that pain was just a gloss over another sensation, which grew steadily stronger. He turned sharply as Vrom entered from his annex, carrying a bulky organic synthesis unit with a precisely temperature-controlled atomizer and fans mounted on top. Vrom placed the device on the floor before Cvorn and quickly moved back. Even the unemotional first-child was now sensing the change in his father and understood that his personal danger had increased.

Cvorn dipped towards the thing, waggled his new palp eyes – an afterthought after the main surgical operation and one he was regretting, because they didn't seem to be working properly. He studied the control made for a prador manipulator hand he didn't possess, then made a connection to it via his array of control units and aug.

'So tell me about it,' he said, strangely reluctant to turn the thing on.

'The power usage is very low and is kept topped up by simple inductance from ship systems,' Vrom stated. 'Even without topping up it will last decades. The hormones and pheromones are generated from your own genome but otherwise precisely match the mix created by these.' Vrom waved a claw towards the mutilated but still living remains of the young male lying nearby and bubbling weakly in agony, as it had been for many days. 'The effect should be the same.'

'But if I activate this now,' said Cvorn, 'the pheromone mix in the air here will be doubled.'

'Yes, Father,' Vrom agreed.

Cvorn pointed his claw at the young adult. He had been reluctant to let it die and lose its hormonal output, but now it was no longer required. 'Remove him for your own amusement, but ensure he dies within the next hour.'

Vrom immediately turned and headed over to the creature, eager for the rare delicacy. The male's bubbling increased since it was still aware enough to know what was in store. As Vrom began dragging it to the door into his own annex, where he would doubtless open up its shell and begin dining on the living contents, Cvorn focused his attention throughout the ST dreadnought. *His* ship now.

First, he needed to seal Sfolk and the other three young adults into their quarters so their hormone production would not spread throughout the air ducts. Through his aug, Cvorn cut their quarters out of the ship's air-supply system, then issued orders to some of his own second-children to go there with air-set resin guns to make those quarters airtight. This wouldn't kill the four for some time; later, if he felt the urge, Cvorn could deal with them on a more personal level.

Next Cvorn turned on the bio- and gas-attack filtration system. The nano-meshes in these would now take out all large molecules and clear the air. This would take some time so Cvorn set an alert to warn him when the hormone levels in the air dropped below ten per cent of their present level. Then he would turn on the device before him. But he was still wary, and a little puzzled.

Surely, even if prador father-captains had never found themselves breathing the same air supply as five young adults and four females, this effect had been known. Why, then, hadn't it been more commonly used? Cvorn thought about his own past.

Cvorn's father had, as was often the case with prador, grown senile and negligent. Whilst chemical suppression of Cvorn's growth had prevented him, his father's leading first-child, from turning into an adult, his father had failed to supplement his fading hormonal control of his children. A long time before he had been capable of acting directly against his father, Cvorn had understood this and had prepared, as had his father's other three first-children. Ironically, if his father hadn't decided that the time had come for Cvorn to be replaced, the result of the ensuing conflict might have been a lot messier and not necessarily in Cvorn's favour. As it was, his father summoned him to his sanctum, where two thralled grazer squid awaited with surgical telefactors and one of the new spherical drone shells into which they aimed to install Cvorn's ganglion. Cvorn knew what was about to happen and therefore had greater motivation to fight his instinct to obey than his brethren. It was the most difficult thing he had ever done – to resist the urge to submit, and then to activate the particle cannon concealed in his claw and turn it on his father. His father had died quickly, the beam punching through the macerating machine he had used in the place of mandibles and into his body, the pressure generated in there by expanding hot gases blowing off the top of his shell, but his pheromones had not faded as quickly as his life.

Cvorn spent many hours crippled by the reaction, sure he had done wrong, expecting punishment, terrified, but as the pheromones in the air faded, he began to feel free and knew he had to act, and now. Already prepared for this too, he went over to his father's pit controls and penetrated his communications, immediately summoning one of his brethren first-children to the sanctum. He gave no indication that it was he doing the summoning and not his father. That first-child arrived and died, burning in the same beam that had taken out his father. The next suffered the same end too, but the remaining first-child, doubtless now aware that its father's hormonal control of it was fading fast, did not respond.

Cvorn's instinct at that point was to go after the other one, but that would have been a bad move. Here in his father's sanctum, at the heart of their undersea home, he was relatively safe and had direct access to the computer system. He locked down the armoured doors before beginning his steady penetration of that system. First, he removed his father's three control units from his shell, incidentally dining on his father's partially cooked flesh and enjoying it immensely. He inserted new nano-connector interfaces into the units, then shell-welded them to his own carapace. The three channels opened to the two grazer squid and his father's four war drones, who had all been Cvorn's predecessors, but the coding he needed to control these had gone with the old nano-connectors. However, his father had been a rather old-fashioned prador who used pit controls to access his house computers and these, if he was careful, Cvorn could work with. And the control codes were probably recorded there too. He spent many days ensconced in the sanctum, eating both his father and his two brothers as he worked, and physically changing.

Urges he could not identify began to wash through him, as he no longer ingested the cocktail of chemicals that had maintained his adolescence. As he worked, his whole body felt looser, odd, and he was always hungry. Perhaps the joy he felt in finally penetrating the house computers, both taking control of it and getting hold of the codes for the war drones and grazer squid, was what helped instigate the change. He was just reviewing the list of numerous attempts by his remaining brother to penetrate that same system, with his limited access outside the sanctum, when he felt a sudden tight convulsion at his back end and heard a ripping sound. Abruptly he could no longer feel his back legs. Looking round, he saw them, and a section of intervening carapace drop away. Then a whole new set of feelings impinged as his new prongs and coitus clamp, as yet not fully developed, were exposed to the air.

As was always the case with pre-adulthood prador, Cvorn immediately felt vulnerable and wanted to hide and protect this new acquisition. He recognized the feeling at once: it was an evolved survival mechanism to get him away from aggressive fully adult prador, including his father, who would immediately attack and try to kill such a competitor. This was a form of selection – with only the fast and the strong surviving. In the far past, before prador society developed, pre-adults went into hiding until the transformation was completed, hunting and eating to build up body mass and armour. As full adults, they then returned to compete for females. Cvorn fought the urge, rationality his armour now because he controlled four war drones.

Contacting those drones, who were less sophisticated than the modern version and so could not distinguish between him and his father, he gave them their orders and then watched on his array of hexagonal screens. These drones were actually original body carapaces reinforced with armour, with major ganglions frozen inside and these interfaced with tactical computing. Other internal organs had been removed and replaced with a power supply and other hardware. Being surface-based and grav-technology being expensive, they ran on caterpillar treads. They were armed with twinned Gatling cannons where their claws had been and underslung missile launchers. Cvorn watched them trundle out of their cache and spread out through the undersea home. Before reaching Cvorn's first-child brother, one of them encountered two second-children. These were already transforming into first-children and were fighting in one of the corridors. A short burst of Gatling fire rapidly converted them into smoking chunks.

The first-child, alerted by this, immediately fled his own small sanctum, headed to an exit portal and out into the ocean. Cvorn was disappointed but understood the impulse. His brother was no longer a first-child either, having also lost his back legs and exposed new tender sexual organs. Cvorn at once changed all the house codes so that the young adult could not get back in. He thereupon watched the drones slaughter all the remaining second-children, and then enter the third-child nursery and there massacre all the males. The females, in their separate annex, would be worth keeping for the usual round of necessary exchanges to prevent inbreeding.

Cvorn next spent many months hiding, ignoring queries from other prador who were his father's allies or associates, aware that if they knew of his father's demise they might well consider this abode vulnerable to attack. Gradually, he grew larger. He went through two further sheddings, and as his final fully adult shell hardened and thickened, his fear began to diminish. During his first venture out of his sanctum, he visited his father's harem to satisfy a strongly growing itch, but used gel contraception. He did not want to inbreed with his mother and knew he needed to exchange these females for some that were more genetically diverse. Returning to his sanctum, he spent some time tending to inevitable mating injuries and decided it was time to announce his presence.

Prador society's muted reaction to his appearance surprised him until he discovered that inter-house communications were abuzz with other news. Exploration vessels had encountered a new sentient race out at the limits of the Kingdom's expansion, and his fellows were making the usual preparations. Of course, the prador were destined to rule the universe, and so would not tolerate other intelligences.

Back in the present, Cvorn felt himself bowed under a deep and heavy nostalgia and tried to shake it off, but the weight of memory continued to bear down on him. He relived the excitement of war preparations, the times he had nearly ended up a victim of his own kind, the allies he had made and betrayed and the enemies that had come close to killing him. He remembered his steady vicious climb up through the prador hierarchy, his steady acquisition of wealth and the commissioning of his destroyer. He remembered his first-children. But just one had survived all those years of warfare against the Polity and he now resided in one of his war drones. He remembered growing old and beginning to lose the mating urge during that conflict, then losing his limbs and the equipment for mating after them. Then it was that he regained some of his cowardice, ensuring layers of protection around him – his ships, armour, weapons and enslaved children. He realized he had become brutal then and that much of his aggression was a product of his fear of anything that might harm him . . .

Cvorn shook himself violently, noted that the alarm was sounding from the device Vrom had brought and through his aug immediately turned it on. He had been thinking about his past in relation to the hormonal effect upon him, not to end up reliving its joys and horrors. So again, why wasn't that effect more commonly used? His immediate thought was that father-captains feared fear itself – that in regressing themselves like this they might end up as cowardly pre-adults again – but Cvorn had felt none of that. He felt now as he had felt when first announcing his presence to the rest of the prador. He felt brave and he felt ready. He also felt something else, something quite powerful and undeniable. Turning, he opened his sanctum doors and headed out. It had been a long time but he still remembered the techniques he had employed to avoid the worst of the injuries. It was time, Cvorn definitely felt, to pay a visit to those females.

The Brockle

The single-ship that had just arrived was one of three used to convey prisoners to and from the *Tyburn* to face the Brockle. The woman inside was a murderess, but there must be more to it or she would not have ended up here. Her hatred of the Polity had led to her joining a separatist organization and she might be involved in other crimes too. The Polity wanted her reamed of information and then sentence executed on her.

The Brockle's latest case had decided that her three sons had no future in the Polity, due to her detestation of the Polity and its AIs. They, despite being legal adults, apparently had no say in the matter. She had tried to force them to accompany her to one of the outlink stations to take a freighter ride outside the Polity. But they had refused, also rebelling further by getting themselves fitted with Polity augs. She had pretended to accept their choice and invited them to her home for a meal, whereupon she had fed them with a self-propagating neurotoxin. This poison, as well as killing them in seconds flat, turned their brains to jelly. So despite the alert broadcast by the augs they wore, they ended up unrecoverably dead.

So prosaic.

The Brockle felt a wave of ennui at the prospect of interrogating her. Maybe if ECS had sent some Golem murderer or the likes of the strange Mr Pace its feelings would have been different. But ennui was followed by angry frustration. Earth Central had informed the Brockle that it could obtain no more of value from Ikbal and Martina after their time with Penny Royal on Captain Blite's ship. It was ordered to release them, returning them via this very single-ship . . . The Brockle's contribution to solving the 'Penny Royal problem' was now at an end.

The Brockle thought otherwise. All the intimate details it had gleaned from Blite's crewmembers proved that Penny Royal, as well as being a paradigm-changing force, was dangerously unstable. The Brockle had requested the other two crewmembers – the couple Chont and Haber Geras – but apparently ECS had intercepted and questioned them on Earth, and released them. This was just plain wrong. It could learn so much more by a joint interrogation of all four. It could make so many comparisons of their experiences. By jointly putting them under pressure and setting them against each other in some VR scenario it could elicit new facts. Didn't Earth Central understand the necessity for this? Didn't that AI understand how dangerous Penny Royal was?

In its seat before the window, which gave a view along the thin central body of the *Tyburn* to the section that still contained the remains of some of the colonists, the Brockle ground its ersatz teeth and felt the need for some rebellion of its own. Through the cams in the interrogation room, it gazed upon Ikbal and Martina. Presently they were lying on the floor, the silver worms of nano-fibres visible around their heads, which had also penetrated within. The Brockle was running them through a perfect recall of events aboard *The Rose* while subtly twisting their mental perspective. And every time it did this, further interesting details surfaced. It then focused its attention on the dock, as the woman exited the single-ship and stood wringing her hands and peering round nervously.

Yes, time to push against the terms of its confinement by Polity AIs. The negotiation to reach agreement had been difficult and it had only consented because here it got precisely what it wanted: suspects to interrogate, minds to take apart. Now it wasn't getting what it wanted.

The Brockle stood and headed out, broke into an unaccustomed jog then, in irritation, melted into a hundred silver worms and shoaled towards the dock. A short while later it exploded into the dock space, seeing the woman separatist from a hundred different perspectives. Quick and dirty, it decided, as it swarmed around her. Then all the worms collapsed in on her with a thunderous crack and enclosed her in a writhing ball.

The Brockle stripped the flesh away from her skull, then the skull away from her brain, which it retained. The shifting bait-ball of worms drifted across the dock, dropping flesh and skin, splinters of bone, and then her headless body. It recorded her brain physically as it took it apart, making a model, and running her mind-state in that. Discarding a slurry of neural matter, it departed the dock, already having extracted enough about her separatist contacts and involvement in other crimes to make a report. Meanwhile, it linked through to its submind in the single-ship. But rather than absorb it, as usual, it delivered some simple instructions: 'Return to Omega Six for next pick-up.' As the Brockle well knew, there was no pick-up waiting there, at the station where this latest victim had been held.

'Understood,' the submind replied.

Immediately the dock began to evacuate, the woman's remains steaming on the floor as they rapidly vacuum-dried. The space doors opened and the single-ship began to manoeuvre towards them with blasts of compressed air. Now, almost certainly, the watcher would be informing Earth Central that the ship was departing without the crewmen. However, by the time the Polity's leading AI responded, the ship would have dropped into U-space. And now there were no more single-ships aboard it could use to return Blite's crew. This was merely a delaying tactic, because in time another one would arrive with yet another prisoner for interrogation.

Back in its viewing room, the Brockle formed itself back into a fat young man, already dispatching the report on the separatist as it stepped back to its chair. Later, it would return and get rid of the headless and now dried-out corpse. Right now, it checked through its units attached to Ikbal and Martina before formulating the replies it would make during the imminent exchange with Earth Central. Then it needed to think very carefully about endings, and new beginnings.

11

The Prador/Human War: Riss

As Room 101 escaped into U-space, Riss continued to try to extract her ovipositor from the wall as the thrum of weapons hitting hardfield defences cut off. Slow data transmission began to re-establish itself. The station had survived! But now, as more and more data and more and more sensors became available, the darkness flooded in. It was filled with drowning minds that were crumbling, falling apart.

'You're with me, now,' said the mantis, closing one limb around Riss's body and yanking the little drone from the wall.

They moved fast from Beta Six, the mite drones falling in behind them, with others joining them and appearing from elsewhere. Hollow booms echoed throughout the station, where air was available to transmit the sound. Power surges and outages continued all around, and Riss detected massive data shifts in the computer systems – shifts that made them difficult to penetrate and therefore understand.

'They're fighting back,' said the mantis, 'but they're as naive as you are and don't understand. Only the subminds and those who returned for repairs, like me, stand any chance.'

Before Riss could ask a question, the mantis routed a data package across. The 101 AI was now killing its children, which didn't make any sense. The station was wiping AI crystal with EM pulses, as it queued up for insertion into new attack ships. It was also using an informational attack against AI crystal already inside ships – in every stage of construction. It was similarly wiping them too in the process. Many minds were managing to fend this off, so Room 101 was physically attacking them in response.

Maintenance robots were swarming aboard some ships in the early stages of construction, but with minds already in place. They were using any method they could employ to destroy the AI crystal aboard these ships. In some areas, other robots were fighting to stop this – the mentioned subminds presumably controlling them. Meanwhile, in the cramped spaces of final construction bays, complete and near-complete attack ships were fighting to survive. Here, the AI had turned the internal station weapons and giant constructor robots against them.

'Attack ship *Jacob* saw the way the wind was blowing,' said the mantis. 'It's gone dark, hoping not to be noticed. *Jacob* is another like me – just in here for repairs.'

Riss tried to obtain information on that ship by again probing the data flows all around. At first, she could glean nothing, but then began to form a virtual map in her mind. She could see the 101 AI at the centre of the chaos, resembling some angry red amoeba jetting out pseudopods at numerous smaller versions of itself around it. These were throwing up defences such as hardfields and shifting as they shattered. Constellations of other minds – those of the attack ships – were shoaling between, sometimes hiding under similar defences, sometimes flaring out like incendiaries when hit by those pseudopods. Sieving manifests, Riss tried to find the *Jacob*, but could not. Next, everything went angry red and something slammed into her mind.

Riss found herself falling into darkness, tendrils of data trying to lever apart the components of her consciousness. A terrible grief and hopelessness filled her. There seemed no reason for existing, no point in continuing with such a load to bear. Riss ceased to fight and began to feel her mind breaking apart—

A flash of light dispelled the darkness and Riss found herself coiled in vacuum in an area of the station without grav. One of the big steel mites was holding her between two of its limbs, having punched an array of micro-bayonet data plugs through her skin to connect to the systems around her crystal. Hopelessness faded, and the little drone's mind began pulling together its parts.

'That was fucking stupid,' said the mantis, hovering nearby. 'You sure are naive.'

The mite released her and backed off as Riss uncoiled.

'I told you *Jacob* had gone dark. And I showed you what 101 is doing to its . . . its children.'

Of course, as one of those newborn children herself, Riss was vulnerable. On detecting her in the system, the station AI had just tried to kill her.

'Don't try that again,' the mantis warned. 'You could end up dead. And worse than that, you could make the AI aware of the *Jacob*. Let's go.'

The refugees, now including others made in the shape of both terran and alien creatures, along with skeletal Golem and some clad in syntheflesh and skin, were moving down the throat of a huge production line. Nearby hung the skeleton of an attack ship, while far behind, one nearing completion was drifting, folded into a boomerang shape by some massive impact. All around debris tumbled, burned, half-melted and often unidentifiable. Dismembered robots clung to some or gyrated free, spider robots swayed like kelp flowers on the ends of power and optic threads.

'Get ready to fight,' said the mantis.

Just ahead, a port opened, and out of it, moving as if doped, came maintenance robots like six-foot-long brushed aluminium cockroaches. They didn't seem to know what they were doing, for they milled around aimlessly, once out of the port. Just making a tentative probe into the virtual world, Riss discovered that for the mite drones, the battlefield was in the informational realm rather than the physical one, and they were confusing the robots ahead.

'Hit them now,' the mantis instructed, accelerating so fast its limbs tore up glowing slivers of metal.

Despite the mantis's speed, a drone shaped like a shark reached them first, accelerating on a chemical drive. It hit one of the roach-like maintenance robots and drove it back into two of its kin, then opened its mouth and began biting with chain-glass teeth turning on conveyors in its jaws. The jets from its steering thrusters were simultaneously stabbing out all around, like some odd kind of firework display. Disconnected heads and other body parts tumbled away. The mantis arrived next, chopping with those sharp limbs and spitting a particle beam from between its mandibles. At that moment, a wave passed through the whole station. They'd just surfaced from U-space.

'We stand a chance now,' the mantis observed.

Riss accelerated while formulating a method of attack to suit a conflict that she just wasn't designed to fight. A missile sped past, made a sharp ninety-degree turn and went straight down into the dark entryway. A moment later, a detonation rippled the deck underneath and numerous roach robots exploded out of that same port in an actinic fountain. This had come from a big war drone lacking any form based on the organic – just a hovering cylinder bristling with weapons. Now, however, the roach robots were no longer milling and Riss recognized that this meant 101 was now aware of her and her allies. Suddenly the little drone found herself confronted by one of the roaches. The thing extruded a tool head from its own skull, two atomic shear fields opening out from it like wings. Riss immediately engaged chameleonware and went into egg insertion mode. She contained no eggs and this wasn't the prey she was designed to destroy. However, her ovipositor was collimated diamond, capable of penetrating even prador armour.

As Riss shot forwards, underneath those shear fields, she felt something tearing into her chameleonware as the roach lowered those fields to intercept her. It wasn't quick enough. Riss was under them in a moment, coiling and stabbing upwards, ovipositor penetrating a simple layer of industrial ceramal – three, four times, precisely hitting certain junctions between the robot's sub-AI processors and transceiver. The roach convulsed, then, waving its limbs aimlessly, began to drift away.

Multiple flashes ensued. Riss saw that nearly all of the roach robots had been disabled or destroyed, but the big war drone was now opening up on something else. Focusing across the production line tube Riss saw more robots swarming out of numerous ports across there.

'Bugger fuck shit,' said the mantis, firing its particle beam across the tube.

Missiles began to impact over there shortly after the numerous strikes from energy weapons, but now something began to reply. Particle beams stabbed back. One a yard across splashed on a hardfield right above the cylindrical war drone. The field held for just a moment, but something glowing white-hot exploded from the side of that drone, then the drone itself glowed briefly and exploded under the direct impact of the beam. One of the mites shot out towards the middle of the tube, limbs windmilling. Then its back opened like a hatch to expose burning components inside. And a swarm of something else, rising on bright drives, began to speed towards them.

They were losing now. Room 101 had turned its full attention, and power, against them. Riss understood that maintenance and construction robots weren't all that were available to that intelligence. This station also replaced damaged weapons and resupplied Polity forces with munitions, which it was now using.

'Oh well,' said the mantis, 'it was worth a shot.'

I'm going to die, thought Riss, *and I have hardly lived.*

But next, on the other side of the chamber, impacts began tearing apart the gathering horde, punching through the walls and raising the blue spectres of plasma explosions. Three massive detonations ensued, CTDs by the look of them, burning mile-wide craters and spewing white-hot gas into vacuum. Green lasers cut through this gas, picking off missiles one after another, and a particle beam sliced across. A shape then abruptly cut the view short – a thousand feet of armour and weapons shaped like a giant flatworm. There was nothing stripped down about this attack ship. It hung there, hardfields flaring beyond it. On the side that Riss could see, the shuttle bay, a munitions-loading hatch and three other airlocks were opening.

'Time to leave, I think,' said the *Jacob* AI.

Blite

Blite had ten days to check and recheck coordinates, to tramp around the ship in a state of irritation, to rant at that antique space suit, which always seemed to feel unoccupied now, and fruitlessly to demand answers. The black AI simply did not respond. Blite remained baffled about the choice of destination until he recalculated, factoring in their temporal debt. Then he got frightened. Again, as they approached their new destination, he found himself aboard the bridge with Brond and Greer.

Brond was once again running his countdown, and Blite was perpetually telling him to shut up.

'Just twenty minutes now,' said Brond. 'Sorry.'

'Leven,' said Blite, 'I want a view towards Crispin Six when we surface. And I want our hardfields up at full strength then too.'

'What's up, Captain?' asked Greer.

He felt a surge of annoyance with her. She had the same data he had, so should have worked it out by now. Then he felt annoyed with himself. He had only worked things out in the last day. Should he tell them they might be about to be fried? No, he didn't think that was going to happen. Penny Royal had demonstrated that it could manipulate time, bend hardfields and feed off the energy of U-space. Penny Royal had demonstrated what Blite could only describe as godlike abilities. And it had kept them safe, or at least alive, so far. Still, the reasons for what was happening now were just as opaque to him as the black AI's recent theft. What it wanted with a massive cargo ship loaded with three runcibles was beyond him.

'Penny Royal is about to drop us right before the blast front of Crispin Six, which is going supernova,' he explained.

'And without hardfields,' Leven added.

'*What?*'

'The AI is not allowing me access to anything but sensors,' said the Golem ship mind. 'And as usual is offering no explanation.'

'A supernova?' said Brond.

'You know our coordinates,' said Blite. 'They put us two weeks, or thereabouts, behind that blast front . . . except, of course, we are now two weeks in the past.'

'And that puts us right on it,' said Brond flatly.

'This ship should be able to take it,' said Greer, with just a hint of doubt.

'Well it looks as if we're just about to find out,' said Blite, eyeing the counter at the bottom of the screen. 'Leven, I want EM readings for as far out as you can get them, all around us. Give me a frame bottom left for that. Can you deploy probes?'

'I'm allowed to do that.'

'Two of them then, at maximum acceleration in opposite directions – tangential to the blast front.'

'Will do – preparing them now.'

'Something you're not telling us, Captain?' Brond suggested.

'You'll see.'

No time remained for explanations as the counter plummeted to zero. Blite rattled his fingertips against the console before him. He was excited and just a little bit scared, but his earlier doubts about the wisdom of pursuing Penny Royal, of continuing to involve himself with the AI, were gone. He realized, not for the first time, that he was putting himself in danger but felt it was worth it. What was about to happen seemed a perfect example of it: the wonder and awe utterly dwarfing the risk.

'Here we go,' said Brond.

Blite suppressed his irritation at the man's need to run a commentary as the *Black Rose* slid out into the real. The grey of the screen laminate darkened and then blossomed with stars, one of them briefly circled and labelled as Crispin Six.

'Probes away,' said Leven.

Crispin Six looked perfectly normal just for a minute, then it steadily began to grow brighter as the light of its destruction started to reach them. It grew incredibly bright, its light glaring into the bridge. It also began to expand, growing as large and as bright as the sun seen from Earth, then growing duller as the screen automatically limited its emission to something that wouldn't burn out their retinas. But it continued to grow.

Blite feverishly studied the data down in that left-hand frame, as the nova blast filled the entire screen with its glare. All sorts of nasty radiation should be reaching them now, shortly followed by the particulate storm. Only it wasn't, and the glare from the screen abruptly turned a dark blood red. The lights in the bridge came back up to compensate.

'You tuned that down a bit too much, Leven,' said Brond.

'No I didn't.'

'What are the probes giving us?' Blite asked.

'Same as ship's sensors at the moment – and they're now eight hundred miles out too,' Leven replied.

'What the fuck is going on?' asked Greer.

'Entropy,' said Blite.

'Uh?'

'The probes just hit the blast front,' said Leven. 'Sending readings to the frame.'

Blite now studied the new numbers. The probes had simultaneously entered areas of space where the radiation would have turned a human being into a whiff of vapour in a microsecond. He doubted that his original ship could have survived that, but perhaps this reconfigured ship was different. The probes were doing okay, so they must have been reconfigured in turn.

'Data disrupting,' said Leven. 'I'm losing the probes.'

Ah . . .

'Perhaps time for an explanation?' suggested Brond. 'Before we die?'

'Okay,' said Blite, 'from that time jump, we were carrying entropy. Negative energy, part of the heat-death of the universe – call it what you will. Penny Royal managed to keep it under control while it was chatting with the king of the prador (and then incidentally stealing a cargo hauler laden with runcibles). But now it needs to dump it.'

'With you so far,' said Greer. Both she and Brond had probably indulged in the same VR games as Blite in their youth.

'Penny Royal has placed us in the path of a supernova blast front, directly between that front and a planetary system called Rebus. This has two living worlds, and on one is a human colony. The entropy dump is basically negating the blast here, sucking the energy out of it and extinguishing it.

The screen was still blood red, and now the data from the probes cut out. How long would they be here, Blite wondered? How long until all that negative energy they were carrying was gone? And would it be enough to wholly negate the blast here? He suspected it would be. Penny Royal wasn't known for its lack of planning.

'So let me get this straight,' said Brond. 'Penny Royal jumped back in time to have a chat with the king of the prador, then used the entropy incurred to blot out a supernova blast and incidentally prevent a human colony being fried?'

'That's it in essence,' Blite replied.

'Fuck a duck,' said Greer.

Blite leaned back and continued staring at the screen. Here was that awe and that wonder, and how nice to know that Penny Royal was so *altruistic*. However, the Polity had planned to evacuate this world anyway, which would have worked if the AI hadn't stolen the runcible gates the Polity had intended for that purpose. It seemed the AI was still cleaning up its own messes, though this time even as it made them. Its motives remained as cloudy as ever.

Trent

'We should all get out of here, now – that is, unless you *want* to be cored and thralled,' Trent urged.

'We're aboard a prador ship. Where are we going to go?' whined one of the three sitting on the other side of the cage. She was a mousy diminutive woman and she looked terrified. He could understand her fear, but could not understand the lack of a response from the two men. One of them looked like the kind of dodgy weasel Trent had been dealing with all his life. The other, the woman's husband, was the sort of shady businessman found in Carapace City. Both seemed like they would perfectly understand the situation, yet they were just staying put.

'Didn't you just hear what we were saying?' Trent waved a hand towards the prostrate Cole. 'We're at the mercy of the shell people, just waiting to be cored then enslaved. You know what your future is.'

'Not mine,' said the businessman, who was sweating heavily. 'Anyway, I believe none of this. Taiken has always been square and reasonable in his dealings. Even if he has gone over the edge, the others won't let him carry on.'

The guy was a coward, pretending he failed to understand. Trent focused on the weasel. 'What about you?'

The man gestured to the door. 'Do go ahead – I'll join you shortly.'

Trent assessed him in a moment. He would allow Trent to open up the cage but he'd then run, hide, try to survive. Maybe he would manage to do so. Did Trent have any right to force the issue?

'I'm going after Taiken,' said Trent. 'He's the key, because without him controlling them, the shell people will return to sanity.'

Wouldn't they?

Trent turned and headed over to the cage door, turning on the small shear. It was fashioned like a normal penknife, with a chain-glass blade that folded out. When turned on, it produced a molecular debonding field around its edge. He studied the cage lock for a moment. It was a simple mechanical kind with a bar engaging in a hole in its frame, the gap between door and frame sufficient. Inserting the blade, he pushed it down. The thing produced a high-pitched buzzing and just sat on the bar while the handle grew hot, then all at once it started going through, steel dust dropping from the cut. It then made a cracking sound and stopped. He'd burned it out.

'So we're not going anywhere,' said the catadapt.

Trent tried to pull the knife out, but it was stuck. He stepped back then, using all his heavy-worlder strength, he drove his boot against the door. He lashed out once, twice and then it sprang open.

'Yes we are,' he said, stooping to pick up the knife as he stepped through. He tried it again but the thing was dead. Still, the blade was chain-glass and very sharp, so he kept it. What now? Operating as he always had before, he would now try to obtain a more effective weapon. Next, he would sneak up on Taiken and simply put a burst of pulse-fire through his head. Even if his sensibilities towards violence had changed, he was clean out of other ideas.

'We need weapons,' he said. 'Any thoughts?'

'The shell people are armed.' The woman shrugged.

Trent gazed at the vessel full of leeches, then beyond it to a room he hadn't been able to see from the cage. Here sat a surgical chair with a pedestal autodoc poised beside it. Other equipment included a small rack, holding six ready-prepared thralling units. He must set this firm in his mind – it was what would happen to them if they just did nothing. Returning to the room containing the cage, he saw the weasel heading through the door into the corridor beyond; Trent followed. The catadapt woman quickly caught up with him, now carrying something she'd picked up in the surgery. It was the autodoc's jointed spare limb and looked heavy enough to serve as a club.

'Shit,' said the weasel.

He was out in the corridor ahead of them as one of the shell-men came round the far corner. This individual walked on four prador legs, but lacked the wide prador carapace. His torso, jutting up from the fore of a short-ribbed body, possessed one human arm, one claw and a perfectly normal head. The man had yet to wipe out his humanity by having mandibles attached to his face. But he still looked like some weird insect centaur. He reacted immediately, drawing a pepper-pot stunner and triggering it. The cloud of paralytic beads hit the weasel full in the face, some outliers striking Trent and the catadapt woman. Trent felt his cheek grow numb and saw her grabbing at her arm. The weasel went over like a falling log while the shellman ran forwards, correcting his aim for another shot.

Trent was momentarily at a loss, but then his training, conditioning and experience took over. The defunct shear knife was a weighty thing with its super-dense power supply in the handle, and the chain-glass blade was not only practically unbreakable but sharp enough to cut through steel – even without its debonding field. He had a split second to weigh it, judge the distance and throw, but no time at all to think of consequences. The knife whipped through the air with all his heavy-worlder strength behind it and went blade-first straight into the shellman's left eye. The man jerked back, his shot going up into the ceiling. His legs lost coordination and he collapsed on them, his torso still upright and the stunner skittering out of his grip. Reaching up with his human hand, he touched the nub of the handle protruding from his eye socket, his expression puzzled. Then with a sigh he slowly bowed over, scraping with his claw as if trying to clear something out of the way, until his forehead finally came to rest against the floor.

'Wow,' said the catadapt woman. She walked over and felt for a pulse at the shellman's neck, as a pool of blood spread out from his face. 'He's a gonner,' she added.

Trent gaped, facing the raw fact that he had killed in one fast unthinking action. He had wiped out a living human being and could never undo that, no matter how much he wished things had played out differently.

'Maybe he's got a memplant,' he managed.

The catadapt woman looked at him oddly as she reached over and picked up the stunner. As Trent walked over she pulled another weapon from the shellman's belt – a neat little pulse-gun.

'Here.' She held the weapon out. 'You'll do better with this than me.'

Trent accepted the thing and it felt familiar, easy, occupying his hand as if that was just the place for it. He stared at the thing, then down at the spreading blood.

'I can't do this,' he said.

'You seem pretty efficient to me,' said the catadapt.

He gazed at her. Perhaps they should swap weapons? No, even at a glance he could see that she wasn't familiar with the weapon she held. If they ended up in a firefight, she would be better with the spread of the stunner. She was his responsibility and if they didn't do this right, she would end up dead. He had to kill Taiken and remove the rot at the centre of this community.

Oddly, given that killing now sickened him and his conscience punished him for it, that seemed somehow right.

'Come on,' he said, stepping past the corpse and leading the way.

They reached a door and peered outside. Taiken's building was just across from them and two guards stood at the door. He guessed that there were others inside too and reckoned he would probably have to go through at least four or five of them before reaching the shellman himself.

'Ooh, nasty.'

Trent whirled and aimed. A figure was crouched over the corpse and trailing metal fingers in the blood. It held those fingers up before its ceramal skull and studied them.

'What the fuck?' The catadapt woman was pointing the stunner at this new arrival, which rather demonstrated how little she knew about the weapon and her prospective target.

'You,' said Trent.

The skeletal Golem, Mr Grey, stood, grinning, but then how could a metal skull have any other expression?

'You know this thing?' said the catadapt.

'It's the Golem that brought me here, in exchange for something from Sverl,' he replied. 'I don't know why he's here now.'

'I'm here to help,' said Grey simply.

'Do you know what's going on?'

'Oh yes, and so does Sverl,' said the Golem. 'The father-captain sent me down to assist you.'

'We'll knock Taiken out . . . capture him . . .'

Grey shook his head. 'No, no – you have to kill him.'

'Why?'

'The pheromone glands are in his body,' said Grey, 'and they stop producing as he dies. While he lives, his children will just fight to release him until they are all either dead or unconscious.'

Great.

'Would you kill him?' Trent asked, feeling disgusted with himself.

'If you ask me to,' said Grey.

'No Polity AI morality there, then,' said the woman.

Grey focused on her.

'Puss puss,' he said.

The catadapt woman looked at Trent, her expression horrified.

'Grey *was* a Penny Royal Golem . . .' he began, trying to explain.

'Stolman reactivated him.' She shrugged. 'Remember I was on the Rock Pool . . .'

'Yeah,' Trent agreed. 'Well, now he's independent.'

'Then use him, if he's offering,' she said. 'You know what's going to happen to us if Taiken stays in control here.'

Perhaps this was the easy way out after all. Then Trent didn't have to do any killing.

'Grey, I want you to go ahead of us. Disable any armed shellmen in our way and, when you reach Taiken . . . finish him.'

'Finish him?' Grey enquired.

Trent hesitated for a moment, trying to still the onset of the shakes. 'Kill him.'

'Okay.' Grey walked up to them and they stepped carefully out of his way. Then Grey was off, speeding across the intervening floor towards the two guards.

'Jesus,' said the woman.

Grey left the ground ten feet before the two guards and landed on one of them. They heard a cracking sound and the other guard turned. Before he could react, Grey was on him too. There was another crack, and something bounced across the floor.

'Come on!' Trent set out at a run.

Grey just went straight through the door, tearing it off its hinges as the two guards collapsed behind. As he ran over, Trent scanned the object lying on the ground. It was a human head, with mandibles. He gazed down at it in horror. He'd said *disable*, but Grey had his own interpretation of that.

'No! Don't kill them all!'

Trent headed in through the door and knew that having someone or *something* doing the killing for him did not relieve the guilt. Penny Royal had opened up his conscience and left it a raw and gaping wound.

Inside, another shellman was lying crumpled against one wall, his carapace shattered and internal muscle exposed, coughing up blood. He wasn't dead, but was certainly disabled. It was a matter of degree.

The door into Taiken's sanctum hung by one hinge and carnage was inside. Shell people lay scattered about on the floor. Someone was screaming repeatedly and others were groaning in agony. Taiken was thrashing about, the skeletal Golem on his back, its hands clamped on either side of his turret head. Almost as if he had been waiting for Trent to be present, Grey now turned that turret head – one full turn, and then another. He lifted the head away on a fountain of black blood as Taiken collapsed, and discarded it.

Trent walked woodenly into the room, watching some shellmen heaving themselves to their feet. Tilting their heads, if they could, and sniffing, if they had noses.

'All done,' said Grey cheerfully, shaking gobbets of flesh from his hands as he scrambled from Taiken's corpse. 'Now it gets sticky.'

At the dais, Trent paused. Everything seemed dark around him. He could see no way to escape his responsibility for the carnage. He raised the pulse-gun and gazed down the polished square-section barrel. Perhaps he had a way out after all.

'It will take a little while,' said Grey, 'but they'll do what prador children always do when they lose their father.'

'What?' Trent said numbly, lowering the weapon.

He tried to understand what Grey had said. Then a furore started behind him and he turned in time to see two shellmen, up unsteadily on their feet, snapping at each other with their claws. However, after a moment, they lost interest and began limping towards the exit. What did prador children do when their father died? They fought for dominance. They killed their brothers and sisters and the winner, once released from phero-monal control, turned into an adult.

'Mr Grey,' he said unsteadily. 'Get them out of here – we'll seal this area.'

'Of course,' said Grey, leaping up and striding over to a shellman who was dragging himself aimlessly across the floor, all his prador legs on one side broken.

'And do it without killing any of them,' Trent added.

What had he done? In an act of self-defence, he had ordered this Golem to kill Taiken. And now, as a direct result, all of the shell people would begin killing each other.

He turned to the catadapt. 'I don't know your name.'

'Sepia,' she replied, studying him curiously.

'See if you can get the other human survivors in here.'

'Really?' She raised an eyebrow, obviously annoyed by his peremptory attitude.

'Please,' Trent added.

'Okay.' She moved off.

Trent now began checking the building. Taiken had obvi-ously been as paranoid as any adult prador, because the doors did have a stratum of armour in them and he could secure them.

However, the shellman had not been thinking straight, because the walls were weak and vulnerable. When Trent saw the behaviour of some of the shell people Grey was driving out, he didn't think that would be a problem. They were occasionally aggressive to each other, but mostly disorientated. In one room, he found the woman and the boy he had seen earlier. The boy was prostrate on a bed, seemingly catatonic. The woman sat on a chair beside it, a smaller boy sleeping on her lap with his thumb in his mouth.

Trent stood in the doorway and stared. On seeing her close up, she no longer looked anything like his sister Genève. This woman before him with her cropped blonde hair and black make-up, her short wrinkled dress and petite form, looked like a waif. She suffered in comparison to women like Sepia, was more delicate and elfin. Yet in that moment Trent knew that he wanted her.

'Who are you?' he asked abruptly.

'Reece,' she replied. 'Taiken's widow.'

'I'm sorry—' Trent began, feeling his hopes dying stillborn.

'Don't be,' she interrupted. 'He would have killed us all.'

'Still . . .'

She stood up and put the younger child on the bed beside his brother, gazed down at her soiled dress, rubbed at one of the marks, then walked over to stand in front of Trent. The top of her head was level with his chest and he suddenly felt big, clumsy and far too dangerous to be this close to her.

'What's your name?' she demanded.

'Trent Sobel . . .'

'Well, Trent Sobel, Taiken was in the war, you know, but he didn't fight.' She studied Trent's face. 'He was on a team that had the difficult job of piecing together how prador society functioned. I met him fifty years after his work there had ended, and by then he had come to admire them.'

Trent didn't bother to point out how obvious that was, given Taiken's subsequent behaviour.

'I did love him,' she added.

'I'm sorry,' Trent repeated, not sure what else to say.

She shook her head in irritation then reached out and rested a hand against his chest. 'We're long past apologies, aren't we?' He found it difficult to meet her eyes. She continued, 'You will get us out of this, won't you?'

'I'll make sure you and your children are safe,' he promised, now sure he would sacrifice his life to that end.

'Good.' She reached up and grabbed his hair, pulled his head down and kissed him hard. He responded, reaching out to pull her closer, wishing there wasn't so much material between them. Finally, she drew back and he released her.

'Later,' she said, turning away to go back to her children.

12

Sverl

Sverl gazed at the snake drone locked in its clamps, and at the spine driven in through its mouth and deep into its body. Soon the data he required would be available, but he was still undecided about what to do with the drone next. His prador instinct was to obliterate the thing. However, his AI logic told him that it might yet be useful and was perhaps still part of Penny Royal's plans. His human side remained undecided, agreeing in part with each of the others. He allowed a painful memory to arise for his inspection, recalling that during his encounter with this very drone, he hadn't even seen it.

The battle had occurred some years after the attack on Factory Station Room 101 and over a small and lifeless Polity world. Sverl was then just getting used to his new dreadnought and had been enjoying carving up space stations abandoned by humans and AIs. Despite being unoccupied, the stations had been left with their weapons set on automatic. The Polity had also deserted a mining operation on the surface of that world and, if the AIs had been using their usual tactics in such a situation, he knew they had probably booby-trapped it.

The Polity had given up on this place since it wasn't essential to their war effort. And the prador had no real interest in acquiring it. This was why the prador ships on this mission were newly minted ones, with the father-captains aboard just trying out some manoeuvres on the space station. It had been, in essence, a training exercise. And it had therefore been puzzling, what with the Polity having abandoned this place, to have five attack ships fly out of a deep shaft carved into one of the moons. They then launched themselves in a suicidal attack against Sverl and his comrades . . .

The Prador/Human War: Sverl

The wide armoured wedge of the space station, now displayed on half of Sverl's array of screens, hurled up fusillades of railgun missiles from its upper face. It then fired particle beams through briefly opened gaps between the hardfields of its weakening defence. Sverl's crew scaled their own hardfields to block those beams. They then replied with beams of their own, as the space station again parted its fields to let missiles through. Those missiles eventually hit Sverl's defences and exploded into plasma. Meanwhile, the rockets he had fired some hours earlier had rounded the planet, entered atmosphere and were now approaching low over a mountain range. Of course, with an AI or human crew aboard the station, this ploy wouldn't have worked, but the automatics that had replaced them were particularly stupid.

Sverl turned his attention to the screens showing the approaching attack ships. They were accelerating, their formation loosening. Sverl's comrades, aboard two other dreadnoughts and four destroyers, were now breaking off to meet the new threat. When these ships had appeared, Father-Captain Vlex, commanding this mission, immediately contacted the rest. He communicated that here was a chance to follow the king's latest orders to the prador fleets. The war wasn't going as well as predicted, what with the Polity bringing new weapons and tactics into play. So capturing Polity technology for study was a priority.

Vlex wanted to capture attack ships. But Sverl wanted to finish off the space station.

'Full barrage in twenty seconds,' Sverl said, confirming an earlier order.

The missiles below were now accelerating up from the surface in two waves of six. The barrage from his ship commenced with railgun missiles pounding the station's screens, and bright blue particle beams carving across them. Sverl checked a counter, watched it zero, then saw it thrown into black silhouette as the first wave of missiles struck the station's defences. Now the station spewed burned-out field projectors from ejector ports, some even exploding directly through its hull. It was as he had thought when the station faced towards him when he arrived: its defence was directional. His second wave of attack struck; nearly all its missiles got through this time. The station bucked as the weapons flared, then dissolved in multiple explosions. Sverl immediately turned his ship; his manipulatory hands locked into saddle controls. Then, with a stab of one claw in a pit control, he fired up his fusion drive – its torch eating up any debris coming his way.

Moving out to join one flank of his fellow ships, Sverl saw the Polity craft coming straight in, breaking formation to go after all of the prador ships. He immediately realized something wasn't right. Usually a group like this would focus their attack on a viable target – like one of the destroyers. They'd hit it with everything they had, while sowing space with EM chaff. Then, faced with three dreadnoughts, they'd U-jump away.

'Distribute EM mines,' he instructed.

A lone ship came directly towards him, releasing a fusillade of railgun missiles. Sverl didn't need to order the intercepting hardfields and watched the whole attack wasted against their shielding. He anticipated some clever manoeuvre next, as would be expected from the kind of AI such a ship should contain. But instead the ship charged straight into the EM mines sown directly in its path. One of them detonated, too close to his own craft, the flash briefly knocking out cam images and causing outages even in Sverl's sanctum aboard his dreadnought. When imagery returned, the Polity attack ship's weapons and fusion drive had shut down as it hurtled on in, dead.

Sverl decided then that this had to be the Polity, in desperation, copying the prador and using attack ships as kamikazes. They had to contain some massive CTD explosives. Rapidly turning his ship to fling it aside on fusion drive, he put his hardfields out to their furthest extent. In the unlikely event that this wasn't a kamikaze, he heeded the king's new orders and fielded the ship in them rather than let it obliterate itself against them. He next caused it to decelerate in a long arc around his ship, expecting that detonation at any moment.

No detonation.

'Something odd about this,' said Vlex.

Sverl checked tactical data and saw that he and his comrades had captured all but one of the attack ships. The one demolished Polity craft had gone after a destroyer that was maintaining a close orbit around the world below. The prador ship killed it with an EM mine but didn't have hardfields strong enough to slow it down, so it merely moved aside. The rising cloud of fire from the planet's surface marked its crash site.

'I suggest we deep scan before bringing them aboard,' Vlex added.

Still holding the apparently dead vessel at a distance, Sverl probed it with his sensors and discovered at once that it contained no U-space drive. Updates from his fellows showed that all four remaining attack ships were without such drives. This accounted for them not fleeing but didn't explain their other odd behaviour. He fired off a sensor probe next and tracked its rapid approach then deceleration down onto the attack ship. It thumped home on the hull and drove in exotic metal scythe legs. Scan results immediately began to pour in, revealing a fusion reactor in safe shutdown, as with the previous scan. But it also showed that it was of the usual Polity design and therefore incapable of exploding. The fusion drive, its electronic controls scrambled, had scrapped itself. The thing was radioactive but no real danger. The ship's weapons cache was empty but for a few railgun missiles. There were no humans or human remains aboard. All the robots were dead, even including microbots and nanobots. In addition, its AI crystal was shattered. He couldn't find anything too dense to probe or anything shielded that might be concealing something nasty. It was a puzzle.

'Biological attack,' said Vlex. 'Check those remaining railgun missiles.'

Update from one of the other dreadnoughts – something had been found.

Sverl focused his sensor probe on the Polity missiles and detected only inert iron with a ceramal nose cone. He then ran a penetration program based on a previous seizure of Polity technology. It took an hour before the program found a chink in the chameleonware, and then that disguise unravelled. In the iron was a super-dense shield, capable of blocking the output of an EM mine. In the hollow interior resided a gyroscopic device that had turned the missile, so that the shield faced the exploding mine. This had prevented the EM mines they had used from crashing the chameleonware in the missile. Another device in the missile was using a diamond drill to steadily bore a small hole out to the exterior. The rest of the hollow contained a soup of organics.

'Got it,' said Sverl.

They spent a further five days checking the rest of the attack ships for anything else concealed under chameleonware and discovered further biological weapons – some even hidden in the fusion reactors. Sverl finally sent armoured second-children aboard his capture to isolate the weapons, for now it was essential to take them back to the Kingdom so prador biologists could design an antidote. His children then opened the ship to vacuum, closed it again and spent many hours spraying a standard bio-weapon sterilizer throughout. Using his saddle control, Sverl personally aimed and fired a cable grab. The exotic metal claw cut into the hull like the scythe legs of the probe, and Sverl hauled the ship in. He brought it into an empty hold, then through into a total-seal annex. There he secured it. He didn't know then that such a precaution was too late, for the real biological weapon had hitched a ride on the armour of one of the second-children and was already aboard.

Sverl knew when it happened. They had just finished up with the world, destroying the remaining space stations and dropping a bomb on the factory complex. Safely ensconced within his sanctum, checking his ship's status and readiness to leave, he had been surprised when his sanctum door malfunctioned. A circuit had blown, which opened it just the width of his claw. A short while later he felt a sudden horrible pain at the base of one of his legs, and a sudden atavistic fear. He did not comprehend his own alarm and its source in prador evolution, and had he but enquired of his children, he would have discovered that many of them had been experiencing both that pain and that fear too. He did not ask. Father-captains never asked after the health of their children. Shaking himself and still feeling a little spooked, he traced the blown circuit, then the fault that had stopped the backup system kicking in. With the door closed again, his fear faded.

Sverl only learned later that Vlex had had a similar experience, as had the father-captain of the other dreadnought that had taken onboard one of the Polity attack ships. All three dreadnoughts had also developed one other mechanical fault, different in each case. Sverl's ship had, for no immediately traceable reason, opened and closed an airlock. Vlex's ship, when it was finally sterilized, was found to have inadvertently fired off a probe before it dropped into U-space. The other captain's ship, again for no apparent reason, dumped the contents of a water tank out into vacuum.

They headed back to the Kingdom with their captures and during that journey, Sverl got lucky, insomuch as he found out what had really come aboard. He could therefore take steps to counter it. Like all father-captains, his lack of regard for his children was vicious. During the journey, his main first-child began to show immunity to the chemical suppression of his adulthood. Sverl summoned him to his sanctum, where a hemisphere surgical telefactor awaited. He'd also brought a brain case in which to install the first-child's ganglion – which was destined to control an armoured ground-assault vehicle.

The child came, reluctantly, its legs quivering. Still possessing his own claws and much mobility, Sverl enjoyed an hour with the child, tearing off its legs and claws. But he was surprised and disappointed at its lack of resistance and how quickly it weakened. He then quickly used a circular saw to cut open its carapace. He had intended to dine on some of the living organs before the first-child showed signs of weakening. However, he now decided to use the telefactor to remove its ganglion at once, before it died. What he found when he opened its shell sent him staggering away in horror.

Something had injected parasite eggs into the first-child, which had hatched out into their juvenile form. The short translucent worms were feeding inside, chewing and digesting connective tissue and depositing a chalky substitute in its place. Sverl did not know what they were, but his fear and horror drove him to research. He soon identified his find and knew that the juvenile worms were at that point in their development where they were about to start dividing, penetrating the first-child's gut and then exiting via its rectum. They would then feed on ship lice until they grew to adult form and mated, moving on to infect other prador. Meanwhile the first-child would steadily weaken as the expanding population inside it moved from connective tissue to muscle. Left finally immobile, it would die as the parasites progressed to their final repast on its major organs, before departing an empty shell.

Sverl understood at once what had happened. This bio-horror had been the real weapon those otherwise empty attack ships had contained. The others had been concealed just enough to be believable. Almost certainly, some sort of assassin drone had deployed the parasite. It had blown the circuit of his sanctum door control, and the pain he had experienced had been it actually injecting parasite eggs. And, checking ship's logs, Sverl realized that the airlock malfunction had been the assassin drone departing.

Sverl considered his options while completely failing to consider the worms that had begun to grow inside him. He knew that upon his imminent arrival in the Kingdom he would be dead if his fellow prador did not see him countering this threat. He also prepared a report on his situation, and the drastic action he was taking.

He ordered a party of second-children to move twenty iron-burner mines to a hold and remain there with them. Then he ordered the rest of his crew, his children, to that same hold. He sealed all the exits, and next sent his small but growing collection of war drones out of their cache to them, just in case. Then, the moment his dreadnought surfaced into the real in the Kingdom, he sent the detonation code. The mines fired up, super-compressed oxygen and hydrocarbons burning slowly but raising the hold temperature quickly to four thousand degrees. The children barely had time to run and pile themselves up at the firmly sealed doors. By the time the fires went out, nothing remained but brittle chunks of charred carapace. He opened the space doors and the ensuing explosive decompression blew most of the mess out into vacuum.

Next, Sverl completely isolated his sanctum and instituted a bio-attack protocol. Airlocks and space doors opened to vacuum all around his ship, blowing out its internal atmosphere. When the doors closed, canisters of highly toxic and acidic gas flooded everything but his sanctum. By now, prador Command was desperately trying to get in contact, demanding a response. The destroyers were all responding, but none of them had taken aboard attack ships. The other two dreadnoughts were just dead and adrift. Sverl sent his report and the response was swift – dreadnoughts moving in to bracket him, weapons doubtless ready to fire.

'This is not new,' one of the surrounding father-captains told him, and sent data on other similar attacks. He gazed upon captured images of the assassin drones that had done this and shuddered to the core of his being. Studying further reports, he understood that his fellows would not destroy his ship, because they could not waste such a valuable piece of hardware. However, they would not help him either. He was in quarantine until he dealt with this, as had some other father-captains. If he did not, when he finally expired, armoured prador would come aboard to sterilize his ship fully in readiness for another captain.

After studying the data from father-captains who had

survived, Sverl sent new orders to his war drones and watched them set out through his ship. They were scanning for certain organics and using lasers to incinerate parasite encystments in living quarters, food supplies and water tanks. He next focused on his two females in their mating pool and regretfully routed the full output from a fusion reactor through superconducting cables to the heat grids. By the time he picked up a laser cutter from his tool cache, fired it up, set it to wide beam and incinerated the remains of his first-child, the water in their pool was boiling. By the time he had searched his own sanctum and burned up the three flattened egg-shapes of parasite encystments, the females were dead and coming apart, while superheated steam was ejecting from their pool, straight out through a port in the side of his ship.

Sverl returned to the data and set up the long series of sterilizations, atmosphere ejections, drone sweeps and the robotic dismantling of equipment to clean it inside. He also ejected and incinerated other equipment he could never classify as clean. This would take many months, but he would need many months to recover. He was now feeling weak and ill. Pus was leaking from his joint sockets, he kept coughing out green slime from his lung and one of his palp eyes was going blind. And he finally admitted to himself what he had long been avoiding: those things were inside him and he had to get them out. He ordered one of his war drones to collect another iron-burner and place it in the smaller abode that his first-child had occupied. The ensuing burn ensured nothing remained alive in there.

Sverl next reluctantly inspected the program those other captains had run through their surgical telefactors, and loaded it to his own. The telefactor returned to its niche to load with extra supplies, then came out again, followed by two secondary surgical robots resembling brass ship lice. Shortly after them came a grav-sled piled with blood and chyme bottles, cylinders of artificial carapace mix, collagen-foam tanks and dehydrated artificial muscle. They came with hundreds of yards of tubing and a big armour-glass disposal tank.

Opening up his sanctum, Sverl headed out and down to the now burned-out and sterile quarters. He settled himself in the middle of the space with the controls of the telefactor before him and stared at them for a long while, utterly reluctant to start. However, he finally forced himself to reach out with one claw and stab it into a pit control to set the program running. The motivator was the definite feeling of something moving about under his shell.

The telefactor slowly revolved as Sverl moved back and settled on the burned floor. It extended a drill on one of its multiple limbs and drove it in beside one of Sverl's mandibles as one of the secondary robots unreeled spare tubing. The factor then worked round him, making more and more holes, and began inserting tubes, cutting all the while. The pain grew steadily, ramped up with the application of a carapace saw. It also died in places where nerve blocks went in. Sverl issued a bubbling scream as the factor folded back a large section of his main shell, but the agony waned as electricity crackled and paralysis spread through him. He could not stop it now. He felt the drone of a cutter behind his visual turret before it tipped over so he was looking into his own gullet – a view usually impossible for a prador. He smelled burning, wanted to scream again but couldn't, then his usual view returned as the telefactor tipped his turret back into place.

Now he saw one of the secondary robots dragging one of the worms away and dropping it into the disposal vessel. He saw pieces of his carapace lying on the floor, their insides etched with worm burrows. The other secondary robot began collecting these and dropping them in the vessel too. Despite nerve block-ing and a cornucopia of prador painkillers, Sverl lost himself in agony when the factor extracted a great mass of worm-eaten muscle. Unconsciousness, something humans experienced, was not possible for his kind, but the extreme pain did kill coherent thought. He came back to some comprehension of his surround-ings some time later, to see a second disposal vessel in place, the other one now full. Agony took him again as the factor removed one of his claws.

And so it went on . . . and on . . .

Sverl finally began to get some intimation that the surgery was ending when he saw the dehydrated muscle being hydrated in a long tray and heard the hissing of a collagen-foam gun. His entire body felt like a raw wound and the pain stayed at a point that seemed just beyond his tolerance, but which he helplessly endured nevertheless. One plus point was that vision had re-turned to his blind eye and some of the paralysis was receding, so that he could move both palp eyes. He looked down to see his claw, pulled out from his body on stretched tendons, veins and nerves opened up. Artificial muscle was being woven in to replace what had been extracted, and he finally saw that claw go back into place – that smell of carapace glue was the best thing ever.

More glue and then the sound of a shell welder, a mixing drum turning to make replacement carapace. Sverl began to come fully back to himself and could now think clearly enough to know that the program was ending. However, he lost concen-tration and it was some time before he realized that all the machines were now stationary around him.

Sverl stood, shakily. He felt terrible: even slow movement was agony and seemed to tear things inside him. He knew that if he moved any faster and exerted any effort at all, then some-thing critical would break.

But it was all over. All he needed to do now was recover. He would have to request food supplies from prador in the other ships, since he had incinerated all his own. He needed to eat now, convalesce, build up his strength, barter for replacement females, rebuild his family . . .

But the worst was over.

Or so he thought.

The Sverl of the present turned away from the immobile assassin drone and walked over to one of his work surfaces. There, he selected a metal collar packed with esoteric tech. He would ignore the prador in him for now and not find some ugly end for Riss. He would, however, be all prador if the drone tried anything.

Spear

In my mind's eye, I saw the *Jacob* accelerate away from Factory Station Room 101. It was leaking white-hot smoke from burned-out hardfield projectors and from the many holes punched through its hull as it dodged missiles and the sweep of energy weapons. Crippled and burning ships tumbled through vacuum all around it, newborn minds being snuffed out in the virtual like embers tossed into a pool. I gazed through the *Jacob*'s sensors and could see the salmon-pink hypergiant sun that Room 101 was now orbiting. Also open to me was the entire reach of the surrounding complex planetary system, which lay beyond human vision. I saw a red dwarf orbiting the hypergiant and a gas giant that once a millennium took a figure-of-eight course. I gazed upon an immense asteroid belt formed mainly of CO_2 and nitrogen ice, and saw this was currently being disturbed. A small black hole was punching through it on its fast orbit around the hypergiant. And I saw green-belt worlds, with the evidence etched on their faces that the Jain civilization had been here.

'*Got it,*' said a satisfied voice.

The galactic coordinates were clear in my mind as finally, amazingly, the *Jacob* managed to engage its U-jump engine. But who had spoken? And what had that individual found? I refocused my attention inside the ship, where the mantis and I were crammed. Along with other drones, we had ended up in a scrapyard mass inside the attack ship's hold. I felt claustrophobic yet was simultaneously aware of clear space all around me. How could this be? It seemed dimensionally distorted – and what the hell was that?

The equally distorted prador loomed over me, mandibles grinding. Room 101 had forged me to kill such creatures, but I had not yet managed to perform this task. However, the instinct was there inside me, as deep rooted as in any organic being. Even though I had no eggs, I flipped myself under the prador ready to drive my ovipositor up into its underside . . . and fell flat on my face.

'Thorvald,' said the prador first-child Bsectil, looking down at me. 'Thorvald Spear.'

I rolled over and tried to flip my ovipositor up again, but instead I found myself gazing up at a pair of booted feet as Bsectil backed away.

'What are you doing?' the first-child asked curiously.

I had no parasite eggs loaded but my knowledge of prador physiology was the best it could be. I could certainly mess up a few nerve nexuses with my ovipositor, which should leave it paralysed. Then I could make mincemeat of its major ganglion. I squirmed along the floor after it, but the movement felt strangely alien and wrong. Something was awry with my grav and my body. I must have been damaged in some—

'Sverl said you would feel some confusion at first,' Bsectil observed.

Sverl.

It was Sverl who'd said *got it* in my head. And, remembering him, I found the dawning reality now facing me somewhat stranger than the one I had just experienced. I stopped squirming across the floor after Bsectil, rolled over and sat up. I had to use my stomach muscles to do so, because I'd temporarily forgotten how to use my arms. I knew at once what had happened. Sverl had penetrated Riss's memories using Penny Royal's spine, and my connection to the spine had dragged me into that replay. But that didn't stop me feeling intensely embarrassed. Finally remembering how to use my arms, I pushed against the floor and stood up.

'So the replay worked. Sverl now knows the location of Room 101,' I said.

'He does,' said Bsectil. 'And after one further stop we will be heading straight there.'

I checked the activity back at my ship and saw two second-children lowering Flute's case from the hole in the side, power supply attached. I checked the channel that connected me to my ship mind, thankfully now devoid of fizzing.

'Flute?'

'I am dead,' the mind replied.

'What do you mean?' I asked, but no reply was forthcoming.

'Do you now wish to see Trent Sobel?' Bsectil asked.

'Yes, why not?'

Bsectil led off again, out of the hold and through the corridors of the ship. During the journey, which lasted a good half-hour, I fully recovered my humanity and was able to separate Riss's memories out of my mind. I also began to get more of a sense of the sheer scale of this dreadnought, and it occurred to me to wonder why the prador had never used dropshafts in their ships. The creatures were, after all, much better adapted than humans to such a form of transport. Finally, we reached the area where Sverl had housed the shell people.

'I will leave you here,' said Bsectil, as the door parted.

'I'd rather you didn't.'

'You will be safe, so my father says,' said the first-child, turning away and moving off.

I took him at his word and entered, the door closing behind me. I immediately smelled smoke and saw a pillar of it rising from the encampment ahead. As I walked towards this, I saw a shellman lying on the ground, prador limbs torn away and his human throat opened. There were also figures milling aimlessly around the burning building from which the smoke was rising. A radically altered human shambled over to me – a shellwoman who had retained her human form but was armoured head to foot. And she just stopped, facing me. She looked dull and confused.

'Father?' she said, then emitted a strange grating sound from her throat.

I gazed across at the others. They all seemed just as disoriented but, while I watched, two shellmen squared off and started snapping at each other with their claws.

'Give it,' said the shellwoman.

I wasn't sure how to respond.

'Over here,' called a voice.

I glanced across to see a catadapt leaning out from behind another building.

'Just ignore her and walk over here,' she added. 'Nice and calm.'

I turned and did as bid, noting the two fighting shellmen losing interest in each other mid-fight and just wandering off.

Now focusing back on the catadapt, I paused, glanced down at my nascuff. I realized I hadn't reset it since my rather torrid encounter with Gloria Markham on Masada. I looked at the catadapt again. She was gorgeous. My inner reptile brain was laughing and pointing out how I didn't see that one coming.

'What the hell is going on here?' I asked the catadapt as I reached her.

'Wait a minute.' She raised one hand – one strong, tanned and quite beautiful hand, cat claws protruding. In the other hand, she held a pepper-pot stunner, which she aimed over my shoulder.

I turned. The shellwoman was close, staring at me intently as if trying to figure something out. After a moment, she winced in pain and then thumped the palm of her armoured hand against her head. When she lowered her hand she looked dull again, distracted. Then she turned and ambled off.

'Come on,' said the catadapt. 'I'll leave the explanations to Trent.'

'Sure,' I said, admiring the shape of her back and then her arse as she turned and led off. Then I sighed, followed, and tried to think like an adult rather than a hormonal teenager. However, the woman ahead was a problem. In the Polity, even in my years before and during the war, it was possible to make yourself into any shape you chose. Most people, of course, chose to be beautiful. It was something one enjoyed over the passing decades and eventually became inured to. The basis of physical attraction then slid into another more complicated realm, based on experiences and minutiae difficult to define. Was my reaction to this woman somehow connected to my experience with Sheil Glasser, soon after I awoke from my memplant? She had been a catadapt, after all. No, it wasn't that – I just didn't know what it was. This woman was beautiful – who wasn't? – but something about her just grabbed me by the throat.

She led me through the encampment, where similar scenes to the ones I'd just witnessed were playing out. Forcing a retreat to a colder portion of my mind, I studied all those around me and remembered Sverl's words. I saw the shell people suffering under ill-made transformations that would eventually kill them, just like Vrit – the shellman from whom I had bought Flute. I saw also that there had been fighting because scattered around there lay dismembered corpses. One of these was the body of a normal man, his severed head lying a few yards away.

The catadapt gestured at it. 'He thought he would do better alone.'

'That didn't work out, I take it,' I commented.

'It didn't work out for two others either, who stayed in the cage where we'd all been kept. Though Rider Cole survived.' She looked at me, then, really looked at me. 'I suspect Trent knocking him out saved his life.'

It always annoyed me when someone made an assumption about what I might know, especially when I really didn't have the facts. Was she trying to establish a connection with me? In irritation, I dismissed the thought and decided not to make any more enquiries.

The catadapt finally brought me to a larger central building and rapped on a door.

'Sepia,' she said. It sounded like a password, but obviously wasn't.

A frightened-looking woman with cropped blonde hair opened the door, then quickly closed it behind us as the catadapt led me through. I found Trent Sobel sitting at a console in some ersatz captain's sanctum, looking tired and utterly defeated.

Glancing round, I watched the catadapt heading off with the other woman. So the catadapt's name was Sepia.

'Thorvald Spear,' said Trent, standing as I approached. 'I should kill you.' He shrugged, shook his head, then reached up to finger that earring of his.

'Trent Sobel,' I said, 'I find you in an odd situation, and I was told that you might need my help.'

He glanced to what I had first taken to be some piece of wrecked equipment, beside the dais at the centre of the sanctum. I realized I was seeing a large skeletal Golem, with some kind of organic-looking tech wrapped around it. It was sitting on the floor with its head bent down between its knees. I took a steady breath. Time to really focus . . .

'Taiken took control of the shell people in the same way a father-captain controls his children,' Trent explained. 'I had that –' he pointed at the Golem – 'kill Taiken because it was our only option. The man wanted us to either become shellmen or face thralling. Taiken's death released the shell people from hormonal control, but now they're behaving like prador adolescents after the death of their father and beginning to kill each other.'

'And why do you care?' I asked, cold now.

'It seems my path to redemption is here,' he said.

'Redemption?'

He stood up. 'Come with me.'

He led me into a small room provided with a bed, a table, some chairs and jury-rigged computing. It looked recently outfitted – clearly Trent's little hideaway. He found a bottle of whisky and two glasses and brought them over.

'Taiken's stock,' he explained, 'though I wonder how many years it has been since he enjoyed it.' He sat and poured. I joined him, and remembered sharing whisky with him and his partner aboard the *Moray Firth* – the glasses tainted with the prions I had later used to shut down their nervous systems.

He explained how Penny Royal had saved him aboard the wreck of that vessel and the AI's subsequent instruction. He then related the rest of his story, and I began to understand Sverl's attitude to the black AI's manipulations. We were just pieces in some complex puzzle. But to what purpose? I had no idea of the overall shape, but felt a strong intimation that this jigsaw of human lives and deaths was the only kind of game that would keep the AI sufficiently interested, engaged. My own part in it remained unclear. On Masada, Penny Royal had provided me with intimate evidence of its own guilt, so my role seemed to be that of executioner. However, on my route to some final encounter with the AI, it seemed I must remain engaged in the game.

'So you want to help the shell people,' I suggested.

'I do now.'

'Because now you are no longer a villain?'

'Because empathy is a painful gift.'

'A conscience is too.'

'I guess.' He sipped his whisky.

'*Sverl,*' I said, communicating through my aug, '*I'm going to need equipment and access to some heavy processing.*'

'*If you could elaborate . . .*' Sverl replied.

I put together a shopping list in my aug and transmitted it. Some of the items were very new and it seemed unlikely Sverl would have them, but it was worth a try. Just half a second later, the list came back, most of the items crossed out.

'*I can provide some of the equipment, but I am sending Riss,*' said Sverl. '*As for the processing, that has been available to you since you acquired your destroyer, with additional functionality since I allowed you to connect into my system.*'

'*And you're sending Riss?*' I questioned, not inspecting too closely what he meant by that 'available processing'.

'*Perhaps it is because I have been changed by Penny Royal itself, that I now see the patterns it follows,*' said Sverl. '*You could not possibly get all the equipment you require up and running in time to be effectual. The shell people are beginning to kill each other even now. And in a short time, because they are not having the medical treatment they constantly require just to stay alive, they will all begin dying.*'

'But why Riss?'

'*The drone is part of the answer, and the other is one easily within your reach.*'

'Why can't you just tell me?'

'*Because I don't need to.*'

Sverl stated the words with finality and when I tried getting in contact with him again, he blocked me. Instead, I concentrated on fully exploring my connection into the father-captain's system. To Trent I said, 'I can probably return many of these people to their base human format. Free them from prador pheromone control and thereby free you from that responsibility.'

'What?' he said, gaping at me.

'Physical damage can be reversed or repaired. We are, after all, dealing with some relatively primitive adaptations, grafts and alterations of body chemistry.'

Trent stared at me for a moment, then said, 'Like you could reverse or repair what was happening to Isobel?'

'These are not one of Penny Royal's transformations.'

He nodded, but he looked a bit less beaten now. I continued, 'However, as Sverl just pointed out to me, that's not our main problem. They are fighting even now and not keeping up with the constant interventions they need to keep themselves alive. So we have little time.' I paused. 'We need something now.'

'What?'

'I'm thinking about it.'

By now, with the larger part of my mind and my augmentation, I was deep in Sverl's computer system. I had made a place for myself and was there uploading stencil programs for the design of nano-machines, complex enzymes, adaptogens and the whole human toolbox of physical transformation at the microscopic and sub-microscopic levels. I had also discovered another body of work in there: Bsectil and Bsorol's combined research. This looked into reversing the damage to them and the second-children caused by being chemically maintained in adolescence for so long. This work wasn't barred to me, and I soon found stuff in there I could use.

'So how do we get started?' Trent asked.

'Taiken must have equipment here,' I said. 'I'll need to make some initial examinations and assessments.'

'I'll show you.' Trent stood up, suddenly energized. I followed him as he moved from his sanctum to an annex containing a surgical theatre. As we entered, I caught myself looking round for any sign of Sepia.

'Will this do?' Trent asked.

It would do for examinations and surgery, and equipment was available for assembling bio-molecules and other organic items. It wasn't the best, but then, according to Sverl, I didn't need the best right now. I just wished I knew what the hell I was going to do.

'It'll do until other equipment arrives,' I said, turning away and walking back out into the sanctum.

Just then, the frightened-looking woman came in through one of the doors, dragging a child behind her. After her came Sepia, armed with a stunner and looking like a warrior maid out of some VR fantasy to me.

'Trent,' said Sepia. 'We might have a problem.' She backed away from the door, pointing her stunner towards it.

'I'm never a problem,' said a familiar voice.

Riss came through the door, squirming like a snake but a couple of feet above the floor. I noted that she now wore a collar about her neck, heavy ceramic with inset controls. Next, she lowered her ovipositor to the floor and seemed to balance on it while opening her black eye.

'We're going to Station 101,' said the drone, with a hint of craziness in her voice that I didn't like. 'And you know what that means?'

'What does it mean, Riss?'

'Eggs!' she exclaimed. 'I can get eggs!'

After living for a brief time in that snake skin, I now understood perfectly what she meant. And that made me like her crazy tone even less. I felt, just for a moment, as if the madness of Room 101 was already reaching out to us here. Perhaps it was my hormones.

'Oh good,' I said. 'And apparently you are part of an answer I require.'

'Just tell me what to do,' said Riss, which was no help at all.

After a brief, embarrassed pause, Trent said, 'Perhaps you can start here.'

I turned to see that the frightened woman was standing close to him, one hand possessively on his arm. He was pointing at the child, who could not have made the choice to have his arm removed and replaced by a claw.

'Yes,' I said, 'that's where I'll start.'

Cvorn

Eager to make the most of the new feelings rising within him, Cvorn wanted to reach his females. He watched impatiently as the first door of the water lock revolved into the wall, spilling fluid from the last time it had been used. The door seals in prador ships were never foolproof, because they had no need to be so. Prador could withstand large changes in atmospheric pressure and losses of air or, in this case, water. And they could easily obtain more from ice asteroids or comets. Cvorn peered at the water running into the gratings about his feet in irritation, but considered how the ship systems reclaimed it anyway. Analysing the feeling, in an attempt to divert his mind from other urges surging through his body, he realized he now disliked an inefficiency he had previously ignored. After fitting his aug, his thinking was tighter, more factual, and his awareness of shortfalls like this was growing. When he was done here, he would set his children and the ship's robots to work to improve this type of thing.

When he was done here . . .

Once inside the water lock, he found the manual environmental controls, then tried to locate them via his aug through the ship's system. Someone had disconnected them, which was odd – more work for his children and robots. Perhaps the problems with this lock were due to infrequent use – he was only using it because he wanted quick direct access to the pool rather than using the chamber above. Through his aug, he set the door behind him closing. As it grated home, circular hatches opened in the wall by his feet, water immediately gushing in. Cvorn hyperventilated in preparation. As a male prador, he could survive underwater for a long time and probably didn't need the

324

extra oxygen in his system. But underwater, it was not good if you had to untangle from a female quickly because you were running out of air – that was when the worst injuries occurred.

Next, he tried mentally to locate the automatics for the inner door, but they weren't in the system either. The water rose quickly and he shivered when it reached his sensitive prongs and coitus clamp. *Damn*. He glanced at the environmental control, reached out with his claw and tapped the temperature up a little way, feeling further irritated when he noted how high the scale could go. This was not only inefficient but dangerous, because if that control was accidentally shifted up to its top sterilizing setting, the females would end up boiled alive in their pool.

The water rose up over his carapace and finally over his visual turret. But before it reached the ceiling of the water lock, an indicator rattled in the fluid to tell him he could open the inner door. He slammed his prosthetic claw against a large impact control on one wall. Such a large, heavy button here to operate the lock was understandable, because any prador here could be in such a state it might end up wrecking something less durable. However, he was finding he enjoyed the newly extended power offered by his aug to control his surroundings mentally. He decided he must do something about that impact control too.

The inner door opened at last into the murk of the mating pool and Cvorn propelled himself out, ready to swim over to the far side. On his previous viewing, he had seen that one of the females had separated herself from the others. The three other females had gathered in the middle around the feeding pillar. He hoped to get past them, and get on with his business before they detected him. However, he hadn't taken his prosthetic legs and claws into account, for they immediately dragged him down.

He hit the bottom with a heavy crump that the other females would have certainly detected through the floor of the pool. He quickly headed to his left, sticking close to the wall in the hope of circumventing them. He could now just see the feeding pillar and the humped shapes gathered around it. They were all rising up on their legs and he could hear the harsh clatter of their powerful far-reaching mandibles through the water. He could also *taste* their readiness for mating and feel the skittering of their ovipositors against the floor. In fact, if he had just waited a little longer, they would have abandoned the pool for the chamber above, where it would have been much easier to hunt them down.

Soon he saw the isolated female ahead, but she was now moving away from the wall and quickly heading towards her companions. Cvorn swerved to intercept her, coming in from the side, and tried to close a claw on the edge of her carapace. She turned slightly as she fled, and one mandible shot out sideways, clanging against his claw and knocking it away. He'd forgotten that trick. It had, after all, been a long time.

The female now joined her three fellows, who all turned to face him. Cvorn halted and gazed at them, remembering how some of his contemporaries had surgically crippled their females by removing their mandibles. Others had ensured the females had guards affixed over their ovipositors, to prevent them being used as a weapon during mating. Still others had even had their females locked into body cages that prevented any movement at all, making mating a completely risk-free exercise. Cvorn, however, was of the old school. He understood the evolutionary imperative that made females so hostile towards the males that wanted to mate with them. It was because only the strongest, most aggressive and most resilient males should be able to reproduce. But that wasn't why he preferred his females to be free-ranging. He'd tried confined or crippled females and it just wasn't the same. Violent sex was much more satisfying.

Cvorn advanced, singling out the one to his left for his attention, then rushed for the gap between that one and the others. The nearest one to his right stabbed out her mandibles but Cvorn intercepted them with his claw, where they hit with a loud thump. Meanwhile, the one on his left shot out her mandibles in turn and tried to get a grip on two of his forelegs – trying to tear them off. Cvorn threw himself sideways to push into the gap, his excitement rising and his coitus clamp clattering against his body. The left female's grip slid off the metal of his prosthetic legs, failing to tear them away, so firmly were they affixed to his body.

The female on the far right threw herself up over her companions. She folded her body, louse-like, and drove her ovipositor towards his visual turret. He knocked the thing down, but still it punched in at the base of one of his mandibles. The pain was terrible, but only increased his excitement. He axed his claw down into her underside, cracking ribs of carapace there, and she rolled away, issuing a stream of green blood. His target female now tried to turn her back end away from him, but he grabbed the edge of her carapace with his other claw and dragged her back, while slicing his legs down upon the eyes of the adjacent female. She retreated just a little, and he turned his upper shell towards her and rammed her, while still hanging on to his prospective mate. His target went over, onto her back, her legs rowing defensively. On the rebound, he swung round behind his mate and slammed his back end in.

His coitus clamp hit its receiving grooves and lodged firmly as he climbed up onto her back. He now closed his claws on her mandibles, wrapped his legs round her and pulled himself down tightly. She fought him as he heaved mightily, while the other two females, recovering, pounded him with their mandibles to try to dislodge him. The shield-like section of shell protecting the softness of her double vagina tore free, blood spilling into the water all round, the section hinging up on gristle. He jabbed his prongs in and out and in again and in a surge of ecstasy squirted his seed inside – the thumping of mandibles against his shell now going through him like throbs of pleasure. After a long dull and mindless moment, while he was only partially aware of the damage the females were doing to him, he rolled off and quickly moved away. He saw the female closing up that shell section, yellow cement quickly bubbling up to seal it into place. This had once been a necessary precaution, in an ocean full of parasites that would have attacked such a vulnerable spot.

Cvorn headed to the far wall, spying out a series of water-cleaning ports he should be able to use as claw holds to get himself back to the water lock. With his heavy prosthetics he had no chance of swimming up there. He noted blood leaking from his leg sockets, where the prosthetics mated with his natural body. He noted some grooves in his carapace and one or two cracks. He felt battered and his satisfaction with the mating was somewhat marred by its speed. As he reached up to the first cleaner port he remembered, far in the past, feeling the same dissatisfaction at the brevity of his matings. He decided he needed more practice. And, as he climbed, remembered think-ing the same back then too.

13

Blite

The antique space suit was empty. Blite had finally nerved himself to open the visor and peer inside. He found only an internal incrustation like soot. He then moved on to search for Penny Royal elsewhere.

Beyond the central corridor running round the horseshoe of the *Black Rose*, there were numerous branching maintenance tunnels. The entire ship was webbed with them like a worm-eaten fruit. Many of these tunnels were big enough for a man, if he was prepared to crawl in some places. They were for various designs of robot, the majority of which were grub-like things capable of performing many tasks themselves or unloading smaller robots where they could not gain access. Over four days the captain explored all these, occasionally encountering those robots. The things politely retreated and dropped back into their side niches to allow him past.

The schematic of the ship, though detailed, didn't really give him the feel he wanted. He needed to go in there and see things with his own eyes, touch them, consider the things he might need to do if there were problems. He wanted to *know* his newly configured ship. And, beside that, he felt the need to locate Penny Royal, rather than talk to that apparently empty suit. Or that black diamond manifestation. But, just as when he had searched before their arrival at the Crispin Six supernova blast front, the black AI was nowhere to be found.

As he stepped into the airlock, Blite understood that Penny Royal, with its ability to radically alter its own shape and design, could enter many areas of the ship where he could not. However, he still wanted to check outside. This was not because of some need to face the black AI, but because, having hung here in the path of the Crispin Six nova blast front for three days, he was growing bored and edgy and finding himself snapping at Brond and Greer.

The airlock evacuated, much faster than the original *The Rose* could have managed, and Blite propelled himself outside, looking for somewhere on the black surface to attach his safety line. He could find nothing. However, since it struck him as unlikely that one of his crew, Leven or Penny Royal itself might suddenly take the ship away, shedding him into vacuum and leaving him to die, he decided to rely on the gecko function of his boots.

The *Black Rose* floated in dark red vacuum, dotted with glittering pink stars. He knew now that without the entropy dump, which was still ongoing, his suit would have been failing about now and he would have been rapidly heating up. Even if he had pulled himself inside before its total failure, with him boiling out of it, he would have been so badly irradiated that even advanced anti-rads wouldn't have worked.

Next, he walked round, following a course between metallic protrusions resembling the low hedges of a maze, on to the front screen. He peered inside to see Greer sitting there, with a VR mask and gloves on – assembling some complicated puzzle, by the looks of it. And while he watched, Brond entered. The man sat down at his console, called something up on his screen then leaned down to take up an old-fashioned touch-board from underneath the console and begin typing. After a moment, he frowned, then looked up. Spotting Blite, he gave a casual salute, then returned to his work.

Blite had seen the man updating this written journal of his, and wondered how he himself might feature in it. He was about to move on but suddenly halted. Greer also had a hobby that recorded more than mere audio, what with all her data-gathering gear and holo-visual . . . Blite suddenly got the strange feeling that he was on to something. He understood why he, and the other two, wanted to be with Penny Royal, but hadn't really considered the reverse. Was this it? Was it their role to be the AI's witnesses? What about Blite himself? He made a leap. At some point, forensic AIs would examine them and he wondered, given the times the AI had actually been in his mind, if it might be recording things there. He suddenly felt cold and just a little frightened, and quickly moved on. He circumvented a sensor spine to head towards the back of the ship.

Just around from the bridge, he came to the circular space door giving egress to the shuttle. This was only visible because the maze walls skirted a clear area, around which a near-invisible black line etched out the door's circumference. Just beyond, he found another black line scribing a stretched-out diamond shape and knew this to be one of the splinter missiles – perhaps one of those capable of U-jumping itself into a target. Beyond this, a row of four inset ports, with amber hardfields deep inside, marked out a laser array. Here and there, on short pillars, stood spherical or extended egg-shaped nacelles, some containing sensor equipment, others holding esoteric weapons. Neatly folded under a red-tinted chain-glass hatch, like some giant burrowing insect made of chrome, lay an exterior maintenance robot. Still no sign of Penny Royal.

Reaching the fusion array at the rear, Blite peered round at the yard-wide tubes of a cluster of seven fusion ports. He stared at these for a long while, aware that their design was quite radical in that they used curved hardfields for containment rather than the usual Tesla bottles. And that fusion actually took place inside them, rather than a short distance behind as had previously been the case with *The Rose.*

'All right, Penny Royal,' he said, becoming frustrated with his search, 'where the fuck are you?'

He began to trudge back to the airlock, but even as he did so, silver veins brightened in the hull's surface – while scattered between them lay a mottling of dark shapes like sword blades. Blite halted and watched as these lines, like threads drawn onto a reel, pulled in to one point ahead of him, the sword blades following like a shoal of shadow fish. A mass of silver and black coagulated before him and just for a second he got that feeling he sometimes experienced during a U-jump, of a tugging at his senses from a direction he simply could not locate.

He felt something straining in his mind, like trying to focus an astigmatic eye. For a moment he had it locked down, and the growing mass of the black AI before him seemed to invert and turn into a tunnel stretching into the far distance. It then seemed to open out in every direction and multiply infinitely. He felt himself hanging within it as threads of power spread out from his body. Gazing then in a direction impossible to locate clearly, he saw a generator, akin to the one they had seen above Penny Royal's planetoid. It was hanging in vacuum alongside a whole series of generators, all feeding in power. But they receded and he found himself hanging in vastness, and it was all Penny Royal, and it was more than his mind could encompass. He shut down.

'I've got you,' it said.

Yes, you have, haven't you, something inside Blite replied.

Blite found himself floating in vacuum, which seemed somehow prosaic and small compared to what he had just experienced. Gradually he became aware of something closing round his ankle and pulling him. He peered down at a silver strand wrapped around it, extending down to the *Black Rose*, which now lay a thousand feet away. Penny Royal reeled him in and, as it did so, he tried to fathom what he had seen. It reminded him of something he had tried many years ago – something many space-farers tried at one time or another.

He had ventured out on the hull of his ship while it was in U-space, but had been within the ship's shielding. Some of his crew had remained conscious, while others, having experienced U-space before, took drugs to knock themselves out. Pre-programmed to do so, the shielding shut down for precisely ten seconds. This was so that Blite, and those inside who had remained conscious, could look at the infinite. Luckily he had used his safety line, because one of those who'd sensibly rendered himself unconscious for the trip later had to come out and retrieve him. It took Blite a week to recover and, at the end of that time, all he could remember was the impression of *something being wrong*, of experiencing something that his mind just wasn't capable of recording.

It was like that, he thought, but even then he wasn't so sure. The feeling was similar, but he could still recollect Penny Royal's infinity. Perhaps his previous exposure to something similar had immunized him in some way.

'What the hell was that?' he rasped.

'I am not a mind reader, Captain,' the AI replied.

Fucking liar.

'I saw something,' said Blite, 'like . . . U-space. And those machines there . . . those generators.'

'I see,' said Penny Royal. 'Just prior to you yelling "spiders" and propelling yourself away from the ship, the entropy dump fluctuated. Since this involves a certain degree of U-space manipulation, you must have experienced some overspill.'

The explanation was too neat. The AI had spoken rather

than dumped something into his mind. And it had not mentioned 'Calabi-Yau frames in juxtaposition' or anything else that he'd struggle to understand. This meant the AI had wanted him to understand it at once, rather than strain his mind around it. As his feet settled against the hull, his boots engaged and the tendril unwound. He felt sure he had been lied to again. But about what and to what purpose, he had no idea. He gazed at Penny Royal, back before him in familiar form – the black head of an artichoke poised on a silver stalk. He remembered that half of the AI had taken possession of the cargo hauler – yet what lay before him looked no smaller than before. What had Leven said about that? Something about U-space phenomenon and the AI doubling in mass before separating?

'So how much longer are we going to be stuck out here?' he asked.

Blite saw a time display rapidly count down ten days – the one he had called up on the Q-dot display on his bedroom wall, when he was a child. He thought about that for a moment, then realized that caught them up with the two weeks of their time jump. He guessed it made a crazy sense.

'Right, okay.' He turned away and began heading towards the airlock.

'Leven knows how long we'll be here,' said Penny Royal, implying that there had been no need for Blite to come out on the hull. Blite didn't believe it, and wasn't even convinced that his impulse to come out here had been his own. He'd seen something more; he'd had something else impressed into his mind. And, he reckoned, he might be no more to the AI than a convenient data-storage crystal.

'Yeah.' He waved a dismissive hand.

He no longer felt impatient or irritable. Right then all he wanted to do was go into his cabin, drink a large amount of a bottle from that crate of Martian vodka he'd bought on Par Avion and curl up on his bed. The thing about wonder and awe, he had found, was that sometimes it sat just a thin skin away from terror.

Spear

Sepia had gone off again, apparently to check on the defences of Trent's new headquarters. She had departed with a lingering and mildly amused glance back at me. Perhaps I'd been too obvious about resetting my nascuff. I hadn't needed to hold up my arm and watch it change from red to blue after resetting it through my aug. I was glad she was gone, anyway – I didn't need the distraction. Despite my libido steadily waning as my nanosuite digested testosterone and hormones, reset glands and twisted complex organic chemicals into different shapes, my visceral awareness of her presence hadn't faded one whit.

Trent had solicitously provided Taiken's wife, Reece, with a seat in the annex to the surgical theatre. Watching how he treated her, I realized I wasn't the only one subject to the whims of libidinous Cupid. Perhaps it was something about the air in prador ships. Reece's other child, who seemed normal enough, was sitting on her lap. Her older boy, Robert, was a bit of a somnambulist – he had been walking round in a trance with his human hand in his mother's. He'd only shown any animation when Trent and I lifted him onto the surgical table. He had fought us, his claw pinching a chunk out of Trent's forearm before we could pin him down and inject an anaesthetic. Now, as the pedestal autodoc bowed over, scanning him from head to foot, I could see the reason for his condition.

Taiken had replaced the boy's left arm with a prador claw

and added a manipulatory arm, which folded against his bloated torso. Both limbs were about the size you would find on a small third-child. Attached to his bones were webworks of shell to support them. The prador nerves of the claw had been connected to the human nerves which led to his missing arm. This was achieved using chemical interface nodes. Artificial nerves had been run from the manipulatory arm into his spine and up to his brain, where a piece of ganglion had been surgically introduced. His blood was a mixture of human and prador blood, heavily laced with antejects. These were produced by an artificial contrivance sunk into his bone marrow. Taiken had also made additions to all the boy's organs and consequently to all the fluids many of them produced. His entire body chemistry had changed. And unfortunately it would never function properly as it was.

A body could only incorporate alien material, without rejecting it, with the use of antejects and adaptogens. But these were suppressing growth in both his prador parts and his human ones. Nothing would knit together. The manipulatory arm would never work. Cancers were springing up like weeds. Scar tissue was swamping nerve interfaces and other interfaces between human and alien flesh, while just keeping the boy alive required constant intervention. In addition, brain growth had stalled and his brain was shrinking. Taiken had turned the boy into a dying chimera and a moron.

Perhaps this boy had not been the best place to start. Having loaded Taiken's records, I knew that the adults were more rugged and many of them had not, despite appearances, so radically redesigned themselves. Some of them even maintained a physical separation between many of their parts – their prador grafts running on their own chemistry and venous system. The prador interface with their human bodies was often an inorganic one in these cases.

336

'So what can you do?' asked Trent, peering over my shoulder at the scan results.

'I can surgically remove most of his major grafts,' I said, 'but I need something more to rid him of the rest and, as noted, our time is limited. The surgery alone here would take the best part of a day.'

Even as I spoke, I was scanning records in my mind, linking to Bsorol's work and trying to isolate some key. The gross surgical work, though time-consuming, would be relatively easy – it would be simply like removing a bullet. But getting rid of the rest would be like taking micro-slivers out of a ceramo-glass grenade. I needed something else. I needed some way of taking them apart and rendering them harmless so the human body could reject them. I needed some panacea I could deliver to all the shell people, and quickly. I first considered nanobots, but the amount of programming involved would have been immense, and the equipment Taiken had at his disposal wasn't up to the task. There had to be a simpler way.

'Enzymic acid,' I said.

It was in Bsorol's work – an enzyme that slowly dissolved prador carapace to allow a new one to grow. The first-child hadn't worked out how to stimulate the new growth and so abandoned the idea, instead working on a method to induce the shedding of old carapace. But the enzyme was still interesting. I called up an image of its molecular structure in my mind and examined it from every angle.

'Acid?' asked Reece. She was now standing up at the viewing window, holding her younger child, and had used the intercom.

'An enzyme is a catalyst of biochemical reactions.'

'I know what an enzyme is,' she replied. 'I'm questioning the use of the word "acid".'

'Enzyme acid is a catalytic acid. It doesn't break down or

combine with the molecular structures it is destroying. It can work very fast. I believe it was used as a weapon against the prador during the war.' I looked over to Riss, who, having followed us into the surgery had coiled on one of the side work surfaces and apparently gone to sleep.

'Various kinds were developed,' the snake drone replied, raising her head, 'but seemed a pointless complication when hydrofluoric acid was available.' The drone's black eye then opened. *'This may be of interest.'* The drone sent me a data package.

So, here was the part of the problem that needed solving. I studied complex formulae, molecular models, statistical breakdowns of performance and other data on four different kinds of enzyme. The difficulty, I immediately found, was that all four would be, to some degree, hostile to human tissue. I selected one of them and began redesigning it in my skull to make it a lot more specific and a lot less likely to kill a shellman outright. Walking over to an organo-molecular assembler, I turned it on, reeled out an optic from the side of the thing and plugged it into my aug. First, I had to test the thing out, so I set it to assembling the original enzyme without my modifications. I lost track of time during this task and, when I looked round, Trent was gone and the woman asleep in her chair. I replayed his earlier attempts to get through to me. The shell people were becoming more aggressive, and one of them had torn a hole through the wall of the building. Some out there, having forgone the treatments that maintained their condition when Taiken seized control of them, had collapsed.

'Many of them will still die,' said Riss.

'I know,' I said as I worked.

The assembler had already produced a batch of the first enzyme and opened a hatch in its side to reveal a bottle of the stuff. I walked over to the sleeping boy and used a simple chain-glass scalpel to cut out a piece of carapace and attached human skin. I cut a sliver of this and took it over to a nanoscope, placed it in the sample clamps then got the enzyme and dripped some on, setting the scope to take the sliver inside. The enzyme rapidly took apart prador tissue and more slowly dissolved human tissue.

The shell people's exterior prador grafts would fall away. Inside them, everything that was of the prador would come apart. Along with all this, their chemically based prador instincts would die too. Many of them would die of blood poisoning, blood loss or one of a hundred other complications.

'*I need those amniotic tanks,*' I said into the void of Sverl's computer system. '*I need help.*'

'*Coming,*' Bsectil replied.

My final altered enzyme, when the assembler produced it, neatly destroyed prador organic matter and left a sliver of human skin pristine. I felt no great accomplishment because Riss's words about likely deaths still weighed heavily. Holding the two cold flasks containing the new enzyme, I studied them. I needed to find some way to get this stuff inside the shell people, but was aware that many of them would die from the effects. However, if they didn't get their portion of this *cure*, they would continue attacking and killing each other. And they would die anyway from the lack of medical treatment to maintain their condition. I made my calculations from Taiken's work and the predicted effect of this enzyme. I took up processing in Sverl's computing as well as in my aug to do this, and on the scales of life and death knew I could save more lives than I would kill, but it wasn't enough.

I needed some way of keeping these people alive as their grafts died. I felt sure that with the processing power open to me and all the equipment available, there had to be a way, but I just didn't know enough. I walked over to a second assembler and stared at it. This device could assemble nano-machines and next to it rested a drug manufactory. Surely I could use something here?

Memory from Penny Royal's spine arose in response to my need. A military doctor called Sykes gazed upon a similar collection of machines. Too many commandos were dying before or during transport from the battlefield to the hospital ship. It was tearing apart this gentle man who had trained as a peacetime doctor of civilian maladies. He called up data in his aug and there studied the parameters of the standard nanosuites most of these soldiers had received throughout their previous lives – the kind of packages he had always recommended. Here were the machines that boosted their immune systems, corrected congenital faults, attacked bacterial and viral infections, quickly closed up capillaries around wounds or swiftly wove clots in severed veins and arteries. They were very useful, these machines, but doctors like him had formatted the whole packages they ran for the general hazards of everyday existence, not for war.

Next, he called up data on the new military nano-package and studied it intently. This was less focused on infections, which were generally slow-moving, and more on traumatic injuries, including amputations, chemical poisoning, munitions shock, beam burns, projectile-killed muscle. It could close off bleeds very quickly and it could weave an impermeable non-reactive skin across open wounds. It could gather toxins and isolate them in bubbles of that same skin. It was a much more aggressive and dangerous package that would need constant reprogramming and tweaking. It could get out of control and inadvertently kill those it was supposed to preserve.

Sykes did not like the thing at all but in the fighting on the planet below it would save many more than it would kill. He used his aug to load its data to the nanobot assembler and set the thing running, feeling he had betrayed his principles . . .

I reached out to the assembler, but before I could touch its controls, my aug had opened a radio link to the thing and was already searching its database. The military package was there and, as I set the machine to make it, I felt thousands of people peering over my shoulder, clamouring for attention, making their suggestions. On an almost unconscious level, I tuned out personalities and focused on data. In that moment, my knowledge became the sum of all theirs. Much of it was of no use, but the cryogenic suspension drug seemed a feasible addition. I allowed the projection of Giano Paulos full access.

He was a historian studying the First Diaspora from the Sol system. Cryo-technicians injected the passengers on the first cryoships with a drug that put their bodies into hibernation. Doctors had already been using this drug on accident victims, putting them into a state of hibernation similar to that of a bear in winter. Someone who might have died from his injuries in an hour would instead take ten hours to die.

Even as I linked to the drug manufactory and searched its database, I saw the problem. In slowing down the shell people's physiology, I would also slow the spread of the enzyme that would destroy their prador grafts. Microspheres were the answer – the drug enclosed in a slow-dissolving collagen that would release it after the grafts died. That might have been my own knowledge – I was now finding it difficult to make the distinction.

What about the pain, the shock? The solution to that lay in the military nano-package. What about conflicts between these? I laid them out in my mind and explored that, feeling a sudden euphoria at the breadth of my knowledge and the skill available to me. It seemed so simple to make adjustments to the military package so that, after the required delay, it would isolate the enzyme acid. I then considered just tweaking that acid to make it deactivate itself after a certain number of catalytic events.

'*You're too deep,*' someone told me, and I felt processing capacity shutting down.

I considered a three-way combination of drugs, nano-machines and adaptogens to stimulate regrowth of amputated limbs or excised organs.

'*It's enough,*' said that someone, whom I now recognized as Sverl.

I snapped back into consciousness of my surroundings knowing that it *was* enough and that further delay would cost lives. Processing came back, but I no longer needed it. I sensed the horde of Penny Royal's victims and their memories retreating like a fast tide and felt a painful regret at the loss of their additional knowledge. However, just a second later I realized that the retreating tide had left its flotsam and jetsam and that the second-hand knowledge I had used now remained with me. I was suddenly aware of the length of my existence as a fact, as if I had never spent a century locked in artificial ruby but had lived every moment of it. Some portion of those thousands in the spine remained with me, etched into my brain.

'Time to get to work, I reckon,' said Riss, now rising up from the floor beside me.

Her black eye was open, and I spotted other openings too. A series of holes had formed in her skin, revealing glittering internals, with spaces seemingly designed to take the flasks I held.

Of course, here was my delivery mechanism.

Riss

Riss felt gravid, loaded and ready for action as she threaded out through the narrow gap opened by the armoured door, but it just wasn't the same. Admittedly the prador-eating enzyme she carried bore some similarity to the hydrofluoric acid she had used on occasion during the war, and the microspheres with their contained drug were a little like the parasite eggs she had once carried, but that was the extent of it. Riss wasn't now heading out to strike terror into the hearts or similar organs of the prador. She wasn't about to inject a hated enemy with a grotesque and hideous form of death. Riss was heading out to *do good*.

Perhaps this feeling of dissatisfaction was simply due to what Penny Royal had taken away. Perhaps even containing parasite eggs and going up against a hostile prador would never feel as it should. Perhaps nothing that filled up her internal tanks and caches could fill that *other* emptiness. Riss knew that she was feeling, and had felt for a long time, something akin to human depression. That is, as depression had been in the days before it could be rubbed out with a five-minute mental reformat – when nothing satisfied, nothing gave pleasure and everything looked bleak. In the same way as some humans had fought that feeling then, Riss tried to use action, business, *doing stuff* as an antidote. She wished that, as with humans, physical activity would generate endorphins to counter the malaise.

Ahead stood the woman she had spotted earlier. The woman had retained her human form but had grown a prador carapace. Now, because she had not maintained constant immune system reprogramming or kept up with antejects and other cocktails of drugs to maintain her condition, she was dying. Down on her knees with her head bowed, she offered an easy target, but Riss decided to study her first. Pus was leaking from the points where the plates of carapace shifted over each other. One such piece had fallen off the back of her hand to expose raw flesh, beaded with blood. Internally she was developing numerous abscesses –

and where internal shell connected her immovable plates to underlying bone, the surrounding human flesh was dying. As Riss observed her, she raised her head and, even though her whole system was flooded with toxins and her brain swollen in its skull, she retained at least enough faculties to speak.

'Kill me,' she said, brown drool running out of the side of her mouth.

Riss flipped her ovipositor forwards and drove it into the woman's chest, punching through carapace and straight into her heart. This was risky because such a wound might kill if the military nano-package didn't quickly repair it, but Riss calculated that the benefit of faster distribution throughout her body of the load outweighed the risk.

Stab, inject and away, now moving fast towards a shellman lying sideways on the floor – a man trying to pull off his prador legs. Riss didn't hesitate: she stabbed and injected again. But no orgasmic release ensued. She had no feeling of satisfaction at having performed her function. Riss moved on, now accelerating and not pausing to inspect – rather as she had done when inside the prador ship and victims had been all around. Some of the shell people were technically dead, like the one Riss found lying next to two normal human corpses in a prison cage. However, that was only under an old definition of death that cited a stopped heart and gradual synaptic decay. With the packages and drugs inside them, with that hibernation drug working and nanobots repairing damage, they still had a chance. Death for a human, after all, was now defined as an unrecoverable state, and these days the human mind and body were only unrecoverable after total annihilation.

'So what the hell are you?' asked a voice as Riss finished injecting the shellman in the prison cage. Another man had stepped out of hiding from behind a glass vessel full of squirming Spatterjay leeches.

'I'm Riss,' the drone replied and moved on – a normal human like that was of little interest to her.

Shell person after person felt the stab of Riss's ovipositor, but she began to feel that just inoculating them as she came upon them wasn't efficient. She paused to map her surroundings and locate every one. Then, checking the rate at which she was using up her loads, she chose the best course. But, as she set upon this course and found herself chasing a shellwoman who seemed much more able than her fellows, Riss recalculated. Analyses of body temperature, heart rate and other signifiers of general health were called for. Riss paused and redrew the map, selecting those who seemed nearest to death first. The basis of this wasn't great, but it was the best she could manage in limited time.

Hundreds of inoculations later, Riss headed back for further supplies that Spear should have prepared by now. On the way, she came upon the shellman who had been trying to pull off his own legs. Riss found him prostrate a couple of yards away from his prador additions. Here now lay a naked man, legs severed at the hips, his arms ending in stumps at the forearms and his jaw missing. Silvery white skin covered the point of division at his hips, it lay around his exposed gullet and covered his arms to his shoulders. He had obviously managed to drag himself a short distance from the collection of prador legs and carapaces before the hibernation drug took effect, dropping his mandibles on the way. From those prador parts Riss could hear a steady hissing and saw steam rising. Even as the drone watched, they collapsed a little. The enzyme acid was dissolving them violently and turning them into a slowly spreading pool of sticky fluid.

Amazing.

Riss felt a momentary surge of something other than her

usual moroseness, other than her perpetual dark mood . . . something like excitement. So unusual, so unexpected was the feeling that she immediately came to a decision. Spear was making enough of this stuff to deal with the shell people and would probably make no more. However, he had made a test batch of the original enzyme acid – the one that also destroyed human tissue – which he hadn't destroyed. Instead he had inserted it into a drug safe in Taiken's surgery-cum-laboratory. Spear had locked the thing with a chip key, but that shouldn't be a problem for a drone capable of penetrating prador ships and bases. Riss would take it and keep it inside, close, ready to use.

The woman the drone had first inoculated was down on her back, large chunks of her outer shell having fallen away. Instead of displaying bleeding raw flesh underneath, more silvery white skin was visible. The regular human Riss had seen earlier was standing over her, a look of fascinated horror on his face. She was in hibernation, like the previous shellman – one beat of her heart detected as Riss approached. But no further overt signs of life were evident as Riss entered the building, the man following closely.

'How many have you done?' Spear asked when Riss came back to him.

'Eight hundred and forty-two,' Riss replied. 'Another seven hundred and sixty to do.'

'The effects?' Spear asked.

Riss routed recordings made of what she had seen outside to the man's aug. Spear turned introspective for a moment, then smiled.

'It's working,' he said.

Riss opened up her body for reloading, ridding herself of empty flasks like a gun ejecting spent ammunition. 'Of course it's working, but still there are those who might die while you're congratulating yourself.'

Spear harrumphed and picked up more flasks from the nearby work surface. While he inserted these into her body, she studied him on other levels, black eye firmly open. Her scanning went deeper than her examination of the shell people outside. The entanglement it had taken her so long to detect and map was still there, now more active than before, and firmly connected to that object up in Sverl's sanctum. Large data exchanges were perpetual, and Riss wondered if Spear had any conception of what he had become. He wasn't just a man now. He seemed to be some synergistic sum of the essence of Penny Royal's victims, a multifaceted being with the kind of mental resources usually only available to an AI.

As the last flask went into place, the drone experienced a moment of confusion, seeing an entanglement echo in U-space and feeling something like an amplifier feedback whine reverberating through her snake body. She snapped the holes in her body closed and abruptly leapt away from Spear to land on the floor some yards away, ovipositor poised to strike.

'You okay?' he asked.

Riss hadn't been okay for a long time, but hadn't often been frightened.

'Nothing,' said Riss. 'No problem.'

She circumvented Spear widely to get to the door, through it and out. Keeping such a physical distance in the real from the man was a futile exercise. It didn't change the fact that Riss now seemed to be quantum entangled, via the spine, to him. What did this mean? She now knew that the spine contained recordings of all Penny Royal's dead victims. But did this now mean it also maintained a connection with all the AI's live ones? The sheer computing power, the ability, the godlike intelligence involved in such a bonding suggested Penny Royal might be a magnitude above even the kind of Polity AIs that gave Riss the shivers. It also suggested, consequently, that Spear ranked higher too.

The little drone truly understood now, on an utterly visceral level, what it meant to be involved with paradigm-changing beings – with beings dangerous enough to bring down civilizations, or capable of raising them up.

Cvorn

As he returned to his sanctum, Cvorn's urge to mate was in abeyance and the other hormonal effects had dropped to a low ebb. Perhaps this was why other father-captains had not gone down this route. He had, after all, subjected himself to these effects by accident and not design. Now, with his mind clearer, he was able to think more about his aims beyond his activities onboard his ST dreadnought.

There was no doubt that Sverl had made a lengthy U-space jump, to give himself time to make repairs to his ship's shielding. He must hope that he could thereby prevent Cvorn from finding out the destination of his next jump, so Cvorn had to consider how to react to that. Immediate attack was the obvious answer, to inflict further damage, but Sverl had to know that and was doubtless making preparations.

Arriving in the corridor leading to his sanctum, Cvorn found Vrom towing away a grav-sled loaded with leftovers. All that remained of the young male that Cvorn had cannibalized for parts was empty carapace, meticulously scraped clean. At some point Vrom must have returned to Cvorn's sanctum because claws and legs were there too, all cracked open. Their contents were now either being digested in Vrom's gut or sitting in his personal food store.

'Father,' said Vrom, halting immediately and cowering.

Cvorn just went straight past the first-child to his sanctum door, auging to its controls and opening it. 'Bring me a reaver-fish,' he said, pausing at the threshold, 'a whole one.' And as he entered, he remembered how sex had always made him hungry and how, in those days, he could really pack in the meat.

Inside his sanctum, he approached the pit and saddle controls before the array of screens and settled himself in position but used his aug to operate the ship's computer system. First, he needed to examine Sverl's coordinates. Though he could use the ship's processing to ascertain their point in realspace, that would take some time, and there was a quicker way. He connected through to the ship's mind – one excised from a first-child over a hundred years ago.

'Give me realspace coordinates for our present jump,' he instructed.

'Calculating,' the mind replied.

There had been no problems of recognition with this mind – no questions about its loyalty to the previous father-captain of this dreadnought. The first-child had been thoroughly stripped down, all personality erased along with all memories of its previous life. All it did was communicate in a very basic way, and calculate U-engine parameters. All it knew was that it received orders from this sanctum, just like the war drones aboard.

After a moment, prador glyphs began scrolling diagonally across one of the screens. Cvorn studied them for a moment but again found using his aug was a better option. He loaded those coordinates, checked them against astrogation maps and studied the data available. Sverl was heading for a trinary system lying far above the galactic plane, beyond the Graveyard, the Kingdom and the Polity. Had he decided to run? Had he decided to relinquish all interest in those three realms?

It didn't matter. All that mattered was whether this new system held something that might give Sverl a tactical advantage – some way of evading Cvorn while making the kind of repairs he could not make in U-space before he proceeded to his next jump. The stellar objects of this system were a white dwarf and a black dwarf whose mass equalled that of the red dwarf orbiting them. The paths of the two masses were eccentric, and there was no way of saying, without making extensive calculations, which orbited which. Worldlets and asteroids abounded, but with nothing large enough to retain much in the way of atmosphere. The whole system had acted as a billion-year-old asteroid grinder, the result of which was a dense ring of fine dust and gas around the white dwarf. This was shepherded by a series of planetoids, and all was perpetually stirred every three hundred years by a close pass of the red dwarf.

There, thought Cvorn.

It seemed quite likely that Sverl, whose capabilities Cvorn did not doubt, intended to surface into the real either in or close to that ring, and use it for cover. The density of the cloud would negate the effects of energy weapons at long range and would heat up railgun missiles, thus lessening their impact. The cloud would also tend to weaken the integrity of hardfields, but since Sverl would project them close to his ship, that effect was negligible. He *probably* wouldn't be able to hide. And though he would have repaired much of the damage to his chameleonware, he wouldn't have been able to make the repairs in U-space that would conceal the mass of his ship – especially when surrounded by gas and dust which would effect its usability. Therefore, entering that ring gave Sverl both advantages and disadvantages.

However, it was still a good choice – probably the best choice Sverl could make.

Cvorn paused there as Vrom came in from his annex with a whole reaverfish on his back, its head gripped in his claws and tail dragging on the floor behind.

'Put it down over there –' Cvorn waved a claw – 'and wait.'

His stomach gave a muffled grumble through his shell and his gullet grew wet with lubricating saliva. The distraction irritated him as he tried to concentrate on his response to Sverl's likely actions. Through the ship's system, he ordered an exchange of railgun loads. In one railgun, he ordered the removal of the iron-cored and ceramic armoured slugs presently lined up for first firings. Armoury robots would replace them with sensor probes, when they finished formatting them for the conditions in that ring; these were to be used mainly for mass detection. He ordered two other railguns to be loaded with the much harder to produce and rarer railgun slugs clad with exotic metal alloy. Frictional heating in the cloud would not weaken these. In fact, if fired at sufficient range, their internal iron cores would melt and build up massive pressure, thus increasing their energy upon impact with an exotic metal hull like Sverl's.

Saliva now dripping out of his mouth and wetting his mandibles, Cvorn conceded defeat and turned from his screens. He walked over to the reaverfish and inspected it, remembering that he must check on the living examples of this species and release one in the mating pool so the female he had mated with could implant her eggs. Vrom moved forwards, the atomic shear flicking on across the edge of his claw, ready to cut up Cvorn's dinner. Cvorn abruptly rebelled at the idea.

When, many years ago, his remaining two legs and claw had ceased to function properly and finally dropped off, he had taken the route of many father-captains before him. Disdaining the very idea of the new prosthetics, beyond grav-motors attached to his shell, he had his closest first-child chop up and feed his meals into his mandibles. However, when his mandibles abruptly stopped working, his condition necessitated him mincing his food in a macerating machine. This was attached below his mouth and tubed into his gullet – and it was this that made him finally change his mind. New prosthetic mandibles came first and, though they lacked sensitivity, he was delighted with them and soon had prosthetic claws installed too. But he continued to have his first-child cut up his food for him. Now, mobile on new legs, sexually active and with corresponding hormonal effects coursing through his system, Cvorn found he had suddenly lost his inclination for pampering.

'Leave,' he instructed.

Vrom's pose was one of puzzlement but, when Cvorn swung his claw round, crashing it into the side of Vrom's carapace, he quickly recovered and retreated. Cvorn now focused his full attention on the fish, reached down, closed a claw around its skull, and snipped. The skull crushed and split, squirting a pale green line of brains across the floor. Cvorn tore up the front end of its head, fed it into his mandibles and began crunching it up. Just minutes later, with a third of the fish gone and his initial ravenous hunger satisfied, he slowed his pace of ingestion and returned his thoughts to Sverl.

Cvorn had done everything he could with the railguns. Now the energy weapons. The particle cannons would never be much good in that dust ring unless they were used close up, but there were things he could do to increase their efficiency there. The particulate the weapons fired was usually aluminium dust, suspended in nitrogen in an electrostatic field. However, by adding heavy elements, tightening the magnetic tube and ramping up power input he could give the beam greater penetrating power.

This wasn't usually done in vacuum conflict because, beyond a certain point, power input outweighed ultimate yield.

As he considered what heavy elements to add from those available, Cvorn abruptly realized he could set things in motion now. He didn't have to crouch before this sanctum's control area to do this . . . with his aug he could do just about anything from any location. Pausing, with a dripping mass of a huge organ resembling a kidney part-way to his mouth, Cvorn understood just how rigid his thinking had been. He should have realized this long before now. He shoved the organ into his mandibles and munched it down, mentally initiating the required changes to the particle cannons.

Other weapons . . . There were few changes he could make to the various available nuclear and chemical bombs, missiles and mines. They were just too slow for what seemed likely to be a running battle over hundreds of thousands of miles. When he finally did get to use them, it would need to be after Sverl's ship was permanently disabled. Then, peeling that ship open to expose Sverl's sanctum would be a job for particle beams. As he reached the tail of the reaverfish he searched his mind for other preparations he could make, but all that was left was some tweaking of the spectra of his anti-munitions lasers, so there wouldn't be so much scatter in the gas of that ring.

He was done: his ship was as ready as it could be – and he had eaten a whole reaverfish. Cvorn moved away from the sticky mess on the floor, now swarming with ship lice, and turned towards his controls. Quite some time remained before his final encounter with Sverl and he started to contemplate how he would fill it – perhaps, after digesting his meal, another visit to the mating pool? But just a moment later he felt intensely weary and his vision blurred for a moment.

What?

His body felt leaden and, as he took a couple of steps towards the controls, a hot tightness began to grow inside him. It was as if some creature was gathering all his organs together and squashing them into one spot. His coitus clamp rattled, then his irised anus abruptly opened, spattering the floor with bright yellow excrement. He moved away from the mess, further squirts of faeces punctuating his journey across the floor to the vacuum disposal port protruding from the wall. But by the time he settled over it, his anus had clamped shut again. This had never happened to him when he had been young. It had only happened in later years during illness, or during the changes he had undergone when he lost his limbs.

Cvorn moved off the port, but not too far away from it, because that tightness inside had turned into deep organ-crushing ache. He felt very tired and found himself losing the thread of his thoughts, his aug responding to his mind with irrelevant data and old memories. He looked around. What was happening with the weapons? What was he doing? Forgetting the disposal port, he walked over to his controls and peered at the array of hexagonal screens. They were scrolling all sorts of rubbish – also in response to his mental confusion. Suddenly a convulsion wracked him and his mandibles extended straight out. It hit him again, then again, saliva pouring in a stream from his gullet. Then a great fountain of half-digested reaverfish and green bile shot out between his mandibles, spattering all over the screens, chunks thudding to the floor and soupy fluids running into pit controls. Another convulsion hit, spraying more of the mess over those controls as Cvorn backed away. Next he lowered his front end to point his mouthparts at the floor, green bile dripping from his burning gullet. That tight pain was still inside but easing a little, and yellow excrement dripped from his half-open anus.

Cvorn was now able to think more clearly. He had been

foolish. The hormones in the air and the recent mating had made him forget one important thing. He might have prosthetic limbs and new sexual organs, but everything else inside him was very old, including his digestive system.

The Brockle

Earth Central had not entirely accepted the Brockle's convoluted explanation for why it had not put Ikbal and Martina aboard the single-ship. And it had said that their agreement must end if the two were not on the next ship to leave. Meanwhile, the Brockle had learned some more about Penny Royal.

Because Amistad had removed the black AI's eighth state of consciousness, the one that seemed responsible for its many ill deeds, Earth Central Security had forgiven Penny Royal's past sins. Then when it retrieved that missing part of itself on Masada, ECS retracted the amnesty. But now the Polity AIs were still doing nothing, because of what Penny Royal might do, or might reveal. In addition, judging by everything the Brockle had gleaned from Ikbal and Martina, the black AI was again having trouble with that eighth state.

The similarities between Penny Royal and the Brockle only made the black AI more fascinating. Penny Royal had, in essence, experienced similar problems to the one that had resulted in the Brockle's agreed confinement here. One of the Brockle's units had gone astray during its last planetary assignment – an investigation that had ended up turning into a minor civil war. The unit had operated as a discrete being for some years and had actually strayed into territory that was not particularly legal. It had interrogated some innocent citizens and left them permanently damaged.

ECS had instructed the Brockle to shut down its rogue unit and bring all of itself in for forensic examination. The rogue had reacted by finishing its work. Through its interrogations, it had learned that a biotech aug network linked all the leading Polity separatists. It penetrated this and released a particularly nasty program into it that made those augs generate an organic virus. The virus lobotomized the separatists and eight hundred of them died when their autonomous nervous systems shut down. That action, it seemed, was just too much – even though these people had been criminals. ECS again ordered the Brockle to shut down the rogue and come in, but the Brockle now realized ECS was wary of enforcement. Positioned where it was on the world, the Brockle could cause many deaths. ECS then informed it that the innocents the rogue had interrogated had required some mindwork; its actions still might have been forgivable, were it not for one of its victims chewing out his own wrists and bleeding to death.

Antonio Sveeder . . .

He had been an innocent man – the only innocent man the Brockle had killed. However, debate continued about other deaths indirectly attributable to its actions on that world. The Brockle had decided on reabsorption because it wanted to know what had caused its unit to stray so far over the line. The answer had been a simple one: in its dealings with human separatist scum, the unit had come to regard *all* human beings as a problem. It had, in fact, formed an opinion not much different from that of many AIs. It felt human beings were what held the Polity back. They needed to upgrade, or rather the AIs needed to force them to do so – or dispense with them. On reabsorbing that unit, the Brockle concluded that it had not been far wrong. And, realizing the strength of its position, it negotiated. It would continue to work for the Polity but only in the forensic examination of the already proven guilty. It agreed to confinement only if it could protect itself. Thus, ECS provided the *Tyburn*, and the Brockle's careful extraction from its world followed.

But all this was beside the point, which was that Penny Royal was demonstrably unstable, and that its instability was directly attributable to that portion of itself culpable of murder. It was having trouble trying to reintegrate this portion – but that it was trying at all meant that it was reintegrating its guilt too so the *whole* AI would be under sentence of death. There would be no debate. No consideration about what Penny Royal might do to redeem itself. But even that paled in comparison with recent news.

Time travel . . .

This put everything the Brockle had gleaned from Ikbal and Martina into the shade. They were dealing with a dangerously unstable, paradigm-changing AI that had not only stolen some runcibles but had been fucking with temporal energies. It had been doing stuff that scared even the prador shitless. It had been playing with energy debts and entropic effects, which, if handled badly, could put out star systems or cause nova chain reactions. And what was still the reaction of Earth Central and the other Polity AIs? Hands off, leave alone, no action. Surely, this news alone should have overridden their fear.

The Brockle felt certain that during its years of confinement, some other paradigm must have changed. When had the AIs of the Polity become so forgiving? When had they become so timorous? It was time to move against Penny Royal – and hard. If they weren't going to do it then someone else had to. And that someone was the Brockle.

The forensic AI stood up from its seat, mulling over what to do. Earth Central had instructed it to put Ikbal and Martina into a coma and leave them alone until the next single-ship picked them up. Their interrogation was over and the ship must return them to Par Avion. The Polity would drop all charges against them and offer the services of a mind-tech, after which they could go on their way. If the Brockle interfered with them again while they awaited the single-ship the watcher would know, and that would be the end of the confinement agreement.

The *Tyburn* had been useful as a prison hulk before and during the prador/human war, but had ceased to be of use a little while after. Prison was a waste of resources, and Polity AIs had decided it was better now to kill the killers and those hardened recidivists who refused mind-work, and impose fines and enforced mental alterations on those guilty of lesser crimes. However, in this time of plenty, crime wasn't a big problem. The *Tyburn* had sat unused for decades until the difficult problem of the Brockle had arisen and it became the only prisoner. If the Brockle again breached its terms of confinement, which meant not doing precisely what ECS told it, it had no doubt that attack ships would arrive sporting U-jump missiles. Previously, the Brockle could fire up the *Tyburn*'s drive and depart if either side broke the agreement. Now, with the advances in Polity technology, Earth Central thought it had the advantage. Perhaps, despite the Brockle's new detectors, it did.

Some subterfuge might be the best option.

Earth Central needed to be convinced that the Brockle had left the Polity. The Brockle needed time to put some plans into action. Therefore, the watcher aboard this station was a problem. It was one the Brockle felt it should deal with, and right now.

14

Sverl

Sverl watched the show amongst the shell people, trying to suppress an internal shudder every time he saw that horrible drone inject the cure Thorvald Spear had designed. There had been no doubt that the man would find a way because, surely, Penny Royal had manipulated events to this end. Sverl accepted this notion, but felt uncomfortable with it. It was almost like the certainty of religious faith and that wasn't a great route to go. But how else should he think? The AI had thrown Spear, like the weapon of the same name, at a target it had set up.

Alternatively, perhaps a better analogy – a favourite of the drone Arrowsmith – would be a chess one. Sverl, Spear, the drone Riss, Cvorn and perhaps the likes of Gost, or even Polity AIs, were being brought into play. They, along with the king of the prador, and maybe many other actors too, were being gently nudged into position by the AI on a massive universal chessboard. What had happened to Isobel Satomi had been the result of one manoeuvre, as were the events on the Rock Pool, and what was happening now was yet another. What would be the ultimate checkmate?

No, not chess . . .

Chess involved an opponent perhaps as able as oneself, and it struck Sverl that Penny Royal did not have one. If he stuck with the analogy, the AI was playing both sets of pieces—

'I'm angry, you know,' said Spear via his aug.

After a brief hesitation Sverl asked, 'And why is that?'

'*You could have done more to help them,*' Spear answered. '*When you knew what Taiken was doing, you could have flooded the area with knockout gas or something.*'

'I could have,' Sverl replied, 'but aren't you humans rather attracted to the idea of free will?'

'*You should know – aren't you partly human?*'

Sverl winced at that. 'I am, and I question my right to interfere.'

'*You saved them once, and most of them ceased to have free will the moment Taiken started using his prador glands . . . but let's be straight here. You either love being a spectator of Penny Royal's manipulations so much that you are crippling your own ability to act. Or your human part has the same lack of empathy as was the case with Trent Sobel. You rescued these shell people from the Rock Pool, then just watched as they began to destroy themselves.*'

'And as a result, I am being given lectures on morality by someone whose life I saved?'

'*I'm just saying that if you had acted sooner there wouldn't have been so many deaths.*'

'And life is important?'

'*Of course it is.*'

'You are alive.'

'*Yes,*' said Spear, puzzled.

'And so are *all* of the shell people,' said Sverl, 'depending on how you define death, of course.'

'*What?*'

'I have been observing, on many levels. Riss has come to understand the sheer extent of Penny Royal's reach but you have yet to do so. Penny Royal's victims are not all dead.'

After a long silence, Spear said, '*The spine.*'

Sverl swung round to eye the aforementioned object, still in

the clamps that had inserted it inside the assassin drone Riss.
'Exactly.'

'It's recording them?'

'Thus far I have ascertained that it contains the stripped-down recordings of thousands of dead minds. But it is also in the process of perpetually recording the entirety of thousands of living ones. I do wonder where Penny Royal draws the line. Does it, for example, record the mind of a victim of one of its victims, or perhaps the victim of an accident caused by one of its victims and, if so, how?'

'Fucking hell.'

'But going back to your original point,' Sverl continued, 'I saved them from the Rock Pool because the danger to them was a direct consequence of what I am and my actions there. I did not intervene in Taiken's experiment because, after all, those people did choose to try to transform themselves into prador. The danger to them was a direct consequence of that choice. In essence I know where to draw my line.'

'But you sent Trent Sobel down here and then me to help him.'

'When I understood Penny Royal's plan for them, I chose not to intervene in that either.'

'But you assisted in it.'

'My assisting was part of the plan too.'

'And what exactly is that plan?'

'Perhaps, in respect of Trent Sobel, Penny Royal wanted to examine the possibility of redemption for a murderer. Perhaps the AI wanted you to become more aware of your capabilities and what you actually are, which is the sum of its victims. Perhaps there was even something there for that horrible fucking snake drone. I don't know.'

'Found your god, have you, Sverl?'

Sverl found that very discomfiting, considering his earlier thoughts.

'Now, on a more practical level, I have things to do,' he said, 'as do you. Bsorol and Bsectil are bringing equipment that you require.' Sverl cut the link and blocked it. He didn't want to talk to Spear any more. The man's perspicacity was unnerving.

Sverl now turned his tripartite mind to other things. The repairs to his ship made by robots and second-children were proceeding precisely as predicted, as were the subtle alterations to internal shielding and the parameters of the U-space engine itself. By the time they arrived at his first destination, all this work would be completed. Sverl had deliberately chosen a system sufficiently far away, and a transition through U-space that was sufficiently long, just for that purpose. He had also chosen a destination that would give him a tactical advantage – when Cvorn inevitably surfaced from U-space in pursuit.

However, the advantage to be gained by jumping directly within that gas and dust ring was a small one. No doubt Cvorn had already realized that his weapons would be less effective there and had made adjustments. Cvorn might also believe that this reduction in weapons efficiency was Sverl's *entire* purpose in entering that ring. Speculating further, Cvorn might even believe that Sverl was trying to give himself time to make exterior repairs to his shielding and thus hide the U-signature of his next jump. It wasn't. Sverl knew he would not have the time. If he tried, during a running battle through that gas, his ship would probably end up even more damaged. Crew aboard would be killed, and his U-space drive might even be knocked out. He intended to make no exterior repairs at all, but he did plan to change the odds drastically.

With his AI component, Sverl gazed through cams and sensors at the other work his children and robots were doing inside his ship. His second-children had stopped working on Spear's ship. Just a few robots remained to make repairs; they weren't essential for the other task he had set for his second-children, for his ship was oversupplied with such robots. Sverl now focused on where most of the second-children were labouring. Their task was the result of an idea that had germinated when he saw the repairs to Spear's ship. It was an idea forced to full flower by the sharp reminder given by Riss's presence here.

Spare components packed the huge hold in Quadrant Three, purchased or otherwise acquired over the long years since the end of the war. An old-style Polity attack ship had been removed from the giant racks along one side of the hold and brought down to the floor. It sat alongside stuff Sverl had acquired during the war. The thing was complete but for the fried elec-tronics inside it, and the sub-AI crystal that had supplanted its actual AI.

Sverl shuddered at the recently reviewed memory. He had captured this ship during that disastrous 'training exercise' with Vlex and the others. It was the ship that had carried Riss, hidden within a railgun missile, to his ship that first time.

Of course, Sverl had been fortunate. He again shuddered at the definition of that word in his case. The prador aboard the other two dreadnoughts had all died while they were in U-space. This had actually been an error on the part of the assassin drones. The parasites should not have killed their hosts until sometime after their arrival in the Kingdom, the aim being for that parasite to spread elsewhere. Only Sverl himself had come close to fulfilling that plan. Yet, following his arrival in the King-dom, he had often wished he had died too.

His earlier self had thought the worst was over after he had removed the infestation from his body, but he had not known about the parasite encystment actually inside the telefactor. Nor had he anticipated the further months of surgical procedures to remove more of those worms, or the secondary procedures because of infections, tissue rejection and organ failures. Or the seemingly endless pain. Yes, he would never forget how he had acquired this attack ship.

His children had now opened up the rear of the attack ship, ready to insert the new U-space drive that was waiting on a grav-sled nearby. In the Kingdom and in the Polity such an operation would have taken place in a major shipyard. Sverl now understood that was because the technical expertise in the Kingdom wasn't as advanced as in the Polity. There was also a little AI obfuscation going on. The AIs were keeping a firm grip on the technology and didn't want it generally known that it was now possible to exchange a drive like any other component. Nor did they want it known that operating that technology wasn't just the province of AIs. Thus they kept their pet humans leashed.

Within a few hours, the second-children and attendant robots had inserted the new drive, and Sverl switched his attention to another area of his ship.

Three kamikaze missiles hung in their cradles, big ugly lumps like squashed spheres with single-burn fusers attached. These already contained U-space drives, and also second-child minds that had been somnolent for many years. Sections of the spheres were detached while spider robots removed the gigaton-range CTDs. Sverl did not want to use these as suicide bombs, though their mission would certainly be a dangerous one. Very soon they would be ready, whereupon the dreadnought's conveyor system would take them to their launch bays.

'Have you come to a decision yet?' Sverl asked through a particular com channel.

'I've yet to understand why you are giving me any choice at all,' replied what had once been his second-child mind, Flute.

'I am beginning to experiment with giving my children free will,' Sverl replied. 'I forced you to use Spear to spring Cvorn's trap, thus creating a conflict in your programming. I do not wish to force you to do anything again.'

'Or could it be that you are not sure you can?' suggested Flute. 'Could it be that my recent . . . transformation makes me more difficult to manipulate?'

Transformation . . .

Flute had been dying. The cooling system in his brain case had shut down. And the electro-synaptic activity in his super-cooled ganglion was being blocked by growing resistance in the installed superconductor grid. This was unfortunately not of the room-temperature variety. Had he been the normal kind of cased child-mind, the resupply of power and the repairs to his case would not have been enough. As it was, his ganglion was now just cold dead meat inside that case. However, Flute was a being with two facets, and one of them was AI crystal. The second-child, knowing he could not survive the thaw in his previous form, had copied all of himself across to the crystal. Flute was now, in fact, an AI.

'That is a factor,' admitted Sverl. 'With your mind wholly residing in AI crystal, you are indeed not so easy to control. In fact, even before you copied yourself across, you were capable of fighting my orders. However, what I require of you this time does not conflict with your programmed loyalty to Thorvald Spear – it in fact increases his chances of survival. I could, there-fore, force you to obey.'

'I see,' said Flute. 'Okay, I'll do as you ask, but on one con-dition.'

'And that is?'

'I want your access to my mind closed off henceforth.'

Sverl felt his prador instincts rebelling against the idea and, as had often been the case before, his human side agreed with the prador. The AI part of him considered other options, including the mind being partly controlled, and reflected that grateful independent allies were often more useful than slaves. Sverl decided to go with the AI's opinion. It was the AIs, after all, who had demonstrated superiority to both humans and prador over a century ago. And Flute had not yet realized how he could change the format of his mind and shut Sverl out anyway – with just a little internal programming.

'Very well,' Sverl sighed, 'I will close off the back doors I left and you will be able henceforth to filter any data I send you via this channel.'

'Nope, not good enough,' said Flute. 'I want the bandwidth of this channel closed by ninety-eight per cent. I want verbal communications along this route only. No data of any other kind, not even images. I'll open secondary computing, with a security cache, aboard the ship for anything more complex.'

'A little drastic, don't you think?'

Sverl observed that Flute's brain case had now arrived on a grav-sled beside the attack ship. Sverl would have liked to use Spear's destroyer for this chore, since Flute was more accustomed to its systems, but that ship was still too much of a mess. The attack ship would do for what he had in mind. All that it required was a little tweaking of its U-space engine – the same tweak he would shortly be applying to the engines of the three kamikazes.

'No, I don't think it's drastic,' Flute replied. 'You've already demonstrated that you're ruthlessly prepared to endanger others if it serves your purpose. You've also demonstrated that the changes you have undergone at the mental level are not as radical as you would have others suppose.'

'You make the mistake, despite all the evidence to the

contrary,' said Sverl, 'of thinking ruthlessness is only a prador trait. Inspect your own mind, consider the war, consider the things that both sides did. You will realize that humans are just as ruthless, that AIs can be even more so, and that both can be as vicious.'

Sverl now sent a program he had been pasting together almost unconsciously. He felt it hit home in the erstwhile second-child and felt it severing links, closing doors. The bandwidth of the communication channel grew narrow, closing from both ends, and Flute receded from him.

After a long pause, Flute replied tetchily, 'I guess I have much to learn.'

'Don't we all,' Sverl replied, now turning his attention to those kamikazes. He asserted his control over their three minds through channels like the one he had just closed and thence to the U-space engines of each craft. When the attack ship that would carry them was ready, he would have to pass information via a different route – supplying data and programs to the secure cache Flute had mentioned. Flute would then have the information to tweak the drive, to make it produce a much larger U-field than that needed by a ship of that size. For, just like the kamikazes, it was a decoy.

Spear

The former shellman was naked, just a torso with arms ending at the forearms. His eyes and lower jaw were missing and Bsectil was gripping him around the chest in one claw. This elicited too many bad memories, my own and those of others. But the first-child carried him gently over to row upon row of other erstwhile shell people laid out on the floor, saying, 'This one doesn't need the tank.'

I watched as one of the many military-format autodocs scattered about this crowd scuttled over to the man and set to work. For every one of those who didn't need to go into an amniotic tank for more critical support, the procedure was about the same. The doc attached a pressure bulb of artificial pan-type blood, injected blood shunts to filter out the captured toxins and inserted thick hollow needles to extract larger concentrations of captured toxins elsewhere in the body. It occasionally fed in tentacle grabs to pull out something too big for the hollow needles. And very occasionally it opened up a patient for still larger items. The program they were running hadn't required much adjustment because it was one used to extract fragments of shrapnel.

Next, turning my attention to the four large amniotic tanks, I saw that they each contained four amputees, with room for two more. The patients trailed all sorts of tubes and wires to the feed systems in the bases of the tanks so they looked like anthropomorphized epiphytes, and a faun of tank robots swam and scuttled around them. These people were the most damaged ones. They had been near death, having sacrificed some of their major human organs some time in the past and now recently lost the prador replacements for the same. They were on support while whole ecologies of nano-machines rebuilt the missing parts, or while the robots inserted artificial replacements. The tanks were cooled. They had to be. The rapid process generated a lot of heat. Already I could see Bsorol operating the small hoist to lift one of them out – this woman now had an artificial heart, though she would never hear it beat since it was a simple rotary pump.

I watched this operation for a while then, inevitably, my gaze slid to one side of the hoist, where Sepia stood observing the proceedings. Again, she occupied my attention more than she should. I glanced down at my nascuff but it was still blue, which meant that I should be shut down sexually. She looked back at me, hand on her hip, and then looked away. Irritated with myself, I dragged my eyes away, finally bringing them to rest on the dead laid out on a long grav-sled.

Thus far, there were twenty-eight fatalities. Seven had died after fights for dominance before Riss could inject them. Thirteen had altered themselves too radically to survive – one had even been attempting to turn his human brain into a ring-shaped prador ganglion. The Golem, which still squatted inside the sanctum of its last victim, had killed the remaining eight. I wondered if it had known about their recordings in the spine, or if it just hadn't cared.

'Thank you,' said Trent.

'There's still a lot to do,' I replied, uncomfortable with his gratitude. 'They'll need physical support, but what about later?'

'What do you mean?'

'If they were normal victims of accidents or combat they could be supplied with prosthetics or tank-grown limbs. And some could transfer to another medium like the Soul Bank, a Golem chassis or some other form of AI. But they're not normal and their problems extend somewhat beyond the merely physical.'

'We need a mind-tech,' he said, looking thoughtful.

I stared at him. 'A while ago I was talking to Sverl and the subject of free will came up. That applies here. We saved their lives but we've changed nothing. Once they're conscious again they may choose to start turning themselves back into what they were before.'

'Why?' Trent looked desperately puzzled.

'I don't know. People change themselves for all sorts of reasons. Some do it just for the novelty of being different and some because they simply hate what they are. All sorts of psychological motivations can be involved.' I paused for a moment of reflection, then said, 'You should understand this. Isobel Satomi's later changes might have been involuntary but the things she did to herself before weren't.'

'It's crazy,' he said, gazing at the bodies on the grav-sleds. 'They need an AI mind-tech to straighten them out . . . mental editing, erasure . . . cutting and pasting.'

As he spoke I considered Sverl, the spine, what had just happened to Riss and what had happened to me. But I replied, 'In your past, Trent, you forced people to obey your will, or the will of Isobel Satomi, but now you are a good person?'

He turned and glared at me.

I continued, 'And now, as a good person, you again want to force people to your will?'

'I feel responsible.'

'It's a novelty that wears off,' I replied, and turned to head away.

'What would you do?' he asked.

I turned back. 'Ultimately what you can do depends on Sverl, and depends on what happens next with Cvorn – who as you well know is in pursuit of us. Perhaps you won't have to worry about these people for long.'

'We could end up dead . . .'

'Yes, so if I were you, and felt responsibility beyond saving lives, I would talk to Sverl. Find some way of putting these people on ice. If I made it out alive, I'd then take them back to the Polity and hand them over to the AIs.'

'You'd boot the problem higher up the chain.'

'Yes. I might save the life of a man whom I found shot

through the head. However, I wouldn't stop him if I saw him take up the same gun and apply it to his temple.' I gestured to the former shell people all around. 'Most of these are Polity citizens and are well educated, intelligent and technically adroit enough to alter their own bodies radically. But, having studied what they were doing, I know that the alterations they were making, even with constant maintenance, were steadily killing them. *And they had to know that.* It seems to me that most of them are like that man with the gun.'

'They were committing suicide.'

'Yes.'

'Maybe it was a cry for help?'

'Maybe, but they were making it a long way from any help.'

'Group psychosis?'

'Maybe that too . . .' I paused to reflect on some other data I'd found in Taiken's files. 'Did you know that most of them are very old?'

'No.' He gave me a puzzled look.

'Most of them are of that age when ennui can become a fatal problem.'

'Ah.'

I turned away again, noting Riss rounding the grav-sled and heading towards me. It was time, I felt, to return to my own concerns. I wanted to see my ship, but first I wanted to retrieve the spine from Sverl. And I wanted to put some distance between a certain catadapt and myself.

'I'm not going to let them die,' said Trent.

I nodded once. Here was a man discovering how, sometimes, conscience and empathy could be a form of damnation.

Cvorn

Cvorn was attempting to deal with his sickness, any way he knew how. He opened his mandibles and lowered his mouth to the tube sticking up from the container, pressed his claw down on the plunger beside the tube and squirted another gallon of the white fluid dispensed by his surgical telefactor into his gullet. It was simple calcium carbonate to negate the excess of acid in his digestive system, a cellular suspension to reline it, and drugs conveyed by nano-machines to his bile nodes to kill their frenetic activity. He swallowed reflexively, and some of the pain in his first stomach eased. It was best to tube this stuff inside past the taste buds around the edge of his mouth, because it was the foulest thing he had ever tasted. Slowly he was recovering, but had found that he could not yet sate his growing hunger. An earlier attempt to eat some jellied mudfish had resulted in another session of projectile vomiting and uncontrollable diarrhoea. Also, though his visual turret eyes were as good as before, he could only see a blur through his palp eyes and they ached abominably around their bases.

'The screens first,' he said, once he felt able to speak without dribbling.

The sanctum was scattered with half-digested chunks of reaverfish that Cvorn's blanks were steadily collecting in large sacks. Cvorn just waited until Vrom had finished cleaning the vomit-spattered screens and the pit-control console. He was still feeling too ill to have any inclination to aug into his ship's system. Vrom then moved back to clean off the saddle control, and as he did this, Cvorn remembered how he himself had ceased to use it many years ago when he lost his last manipulatory limb. Perhaps he should finally replace them with prosthetics? No – right then he'd lost any inclination to return himself to a more youthful form.

As Vrom set to work on the floor, Cvorn lowered himself onto the control saddle. He knew the leaden feeling in his legs was psychosomatic. Stepper motors actually drove them, supplied with power from internal laminar storage. But it was still a relief to take the weight off his feet. He then inserted his claws into two pit controls. Despite his claws having nowhere near as much dexterity as manipulatory hands, the pit controls were good enough for some complex work. Flexing his claws open and closed on sliding scales pulled up numerous prador menus and options on his screens. First, he checked up on the state of his ship's weapons and found that everything he had wanted done was complete. Fifteen hours from now, he would drop into realspace with his railguns and energy weapons fully operational. And he'd immediately go in pursuit of Sverl.

Next, he checked up on his old destroyer, now filling one of this ST dreadnought's huge docking bays. He'd ordered a second-child aboard, in the expectation that he would not be seeing either it or his old ship again; the child was still in his old sanctum, squatting over the tail portion of a mudfish, steadily snipping off its proto-limbs and feeding them into its mandibles. It looked perfectly contented and seemed to be enjoying its repast, but then it was out of the way of competition with its fellows or from any likelihood of getting its shell cracked by Vrom. Cvorn envied its digestion and now resented the creature itself.

'Child,' he said, speaking through the intercom in that sanctum.

The second-child leapt up and away from its meal, dropping the proto-limb it had been chewing on and cowering.

'Child,' Cvorn repeated, then was momentarily at a loss as to how to continue. However, remembering the preparation he had made for his attack on Sverl, he began to think about his old destroyer, and another angle of attack occurred to him. Dividing Sverl's attention might be a good idea. He found himself instinctively processing relevant tactical data in his aug and realized he was now starting to feel better.

'When we arrive in realspace, you will launch,' he continued, now thinking and planning as he spoke. 'You will head out on a course, relative to mine and Sverl's position as detailed in your system.' He sent the data by aug, but kept a link open to the child, ready for updates.

'Yes, Father,' said the second-child, its clattering speech muffled by the flesh still sticking to its mandibles.

Yes, if he sent his destroyer out it could flank Sverl and at least limit the number of courses he could take while fleeing. In addition, Sverl would necessarily be concentrating most of his resources on defending himself from Cvorn's attack. Cvorn checked figures and analysed tactics. The destroyer carried some serious weaponry but, for the task in hand, perhaps something else . . .

Cvorn rose up off the saddle control as he considered this, the leaden feeling in his prosthetic limbs dissipating. Via aug through his ship's system, he sent requisition orders to numerous arms caches, where robots immediately began loading various items into internal transport tubes or onto grav-sleds. Like most prador, he felt uncomfortable watching machines show even meagre intelligence, but he couldn't deny that it was useful. The exigencies of the war had resulted in more and more robots aboard prador ships – the kind of concession that led eventually to artificial intelligence, and then to the likes of Sverl.

As he watched the robot preparations, he considered how he would change things for the prador race. The king would inevitably take a final trip out on the ocean of the prador home world, hydrofluoric acid eating his insides. Cvorn would usher in a new age. Perhaps he could institute some new form of technology based on the old ways, with more ganglions taken from prador children running such automated systems. Robot limbs like the ones he had just watched could be controlled directly by prador, just as he controlled his prosthetics. Of course, this would require more children. Rather than take the ganglions from second- and first-children that had ceased to be useful in their normal form, he could breed children especially for the chore.

Third-children were an option too. Prador fathers had never used them before. They left them much to themselves in their crèches to fight for dominance. Only the survivors made the transition to second-children. Chemical reactions in their bodies, caused by them dining on numbers of their fellows, drove that change. But, yes, he could use them before that happened.

Future possibilities looked good, and they looked good for the prador, but first he needed to get some things done. He issued further instructions and watched as his destroyer opened a munitions bay door. A short while later, second-children turned up with grav-sleds loaded with robot missiles. But before loading them, they began manually extracting drum belts of inert railgun slugs to make room.

'You will flank Sverl,' he said to the second-child. 'You will sow minefields in his path and fire missiles to the locations I designate.'

'Yes, Father.'

Those missiles were a perfect example of where the prador had gone wrong. They contained semi-intelligent computing, though at a level way below both the prador and Polity definition of AI. Surely he could install third-child ganglions in such weapons, in much the same way as the ganglions of their older brethren were installed in planet-busting kamikazes.

'Your munitions are being loaded now,' said Cvorn. 'Oversee this operation and ensure you are ready.'

'Yes, Father,' repeated the second-child, casting a glance at its unfinished dinner, then heading over to the destroyer's controls. Cvorn watched it climb onto the saddle control and insert dextrous manipulatory limbs, and felt a moment of peevishness. He decided that if it survived the coming encounter, its next encounter would be with a surgical telefactor. He would then use its ganglion, supplanting the sub-AI computing running this ship's weapons caches.

Having thought about children – their present utility and future uses – Cvorn now turned his attention to the mating pool. The female he had fertilized was squatting by the food pillar, the other two just out from it, protectively on guard. This was nothing to do with instinct – just filial loyalty. Before prador first began banging lumps of diamond slate together and thinking about how much more protection it offered when stuck to their carapaces with wrack resin, competition for mates and for the production of children had been fierce. A female already fertilized by one male was just as much a target for mating as an unfertilized female – even though they tended to fight harder. If a male managed to subdue her and mate with her, he used his prongs first to extract the already fertilized eggs before injecting his own seed. This then stimulated the production of more unfertilized eggs. The other two females must have been fighting their instinct to head to the surface to protect their fellow.

As expected, the female was gravid and ready, the blush and swelling around the base of her ovipositor being clear indicators. Cvorn now checked surrounding sub-systems and found the annex reaverfish tank. There were twenty of the big piscines swimming around in there, perpetually checking on their own feeding pillar, occasionally snapping at each other in irritation.

Vlern's children had clearly been thinking for the future, because all three sexes were present. And chains of reaverfish egg cases drifted amidst kelp trees growing in niches all around. Some of these had split open and fish fry shoaled under the spread of the thick pulpy leaves. Because so many adults and fry were present, it didn't matter which one Cvorn selected, so he just opened the series of doors in the tunnel leading between tanks.

Immediately one of the fish swam over to investigate, but then quickly turned away, perhaps detecting something in the water it didn't like. A second and a third fish did the same, then Cvorn found the virtual control to release a blood concentrate into the tunnel. The moment he did this, fish after fish headed directly for it. Cvorn discovered the necessity for that series of doors, when he finally managed to slam one shut behind the leading fish. It swam eagerly into the mating pool, the last door closing behind it, then it became more hesitant. It swam out, its head swinging from side to side as it tried to pick up more of the taste that had brought it here. It detected a taste it did not like at all, and shot back once more towards the tunnel. There it tried to slam its head through the closed door.

Now the two unfertilized prador females began cracking their mandibles together, sending out sonic shocks. The fish moved away from the door, searching for another escape route, but with the shocks slamming through its body it became steadily more confused. The fertilized female scuttled out at high speed, leapt off the floor and began propelling herself with her blade-section limbs. Swiftly closing on the reaverfish, she cracked her mandibles together, repeatedly punching in sonic shocks at closer and closer range. She then grabbed the fish in her mandibles and dragged it down to the bottom. There the female humped her back and drove her ovipositor deep inside it.

The injection was over in a moment and the female released the fish, which moved away, and headed back to her companions.

Ever so slowly the fish recovered and just circled around in the mating pool. Cvorn now opened another hatch to another annex pool. The fish was a large lump of meat and, though it was now issuing the chemical signature that prevented the injecting female from attacking it, the other females would soon forget and go after it. Cvorn released blood concentrate in the new tunnel and the reaverfish went through. It headed straight over to patrol round, where it expected to find another feeding pillar, but it found nothing. In a few hours the prador nymphs would start hatching out, and would begin eating it from the inside out. Like the parasites the Polity had resurrected during the war, they would first avoid eating any organ that would kill their host quickly. However, as they grew into what some prador described as fourth-children, their appetites would change.

Eventually the fish would die and be consumed, whereupon the fourth-children would turn on their weaker brethren and eat them, in turn. With lungs wholly displacing their gill systems, the males would head for the surface via a ramp that led into a third-child crèche and to yet another feeding pillar. There they would viciously compete while their ganglions expanded and they steadily turned from savage mindless predators into savage predators with brains. Older prador would then take these male third-children from the crèche to begin the next stage of their education. This, as Cvorn well remembered, usually began with a beating from a second-child. Education thereafter was a weeding-out process. Those that didn't learn quickly enough became lunch for their older brethren.

Blite

Blite jerked into wakefulness and rolled out of bed, trying to figure out if he had been dreaming it, or if the *Black Rose* had really submerged into U-space. He felt bleary and nauseous. All the waiting around at Penny Royal's command, for who knew what, had made him delve into his liquor supply more than was his custom. He sat on the edge of his bed, rubbing his face, and reached over to the drawers set in the wall beside it, opened one and took out a small bottle. He eyed the dwindling contents, then tipped out two aldetox tablets and dry swallowed them. As he stood up and walked over to his cabin dispenser, he realized that, yes, he could feel the almost subliminal hum of the U-space engines. On autopilot, he used the touchscreen to order a pint of black tea sweetened with honey – aldetox worked better with some liquid in your stomach.

'Seems we left a little early,' he said, expecting either no reply or a terse and dismissive comment to issue from the air. Surprisingly, a tinkling sound came from behind him and he turned to see a black dot heading towards him from an impossible distance to grow into one of Penny Royal's black diamonds. It hung there, with the air distorting about it; the captain, just for a moment, sensed vast amusement and a kind of joy.

The feeling abruptly cut off as the diamond disappeared with a sound like a dropped wine glass and Leven's voice abruptly issued from the ship intercom.

'Must I?' said the ship mind to someone, then, after a pause, 'It seems I must.'

'What is it, Leven?' Blite asked.

'Just listen,' said the mind, continuing, 'The further beyond Penny Royal's particular definition of average a being has gone,

379

either by augmentation or by some other mental transformation, the more difficult it is to predict its actions.'

'So it's predicting actions, not zipping into the future to check?' Blite turned back to his dispenser, took out the insulated beaker of tea and sipped it to check its temperature. It was perfect, as usual with anything produced by this new ship. He gulped down about a quarter of it.

'In a sense it is doing both,' Leven replied.

'What does it mean by that?'

'Its future self informs its actions and it knows when action is required.'

Blite felt the skin crawling on his back again. He thought he understood that, and he didn't like the implications. In previous conversations with the AI, if he pursued something, he got explanations that lay just off the edge of his comprehension. Or he was left with his skull feeling as if it had been reamed out. Now his ship's mind was translating these communications. Maybe he would learn more this time.

'So what actions are difficult enough to predict that they warrant our early departure?' he asked.

'Penny Royal can predict the action of the mid-range augments – both human and prador cases – for up to a few months before chaos factors throw calculations into disarray. Higher-functioning entities are difficult, apparently. Polity AIs, Penny Royal has told me, have chosen not to interfere, otherwise all his plans could have come to nothing. Sverl, with his conflicted tripartite mind, is difficult too, but sufficiently within required parameters. The king of the prador is a whole order of magnitude more difficult than Sverl – close to the Polity AIs but with more random elements introduced because of his steady transformation and opaque goals.'

'So how far ahead can Penny Royal predict the king's actions?'

'A matter of weeks, usually.'

'The king's done something, then?'

'Penny Royal is uncertain about its prediction of the king's actions within that time-span.'

'Try to be a bit clearer, Leven.'

'I'm trying my best. It seems, for reasons that extend into esoteric mathematics even I have trouble grasping, that the king might do something . . . unexpected.'

'So where are we going?' Blite asked, not feeling any wiser, but certainly starting to feel a bit less hungover.

'A supply station with a prador designation,' said Leven. 'Penny Royal has to check to see if the king is—'

'Doing as predicted,' Blite interrupted. 'I get that.' He paused and took another sip, then continued, 'But what about the entropy dump? What will happen to the worlds of the Rebus system when we leave without stopping that supernova blast?'

'The entropy dump is complete, I'm told. We are now . . . up to date.'

'So we didn't have to stay in position for two whole weeks . . .?'

'No, less than two weeks of negation was the best option for Rebus.'

'And now?'

After a long pause, Leven continued, 'It seems the Polity observers will not have to evacuate the human population of these planets as planned. They will soon learn that moving the population to a planetary cave system will be enough to ensure their survival. Meanwhile, the brunt of the supernova blast front – striking both the world and the gas giant's moon – will be nowhere near as powerful. Both of the unique ecologies under observation will be damaged, but will survive.'

Blite swallowed some more tea. 'Which is of course quite convenient, what with *someone* having made off with the evacuation runcibles.'

'Quite.'

'And those ecologies were the most important thing to Penny Royal, just as they probably were to the Polity AIs who had aimed to evacuate that place?' he questioned.

Again, that pause, then, 'Yes, humans are not rare and either way they would have survived. All that will be lost is their social structure. Once subject to Polity intervention and assistance to survive the damage to their world, they will have to change. If they had been evacuated, it would have been lost anyway.'

'Oh, that's all right, then,' said Blite, knowing he was being unfair, but at that moment not caring. 'But the main objective wasn't really anything to do with those worlds was it? It was all about the runcibles. So what does Penny Royal want them for?'

'That I don't know and am not being told,' Leven replied.

'Figures,' Blite grunted. 'No more questions,' he added. Leven hadn't actually complained. However, even though his voice was computer generated, Blite could tell that he hadn't enjoyed the position of translator. He had started to get a little shrill towards the end.

Blite gulped down the last of his tea, eyed his shipsuit slung on a clothes horse beside his bed and headed over to his sanitary unit. He needed a piss and hadn't been inclined to do that while the AI was present in his cabin. Then it was time to get ready but he wasn't in any hurry. After a shower in the same sanitary unit, he had a long-overdue haircut and a shave. He donned underwear, black jeans and white shirt. Next came an ersatz enviro-suit jacket and intelliboots that closed up comfortably about his feet. He then left the cabin.

Upon his arrival on the bridge, he wondered if Penny Royal had been playing with their minds because Brond and Greer had also cleaned themselves up. Brond was clad in something similar to an ECS combat suit with its white and yellow-gold colouring, as if on some chameleoncloth setting of a desert world. His head was shaven. Greer had plaited her hair, or perhaps some grooming machine had done it for her, and coiled it on the back of her head. She wore skin-tight pale blue knee-shorts and a tight cream top that exposed the ribbed muscle of her belly. She looked the most feminine Blite had ever seen her, despite the belt around her waist holding a pulse-gun on one side and a ceramal combat knife on the other.

'Seems we're all getting ready for a party,' said Brond.

Feeling uncomfortable, Blite gazed at them for a long moment, then went over and sat in his seat.

'Leven, what's our status?' he asked.

'Five ship hours from our arrival time and bending relativity to breaking point,' the Golem ship mind replied.

'Time travel again?'

'Yup.'

So where was the next resulting entropy dump? At this prador supply station? Blite stood up again and gazed at the representation the screen laminate was showing – the black of space with stars dopplering past them. Then he suggested, 'Breakfast?'

'Sure – I'm ready,' said Brond.

'Me too,' said Greer, looking slightly puzzled as she ran her hand over her flat stomach.

Blite shivered. They all cleaned themselves up and put on fresh clothing, and all three had yet to eat. Was this just one of those cases of a crew falling into a strange consonance with each other, or was the black AI onboard neatly controlling them, setting them running together like all the other components aboard this ship? Or were they simply reacting to some overspill from the AI? Together they trooped out to the communal refectory.

They spent an hour eating and talking generally about past events, then a further hour in speculation about what Penny Royal's ultimate goals might be.

'We're pets,' said Brond at one point.

'I think you're wrong,' Greer replied. 'We're an audience.'

Blite considered both their contentions, remembered his thoughts about them being witnesses, then came up with a further contention of his own. 'In a way I reckon you're both right, but I think we're something else too.'

They both waited patiently for his explanation. Noteworthy, he felt, how during that last few hours there had been no friction, no contention. They were all being perfectly reasonable and logical and he himself had felt none of his usual surges of irritation. Something in the air supply?

'I think we're a tie to reality. I think we're a sample of normality.'

'Normality?' wondered Greer, raising an eyebrow.

'Relative normality,' said Blite, trying to solidify some vague thoughts. 'Penny Royal doesn't need us – our presence aboard this ship is irrelevant to its actions. So why are we here? I have to wonder if, through us stupid, petty, completely physical and relatively normal humans Penny Royal maintains a grip on reality.'

'Vague,' said Greer.

'You're saying we keep Penny Royal grounded?' suggested Brond.

'Yeah.' Blite nodded, still struggling to put what he felt into words. 'Here aboard we have a being capable of manipulating time, of putting the king of the prador on the back foot, of scaring off Polity AIs. I would say Penny Royal is like some world dictator slumming it in a bar to find out what the plebs think.'

'I can live with that, I guess,' said Brond.

'Or I'm a mouse trying to guess the motives of a nuclear physicist,' Blite added.

Blite headed back to his cabin, leaving the other two to their own devices. He called up all available data on Penny Royal on a wall screen, collated by sub-program into a documentary format, then lay back on his bed and watched it. Penny Royal had been the mind of a destroyer that went AWOL after exterminating a human force of some eight thousand soldiers on a world called Panarchia. After that, it had turned into an extreme version of the kind of villains – crime lords – that occupied the Graveyard. Or you could say Penny Royal became an AI equivalent of something out of one of the old religions: a fallen angel, Satan. The black AI was something people went to for some advantage and sold their souls in the process. Dealing with Penny Royal could make you fantastically rich and make your dreams come true, but it could also leave you either dead or in some very personal hell.

After the AI's near-terminal encounter with some Atheter technology, the war drone Amistad had saved it and brought it back into the Polity fold, apparently forgiven. It had behaved itself for a while on the planet of Masada, but went AWOL again – in Blite's old ship. This time, it was seemingly on course to ameliorate some of the mayhem it had caused. Apparently, Penny Royal was seeking redemption. But it was following an unnecessarily convoluted route and had opaque motives. Blite also felt sure that it had some goal other than redemption in mind. He sensed that it had stretched out and shaped the game it was playing to that end, but that end purpose eluded him. Certainly, it involved those generators he had seen, it involved three Polity runcibles, and it involved the black AI. He now felt sure he was seeing just one small portion of its whole too: the one facet displayed to the small world of human intelligence.

15

Riss

The collar Sverl had locked her into was very effective. It sat tightly around Riss's neck, its inner face a form of remora pad. Once it had been stuck in place, it injected nanoscopic hooks deep inside to root. Riss had tried attacking these internally using her nanobot immune system, but the collar issued a reprimand – a focused EM pulse that left her blank and confused. In the process she lost conscious control of those nanobots so they returned to their usual tasks, and the hooks just regrew.

Besides making itself very difficult to remove, the thing's main function was to interfere with Riss's many systems, including chameleonware. It had all the 'ware's components and systems located. And when Riss tried to activate them, they too became subject to one of those directed EM pulses. So now the drone could not use the light-bending effect of her outer skin. She was also denied the underlying powered layer that could bend other radiations. Or the skin microscales that negated any air disturbance. She could not rapidly pulse viruses into any form of directed scanning. She could not use the grav-motor that matched frequencies with grav-plates so no detector would pick up her weight, its effect also twisted through and reflected by a complicated arrangement of hardfields that could defeat most mass detectors. Nor could she use her method of displacing U-com and other U-space systems, so detectors always found them at the wrong realspace location. Riss had even tried moving her internal components, but the collar had tracked them. Sverl knew his stuff, and Riss realized that to remove the collar would require some drastic action that present circumstances did not warrant.

A secondary function of the collar was to prevent any interference with this dreadnought's computer systems. The moment she tried any of that, it went into rhythmic pulse mode, scrambling her penetration so she could only glean scraps of data and could influence nothing.

'So where now?' she asked.

'Sverl first,' Spear replied. 'I want that spine back.'

'Right. Sverl,' said Riss.

All scans of the collar revealed that its purpose was dual: it scrambled both chameleonware and attempts at computer penetration, but it hadn't prevented her taking Spear's cure inside and injecting it into the shell people, and it showed no signs that it could have. It also hadn't stopped her from returning to the medical area where Spear had made that cure and breaking into the drugs safe. But then that had been a low-order computer penetration that might not concern Sverl. And it hadn't prohibited her from removing the flask containing the original enzyme acid and loading that – which really should concern Sverl.

An option was now available to her. If she got close enough to Sverl, she reckoned she could beat any of his defences and have time to drive in her ovipositor at least once. The enzyme acid would dissolve all Sverl's prador organic tissue. Because it wasn't as specific as the version Spear had made from it, it would also attack his human tissue. Surely Sverl could not survive that?

As they approached the doors leading out of the fourth quadrant of Sverl's ship, Riss probed ahead and examined the locking mechanisms and their computer controls, which weren't very complicated. She felt sure she could open these doors but it would be an unnecessary demonstration of the abilities the drone still retained. Sverl might decide to upgrade the collar and hamstring her further. A moment later, the first door opened. Spear walked through and she followed.

The next door took them out into one of the main corridors, where a second-child paused to gaze at them, started snipping its claws at the air in irritation and began to edge closer. Riss could take the child down in a second and knew the acid would not even be necessary, but again it was probably best to remain low profile. The clattering and bubbling of prador speech issued from a PA speaker – Sverl specifically telling this child to back off. Sverl then gave that same order, concerning all humans, generally throughout the ship. Riss noticed that assassin drones weren't mentioned in this amnesty. The second-child abruptly turned away and moved off.

'I've been checking on things,' said Spear as they headed in the opposite direction.

Riss had been monitoring the man since they first met, but had now delved into his aug on levels with which he might not be comfortable. Though the collar prevented Riss from penetrating this ship's system, it did not react when Riss penetrated other computing hardware, Spear's aug being one such example. Sverl trusted Spear, so had allowed him access to the ship systems. Riss was using him as a stepping-stone to access them herself – so knew precisely what Spear had been checking and had already guessed his aims.

'You have?' Riss enquired innocently.

'Sverl set his children and robots to work on restoring my ship, but recently pulled them off for other projects.'

Yes, the second-children were working on an old captured attack ship and three prador kamikazes. Riss had leapfrogged from Spear's aug to grab all the data available on this work, established a link and was watching still. At first she had thought the attack ship and kamikazes were being prepared as weapons to use against Cvorn, but had then been baffled when the second-children started removing the CTDs from the kamikazes.

'But in my ship, they did manage to tear out everything that was scrapped anyway and replace some items,' Spear continued. 'We don't have a U-space drive or fusion drive, and a lot of armour is missing. But the robots Sverl left on the job have been restoring the ship's loom and control nexi, ready to integrate all replacement components. They've repaired much of the bridge as a point from which to oversee that integration.'

Do you know about Flute? Riss wondered.

'It's a standard procedure,' said the drone. 'If you can't do the heavy stuff, get the light stuff done ready to receive it.'

'They replaced the burned-out screen fabric too,' said Spear.

When they arrived at Sverl's sanctum, the diagonally divided door stood firmly closed, while outside, resting against it was the spine. Seeing this, Riss immediately wondered if her collar might also give the prador access to things she didn't want him to know. No, Sverl was just very busy preparing for the coming encounter with Cvorn . . .

As Spear picked up the spine, Riss detected a surge of U-space data transfer, immediately followed by an intense phys-ical reaction and out-of-parameter functions in his aug. The man had just started to experience someone else's memory and used aug-mind synergy to suppress it. Riss backed off mentally – some of the stuff going on in there defied analysis and was therefore dangerous. Spear rested the spine on his shoulder, turned and trudged off.

'What about Flute?' Riss asked, squirming to keep up.

'Dead,' said Spear. 'I got some connection, but he told me he was dying. After that, no connection.'

He didn't know. Riss decided to throw him a bone. 'Remember that Flute was a combination of deep-frozen prador second-child ganglion *and* AI.'

Spear went quiet, and now risking another mental peek Riss found him talking to Sverl.

'*What is Flute's status?*' Spear asked.

'*The second-child brain died,*' Sverl replied.

'*A precise statement,*' Spear observed, '*and lying by omission.*'

'*He recorded across to his AI component.*'

'*I want him back.*'

'*When he has finished carrying out one last chore for me you can have him back.*'

A second later Spear was into Sverl's system, tracking Flute, locating him in the old attack ship, then pulling up information on the kamikazes. That was almost as fast as a haiman – the nearest the Polity had come to amalgamating human and AI.

'*I see,*' said Spear. '*U-signatures.*'

What's this? Riss was baffled.

'*Precisely,*' Sverl replied.

'So there you go,' said Spear aloud.

'What?' Riss asked, rapidly withdrawing her probe.

'Now I know what happened to Flute,' Spear continued, 'and now you know, supposing you didn't already.'

'Didn't already?' Riss repeated.

'Stop being coy – I can feel you in my aug like a splinter in my finger, Riss.'

Not for the first time, Riss considered killing a man. Humans were easier to off than prador. Even without the enzyme acid, which would chew through Spear's body just a little bit slower than it would go through Sverl's, Riss could punch holes through his heart or brain stem. And even without a collimated diamond ovipositor, Riss could still simply strangle him.

'Sverl is blocking me,' the drone said.

'Understandable, really,' said Spear. 'You told me that Penny Royal hollowed you out and left you without purpose, which is a vague description coming from a machine, but I sense that since coming aboard a prador dreadnought, your homicidal instincts have been on the rise.'

Riss immediately began checking the induction probe she had been using to hitch a ride on the man's aug. Could it be a two-way street?

'I sometimes wonder, Riss,' Spear continued, 'if all Penny Royal took away were the remnants of hope. You were fashioned for one purpose and that ended with the end of the war.'

'I know what Penny Royal took,' Riss asserted, not really knowing at all.

Spear continued relentlessly, 'During a war, weapons get superseded and dispensed with. After a war they're melted down and turned into ploughs.'

'Shut the fuck up, Spear,' Riss hissed.

'Ah, not so empty after all.'

Riss found herself stationary on the floor as the man trudged on ahead, trying to control a surge of rage that was as integral as her power supply. As this waned, she felt bafflement again. What was that? And why had Spear spoken like that? Riss abruptly went after him again, induction probe at full strength, just catching the tail of another surge of data exchange between the spine and the man.

Was that you speaking then? Riss wondered.

Eventually they arrived at Penny Royal's erstwhile body, the destroyer Spear had renamed the *Lance*, like the spine he carried on his shoulder. The ship had been moved, much had been torn out and much reconstructed, and now a ramp led up to its open shuttle bay. Spear made his way through the partially recon-structed interior to enter the bridge. Riss followed and watched the man walk across the charred floor, to stand beside a portable prador saddle control. He hoisted the spine off his shoulder and rested it against the saddle.

'We all have our loads to bear,' he said, 'and that's a heavy one.' He turned to look directly at Riss. 'I'm sorry, I don't know why I said what I said before.'

He turned away again and dipped his head to peer at the saddle control. After a moment, it hummed and buzzed to itself, glints of light igniting in small pit controls made to take a second-child's manipulatory hands. The screen fabric came on all around, turning the ship transparent and showing them the hold in which the destroyer sat. Out on the floor a single constructor robot was perambulating, a coil of high-pressure fuel line sitting on its flat back. It moved out of sight – entering the ship some-where to the rear.

'I think we can do better,' said Spear.

He was auged into the control, now making linkages to the entire computer system of Sverl's ship. The screen fabric turned grey, swirled through with shots of nacre. It looked like a mal-function until Riss turned and saw the jut of a sensor spire in one direction, and some bulbous nacelle extended on a pylon in the other. The cams could not quite convey what lay out there – they were looking at a machine interpretation of U-space.

'Just a few minutes now,' said Spear. 'Penny Royal's timing comes close to perfection, though Sverl facilitated that by not allowing us into his sanctum. If we'd gone in and you'd been un-able to resist your urge to try killing him, we would have been late.'

Riss just gazed at the man, and yearned for the simplicity of murdering prador.

Blite

The screen display of the *Black Rose* blended smoothly with reality as they returned to that state. The stars slowed in their dopplering course past them, and objects ahead glimmered and expanded into view. An iron sphere sat in vacuum ahead, other objects positioned in an arc underneath it like lashes below an eyeball. And some other large object lay beyond.

'Leven,' said Blite, but before he could continue, magnification increased to bring these objects closer and data began scrolling down a subscreen in a bottom corner.

The prador supply station sat out in clear vacuum many light years from the nearest star. It was a slightly flattened sphere with a square-section protuberance girdling its circumference. Around this, three ships had docked like fish feeding on a bread ball, and Blite at once recognized the long brassy teardrops as the ships of the King's Guard. All of them were here – the other twenty-seven arrayed in an arc below, neatly lined up like a series of text slashes. Some distance beyond hung a cylinder about which smaller vessels and vacuum construction machines swarmed – scaffolds spreading out from one end to etch out some saucer section. Blite just glanced at this – his focus was mainly on those King's Guard ships. Then he scanned the data coming in, blinked in disbelief, and returned his attention to that other object.

'What the fuck is that?' he wondered.

The structure looked small in perspective, but that was because it lay some distance back from the other objects here.

The damned thing was immense: fifty miles long and maybe ten miles thick.

'The King's Ship,' intoned Penny Royal, seemingly right beside his ear.

He glanced round, half-expecting that antique space suit to be standing behind him, but the AI had not seen fit to materialize in any form.

'The King's Ship?' he repeated.

'Six hundred years,' said Penny Royal, 'or less than one.'

'What?'

A frame opened on the screen and, once again, an armoured prador was there. Blite experienced a familiar surge of irritation, knowing he was just about to witness yet another baffling conversation between this Gost, who was apparently the king of the prador, and Penny Royal. Then he felt glad, because the irritation was surely his own.

'You again,' said Gost.

'Yes,' Penny Royal replied.

'What now?'

'If you lead your Guard to Room 101, you will die,' the AI replied.

'Sverl cannot be allowed to exist,' said Gost. 'He might be used by subversives to destabilize my Kingdom. This will lead to damaging civil war during which, as I suppress those subversives, they will launch attacks against the Polity. They will hope for a response that would unify all prador under them.'

'This will not happen.'

'I calculate that, without my intervention, it will.'

'I know that it won't.'

The armoured prador on screen rattled its legs against the floor, evidently in frustrated irritation. Blite knew the feeling.

'I need more,' it eventually said.

'It is time for you to board your ship,' said Penny Royal. 'Already you are reaching the stage in which you need larger armour to conceal your development. You need the space to grow, physically and mentally. You will call yourself Oberon.'

'Very good,' said Gost. 'And you're a Delphic oracle.'

'You understand human thought.'

'I still need more.'

'I can show you a future,' said Penny Royal.

On screen, the armoured prador abruptly whirled around. One of those black diamonds had appeared in its sanctum. In response to this object, ports all around the walls slammed open to reveal the mirror throats of particle cannons. Seemingly under their regard the diamond separated into six pieces – with something extremely dark and deep lying central to them and only just visible from Blite's perspective. The king emitted a bubbling scream and retreated out of view. Then the whole scene disappeared in a crash and explosion of blue fire as the particle cannons fired. White-hot chunks of metal and boiling smoke filled the frame before it blanked.

'What the hell happened?' said Brond.

'Patience,' said Penny Royal.

Blite now looked up at the main view ahead, which had drawn closer. The Guard ships were breaking formation – steering thrusters blading out into darkness and the hot stars of fusion drives igniting. Those docked to the station were detaching too, while anti-munitions lasers probed out, picked out by wisps of vapour issuing from the station.

The sounds continued, slowly died, and then out of the blankness Gost said, 'I don't believe you, and I will still take my Guard to Room 101.' Blite wondered what he had been shown by the black AI.

'You will believe me,' said Penny Royal, 'and now I will give you time to think.'

A surge of *something* passed through the *Black Rose*. Blite experienced a falling sensation twinned with an odd feeling of déjà vu. Another surge followed this – setting steering thrusters at full power with the fusion drive igniting. Blite groped for his seat strap, expecting battle, but he still focused on the screen – to see the station and the Guard ships simply die. Fusion drives and steering thrusters went out, the lasers blinked off and light issuing from view ports and bubbles died. Everything went dark; the ships were no longer accelerating, and the constructor robots about the King's Ship were drifting on courses set before this event. Even far beyond this scene, the stars grew dim.

'Entropy dump,' said Brond.

Blite looked at the data and could see that they were now under huge acceleration, as he replayed that conversation in his mind. He couldn't quite grasp what the AI had been getting at – but perhaps he would when he viewed a recording of it later.

Next, the lights in their bridge dimmed, the data stream disrupted and for a second he found himself weightless. A microsecond later they were dropping into U-space and power returned. *Edge of the entropy dump?* he wondered. That rather frighteningly indicated that the ship could direct it like a weapon.

'Where now?' he asked.

'The War Factory. Factory Station Room 101,' Penny Royal replied.

Cvorn

Vrom was gone and the sanctum gleamed after his cleaning efforts. Even the ship lice had disappeared into their niches and crevices around the stone-effect walls, or under the glowing dead man's fingers of sea lichen, because they had nothing to glean from the floor. Vrom had been even more meticulous than usual – probably sensing his father's mood and wanting to ensure no punishable infractions. Cvorn still did not feel so good. He felt like a second-child after a thorough beating, and the vision in his palp eyes had worsened further and their movement felt stiff. He was also anxious about what was to come.

Everything was ready and Cvorn could not be any more prepared, or more on edge. He stomped around his sanctum, perpetually going over his plans but unable to spot the glaring error he was sure was there. At one point, he began using his screens to review other plans concerning the alliances he would make and eventually break, once he had captured Sverl. But these were also plans he had checked over ad nauseam and just thinking about them now brought on a deadening boredom, so he sent them back into storage.

He had to do something.

Cvorn returned his attention to the shoal of reaverfish, the prador females and the lone reaverfish he'd let into the mating pool. He found his tension easing as he watched them and went into a kind of fugue state as the hours slipped by. He even caught the moment when the lone reaverfish began shuddering and shaking as it felt something seriously wrong inside it. When he finally dragged himself back to the present, he found that only an hour remained until his encounter with Sverl. He was hungry again now, but didn't dare risk his delicate digestive system until after the battle. He didn't really need to check his plans again, but his earlier paranoia that he had missed something was returning. Nearly everything was as it should be, but an alert glyph it took him a second to recognize drew his attention.

Vlern's children . . .

Sealed into their quarters all about the ship, three of them were running out of oxygen and sinking into somnolence. However, the fourth had either been astute enough to prepare for something like this, or had got lucky. The young adult Sfolk not only had his own oxygen supply but he had also found a diamond saw with its own power pack and was steadily cutting through one wall. This despite Cvorn's precaution of cutting electricity to all but the cams in his quarters, meaning most power tools were of no use.

Cvorn observed the scene, his guts bubbling with the intensity of his sudden anger. He wanted to go down there right then, open Sfolk's quarters and simply tear the creature apart, but did not have the time. He could send Vrom, or some of the others, or maybe a war drone. But that wouldn't be as satisfying. For a moment, he just stared in frustration at the screens, then, remembering his ascendancy in the Dracocorp aug network, he felt a sudden fear. *How had he forgotten that?* Opening bandwidth, he sought to seize mental control of the young adult, but it was like trying to get a grip on jelly. Presently the jelly collapsed and the connection closed.

'Desist,' he ordered through the cam-com.

Sfolk backed away from the hole he was making in the wall, still gripping the diamond saw in his claws, then tilted up and gazed at the cams in the ceiling.

'The others were naive,' he said. 'I knew not to trust any gift from you. I routed the aug through a thrall unit interface set to shut down after a period of time if I didn't log in.' Sfolk abruptly dropped the diamond saw. 'I guess this wasn't quiet enough.'

What?

Sfolk scuttled over to an open tool chest and took out another item, turned back towards the hole he had been making and raised the object. With a crack, he activated it and billowing smoke highlighted the intense green beam of a quantum cascade laser. It swiftly sliced through material the diamond saw would have taken an age to cut.

'Vrom!' Cvorn clattered, quickly routing his present screen view to the first-child. 'Get down there and kill him! When you've dealt with him, kill the others!'

'Yes, Father,' Vrom replied.

Cvorn winced. The base of his left palp eye had started hurting as if someone was stabbing in a carapace drill. He tried to ignore the pain while making an aug connection to his own war drones, dispatching them to the same quarters. However, Sfolk's behaviour was puzzling, because he could not hope to escape . . .

Suddenly feeling panic, which made that palp eye hurt even more, Cvorn brought up a ship's schematic in his mind. The wall Sfolk was cutting through opened into a main tunnel. Even though Vrom would take a while to get there, two war drones, carrying enough weapons to go up against a Polity assault boat, were speeding in that direction and would arrive soon enough.

Something was wrong.

Cvorn deliberately forced himself to be calm and examined the schematics more meticulously. They definitely showed that main tunnel just on the other side of that wall and all the measurements were correct. However, when Cvorn expanded his examination of datum lines and the measurements of the ship as a whole, things ceased to add up. The schematics were wrong. Sfolk had almost certainly interfered with them. Cvorn began working on them, observing the drones – two armoured spheres ten feet across and pocked with missile and energy weapon ports – arrive in that main tunnel and slow to a halt.

'Request clarification,' said one of them. 'Further orders required.'

Wordlessly, Cvorn auged his instructions through, and they

both turned towards the wall supposedly adjacent to where Sfolk was cutting, and powered up their particle cannons.

Cvorn continued analysing the schematics in his aug, running a search program and trying to correct obvious errors. Some liquid ran into one of his turret eyes and he blinked it away – too wrapped up in present concerns to heed it. It struck him as likely that what Sfolk had done had been originally in preparation for seizing control of this ST dreadnought from his brothers . . .

There.

The schematic expanded, holes appearing throughout it. However, though this was *probably* where areas were missing, it was wrong in the area where the drones were cutting, because still it showed just that one wall between Sfolk's quarters and the main tunnel.

'Cvorn,' said Sfolk, his laser shutting down, 'you can augment, put on legs and take my brother's prongs, but your brain is still old.' The young prador now dived into the hole and disappeared out of sight.

Out in the corridor, as Vrom arrived, the drones cut through to expose a vertical maintenance shaft made for first-children, but which was still large enough for the young adult to squeeze down. It was too small, however, for the war drones to enter.

'Vrom,' Cvorn instructed, 'get what resources you need, go after him and kill him. But take nothing that will in any way hamper my attack on Sverl.'

'Yes, Father,' said Vrom, then turned away to begin clattering into the communicator beside his mandibles. Cvorn watched and waited until a small squad of heavily armed second-children arrived, along with one of the ship's internal security war drones – a thing shaped like a melon seed over five feet long. This ignited arc lights in its fore and headed down into the maintenance shaft.

The second-children followed, and Vrom a short while after, when he had donned all the hardware they had brought for him.

I really don't need this now, thought Cvorn, aware it wasn't a new thought. He eyed a counter in one of his lower screens and, with a further thought, banished the present views in preparation for those outside the ship, rattled his feet against the floor and spat some acid gathering in his gullet. Belatedly he linked to a cam view showing his own sanctum – the only way he could get a good look at himself – and focused it in on his visual turret. His left palp eye was lying over, some pustule having burst underneath it. He reached up with his claw and gently took hold of it and tried to move it back upright. More pus oozed out round its base, then when he released it, it fell forwards and popped back out of its socket. It tumbled down his visual turret, bounced off his mandibles and landed on the floor. Cvorn stared at it, at its withered tail of nerves and veins, then turned away as a ship louse came out to investigate. He returned his attention to his screens. It didn't matter. He had more important concerns.

Now Sverl, now you're mine.

Spear

The new screen fabric within the *Lance* glimmered. It formed a bright circle, expanding from a point at the centre of the ceiling, then spreading out and settling down the walls. With a horrible twisting sensation, probably due to damage Cvorn had inflicted earlier, Sverl's dreadnought dropped into realspace. As the view was revealed I thought that something had gone seriously wrong. But, updating from Sverl's system, I understood that we had surfaced actually inside the ring of dust and gas. That was why it looked like some ancient city smog out there.

'You'll have to enhance the view,' said Riss.

'No, really?' I said, wondering why I had been growing irritated with the drone lately.

Sverl's sensors were bringing in a lot more than mere human visual data, so I started to make use of that. The smog cleared on the screen and the stars came back into view, but none of this made me any wiser. I ran the data through a program in my aug and routed it back to the screen fabric, truncating distances and bringing the trinary system about us into the human compass.

The white and black dwarf stars orbited each other far out to my left, whilst the red dwarf sat over to my right. I made a slight adjustment to bring the ring of dust and gas surrounding the white dwarf, in which we sat, into view. This gave the odd effect of sitting inside a massive tunnel that curved off into the far distance. Scattered inside and outside this were asteroids and asteroid clusters, while sprinkled along the ring were planetoids, smoothly spherical after billions of years in this stellar tumbling machine. The whole scene would have been a bit too much computer model and not enough reality, but for the processing I was also running in my aug. This truly gave me a sense of scale and of *being* there.

'U-signature,' observed Riss.

I was already on it, because the drone had only picked it up through my aug connection to Sverl's system. I etched out a frame beyond our tunnel and there, rucking up a trail of generated photons like fairy dust, Cvorn's ship scored itself into the real. I brought the frame closer for more detail. This was my first real look at this ST dreadnought and it was fearsome indeed. However, I also saw, straight away, the mistakes that had made this design of ship vulnerable to the Polity. Packing all those weapons in one area wasn't a great idea.

'Putting all your eggs in one basket, so Arrowsmith would say,'

Sverl told me, revealing the breadth of his abilities, for surely in such a situation all his concentration should be on Cvorn.

'The prador have such a saying?' I asked out loud.

'*Similar,*' said Sverl, '*a direct translation is "putting all your seed in one female" but the meaning is the same.*'

Cvorn was opening fire already. A swarm of railgun missiles began to depart his ship while, on one side, space doors had opened to allow something to nose out. All appeared to move in slow motion. Even when Cvorn fired his particle cannons, the beams groped out at the speed of mercury in a thermometer dropped into boiling water. Finally, the object drew clear of those space doors and I recognized a prador destroyer.

'*Cvorn's original ship,*' Sverl updated me.

Twin particle beams crossed vacuum towards us, while a single beam drove back the other way, its hue turned violet by the dust and gas through which it was passing. Even without my link into Sverl's system, I could tell we were under heavy fusion acceleration. The *Lance* was shuddering and internal ship's gravity was failing to compensate for the drag of acceleration. I could also grab detail on the other things Sverl was doing, such as firing his own railguns and now opening up two sets of space doors in his hull, but I wanted it laid out before me. I ran the incoming data through another program and displaced myself, which was easy enough to do with the data. The scene flickered, major objects not changing position very much but some closer asteroids whipped to different locations. Now I appeared to hang in vacuum ten or twenty miles out from Sverl's ship.

I watched protective hardfields spring into being, dust swirling behind them as they interfered with ancient currents here. Upon reaching the perimeter of the dust ring, the twin particle beams turned violet too, but against the hardfields they splashed ruby fire. Meanwhile Cvorn's old destroyer was accelerating off at an angle and beginning to fire a series of missiles. Turning my attention back to Sverl's destroyer, I saw the first kamikaze leave one bay, while the old attack ship he'd kept was steadily heading out of another. I understood Sverl's aim here and knew Riss had not – but felt no inclination to keep the drone informed.

Even though Sverl's dreadnought was under full acceleration, Cvorn's ST dreadnought was moving fast and closing. Ahead of it, its first railgun missiles began to impact against our hardfields and I felt a steady shuddering thrum through my body. Next, a ball of fire exploded from some port in the side of Sverl's dreadnought – a hardfield generator burning. All the energy it had absorbed had been converted into heat and motion, but thankfully it was expelled through a disposal port. A short while later fire exploded from other ports and continued burning inside. Sverl hadn't had a disposal tube lined up for that one and, checking the ship's system, I saw that it had burned a half-mile course through the ship's interior.

'*He has designed his weapons well,*' Sverl noted.

'*Not too well, I hope,*' I replied.

'*We shall see.*'

The first kamikaze and the old attack ship were now clear and accelerating.

'*Good luck,*' I sent, expecting no reply.

'*I hope not to need it,*' Flute told me.

I saw two more hardfield projectors go, and the storm of explosions against our protective fields created a thousand-mile-wide cloud of red and orange fire. A particle beam licked through and began grinding against the hull like a hot iron on wood. Railgun missiles followed, and Sverl responded with anti-munitions lasers. These laced the cloud like the threads of a spider's web under the glare of sunset. All were accurate, but with energy spent on gas and dust, they did not instantly destroy the missiles. Instead they tracked them in the hope of melting or otherwise weakening them to soften their impact. Inevitably, some found their target.

I staggered as three struck, massive plasma explosions reaching out into space, leaving glowing dents in the exotic metal hull armour. One had hit close to the space doors from which one of the last two kamikazes was departing. This sent the craft tumbling, steering thrusters firing to try to stabilize it. Sverl had already closed the space doors Flute and the first kamikaze had used and now hurried to close the doors the last two had utilized. They were a weakness; if just one of those missiles had passed through them, the damage inside would have been massive.

Missiles fired by Cvorn's old destroyer were now turning in towards our flank. Given time, these would force Sverl to redirect some of his defences, thus weakening his main defence against Cvorn. With his superior firepower, Cvorn would eventually break through and tear Sverl's ship apart. Sverl, of course, could flee. He could drop his dreadnought into U-space and run. But, with incomplete shielding, he could not hide his U-signature and Cvorn would follow. Wherever Sverl arrived next, the same scenario would play out, only each time Cvorn would wreak more damage on Sverl's ship. Sverl had known this right from his first encounter with this ST dreadnought – hence his new tactics, hence the kamikazes and the old attack ship.

'How long?' I enquired.

'Minutes only,' Sverl replied.

Minutes were a long time with shoals of railgun missiles bearing down and two particle beams tearing at the hull. I noted that the tumbling kamikaze had stabilized and was accelerating to position. The three other vessels spaced themselves out evenly around the dreadnought and matched acceleration. They were ready.

More railgun missiles came in, exploding continuously against the hull. Anti-munitions lasers began stabbing out at the other missiles fired by Cvorn's old destroyer and now powering in under their own drive. I found myself perpetually having to regain my balance and finally went down on one knee with a hand against the floor. The screen fabric was flickering now and black spots were appearing, because the assault was steadily destroying Sverl's sensors. The illusion was failing, and it finally dissipated with the smell of smoke. I was left kneeling inside a near-useless Polity destroyer, inside a prador dreadnought taking a hellish pounding. Suddenly I felt very mortal. If one missile got through to my location, I was dead. If one knocked out Sverl's U-space drive, I was dead. If the odds of four to one in our favour didn't work out, I was dead.

Viewing via my aug now, I saw the last kamikaze reach its required position just as Cvorn's ST dreadnought entered the dust ring. The dreadnought started firing a series of railgun missiles – marked as somehow different by the huc of the glow they created as they heated under friction. I didn't need to analyse spectra or talk to Sverl to know that the killing blow was on its way.

'Now,' said Sverl.

I felt reality lurch and twist around me, drag at me, trying simultaneously to pull me apart and crush me down into singularity. My body reported agony, but it was too intense for me to even scream, and I negated it with a pre-prepared aug program. This effect could have been due to damage to our drive or its shielding, but was also one I could not distinguish from something that had been described as happening during the war. Ships sometimes U-jumped while clustered too close together. It was never a good idea to jump when U-fields could interfere – the ships had a very good chance of surviving, but the crews had a very good chance of dying. This was due to the intense internal electromagnetic disruptions. But sometimes the choices were stark when under heavy attack, during which survival was a matter of decisions made in seconds, or microseconds.

It passed and the screen fabric turned grey swirled with nacre, where it was still receiving data. Now it was time to test those four-to-one odds.

'*Where are we heading now?*' I asked Sverl.

'*Room 101.*'

'*Surely another location—*' I began.

'*That was my best shot just now,*' said Sverl. '*The only option I have left to try, if Cvorn manages to follow us, is to lead him straight into that station's automated defences.*'

'*Which we would not survive anyway,*' I said.

'*Quite,*' said Sverl.

I blinked, set the screen fabric to emit just a plain white light, and stood up. I could still smell smoke and the ship was still shuddering as damaged structures realigned. I could hear distant crashes and clangs and at one point the rumble of an explosion. I focused on Riss, most of her body coiled on the floor, ovipositor sticking straight up, head raised and black eye open as she watched me.

'Do you understand the strategy now?' I asked.

'Yes,' Riss replied, 'I understood the moment that first kamikaze launched, when it began to power up a U-drive set to generate an unfeasibly large U-field. The kamikazes and that old attack ship are decoys, and Cvorn won't know which U-signature to follow.'

'Good.' I nodded.

'I also get that Sverl hasn't worked out the one survival option that remains open to us, should things go tits up.'

I noted that 'us'. Riss wasn't particularly concerned about Sverl's survival.

'Then perhaps you should elaborate.'

Riss swung her head around, inspecting our surroundings.

'Think of Station 101's automatic defences,' said the drone.

I understood at once. *'Sverl, listen to this . . .'*

'Of course,' Riss added, 'it's a survival option limited by the space available . . .'

The Brockle

The micro-fibres had penetrated throughout the *Tyburn* like the mycelium of some fungus. They had attached themselves to pin cams everywhere, though even that wasn't entirely necessary. Where they terminated at surfaces in the old prison hulk they had grown microscopic nodules, much like fungal fruiting bodies but packed with sensory equipment. These nodules were especially prevalent in the dock and the rooms the Brockle chose for interrogation. Their terahertz scanning could record and transmit the functions of the Brockle's shoal body entire, and other scan bands could render close copies of the forensic AI's thought processes. However, the watcher allowed some privacy, since that depth of scanning generally shut down when the Brockle had no one to interrogate.

The Brockle stood and walked slowly to the interrogation room that contained the comatose Ikbal and Martina. It paused outside the door, aware that deep scanning had not shut down in there. However, in this tunnel it would be at low ebb – just registering that the Brockle had arrived. It reached out and rested one hand flat against a wall – replicating an inadvertent action of the human it mimicked – and at a microscopic level it inspected the scan nodes under its palm. Each node was a highly complex chunk of nanotech, but the micro-fibres feeding back to the watcher's location were simple photon tubes to convey data in that form.

The Brockle now sweated nano-machines from its palm – simple locators with laser drives to convey them where required. These penetrated the points where the micro-fibres attached to the sensory nodules and began propelling themselves back along the photon tubes. These would not be detected, for they were simply too small to interfere much with the data flow.

Lowering its hand, the forensic AI stepped back and waited patiently. In its mind, it located the position of its nano-machines on an old schematic of this ship and traced their progress. Until now, it had never really made an effort to locate the watcher and it observed the progress with interest over the ensuing hours. The nano-machines passed through various junctions and began heading towards the ship's nose – where the colonists had slept in their hibernation capsules. It felt vaguely surprised about this, because it had expected the watcher to be nearby. The machines were just beginning to head up through the connecting stalk of the ship when abruptly they ceased to move. This could mean that they had reached the watcher's location, or it could mean that it had shut down the relevant micro-fibres. No matter – the Brockle knew where to go now.

It turned away from the interrogation room and headed towards the dock, opening one of the rear doors and stepping out onto the metal grating. Here it paused to gaze at the vacuum-dried remains of its last victim and decided that it wouldn't bother clearing up here after all. Turning right, it went through a smaller door into the short tunnel Trent had entered before he left. It closed the door behind it, because the section lying beyond the next door was unpressurized. Here the signs of decay were more evident and, as it walked, it detected that one of the portals was developing a small atmosphere breach around its rim. No matter.

At the end of the tunnel, it squatted down before the second door, which was welded shut. It reached out and touched a finger against a weld, issuing high-vibration microscopic diamond cutters from its fingertip. Drawing its finger round, it turned the welds to dust, finally, after a couple of passes, revealing the rim of the door. It next turned the handle, having to exert more pressure than any human could possibly have managed. The door cracked off a decaying seal and air began to hiss out through that. The Brockle began to heave the door open, the seal tearing and flapping in the blast of air as the tunnel it occupied evacuated. By the time the door stood open, all the air was gone.

The tunnel beyond stretched straight along the stalk connecting the drive-section to the colonists' section – a place that might still contain their hibernation capsules. No grav here. The grav-plates behind were a recent installation, for the ship had been built before such technology existed. The Brockle pushed itself through and, using handholds jutting from the walls, propelled itself along the tunnel. It paused beside a name etched into a wall, *Freedom*, and considered the irony of the new name this ship had acquired. Next, it pondered the idea of separating into its individual units, for in that form it could travel faster and be more effective. But in an odd hat-tip to the history of this place, it decided to retain its human form.

The door at the end of the tunnel led into an airlock. Upon opening this, it discovered the seal to be a more modern Polity version and, once it stepped inside and closed the door behind, the airlock pressurized. Just for a second the Brockle wondered if the watcher might be some living creature that needed air, but under analysis the gas turned out to be a mixture of argon and the kind of preservatives usually sprayed into museum cases. With the lock charged, it opened the inner door and pushed itself through.

The colonists' section still contained the honeycomb frames to take hibernation capsules, with tubeways running through each collection of six for inspection. But for a scattering of capsules, the frames were empty, so perhaps the occupants had reached their destination. Those capsules still in place – cylinders of early chain-glass with metal end-caps and trailing fluid tubes and skeins of wires – still contained their fluid. It was no longer pale green, but dark brown with the emissions of decay. Passing by one of these, the Brockle spied bones inside. It paused, and decided it was time to scan.

Just a minute of induction detection located a power nexus ahead. The Brockle continued along the tubeway to reach a honeycomb frame that contained just one capsule. In this the fluid hadn't degraded – was still that healthy pale green – while the body inside looked intact. The Brockle moved to inspect it more closely. The naked corpse of a man floated inside. The Brockle stared at it in puzzlement, not quite sure why this body bothered it so, until it saw the chewed-out wrists.

Antonio Sveeder.

Here lay the corpse of the Brockle's only innocent victim, dead but preserved by old hibernation technology. The presence of this corpse here made no sense. Why had it been moved here? Why had Earth Central installed it in this container? Then the forensic AI saw that green preserving fluid was not all that surrounded Sveeder. Masses of semi-transparent micro-fibres ran through the fluid, penetrating the body throughout. This was the watcher? How could a dead man be a watcher? Abruptly the Brockle felt a surge of irritation, lost its human hue and absorbed its ersatz clothing, then broke into a hundred units shoaling round the hibernation capsule. One of the penalties of taking on human shape it found was that, when in that form, it tended to think like a human being. Perhaps it was because that was precisely what the Brockle had been. In distributed form, it could think more clearly, and now it needed to act.

Touching the chain-glass with one of its units, the Brockle forced a decoder molecule into its surface. The glass turned white, then the cylinder exploded, a pressure differential propelling fluid and decoded chain-glass out from the body. The Brockle waited a short spell, observing the body just hanging there with great globules of the fluid still clinging amidst the skeins of micro-fibres, then moved two of its units into contact. Injecting fibres of its own into the dead flesh, it began exploring the body, soon understanding what EC had done, but failing to understand why.

Polity AIs had interfaced Antonio Sveeder's brain with an organo-metal substrate, quite similar to the Brockle's own, to create a sub-AI system based on the man himself. It was a pointless exercise because now little of the man's own brain remained. Tracing connections to the substrate, the Brockle found a larger than normal data optic leading across the honeycomb frame to the wall, then spearing towards the nose-cone of the *Tyburn*. It sent one of its units to follow it. That unit shortly reported that the optic connected into a U-space transmitter, so the Brockle immediately severed the optic. Delving further, it quickly put together the entire function of this watcher. Then with a feeling almost of betrayal, it noted an anomaly with the remaining, and quite badly decayed, organic brain.

The man had possessed a memplant!

Damn, this meant that Antonio Sveeder had only died an organic death and now probably resided in a new body of some kind. Surely this also meant that the Brockle's sentence for murdering him wasn't—

The Brockle froze. Some sort of sub-system had activated when it severed that connection to the transmitter. Electrical activity occurred in the body, neuro-chem was flooding some areas of organic brain, and nano-fibres throughout were writhing as they stretched and contracted. Antonio Sveeder's chest rose and fell, ejecting fluid from his lungs and, after a moment, he opened his eyes.

'So you have chosen to breach the terms of your confinement,' he said in a phlegmy voice, but one instantly recognizable by the unit that had interrogated him. 'Think very hard before you go any further. Do you really want to become an outlaw? Do you really want us to hunt you down?'

Stupidly over-dramatic, the Brockle felt. But because Earth Central had designed this set-up, it stabbed to the core of the forensic AI's being. The Brockle responded in kind. Its entire shoal being fell in on the corpse, exuding meniscus blades and hard little limbs, and tore it to shreds.

16

Cvorn

Cvorn stared at his screens in disbelief, at the swirling dust and gas, at the particle beams punching through and the swarms of missiles closing on a target that was no longer there. He had expected Sverl to U-jump before receiving too much damage to be able to do so. He had expected then to follow Sverl to another location and some desperate harpooned-fish defence, and there peel his ship like the shell of a mollusc to get to the soft centre. Now he wanted to rage, shriek and tear something apart.

The data. The damned data.

Cvorn ran it again in his aug, and again. Here was the hole he hadn't seen. Here was the option he had been unable to cover. The Polity had done stuff like this during the war when the prador had centred on a major target amidst minor ones, like a dreadnought amidst attack ships. They had intersected all their U-fields, then twisted and changed them so that the attack ships threw out fields large enough to be considered a dreadnought. During U-jump transition, mass readings became indistinguishable, and then all ships headed off to different locations.

Cvorn ground his mandibles together, backed off from saddle and screens and turned full circle, stamping his feet against the floor in frustration.

Damned data.

Sverl's shielding was so damaged he had had no chance of preventing Cvorn obtaining his ship's U-signature and thus his next destination. He had known that, and so confused the issue. Cvorn did not know which field related to which ship. The five vessels had also headed off to destinations all at wild variance. He now had a one-in-five chance of choosing the right one, unless he got smart and figured something out.

Cvorn still wanted to tear things up, but instead he shut down his weapons and issued recalls to those missiles he could call back. Meanwhile, he headed across to the other side of his sanctum and pulled open a medstore. He took out a sausage of smart cement, snipped a piece off and slapped it over where his left palp eye had been. As the cement softened and deformed to ooze in and fill the hole, leaking analgesics and pathogen killers, the pain there died and Cvorn began to get over the urge to throw a tantrum.

'You,' he said, opening communications with the second-child aboard his old destroyer, 'recall what missiles you can and return.'

'Sure thing, Father,' said the second-child. Cvorn studied its image down in one facet of his screen array and wondered if it was time to have the child replaced. It had perhaps spent too long away from its family, and certainly too long away from the airborne pheromones that enforced obedience. Then, while he gazed at the second-child, he realized the odds had changed. He could send the destroyer the child occupied after one of the five vessels, and have it report by U-com the moment it found out which it had pursued.

This glimmer of hope, on top of the pain in his visual turret fading, raised Cvorn's mood and he began to think more positively. Returning his attention to the U-signatures, he began to try gleaning what he could from their minor differences. He related them to astrogation and soon learned that every destination was a planetary system. He now began examining these closely.

The first he checked, because it had at once seemed familiar, turned out to be the world where Cvorn had originally set his ambush to catch Sverl. Now, supposing this signature related to Sverl's dreadnought, why would he go there? It seemed an odd choice – did that make a more likely one? That might be the case, so Cvorn marked that world as a definite possibility.

The second signature related to a binary star system at the far edge of the Graveyard. Examining data available on this, Cvorn could see no way in which it could give Sverl any kind of tactical advantage. But then perhaps that was the point.

One more signature was to a hypergiant sun. This lay outside the Graveyard and, with its complex collections of surrounding astronomical objects, offered possibilities for Sverl. Cvorn began analysing the system and at once saw that it did offer more such advantages than the other two, and so listed the destinations in order of advantage to Sverl. However, even as he did this, he felt a leaden depression, knowing that the system with the most advantage might mean Sverl was heading there or that it was the most likely decoy. Then there were the two remaining destinations, which were highly problematic.

One lay inside the Polity and one lay inside the Kingdom. The first Cvorn felt he did not need to study at all because Sverl would most likely not get there. He'd be picked up by a Polity watch station – then be knocked out into the real either by its USER or by a U-space mine or missile deployed by one of the new Polity attack ships. Perhaps that was his intention. Perhaps he intended to scream for help from the Polity, hoping to turn Polity defences against Cvorn, and see Cvorn destroyed. Then at least he might survive as a captive of the AIs.

The Kingdom did not have quite such efficient U-space defences, but it did have detector gear. Sverl would probably get through there and head just beyond the secondary and much tighter U-space minefields surrounding the home world. When he arrived he would almost certainly be surrounded by the home world King's Guard squadron just moments later. Cvorn was sure the king would be aware of the threat to his rule that Sverl represented. He would therefore annihilate his ship without further ado. This destination struck Cvorn as the least likely. But then again, did that in turn make all the others more likely decoys? What would Sverl gain by heading there? He would die. But if Cvorn followed, he was certain to die too.

Frustrated and feeling that he was getting nowhere, Cvorn struck the Polity and Kingdom destinations from his list and focused on the others. Now he examined the U-fields more closely and compared their parameters to a recording he had made from Sverl's ship during its last U-jump. None of them matched completely. This could be because of the mass Sverl's dreadnought had shed by sending out that old attack ship and kamikazes, also because of the damage Cvorn had inflicted. The closest match was the one heading to the ambush world, while the one most at variance was the one heading to the binary system. He studied the parameters over many hours, glancing at the alert that told him all the self-drive missiles were back in their weapons cache. Then he noticed the alert informing him that his destroyer was ready to dock, to which he briefly responded by telling the second-child aboard to stand off and wait. Nothing revealed itself – nothing to change the odds. Then, despite striking them from his list, he ran a U-fields comparison for those vessels heading for the Polity and the Kingdom. It was with a feeling of inevitability that he studied the results and found they were the closest match to Sverl's original field.

In the end, it came down to a very simple reality. The hypergiant was the one that gave Sverl the greatest tactical advantage, and was the most likely decoy. Sverl was very smart, so in a way

Cvorn felt that the other prador might exclude the hypergiant. Sverl might head to a location that was neither the most likely decoy nor the most tactically advantageous. After all his checking, all his calculations, all his thought on the matter, Cvorn realized he could rely on only one thing, and that was instinct. He liked the ambush world; just its sheer oddity as a choice made him feel that this was where Sverl would head.

'Child,' he said to the second-child aboard his destroyer, 'you will at once head to this destination.' Cvorn sent the coordinates of the hypergiant. 'Upon your arrival open constant U-com and keep me updated with what you find there. I will pick up on it when I surface from U-space.'

'Will do, Dad,' said the second-child.

This reminded Cvorn that he definitely needed to straighten that child out, but he wouldn't do it yet.

He next sent the coordinates of the ambush world to his ST dreadnought's ship mind, and ordered immediate pursuit. The dreadnought accelerated on fusion, since even it did not possess the tech for a standing jump into U-space. Twenty minutes later Cvorn watched his destroyer disappear, and ten minutes after that he felt a wave of distortion pass through his body as his own ship submerged into that baffling continuum.

Trent

'So what's this all about?' asked the catadapt woman, Sepia.

'I've no idea,' Trent replied, observing the prador moving towards them. He turned to Rider Cole, 'You?'

The mind-tech was squatting over the shellwoman whose body was complete, but who had lost an outer prador carapace. She now wore a skin of silver grey. He had attached a reader induction ring around her head and was studying data on a touch screen. He looked up.

'No idea either,' he replied, his expression slightly lost.

Trent had not liked the idea of letting Cole make even a cursory examination of the shell people, because the man might be tempted to start tinkering. But what choice did Trent have? He needed to do something to stop these people committing slow suicide. Cole was assessing them for any organic damage, caused either in the past or by the recent hormonal control. He had said that he couldn't do much anyway while they remained in such a state of somnolence. Trent didn't believe him.

Cole abruptly shook his head and stabbed a finger towards the approaching prador, scattered about a grav-sled bearing a large bulky object into Quadrant Four.

'But that thing looks old and it looks like human manufacture.'

Trent eyed the thing. It was a huge squat cube decorated with thick pipes, power sockets and exterior tanks. It had sets of cooling fins both on its surface and as separate components sitting on coils of superconductor. One face was clear of such items and inset in this was a ring, punctuated all round with circular hatches. With all the exterior gear and attachment points, it looked like some large component extracted from a ship, or maybe an autofactory. He recognized something about it, but couldn't nail it down.

As it drew closer, Bsorol moved over, leading a small party of second-children. Trent knew that the first-child was all right, but he didn't like the idea of second-children milling about so many somnolent and vulnerable human beings. He headed over, Sepia falling into step beside him. But Cole remained intent on his studies of the shellwoman's brain structure and slow neural firings.

The sled arrived beside the line of shell people laid out on the floor, and immediately one of the second-children went over and picked up one of them. Meanwhile, other children were opening power ports in the floor, reeling out cables and plugging them in, and the object on the sled started to emit puffs of vapour.

Trent broke into a run, heading for the second-child now cradling a shellman sans legs and with a deep sealed cavity where his intestines had been. 'Wait! What the hell are you doing?'

Bsorol clattered something and the second-child dropped its load heavily on the floor and rapidly backed up. Trent stooped down by the man, turned him over onto his back and checked the small circular monitor attached to his chest while Bsorol clattered some more then cracked a claw against the second-child's back. Trent flinched even at this common violence of prador society. The second-child bubbled grudgingly and went off to help its fellows with the power lines. The monitor showed a mild concussion that the man's nano-package was already repairing. And, even as Trent watched, the man stabilized and settled back into hypersleep. Trent stood and headed over to Bsorol.

'What's going on?' he asked.

'Father's orders,' Bsorol replied, waving a claw towards the thing on the sled.

'I think I know what that is,' said Sepia.

'What orders?' Trent asked.

'He wants them to survive and we have to prepare,' said the first-child.

'For what?'

'You need to talk to Thorvald Spear – he will give you detail.'

'It's a zero freezer,' said Sepia.

Bsorol turned slightly to face her. 'It has the capacity to deal with all of them, whereupon they will have to go into insulated containers with independent refrigeration.'

'What?' said Trent. He now recognized the thing – not the whole of it because he had never seen one entire, but the hatches. Polity Medical had used these things in some hospital ships during the war, when casualties had been coming in too fast for capacity. Trent, who had been born after the war, had visited some of the highly popular war virtualities. In one he had seen a freezer like this being used.

'You're going to freeze them?' he asked.

There were dangers, especially in freezing people as damaged as these. Trent wanted to object, to stop this, but was also attracted to the idea of putting the problem that these shell people represented on hold.

'Spear has more information, you say?'

'He will explain,' Bsorol confirmed, now turning to the second-children. Having plugged the zero freezer into the ship's power, they were now gathering before him. 'This child will take you to him.' Bsorol gestured to the second-child he had earlier berated.

Trent eyed the creature. He hoped that it was too frightened of Bsorol to do anything nasty, but did not think for a moment that anything beyond fear, or a large gun, might stop it. He groped down towards his hip where once he had holstered his pulse-gun and wondered if the empathic feelings Penny Royal had burdened him with applied to prador. He didn't need to think for long. He had winced when Bsorol hit that second-child earlier. He had felt its pain.

'Are you coming?' he asked, turning to Sepia.

'You're going to see Spear?' she asked.

She appeared nonchalant about it but Trent guessed her

feelings were otherwise. In him, when they were in the cage, she had seen someone she had categorized as an operator, accustomed to violence, and just the kind of ally she had needed. Perhaps she had, briefly, considered him as someone she would have liked to know better. But he hadn't behaved as expected, and when she saw how he was with Reece, she'd become distant. However, the moment she and Spear got close to each other, it seemed the air between them fizzed. Trent understood that his earlier self would have been jealous, even though he had no claim on Sepia. That wasn't the case now.

'Yes. Spear,' he said.

'Yeah, sure,' she replied. Next, glancing at the second-child, she dropped a hand to the pulse-gun she wore. She'd also found a laser carbine that she carried slung on her back. Perhaps her disappointment in Trent as protective muscle had made her more careful about her own safety.

'Let's go,' he said, gesturing to the second-child.

The creature snipped its claws then clattered something. Bsorol whipped round to face it, whacked it on the back again and clattered a reply. It cringed, bubbled, then turned away to head towards the exit from Quadrant Four. As he followed, Trent imagined the content of that conversation. The second-child had probably sought some confirmation that these were humans it couldn't eat and Bsorol had clarified the matter.

'Like a lot of people in Carapace City, I always watched the news feeds about new arrivals,' said Sepia as they stepped out into one of the ship's corridors. 'If available, those feeds presented potted biographies. You were Isobel Satomi's most trusted lieutenant, a dangerous man, a killer. What happened?'

Trent felt himself go cold. It was almost as if she was keying into his earlier thoughts.

'Penny Royal,' he replied briefly.

'What?'

'There's a possibility that it wasn't the black AI, though,' he said contemplatively. 'I was handed over to the Polity and then into the tender care of a forensic AI.' Trent blinked – memories of a bloody maelstrom sunk deep in his mind surfacing for a moment. 'It could have been the Brockle, the forensic AI, that changed me. But I'm sure it happened before then. I'm sure it was Penny Royal that tampered with my mind.'

'Uh . . . forensic AI . . . you're an outlaw who was sentenced to death by the Polity long ago. How the hell did you get away?'

He glanced at her. 'It just released me. It's complicated, but I'm sure part of the reason it did so is because of what Penny Royal did to me. I'm no longer the threat I was.'

'That's not enough – death sentences are supposed to be immutable.'

'There was some pressure as well.' He shrugged. 'Politics.'

She nodded acceptance of that. She was a citizen of the Graveyard and so, unlike most Polity citizens, did not trust in the unalterable justice of the AIs. Those who had lived outside the Polity for any length of time began to see the rust under the paintwork and soon understood that things were never as neat and definitive as often portrayed in that realm.

'So what did Penny Royal do?'

'It gave me empathy, or a conscience, or both, though I would say that one is a product of the other,' Trent replied. 'I feel the pain I cause.'

They walked on in silence behind the second-child, then Sepia asked, 'Do you regret the change?'

Trent was about to reply that yes, he certainly did, but then reconsidered. Sure, possessing such empathy limited his ability to act. It was painful, traumatic, but only because he functioned in a world where pain and trauma were common. However, he now felt larger, more connected and open to ways of thinking that hadn't been within his compass before. When he reflected on how he used to be, he saw a limited man, a cipher. The traumas of his early life and the violence of it thereafter had severed and cauterized his emotions and thought processes. He also saw a man who could never have felt the way he now felt about Reece, but whether that was a good thing, he wasn't sure.

'I don't know,' was all he would concede.

Was that really what Penny Royal had done? He labelled the change he had undergone as the addition of empathy and conscience, but maybe the black AI had given him nothing at all. Maybe Penny Royal had merely decalcified his brain, scraped the crap off all those functions that had shut down and set them running again. Perhaps conscience and empathy had been petrified and, because they were working again after so long, they felt very raw.

The second-child finally arrived at a wide diagonally divided door, inserted a claw into a pit control beside it for a moment, then stepped back. The door opened into a massive airlock with an identical door at the other end. The prador gestured them inside.

Sepia led the way in, saying, 'I notice only the first-children have translators.'

Trent followed her in, a short while later the door rumbling closed behind him. 'Maybe it's better we don't understand what the second-children say about us.'

'Maybe it's better they don't understand what we say about them,' said Sepia. 'Seems to me they're a little lacking in self-control.' She raised her voice with the last few words as the doors opening ahead of them released a cacophony.

Spear's destroyer sat in the huge hold beyond. Welding spatters were spraying the floor, from robots clustered over it like wasps over a rotting banana. A jointed arm towards its rear end was extending what looked like a complete fusion drive. Second-children were scurrying here and there. Some wore exoskeletal worksuits bristling with tools, others were loaded down with materials. It took a second for Trent to realize what was odd about the picture, then he noted various objects just hanging in the air or scribing straight courses between workers. He understood that grav was off in that area.

While studying the vessel, Trent remembered his first sight of it from the *Moray Firth*. He and Gabriel had speculated on whether Isobel would give either of them the captaincy of it, after she inevitably ordered them to murder Spear. That was before Spear used a prion weapon to paralyse them and head away with this ship. That was also before Isobel, while transforming into a hooder, had eaten Gabriel.

The second-child who had guided them here clattered something and scuttled off. Trent watched it go, then turned back to the scene before them.

'What can you tell me about him?' Sepia asked.

Trent didn't need to ask who the 'him' might be. 'Ex-bio-espionage agent during the war. Resurrected only recently after mouldering in a memplant for a hundred years, but still fucking dangerous. He played Isobel easily and took that ship right out from under her.' Trent nodded towards the Polity destroyer. 'He could have killed her and me, but didn't.' He glanced at Sepia. 'And you've already seen how smart he is.'

'I've seen,' she said.

'So what do you think of him?'

'He looks at me as if he wants to eat me,' she said.

'Surely you're used to that?'

'Yes, but I get the impression that there might be screaming and blood involved when it's one of them doing the looking.'

She stabbed a thumb behind in the direction the second-child had taken.

'I guess he might seem a little intense,' said Trent.

'Fucking terrifying might be a better description.'

'Enough to drive you away?'

'Definitely not,' she replied. 'Shall we go in?'

As they stepped into the hold, a voice called, 'This way!'

The snake drone Riss rose out of a floating pile of debris, hovering in mid-air like some weird exclamation mark, then nosed out and writhed towards the destroyer. Her movements were just like a snake, only one that had found invisible ground level, a yard above the floor.

'What's this about, Riss?' Trent asked, now trying to dismiss the previous conversation from his mind. He was uncomfortable with it and with the fact that he had wanted to continue, to ask Sepia about Reece. It was the kind of exchange he would never have had before – all that relationship stuff. The full extent of his *relationships* up until the events on Masada had usually involved a secured payment beforehand.

'It's about our best chance of survival,' the drone replied.

Trent moved to the edge of the hold and from there propelled himself to the mass of cables. He landed heavily, as it had been a while since he had moved about in zero gravity. Sepia sailed past him after the drone, neatly catching the edge of the airlock it had entered, flipping over and coming down on her feet. Trent followed, landed a bit better this time and propelled himself inside after her – then crashed down on his shoulder.

'Grav's on in here,' she observed.

'No shit,' he replied, struggling to his feet.

They found Spear on a bridge lined with screen fabric displaying various scenes from the work ongoing all around.

'They're zero freezing the shell people,' said Trent.

Spear gazed at him for a moment, then at Sepia, but the charge between them seemed to have waned a little. He then pointed up at one of the screen frames, which showed the open hold of the destroyer. 'We'll put them in insulated caskets – one hundred per cent heat sealed – and pack them in there. They won't take up all the room, but that's because not one of them is actually a whole human being. It's good that they aren't, otherwise we wouldn't have room for Sverl's second-children.'

'What?' was all Trent could manage.

'We're tearing out the human quarters now to make room for Sverl, Bsorol and Bsectil – plus Sverl's war drones. And we should be able to fit other encased child-minds into the weapons cache.'

Riss issued a contemptuous snort at this.

'We're leaving?' asked Sepia.

Spear glanced at the drone first, obviously annoyed at its attitude, then looked at Sepia. 'Perhaps the best way I can put it is that there is a one-in-five chance that we will have to if we want to stay alive.'

'Back up a bit there, will you, and explain?' said Trent tiredly.

'Did you understand what happened last time we surfaced into the real?' Spear asked.

'No,' Trent replied.

He did know that Cvorn had attacked them. He had found himself hanging onto a wall pit control while the ship shuddered around him and grav fluctuated. And he did see part of the upper wall of Quadrant Four bulge and break open like a ripe boil, to spew white-hot gases high above. This was apparently from a shield projector melt-down. But he knew that wasn't what Spear was getting at.

'Let me explain,' said Spear.

Trent listened and pondered why, once again, frying pans and fires seemed to be part of his destiny.

Sverl

Sverl perambulated about inside his sanctum, inspecting terrariums, aquariums, his little glasshouse and some freestanding plants. He studied some of the other projects he had used to occupy his time ever since the war. He eyed a process for cold-growing AI crystal, much as it grew inside him, and another to isolate his original genetic tissue from the mish-mash he now contained. The idea had been that one day he might even be able to grow himself a new prador body. He checked on an attempt to isolate the human genetic tissue within him and identify it by running searches through the massive collections of genomic files in the Polity. As he moved on to peer at the strewn-out parts of a disassembled piece of U-space drive, he realized he wasn't contemplating what to work on next, but saying goodbye.

For many reasons Riss's idea was a good one. Cvorn would finally trace them to Factory Station Room 101 and might arrive before they had completed their business there – whatever that might be. But whatever happened, his dreadnought would not be able to survive another encounter with Cvorn. It was already severely damaged, low on munitions and low on stored energy. He needed a method of escape but he also needed a way of actually getting aboard the Factory Station. Riss's idea that they use Spear's destroyer to access it, because the automated defences should not react to it, solved both these problems. What would happen thereafter, he had no idea. But Penny Royal was due here, so they could finally confront the black AI. That was all he needed to know.

Not bothering to return to his prador controls – he performed most tasks mentally now – he studied how things were progressing with Spear's destroyer. His robots and children had almost repaired it and the only thing it lacked was a mind that could drop it into U-space. They wouldn't need that for the short trip from this dreadnought to Room 101. And, anyway, it was a position Sverl himself could occupy if Flute did not return from his decoy mission. The shell people, all zero frozen and secured in their containers, were now on their way down to the ship. Bsorol and Bsectil were already there, installing Sverl's war drones and other mind cases in the weapons cache. The remaining second-children were on their way too. All that remained was for Sverl to head over, but still he was hesitant. Now was the time for a course he had been avoiding. He had admitted to himself that his ship, complete and unguarded, was vulnerable. Cvorn would annihilate it as it was, so now it was time for drastic measures to try to save at least some of what he had here.

Like all prador dreadnoughts, Sverl's ship, when constructed, was an indivisible chunk of technology. Wrapped around its father-captain like layers of armour, it either survived or died with him. However, Sverl had noted the utility of the idea used in some wartime Polity ships of breaking them into a series of components and firing them off on different courses. This option might render a ship unusable, but Polity forces could retrieve surviving components to reassemble them into a whole ship, or to serve as parts of another one. Sverl had taken the idea and applied it to his own dreadnought. The first problem he had faced was that the major complete component was the exotic metal hull wrapped around the rest. It had been necessary to cut it, which made it weaker – a weakness that was part of his problems now with Cvorn. He had then made lines of division, liberally scattered with planar explosives, shear fields, hardfields and rocket motors to provide motive power. He had distributed power sources and other items between them and thus, in the end, Sverl had indeed divided his ship into its eight quadrants. They all contained living quarters, holds, supplies, weapons and other essential items. Two respectively contained the fusion engines and the U-space drive, while the latter also contained Sverl's sanctum.

Sverl set into motion the automated preparations for division, diverting energy to distributed power storage and lining up command sequences in the system. It took just a moment for the ship to be ready, since it needed little physical preparation – its main task being to close and seal bulkhead doors. Shortly after it surfaced from U-space, the planar explosives and shear fields would be ready to sever physical connections. The hardfields would be ready to throw the quadrants apart, the rockets would send them on courses about the numerous astronomical objects in Room 101's system.

That's it, then . . .

Sverl turned and headed to his sanctum door. As the two halves rolled back into the wall he paused, realizing that, though he had often opened and closed these doors to allow others to enter and leave, it had been many years since he himself had stepped beyond them. He stood there, staring into the corridor beyond, analysing his reaction in intricate detail. Then he understood that such an analysis wasn't required: he was just a tad agoraphobic and frightened.

'I need to get out more,' he said, using human words, and headed out into the corridor.

Within a few minutes, he reached a wide dropshaft – the kind of transport not usually found aboard a prador vessel – programming his route ahead. Irised gravity fields dragged him through his ship, finally depositing him through a ceiling hatch in a grav-plated corridor. He landed with a heavy thump and behind he heard shrieks and panicked bubbling, and turned to eye a couple of second-children he had just avoided crushing. They backed away from him in confusion then, as his pheromonal output reached them in all its intensity, they paused.

'Father?' one of them clattered.

'Of course,' he clattered back.

All his children had known about the changes he had been undergoing, but few of them had actually seen him. Certainly, few of his second-children had come face-to-face with him in decades.

'Shall we proceed?' he asked, waving a claw ahead.

Hugging close to the wall, they scuttled past him, heading on towards the hold containing Spear's destroyer. He sighed to himself and followed, stepping through after them into organized chaos.

The shell people were now arriving – within hundreds of coffin-sized caskets loaded on a series of grav-sleds now the grav was back on in here. If each of these caskets had only been capable of holding one shell person, then there would not have been near enough of them, nor enough space in the destroyer for them. However, some of these contained as many as three or four people, frozen together and interlocked like a meat supply. All of them were filled with special anti-freezes and cell preservers, so that even at a temperature just ten degrees above absolute zero they would become pliable. They could then be separated and placed individually into whatever medium or device would be required for their revivification.

Sverl eyed this scene and peered closely at the small gathering of humans towards the nose of the ship. They in turn were watching Bsorol and Bsectil guiding war drones through a hatch into the weapons cache. He then observed the two second-children with him head over to load caskets. Only once those were aboard could the second-children obey their orders and climb in afterwards. They would pack themselves as tightly as the human amputees, along with, of course, their wide selection of weapons and tools. He moved out, and at once all activity slowed and all eyes, whether set in skulls, visual turrets or up on stalks, turned towards him. He felt suddenly nervous and found himself running a program to control his limbs rather than just using his prador ganglion. Next, slightly irritated, he sent an order directly to Bsorol's aug and the first-child clattered loudly, putting his prador words through the hold PA. As work recommenced, Sverl walked over to his first-children and the humans.

Here stood Spear, Trent, the catadapt Sepia and the mind-tech Rider Cole. These were all the conscious humans now aboard, for Taiken's wife had chosen to take herself and her two children through the zero freezer. Sverl had noted Trent Sobel's bafflement at this and supposed that his new empathy had its limitations. The catadapt and the mind-tech, who had never seen Sverl before, were gaping at him.

'Fucking hell,' said Sepia.

Sverl ignored her, instead coming to stand before Spear.

'My place is ready?' he said, speaking human words. The question wasn't strictly necessary, because he was continually viewing the changing interior of the ship in one portion of his AI mind.

'It's an extended annex behind the bridge,' said Spear. 'You obviously won't need to see the screen fabric.'

'These others?' Sverl gestured with one claw to the other humans.

'A bit cramped – but I've had extra acceleration chairs fitted in the bridge.'

'We're all going to be nice and cosy,' said another voice.

Sverl eyed the snake drone Riss, realizing he had been trying to ignore the thing. He then studied it on a deeper level and noted its attempts to free itself from the collar. No doubt, once outside Sverl's dreadnought, Riss would eventually break out of the thing. Whether Sverl would then have to destroy the drone depended on what it did when free. If it came anywhere near him with that ovipositor, it would discover that Sverl's prosthetics and internal bracing skeleton hid a multitude of sins.

'I will install myself now,' said Sverl, moving round the group to Bsectil and Bsorol, sending a coded transmission directly to their augs, *'Join me when you're done here – and bring your full kit.'* For most prador, this would have meant armour and weapons, but for these two it meant more than that. Each of them had his own specialized tool kits as well as weapons. Each of them was somewhat more effective than the average armoured prador.

'The EMR pulse-gun?' suggested Bsorol.

'Of course,' Sverl replied. If the snake drone got uppity, it would quickly learn the error of its ways.

Rounding the nose of the ship, Sverl observed where a large section of hull had been folded out and fitted with a ramp leading into the interior. He clambered up this and entered the afore-mentioned annex, which backed onto the screen fabric-lined bridge, an arch open between. The area was without grav-plates, otherwise Bsorol and Bsectil would not have been able to fit inside too. Occupying the area still pulled down by the grav of the hold, Sverl found the specially made indentations in the floor into which he inserted his feet and secured himself. He opened himself up to his ship's systems again and, despite his nervousness about relocating, found it made no difference to his control of his environment. That might change, however, should Cvorn arrive and force them to head for Room 101, while Sverl's dreadnought deliberately tore itself apart behind them.

'*Now we are coming to the crux,*' said Spear, communicating via his aug.

'*Yes,*' Sverl replied.

'*While we have avoided being destroyed by Cvorn, the vagueness of our quests has been cast much in shadow.*'

'*Yes.*'

'*We are either going to Room 101 in pursuit of Penny Royal – or at that AI's behest. We're pawns being moved into place.*'

'*Yes.*'

'*Aren't you uncomfortable with this?*'

'*No,*' said Sverl, and he really meant it.

'*I'm not uncomfortable with what we're doing,*' replied Spear, '*though I am somewhat disturbed by a notion I cannot shake – that I am pursuing a set destiny. Sometimes it seems that everything I do resembles the actions of one with a religious faith.*'

'*But what are the alternatives?*'

'*Too numerous to list.*'

'*But they are all commonplace, prosaic.*'

'*And there you nail the heart of it.*'

'*We have just hours now,*' said Sverl. '*There is no turning aside and Cvorn is a driver of this. I wonder if that was his sum purpose.*'

'*And when his purpose is over?*'

'*Discarded, like a blunt screwdriver,*' said Sverl. '*I would bet that the series of events leading to his destruction are already in motion.*'

'*Let's hope so.*'

17

Spear

The massive space doors of the bay drew open, stretching between them the meniscus of a shimmershield – another example of the kind of technology not usually found aboard a prador ship. I gazed out through this thin veil into the heart of U-space and felt it was reaching in through my eyeballs in an attempt to liquidize my brain. I found myself down on my knees, with my eyes squeezed tightly shut. My fingers were digging into my eyelids as if some part of me had actually decided that the only option was to reach in and tear out my own eyes.

'Told you so,' said Riss.

Chunks of memory surfaced and coagulated into a whole. Others, victims of Penny Royal, had glimpsed this continuum unshielded. They had all survived it and their memories of it had been hazy, which was why I'd thought I could gaze upon it without ill effect. I understood then that the vagueness of their memories was due to the human brain being an inadequate recorder of what lay out there. It simply could not encompass something it had not evolved to cope with.

Yet, even as I understood this, I did begin to cope, sorting data in my mind, my aug and in the Penny Royal extension to my mind that lay inside my ship. I can only compare the experience to reading some text from a universe that was scattered with unknown words, but still, at least, managing to put them into context.

I staggered to my feet, turned and headed towards the open airlock of the destroyer, Riss sliding along drily beside me, and entered. I'd managed the whole of this without opening my eyes. And when I opened them, as the airlock sealed behind me and I stepped inside, everything possessed a shadow that stretched into that unknowable dimension.

'I don't know why you did that,' said Riss.

I gazed at the snake drone and now it was transparent to me. I could see the shadowy extensions of its U-space communicator and other U-space hardware stretching out from some of its internal components. I could feel one of those extensions reaching out to me, and I could sense the tug of others reaching out to the spine.

'You don't?' I asked. 'Then perhaps you're as empty as you say.'

Riss closed her black eye and moved on ahead of me, a little huffily, I thought.

On the bridge, Sepia, Trent Sobel and Rider Cole waited – not yet strapped into the three waiting acceleration chairs. These were crammed into a space between the bridge's renewed horseshoe console and one screen wall. Sepia was still a distraction and I tried to ignore her, then worried about offending her. Glancing into the rear annex, I saw Sverl squatting with Bsorol and Bsectil on either side, propped horizontally against their father in a space too small for all three. The grav of the hold where the *Lance* rested was dragging them down. A moment later I felt my weight alter slightly then stabilize and the two first-children propelled themselves upwards to now hover above Sverl, who had obviously turned off the grav out there.

'I have also tried this viewing of U-space,' said Sverl. 'My prador and human parts always react badly, but my AI component

437

just accepts it as part of a reality that isn't the linear one of organic evolution.'

'Me too,' said Sepia, 'and I had a headache for three weeks, which only mental editing dispelled.'

'There can often be damage,' said Cole, eyeing her intently.

She shook her head in annoyance either at him, or at my stupidity, then stepped over to one of the chairs. She had to unstrap her laser carbine from her back before sitting, and placed it across her lap. Cole sat in the chair beside her, unrolled a computer scroll and began doing some complicated touch-work on it.

Trent just stood staring at the grey swirls in the screen fabric and said, 'How long?'

'Minutes only,' I replied. Next, auging into ship's systems, I changed the imagery to give a facsimile of the realspace our course was taking us through . . . if you made your calculations in a linear organically evolved manner. Stars sped past us, and in the screen fabric ahead, one grew steadily brighter. I could show no more than what was already in my ship's astrogation files. Had that star ahead gone supernova, this facsimile wouldn't show it. Nor would it show the position of Room 101, because that was something that Polity AIs had excised from all Polity files. I threw up some frames giving a countdown and realspace distance, then I occupied the acceleration chair positioned inside the horseshoe console. Trent eyed me for a moment then stepped over to the remaining chair beside Sepia and likewise made himself secure.

The sun ahead expanded and shaded to salmon pink and I now began to get some sense of this hypergiant's immensity. I contracted distances to bring the orbital red dwarf into view, a gas giant out beside it on its millennium-long figure-of-eight course. I saw the whole of the asteroid belt of CO_2 and nitrogen ice, and put a frame over the small black hole now passing through it – leaving a swirl of shattered asteroids behind. The green-belt worlds were there too, quadrate patterns in their surfaces marking out the decaying foundations of an ancient and now long-dead civilization. Everything matched up to Riss's memory, except Room 101, which the astrogation program had of course failed to include. We fell fast into this, past the red dwarf and the asteroid belt. The sun expanded to fill one screen wall, the truncation of distance perpetually adjusting. But of course none of this was *real* and, had I been able to gaze upon it all without computer assistance, my eyes would have burned out in a microsecond in a glare millions of times brighter than Sol.

Next, I felt the twisting around me, as reality cast U-space shadows into madness. With a crump I was sure I imagined, we surfaced into the real as if through some icy crust, and everything all around readjusted. Factory Station Room 101 was too small to be visible to human eyes at this distance. And, as I called it into being in a frame, I sank more into the aug perception of our surroundings through the ship's sensors. Why, I wondered, was there always the need to translate things for limited human senses?

There lay Room 101: a giant Polity factory station utterly dwarfed by its immense surroundings. It was completely familiar to me. Its harmonica shape was that of so many other wartime factory stations, and Riss's memories of it were still sharp in my mind. Still, seeing this eighty-mile-long object stirred my awe. As I continued to study it, I began to notice disparities between memory and fact. The station no longer possessed the clean lines it once had; it was lumpy, as if cancerous. Large areas of utter blackness looked like holes in its structure, but analysis revealed these were high-absorption solar leaves scaled across its skin. There were growths and incrustations on its hull and it truly looked like a wreck. Not the usual kind one would find out in vacuum, but the wreck of a ship under a sea. It seemed that the fauna and flora of surrounding waters had occupied Room 101, and it was sinking softly into decay.

'I'm taking my ship in closer,' said Sverl. *'No need to hurry just yet.'*

I felt the kick of the fusion drive, despite the active grav-plates on my bridge. The perspective slowly changed, but I kept a sharp eye on the data that was being steadily collected by the dreadnought's sensors elsewhere in this system. And there, within just an hour of our arrival, another U-space signature. I immediately opened up a frame on it and expanded the thing into view, relaxing slightly when I saw a mere prador destroyer.

'Cvorn's,' Sverl informed me.

It was almost half a system away, poised just out from the red dwarf, but I immediately surmised that Cvorn had sent it after one of the U-signatures. It was probably talking to him even now. Fretting about this as I watched the ship, it took me a moment to realize that something was going on there, because I could see distortion beyond the ship silhouetted by the red dwarf.

'Expand your frame,' Sverl told me.

I issued the mental instruction, now including the whole dwarf star, but could see nothing. I expanded it again then to see a cluster of bright objects in low orbit around the sun. Sensor data was vague for they had hidden themselves well close to the photosphere, but they became clearer as they accelerated out. I put a second frame over them and magnified, just in time to see lines scribing out from them, white against the red. A few seconds later Cvorn's destroyer was blowing out hardfield projector debris and just a second after that, four intensely powerful particle beams hit it all at once. They just carved across it, splitting it like a peach, subsequent explosions blowing the two halves apart.

'*I'm breaking my ship now,*' Sverl replied. '*Launch at once.*'

With a thought, I brushed away docking clamps, but rested my hands on hand-imprinted ball controls in the console to set us moving. Light pressure on the left fired up the fusion engine, rumbling throughout the ship, and set it heading towards the shimmershield. About this, the space doors glared in the pink sunlight, with filtering set close to maximum. I could sense the hold behind burning in the fusion torch. The shimmershield then winked out and, in a blast of escaping air, and a cloud of debris left from my ship's reconstruction, we fell out into the hot glare of the hypergiant. Even as we went, I applied to Sverl on another level and got data on those ships, and a closer view. They were King's Guard ships.

Next, I took in the sight of Sverl's dreadnought etched about its surface with lines of fire, jetting long flames and beginning to slide apart.

'*Look to your defences,*' said Sverl.

I was already as deep into the system as Flute had been. I therefore managed to throw up a hardfield behind us, at the very moment some titanic explosion went off on the other side of the dreadnought. Checking the weapons cache, I saw that Sverl had resupplied it. In addition, I began making selections. As the giant ship continued to come apart, I saw one of those segments targeted by multiple particle beams beginning to radiate and explosions like volcanic eruptions were appearing all over its surface. I ramped up acceleration to take us away, firing off two chaff shells behind, and then I saw that fleet of massive ships bearing down on us. They'd U-jumped from close to the sun, very accurately indeed.

'*Let me into your system,*' said Sverl. '*We U-jump or we die.*'

Cvorn

Cvorn gazed up on his screens at the images the security drone was sending from his ship's interior and just wished he could roll back time. He wished that, rather than sending Vrom off to hunt down Sfolk, he had instead summoned his first-child here. Vrom had obviously outlived his usefulness as a first-child but should have been recycled as a child-mind in a war drone shell. He had failed his mission to take down Sfolk and now it was too late. The screen image showed a steaming pile of severed limbs and claws and a main body divided into neat segments.

Panning round, the security drone took in the rest of the scene. Two of the second-children were still alive, though one of them, with its legs missing on one side and its visual turret smashed, was hardly worth salvaging, even though it could re-grow its limbs, and the visual turret could be repaired. In the past, Cvorn would have considered this option, with his previously limited ability to produce replacements, but not now. Now, in the birthing tank aboard this ship, his own nymphs were steadily devouring the corpse of a reaverfish – his own fourth-children. Within a few years, he would have plenty of replacements.

The other surviving second-child did look easily salvageable. It was attempting to drag itself off the spike on which Sfolk had impaled it – the same spike Vrom had occupied earlier while Sfolk sliced him up with a carapace saw. This child had missed meeting the same fate when the rapid return of the security drone had curtailed Sfolk's entertainment. Before the cam images Sfolk had been sending had cut off, Cvorn had watched it all.

'This is what I'm going to do to you,' Sfolk had said as he sliced off Vrom's limbs, 'though there will be refinements.' Vrom's screaming and bubbling had gone on and on as Sfolk explained those refinements. The medical technology to extend Cvorn's life, the dissolving of his prongs and coitus clamp in hydrofluoric acid and the cauterizing irons. There was also the final flourish of installing Cvorn's major ganglion in a brain case, where it would endlessly re-experience the whole aug-recorded episode.

Sfolk, Cvorn decided, was obviously resourceful and smart. But he wasn't quite smart enough to understand that he had just detailed what would happen to *him* if Cvorn captured him alive. However, that was unlikely, since Cvorn now intended to make no real attempt at such a capture – the order was kill on sight.

The second-child finally, with much scrabbling, made it to the top of the spike and fell off, landing on its back on the floor with a thud. It struggled there for a while, then finally righted itself by bashing its claws down and flipping over. It stood there shivering, foam dripping from its mandibles. The spike had penetrated between its arrays of manipulatory limbs, through its alimentary tract, inside the ring of its major ganglion and out through the top of its shell. Sfolk had known what he was doing – ensuring he wouldn't cut any arteries or hit anything critical. The child would steadily recover – that recovery speeded up by Cvorn's decision.

'You, child,' he said, 'what's your name?'

'Vlox, Father,' it replied.

As he used his aug to order another five security drones initiated, and gave them their orders, he said, 'You will now come to Vrom's quarters, where you will utilize his food supply. You are now my first-child.'

The title always came first. Within a very short time this

child would begin to change, feeding on a first-child diet free of the chemical suppressants that had kept it as it was. However, it would still consume suppressants that would prevent it attaining adulthood. It would rapidly build up a dense bulk of stored fat and would shed its shell. The underlying new shell would remain soft for a few months as it rapidly converted that fat into muscle and other body tissues and grew in size. During this process, its injuries would heal quickly.

'But Sfolk, Father?' the new first-child enquired.

'Any sabotage he tries, I will detect at once,' said Cvorn, more confidently than he felt. 'If he tries to reach a shuttle or other craft to escape when we next surface into the real, I will detect that too.' In reality, Cvorn doubted Sfolk would try that. Inside the ship, he was safer than he would be on the outside, where Cvorn could fry him with major weapons.

Cvorn paused for a moment, checked the ship's manifest and found another four security drones in storage. He released them and gave them the same orders as the others. That was all of them and surely enough to keep Sfolk on the run and out of the way during their next imminent transition from U-space – and whatever might ensue.

Cvorn now took a moment to check on the progress of his offspring. He called up an image of the annex pod to the breeding pond and saw that just a few fourth-children clung to the bony remains of the reaverfish. Others were propelling themselves about in the tank and, even as he watched, two of them attacked another child that hadn't developed properly – the paddle legs on one side of its teardrop-shaped body seemed deformed. They tore into it with sickle hooks, which would be supplanted by growing claws when they finally left the pool. As it struggled to escape, they ripped soft carapace off its back end, whereupon innards spilled out in a long Gordian tangle behind.

This they fed upon while their victim struggled to escape. All was as it should be there.

Cvorn next briefly watched the erstwhile second-child head towards Vrom's quarters. At the door, it reached out and used the pit control. Only a little while before, this would have sliced off its claw. Instead, the door opened and Vlox entered. But there was no time now to take in anything more.

They had arrived.

The ST dreadnought surfaced into the real, sensors picking up the glimmer of photons forced from the quantum foam all around. Cvorn ranged out with his sensors, seeing the ambush world and noting that his departure from the hollow moon had put it in a decaying orbit that would bring it crashing down a hundred years hence. He quickly ascertained that no ships were in view and felt a sinking sensation in his sensitive gut as he wondered if Sverl had managed to make full repairs to his chameleonware. His belated discovery of a vessel lying half a million miles away, with U-space disturbances still new in its vicinity, dispelled this sensation.

With a thought, he turned the ST dreadnought towards this and engaged its fusion engines, as the distant ship's apparently recent arrival puzzled him. The reason became evident when further sensor data began to come in, and Cvorn swore eloquently in prador. By expanding its U-space field enough to encompass a prador dreadnought, the old style Polity attack ship had created a mass/field energy debt which had a delaying effect. That was why it hadn't been here long. And it wasn't Sverl's ship out there, but one of the decoys.

The attack ship began accelerating away and Cvorn tried to decide if it was worth pursuing. Perhaps it would be better to just charge up his U-space engines and jump to the coordinates of one of the other signatures. He then noted that the attack ship was trying to open communications with him and, taking the necessary precautions, he allowed this.

'Oops,' said the mind in that ship, 'wrong ship.'

'Who are you?' Cvorn asked.

'My name is a human one: "Flute". Which is also the name for a musical instrument humans use. It's funny, but I can't actually remember what my old name was – I reckon I left it in my old ganglion.'

'What?'

'It's refrozen now so I suppose if I was to charge it up and sift corrupted memories, I would be able to find my old name again. But what use is it to me now?'

The mind was babbling with the obvious purpose of delaying Cvorn's departure after one of the other signatures. Cvorn shouldn't waste his time on it.

'It's rather nice to be able to think as clearly as I do now,' Flute added. 'And at least I haven't ended up with a senile old brain like yours.'

Then again . . .

Cvorn opened fire with a particle beam. It stabbed across the intervening distance where inevitably a hardfield intercepted it. However, such a small ship would struggle to engage its U-space drive while thus defending itself. The attack ship turned, setting itself on a course to take it towards the world. Cvorn fired off a swarm of sub-AI missiles – their course set to take them between the attack ship and that world. The mind's tactics were obvious: it could go in low and slingshot into the atmosphere. Meanwhile Cvorn, with a larger and less manoeuvrable ship, would have to take a longer course. At some point, the world would get between them and, leaving atmosphere, the attack ship would then be able to drop into U-space before Cvorn could recommence his attack.

'So where has Sverl gone?' Cvorn asked.

'Now, if I told you that, we wouldn't be able to play any more.'

The attack ship changed course, now heading for the hollow moon. Cvorn sent a signal to divert his missiles in that direction and considered launching some more. But how much time and resources was he prepared to expend on capturing a mind that Sverl probably hadn't informed of his destination anyway?

'I can give you a clue if you like?' said Flute.

'Please do,' said Cvorn.

'He's gone to the most likely of the least likely destinations,' said the mind. 'Then again, I might be lying.'

'What is Sverl's purpose?' asked Cvorn, annoyed by this exchange but knowing that such ship minds were often naive and could sometimes betray themselves.

'To survive and grow, as is the purpose of us all,' said Flute. 'Hey, shouldn't you be railgunning that moon by now? The debris cloud should make things difficult for me.'

Cvorn brought his railguns on line to target the moon and was about to do just that—

—when someone began talking to him down another communications channel he had kept open through U-space.

'Well, here I am, Dad,' said the second-child aboard his old destroyer. *'There's some seriously weird . . . shit! What the fuck is—'*

The channel closed with a brief surge of energy and the kind of squawk emitted by a fried U-space communicator.

'Good try,' said Cvorn to the mind in the attack ship.

'Whassup?' said Flute.

Cvorn calmly recalled his missiles and shut down his particle beam. He sent new coordinates to his own ship mind for now he knew precisely where he was going. To where something had just annihilated his old destroyer.

Blite

Seen through the atmosphere of this green-belt world, the hypergiant sun had a violet hue. It appeared no bigger than Sol did from the surface of Earth because the distance from the sun was much greater. However, because of the intense output of the hypergiant, Blite had his visor filtering heavily. A single cloud mass, resembling some organic grey battleship, rested on the horizon over to one side of this orb, while across its face flew creatures resembling birds at a distance, but more akin to pterodactyls when close. He turned from this scene and took in the one behind.

The *Black Rose* possessed its own avian qualities: it was black and this light had picked out the scaling of its hull so it resembled some giant raven expiring on the ground. It rested on a bed of vegetation that looked like a mat of gnarled tree roots. Perhaps they were roots extruded from the wall of alien red jungle, lying just a mile away. However, Blite stood on a soft mass of shredded organic matter which extended in a line from his ship to the exposed remains of some built structure. Here lay foundations – adjoining sets of triangular walls just waist high. They were made of a blue and slightly translucent ceramic that was incredibly hard. These were the remains of Jain buildings, so Penny Royal had said, and the AI stood in black thistle form within it. Its own silver roots had spread all around as if it was feeding on the ruins. Blite headed over.

'I don't need to tell you that they've arrived,' he said.

A twenty-foot-wide projection of outer space shimmered into being beside Penny Royal. The view was similar to the one Blite had obtained from the probes he'd scattered around this system upon their arrival. The captain now watched the current replay.

The King's Guard, fresh from destroying Cvorn's old destroyer, U-jumped close to Sverl's ship and attacked it while Spear's Polity destroyer departed. He saw Sverl's ship breaking into segments, which kept the King's Guard ships occupied while the destroyer managed to gain some distance. There was a brief conflagration as the Guard belatedly focused their attack on that small ship too late, because it U-jumped across the system to within just a few thousand miles of Room 101.

'I thought you didn't want the King's Guard here,' he said. 'I thought that was the whole purpose of those risky jaunts through time.'

'Incorrect,' said Penny Royal. 'I did not want the king here.'

'Why?' asked Greer, who had just joined them.

Blite glanced at her, wondering what had compelled her to come out after him.

Penny Royal didn't reply, so she continued, 'Yes, you say he would have died here. I know that, but I fail to see why.'

Penny Royal emitted something that sounded suspiciously like a sigh of boredom, whereupon Greer staggered, clutching at her head. Blite watched her, wincing slightly because he knew what was happening, and waited. Eventually she lowered her hands and turned to him. Her face was pale and he had no doubt she felt sick. Woodenly she said, 'The King's Guard will carry out their orders, hit their target and leave. If the king was here he would have done more and ended up dead.'

Blite had to wonder just what memories Penny Royal had resurrected in her mind to impart that information.

'So what do we do now?' he asked.

A glimpse then through the eyes of his younger self, as he peered into an archaeological dig on one of the first Diaspora worlds.

'Stop being opaque!' he snapped, not wanting Greer's recent experience.

The AI's spines rattled and shifted and it lifted some small object up at the end of one of its tentacles for examination. Blite meanwhile turned away from the dig site in his past and found himself playing chess against Brond in his head, shortly after recruiting the man. Brond's king was on the run and quite soon Blite would have him. Overlaid on that was his present knowledge that he had been thoroughly mistaken, and that Brond had lured him into a trap. Then the whole scene shattered.

'Clear as mud, as usual,' said Blite, glancing at Greer, who shook her head in annoyance.

'Explain to a child the reason, and it will still ask why,' said the AI.

Fuck you, Penny Royal, thought Blite, and peered closely at the object the AI was holding. It looked like a small egg, quadrate patterns visible all over its surface. The egg grew as bright as a welding arc and disappeared with a crack, leaving a wisp of black smoke.

And fuck you again, thought Blite, turning away and stomping back towards his ship, Greer quickly falling in beside him.

'Curiosity,' said Penny Royal.

Blite halted and turned around, Greer too.

'I wish you wouldn't keep on dragging me into this,' said Leven from Blite's suit.

'I'm not.'

'I'm not talking to you.'

'Oh.'

'Here goes, then,' Leven translated. 'The King's Guard have been ordered to remove the threat Sverl poses to the king's rule. And they are intelligent enough to know the entire substance of that threat: that Sverl is an amalgam of prador, human and AI,' said Leven.

'Wait!' said Blite. 'You hearing this, Greer?'

'I'm hearing it, Captain,' she replied.

'Now may I continue?' asked Leven tightly.

'Yeah, go ahead.'

'In the past Factory Station Room 101 was able to fend off an entire prador war fleet – but is no longer capable of the same now. The erstwhile Polity station is much weaker and prador weaponry has changed. Those Guard ships are fully capable now, though with some effort, of getting enough CTDs past station defences to vaporize it completely.'

'What about this "curiosity"?'

'The King's Guard will adhere to their orders and make efforts to destroy Sverl, to remove him as a threat to the king's rule. Most likely they will do this by simply destroying the station. If the king had been here, rather than order the destruction of Room 101, he would have ordered an assault upon it. This is because he is curious, because he wants to know what Penny Royal is doing and why. Such an assault would have resulted in the king's death.'

'So basically Penny Royal has answered Greer's question but not mine,' said Blite.

'I haven't finished yet,' said Leven, obviously irritated.

'Sorry.'

'Okay, the events here will, apparently, lead to some sort of resolution for two . . . problems . . . well, the nearest I can get to it is "actors in a play". Simplistically, Penny Royal is clearing up its own messes,' said Leven, 'and incidentally solving some other problems along the way.'

'One of those is Sverl? Sverl is one of those actors?'

After a long pause Leven replied, 'Yes.'

'And the other? Is that Spear?'

The reply issued from Penny Royal like a ghost muttering in the wind. 'Spear is not a problem, but a solution.'

'And what about the answer to my question – what do we do now?' asked Blite.

'We wait here, apparently,' Leven replied.

Blite did not bother asking anything more. He knew, on some unconscious level, that his audience with the black AI was over. Suppressing irritation, he walked away.

Riss

'Identify yourself,' was the essence of the demand, but it sounded like one made by hundreds of individuals. As Spear's response wasn't immediate and sensor data showed numerous weapons turrets and other armaments focusing on the *Lance*, Riss considered taking over. However, that would entail a mental tussle with Spear that might delay things fatally. A moment later Spear sent the Polity identification codes recorded in the ship's system – it had just taken him a few seconds to find them, that was all.

'Resupply or refit?' was the essence of the ensuing question. As with the demand, it wasn't phrased in human words.

Spear chose 'resupply'. Then whatever he was talking to, at a level somewhere between code and language, replied. 'Proceed to these coordinates,' it said, and sent a data package.

Keyed into the sensors, Riss now watched the King's Guard ships materialize some tens of thousands of miles behind them. The station's first response took the form of coolant ejections and shade-side shots of coolant lasers. Then the massive structure warmed up by a few degrees in just a few seconds as even bigger weapons arrays powered up. Even so, Riss could see evidence that things definitely weren't as they should have been. The station was a mess: riotous growths of nano- micro- and macro-tech gone insane. Some weapons arrays warmed up, then immediately powered down again, others were tardy, and quite a few looked heavily damaged. Also, unlike during the last prador attack on this station, no ships were launching – none at all.

The King's Guard ships looked decidedly more lethal. In response, they began closing into a tight formation, simultaneously firing swarms of railgun missiles and probing with particle beams. Spear released two more chaff shells and abruptly altered course, raising protective hardfields again a moment later. Beams intersected on their previous position, then began probing out randomly through the chaff. One of them just grazed one of the *Lance*'s hardfields and the ship shuddered. Riss detected a hardfield projector taken just to the edge of overload. Spear launched two more missiles and changed course again. The two fission bombs they contained exploded – their EM output enough to defeat even sophisticated scanners for a little while. Then probing beams were splashing behind them like flame-throwers hitting a glass wall. They were now inside some set perimeter and coming under the station's protection. It had also opened fire.

The firing wasn't neat or coordinated, but the sheer volume of weapons fire was enough to have the Guard ships scaling hardfields together in front of them. High-intensity green lasers hit first, turning hardfields iridescent. And ship-killing particle beams splashed on them next. Some hardfields went out, to be instantly replaced, the ships behind explosively ejecting the molten ruin of field projectors.

If Riss had possessed breath to hold, she would have let it out now.

'I'm guessing these are here for Sverl,' Riss said to Spear via his aug.

'I guess,' Spear replied. *'And now they want to talk.'*

Spear turned from her to gaze up at the screen fabric, where a frame opened to display a huge prador clad in black armour striped with iridescent blue. The creature was occupying a severely cramped sanctum, machines jammed into the spaces all around it.

'You are Thorvald Spear,' said the prador.

'And you are?'

'Fleet Admiral KG1 is all you need to know.'

'That's not very friendly.'

'I am prador,' said the admiral.

'So what can I do for you, Fleet Admiral KG1?'

Exterior sensors now showed the *Lance* flying into the open mouth of a massive final construction bay. Factory Station Room 101 loomed hugely around them, so they seemed like a small weaver fish swimming into a cave in an undersea cliff. And that analogy was a close one, because strange corals and other growths occupied this cliff. This was also a surface with seemingly volcanic vents opening across it, as the station ejected its own overheated projectors and some missiles got through.

Inside this construction bay, Riss spied giant robotic arms and resupply towers. The drone shivered down all its snaky length – reminded of past times. However, those arms were still and most of the movement here was elsewhere. What looked like massive worm casts covered large areas of the bay interior. An abundance of constructor tentacles writhed from these and elsewhere – ribbed and braided snakes sometimes miles long. These terminated in spiderish tubeworm splays of individual tentacles. Studying an image of one of these heads more closely, Riss saw that the single appendages terminated in coffin-sized objects like polished pistachio nuts. She recognized 'structor pods – so named because they were made both to construct and 'destruct' – and there were thousands upon thousands of them.

'The Prador Kingdom has no quarrel with either the Polity or with you, Thorvald Spear,' said the admiral. 'However, the grotesquely changed prador, Sverl, is a threat to our security and I have been ordered to negate that threat.'

'Right now that might be a little problematic for you,' Spear observed.

'I agree. Room 101 is a formidable space station. However, it is no longer runcible-linked for resupply, is no longer manufacturing weapons and is entirely reliant on its static defences. There is also evidence that its main AI no longer controls it and, though there is a possibility I will take losses, I know I can destroy it. I therefore suggest that you turn around and bring Sverl back to me.'

'I'm not really seeing any upsides for me just yet,' Spear observed.

'*There's something decidedly odd about these King's Guards,*' he shot at Riss. '*Even in translation I've never heard of prador being so reasonable . . . well, until Sverl . . .*'

'*A curious definition of reasonable,*' said Riss, but she was more interested in studying the signal the *Lance* was receiving. Room 101 wasn't even blocking it, so she recorded the channel and coding. It might come in handy.

'The upside is that if you hand Sverl over you get to live,' said the admiral. 'Hiding away in that station is a sure way to die.'

The ship shuddered; something was getting through into the construction bay and causing an explosion that tore free a crane almost a mile high from its mountings. Seemingly in concert with this, the signal mutated to carry an aug frequency. Riss observed

Spear sorting it and listened in to what the prador on the screen wanted to pass on in secret.

'I am not yet using all my armaments. You have one of your solstan days. You either hand Sverl over, or you give me evidence that Sverl has met with an accident. Your choices and your time are limited, Thorvald Spear.'

That was smart, thought Riss, and agreed somewhat with Spear's earlier observation. The usual prador archetype would be hitting them with everything available, not talking. This Guard had tried that initially, but now they were inside station defences, it knew it could not take them out without losses so was negotiating.

'You should have put Sverl in a hold,' Riss said to Spear. *'You could have ejected him out into vacuum the moment they appeared.'*

'And thus the King's Guard would have no quarrel with me?'

'Yeah, thusly, motherfucker.'

'I see, so Penny Royal managed to empty you of your purpose for existence but neglected to remove the hatred that was one of its drivers?'

'Our best course would be to hand Sverl over, or at least put some distance between us and him when they fry him.'

'Sverl is an ally, Riss,' said Spear.

'Let me kill him,' said the drone.

'You already know my answer to that,' Spear replied.

Stupid human, Riss thought, and began to pay some serious attention to the restraining collar with which Sverl had burdened her.

They were deep into the construction hold now and the ship shuddered in the grip of numerous hardfields. The frame showing the prador admiral blanked out, but didn't disappear as would be usual. Riss did some checking and found that though the prador had cut the com, something else, from within the station, had inserted itself in that channel.

As the destroyer reached the wall of the hold, clangs reverberated throughout as clamps locked into place. Riss rose up off the floor, hovering, and gazed back towards the rear annex. Sverl had surprisingly little to say now. Perhaps he was considering his options. Meanwhile, Riss was considering one of her own . . .

With the ship safely docked, Spear unstrapped himself, stood and stepped out of the horseshoe console. 'Sverl?' he enquired, looking back into the rear annex.

After a long pause Sverl replied, 'I trust that Penny Royal has a purpose beyond the destruction of me and this station. I trust that Penny Royal has not lured me here just to . . . *solve* me.'

'That seems to be a high degree of trust,' said Spear. 'That might have been exactly Penny Royal's intention.'

The ship shuddered again – something else hitting it out there as if to remind them of their danger.

'I am remaining here on this station. You may leave.'

'And I must trust that those ships out there won't destroy me and my ship out of hand?' said Spear, his tone completely lacking in nuance. He turned to look at the others on the bridge. 'I welcome your input.'

'I think we've got a problem,' said Sepia, flicking a glance towards the rear annex. 'A heavily armed one.'

'Trent?'

'Why is Sverl a threat to the Kingdom?'

'Because he is part human and AI and his transformation can be used as an example of Polity perfidy to foment rebellion.'

'I wonder if the King's Guard would want to leave any witnesses to that, then.'

There it was, Riss felt. *Nothing personal, Sverl, but our best*

chances of surviving are if we remain here and you don't survive.
The Guard out there know that, too.

'I will make it simple for you. You can go or you can stay,'
said Sverl. 'I will not leave you any other . . . options.'

Had Sverl somehow heard the aug message Spear had
received, Riss wondered.

'Sverl, I don't quite—' Spear began, just a second before
explosive decompression picked him up and dragged him
towards the rear annex, and the glare of the hypergiant entered
like a thermite blast.

Riss reacted at once, hurling herself towards the arch between
annex and bridge and driving her ovipositor deep into the wall.
As Spear came within reach, she coiled tightly around him and
held him in place. The other humans were still strapped in, so
were safe for the moment. But the internal temperature was
already rising and some objects were beginning to spill smoke.
Still holding tightly to Spear, Riss saw that the entry hatch made
for Sverl and his two first-children was gone. She didn't need to
analyse the burns around it to know they had blown it. Sverl was
outside the ship, a meniscus extruded by his prosthetics protecting his soft bulky body from vacuum, and darkening to block the
intense light. Gripping him on each side, his two first-children
had ignited thrusters mounted in their armour to take him away.
Checking further through the ship's systems, Riss saw that, yes,
the hold space doors were open and the second-children were
spilling out and firing up the thrusters in their armour to take
them after their father-captain. And the weapons cache was
open too – releasing Sverl's remaining war drones.

Riss desperately wanted to go after Sverl and end this now,
but if she let go of Spear the man would die. The air blast waned
– they were now in complete vacuum. Just minutes remained
now before it killed Spear.

'*Riss,*' said Spear via his aug, '*you can let me go now.*'

Riss focused on him fully, and now saw the segmented hood of a space suit up over his skull and his visor closed and polarized. How had she forgotten that the man was wearing a space suit? She knew why. She wasn't thinking straight, hadn't been thinking straight for the best part of a century.

Riss uncoiled from the man and flung herself to the lip of the blown hatch to see Sverl and his children heading away. Stay or go? Riss hesitated for just a second, then used her internal grav to fling herself from the ship and in towards the wall of the construction bay. A particle beam scored past, and a Gatling cannon flashed from the prador group. That fucker Bsorol. As the drone propelled herself to cover, she glimpsed the prador heading into the mouth of a tunnel in the construction bay wall. Riss waited until the last of them went out of sight, rose up, then had to duck the swipe of a complex tool grab. The construction robot was small compared to other things out here, but still much larger than Riss. It tried to grab her again, but Riss squirmed away through the air. She grav-planed to the hold wall, engaged the remora function in her skin and squirmed down that. A crash shook the surface underneath her and Riss looked up to see the construction robot tumbling through vacuum, another robot wrapped around it and apparently trying to tear it apart. Beyond it the head of a massive constructor tentacle was open like a giant organic star and multi-limbed construction robots were propelling themselves from open 'structor pods. Other pods were issuing shearfield blades and ripper arms.

The fuck?

Elsewhere other robots were grappling with each other too. Apparently, their arrival here had started some sort of conflict. There seemed to be no coherence and no cooperation out here at all. Riss moved on, focused on her target, then paused, something else grabbing her attention.

Uh?

She could see the Penny Royal Golem, John Grey, crouching by the nose of the *Lance*. He had to be under Sverl's control, but what was he waiting there for? However, even as she watched, Grey suddenly moved out and headed off, streaking across the wall of the construction bay and disappearing into a small hatch.

Sverl. Must concentrate on Sverl.

As she entered the mouth of the tunnel, the prador were no longer in sight. But the flashing of weapons indicated their position around a curve far ahead. However, Riss knew that she must rid herself of this collar if she was to get to her prey. She gave chase, coming up behind other pursuers – more construction robots like the one earlier. Each resembled a number of segments chopped out of a steel centipede, with their waterscorpion limbs to the fore. Creeping up on the last one, she saw her opportunity. These things weren't weapons, but they certainly carried a lot of hardware, including diamond saws and atomic shears . . .

18

Spear

The other three had all prepared themselves, following the descent of the ship's interior into vacuum. Cole and Sepia had managed to fold up the hoods and flexible visors of the survival suits they had worn under their clothing, while Trent was wearing a suit similar to my own that had reacted to the pressure drop. Working through my ship's system, I closed up the weapons cache hatch and the hold space doors. And as I did this I noticed perpetual interference on the virtual level. Attempts to penetrate my ship's computing were constant, but weak and incoherent. When I tried to analyse these I found external programs fighting one other, and in fact weakening each other. Further analysis revealed that they were old news – the kind of viral attack used during the war. Even at full strength, they wouldn't have been good enough to get past the system's standard informational warfare defences – let alone crack the codes that gave me control of both system and ship.

The blown hatch was more problematic, what with the potentially dangerous level of light penetrating. Luckily, we weren't in the full glare of the hypergiant, or we would have been getting a lot more than just singed. I would have liked the hatch back, but it was now tumbling away towards one of those tentacle-headed constructor monstrosities. And, even as I watched, one tentacle fielded it, while pods at the ends of other tentacles spilled numerous scorpion-format robots all over it. However, I did still have a hardfield generator available, which would darken to the right degree. I focused it in the gap, but not quickly enough.

Just moments before the field came on, a closer tentacle thrust its pod end inside. I swiftly altered the programming of the projector, so that the field only conformed to the frame of the hatch. With a flash of discharging energy, it sheered straight through the tentacle, but even this was too late. While the severed limb thrashed, the pod at its end divided horizontally and its back end hinged open. Packed inside was something that looked like a complex technological chrysalis – all folded limbs and tubes, polished metal and gleaming lights. The severed tentacle bucked again, spilling this thing, and as it rolled out it began unfolding above the deck. There it thumped down and engaged two long-toed gecko feet.

At first it just seemed a metallic lump, fashioned somewhat organically. Then, as my visor adjusted to the light drop, it rose up. It hunched, twinned sets of arms opening out, these terminating in complex tool hands – with the glimmer of shear fields along curved fingers. It trudged through into the bridge, noticeably collapsing down a little as it came over the grav-plates, then straightening up again. Its head, a squid-like contraption with three glowing blue eyes, had been swinging from side to side until that moment. Then it focused on me, ribbed metal tentacles furling and unfurling. The presence of this machine confirmed that something was decidedly wrong here, supposing I actually needed any confirmation. On top of the weird growths out there and the barely understandable communications I had been receiving, this thing did not look familiar at all. I could remember the kind of robots usually found aboard wartime factory stations and this thing wasn't one of them. Sure, during the war there had been an inclination to create robots with a more organic look – like Riss – but aboard stations they had always been more utilitarian.

I glanced across at the other three, who were quickly unstrapping themselves. The only one armed was Sepia. And, while I wondered how effective her pulse-gun and laser carbine could be, I wished she did not have them. They might make her more of a target. I backed away, moving over to one wall to reach out carefully and touch a control to release a series of clamps. Penny Royal's spine fell into my hand, memories surging in my hindbrain like a stormy sea and an utter sense of connection establishing itself. An icon flashed in my visor to tell me atmospheric pressure was up again, and the visor and segmented helmet closed back down into my suit's neck ring. In the air, I now smelled hot metal and something caustic, like the mist off an acid bath. Next, Trent, Sepia and Cole were on their feet, Sepia bringing her laser carbine up to her shoulder. Part of me wanted to tell her to lower it, yet another, larger part, was assessing how useful she would be.

'I am seizing control of this ship,' said a voice. 'Drop your weapons and provide access codes.'

I glanced up at the frame still open in the screen fabric – now displaying a standard com icon of a silver human head. The speaker was using the channel the prador had used, but was clearly much closer. However, the communication wasn't coming from the unwelcome new robot we'd acquired.

'Who are you?' I asked.

'Construction bay AI designation E676.'

I found myself probing back along the signal, not sure how I was doing this, and glimpsed a mind and then a wider view. E676 was physically transferring itself to a spiderbot carrier. I now knew exactly what was happening – why robots were swarming and fighting each other out there, why the constant attempts to take over my ship's system. The AIs here had heard what the King's Guard had said to me. They wanted off this station before he carried out his threat. The robots wanted my ship. The one talking had been just that little bit faster than the rest.

'Give me your access codes,' it demanded again.

'Go fuck yourself,' I replied succinctly.

The robot reacted.

It leapt, one of its tentacles stabbing out and whipping across. It hit Sepia, picking her up and smashing her into the wall. It then caught Cole and sent him spinning as it came down on the bridge's horseshoe console. It was horribly fast, and in response my time sense changed. My thinking ramped up in a synergetic curve between my aug and my mind. Rage arose in me too, because it had hit Sepia and she might be dead. I saw Trent diving, going into a neat roll that put him underneath the sweep of another tentacle as he snatched up the carbine. On another level, the memory horde, residing in the object I clutched, responded with a tsunami of data. It drained into my mind and my aug, and an instant later became firm knowledge. Some of the people there had been robot designers, programmers and maintenance technicians. From their knowledge, I quickly understood that this thing was an amalgam of two small construction robots, while its upper squid-like head was in fact a type of war drone.

'Hey!' I shouted, moving now with what I felt to be glacial slowness, and the thing began to swing its head back towards me. By now Trent was up in a squat, aiming and firing, burning out its eyes and frying tentacles. Reaching out to my ship's system, I knocked off the grav at the same time as throwing myself forward, legs ahead. A tentacle skimmed over me, while a second one smacked the carbine from Trent's grip – before catching him under the chin and sending him flying backwards.

The controlling mind wouldn't be in the parts originating from a construction robot – at least that was my calculation. I closed my legs around the thing below its head. Simultaneously, I swung the spine round and drove it hard into the lobe-like structure behind the front of its tentacular head. The shock juddered up my arms but the spine punched through armour, impaling the thing. I released and, bringing grav back up, landed in a squat, then stood and turned. The robot keeled sideways and crashed to the floor.

'Riss,' I said aloud, simultaneously sending the message by aug as I headed over to Sepia. 'Leave Sverl alone and get back here.'

'Sorry, no can do,' Riss replied, her words almost lost in static.

'Sverl is an ally,' I reiterated. For a moment, I got a flash of something through Riss's eyes. The drone had its ovipositor stuck deep into what looked like a standard design of construction robot. It was down on the floor with its limbs moving randomly. On another level, I could sense the drone circumventing a block and penetrating that robot's simple mind.

'You would kill yourself . . . not taking . . . logical step,' said Riss. *'Sverl has to die . . . are to survive. It's simple.'*

'Or you have simply rediscovered your purpose in existing?' I suggested.

'Fuck you,' said Riss, those words coming through quite clearly, and she cut the connection.

I tried to reach out to her, and found something in the spine responding. In a moment I realized it was the *copy* of Riss in there. Sinking into that and fast-analysing it with a multitude of programs running in parallel, I searched for strengths and vulnerabilities. Annoyingly, I found that I had provided the very weapon she intended to use next. But in a close parallel search,

I found the relevant vulnerability. It was a code a Polity AI had once used, which made her dump the parasite eggs she had contained. I could use it to make her dump the enzyme acid she carried. But to do so I had to get close enough to send a powerful enough radio signal.

'Sverl,' I said, opening another channel.

'Yes, I know about the snake drone,' said Sverl.

'I will come to you,' I said.

'Your presence is irrelevant,' he replied, and cut me off too.

I squatted down by Sepia, and aug-linked to the biostats from her suit. When the stats told me she was alive, and not badly injured, I felt some of the tightness leave my chest. I gazed at her face, at the blood leaking from her nostrils, and stepped back. I needed to ensure we were all safe.

I next focused my attention out through cams on the *Lance*'s hull. Robots were still fighting each other out there – some were clinging to the hull too and trying to drive in diamond saws and drills. Some of those tentacle umbilici were also approaching. Still running extra programming, I assessed the situation, briefly considered tactics, then set things running. Anti-personnel lasers extruded and began firing, ripping into anything vulnerable to them. Steering thrusters fired up, plasma flames frying anything in reach. I fired the particle cannon, destroying one of the larger umbilici, but was unable to reach the rest. I then triggered the emergency explosive undocking procedure. The *Lance* jerked and rolled, then rose, the shattered remains of docking clamps falling away. I fired again, particle cannons and railguns spreading a steady wave of destruction from where we'd been secured, scrapped and burning robots tumbling out into the bay. I hit the nearest big grabs threatening us and turned them to glowing scrap, then I brought the ship back down again, engaging remora feet.

'Attempt to take my ship again,' I said, 'and I will cut through to this location –' I sent the coordinates of E676 back to the AI – 'and will burn everything I find there.'

After a long pause E676 replied, 'Understood.'

I glanced over towards the fallen robot. It was utterly still but for something shorting out where its tentacle face touched the floor. I walked over and took hold of the back end of the spine, but it was jammed in solid. It needed to be thinner to slide free. It needed to change its shape just as Penny Royal did with all its parts. Geometric patterns fled through my consciousness and the thing made a sound like blades passing over rock, loosened in its hole, and I pulled it out. The thing was narrower now and indented with deep grooves, small crystalline structures folding down its length.

'Jesus Christ!' said Sepia. She slowly pulled herself upright, wiping at the blood below her nose. Such an archaic curse, I thought, and considered asking her where it had come from. Some sensitivity to my surroundings returned then and I realized she was staring at me with something close to terror. I glanced down at the robot again, then at the screen fabric. The rose sunlight from the hypergiant illuminated it well, giving us an excellent view of the glowing wreckage out there. I then looked across at Trent. The man was watching me carefully, his expression unreadable until memory presented me with many similar examples. People displayed this kind of dumb acceptance when things were just completely out their control. It was often writ on the faces of those who were confronted by Penny Royal.

Now I analysed what I had done. I had been a soldier, but I was no highly trained killer like Trent. I wasn't physically boosted or augmented, yet I had just, in the matter of a minute, brought down a robot that was part war drone. Next, as if that had been nothing, I conducted two brief conversations before taking on and defeating a station AI. I understood then that the bleed-over from those other dead minds was affecting me on every level. Not only was I acquiring knowledge I hadn't had before, but skills too. And all were working synergetically within me.

'I'm going out after Sverl,' I said. 'I have to stop Riss.' I glanced at Sepia again, whose stats told me she had cracked a couple of ribs. The prostrate Cole was unconscious but in no danger. I then focused my attention on Trent.

He reached over and picked up the laser carbine, frowned as he inspected it, then glanced speculatively into the rear annex.

'Of course you are,' he said.

Sverl

Sverl felt truly frightened for the first time in many decades. Things seemed to be slipping out of his control, because they had slipped out of his understanding.

What happened to Grey?

He'd felt his links to the Penny Royal Golem, John Grey, dissolve and dissipate. This happened just as the King's Guard delivered its secret message to Spear. These factors, then Riss's communication, had all increased Sverl's sense of danger. He suddenly no longer trusted Spear – the man had obviously been undergoing some drastic changes anyway. And he was sure that Spear's reply to Riss had been just for Sverl's benefit. He must know Sverl had penetrated their communications. That the man was now controlling Grey was also a distinct possibility. Thereafter, all Sverl knew was that he had to get out of Spear's ship . . .

In terms of choices, why should he die, so Spear and the

others could survive? Should he sacrifice himself to prevent the destruction of Room 101? Was this what Penny Royal wanted of him? No, the AI was playing some other game here. Its interest in him had to be more than that, surely?

Just then, the station shuddered – another missile from the King's Guard getting through. These strikes acted as a constant reminder of the reality of the situation. Was it a reality he was trying to deny, Sverl wondered.

He now clung to a series of pipes, crusted with odd metallic moulds and running the length of a warship assembly tube. Perhaps it was even the tube in which Spear's ship had been built. As he did so, Sverl tried to see his way through his steadily waning panic. The certainty that Penny Royal intended more for him than his destruction here arose from the portions of his mind where that earlier panic was deeply rooted. In the human part of his mind, it came from what he might describe as the religious impulse. There was a need to attribute responsibility to a higher being, whilst feeling self-important enough to believe a higher being was interested. Certainty also arose in his prador self – from a similar arrogance and a greater belief in his own immortality. And, annoyingly, it had moved from both of these into his AI self. Sverl considered the idea of shutting down the two organic sources, to look at the situation more realistically, but just couldn't do it. The mere thought of doing so now caused panic to return – the organic portions of his mind hanging on for grim death.

Penny Royal would not allow anything to destroy Room 101; Penny Royal would not let Sverl die.

'Where now, Father?' asked Bsorol, eyeing some centipede robot crawling along the pipes towards them, seemingly grazing on those metallic moulds.

Where now? Where was Penny Royal?

'We need to establish a base,' Sverl replied, trying to appear utterly firm. 'From there I'll be able to search through this station's systems and eventually locate Penny Royal. When I have located the AI we go to it, and I at last get some answers.'

Answers? To what?

One of Sverl's war drones slowly cruised down the length of the pipes to pause over the centipede robot. The thing stretched as if trying to reach it and the drone zapped it with a maser. At once it turned around and scuttled away. The drone swivelled round to return, then something hit it hard on the side, exploding and sending it gyrating away from the pipes.

'Just one response!' Bsorol snapped over the command channel. 'We don't have an endless supply.'

A second war drone fired a missile and the thing sped off, igniting its drive a short distance away. It shot down towards where the end of the assembly tube was filled with one of those massive worm cast growths. There, it hit and exploded – a brief flash was visible and a spreading cloud of debris. Sverl meanwhile keyed into data exchanges. The distant attacker had, again, been a highly mutated maintenance or construction robot. It seemed that was all the fragmented society of AIs here had available inside the station. There were no Polity war drones, thankfully – well, except for one . . .

'They'll try some sort of sneak attack next,' said Sverl.

'Yes, Father,' Bsorol agreed, obviously still waiting to hear where they should go.

Sverl tried to pull back from his fear – for surely it issued from his amalgamated organic brain – and tried to think with the clarity of AI crystal. To know why Penny Royal would come here, he needed to resolve this place's mystery. Nobody had a clear idea of what had happened here. The place had been under prador attack and it had escaped. But why had the Factory

Station Room 101 AI taken the station out into the wilds like this, and here begun killing all its fellow AIs? What was the madness that infected it? And where was it now? There were intelligences scattered throughout the station – but there was no sign of the Room 101 AI. Had the others destroyed it?

'We go that way,' said Sverl, gesturing with one claw along the length of the assembly tube.

He had already snatched a station schematic from the mind of a maintenance robot, and now knew the physical location of the station AI at least. Sure, with its subminds and data nodes spread throughout the station it had been a partially distributed intelligence. But still, the bulk of its thought processes had run inside a large chunk of AI crystal. And this sat inside an armoured vault lying twenty miles ahead.

Bsorol settled beside him, reaching out and closing a claw around one of his limbs and used his suit impeller to set them in motion. As they travelled Sverl began to reach out, mentally, trying to reacquire his connection with Grey. At least he might find out if Spear had control of the Golem. This time a connection established at once.

'*Hello Sverl,*' came the reply.

'*What happened, Grey?*' he asked. '*Does Spear control you?*'

'*He does not yet know that he can.*'

'*Are you still free?*'

'*No, I never was.*'

'*Who controls you?*'

'*The same as always.*'

'*Who?*'

'*Who do you think?*' Grey replied, and cut the connection.

Sverl felt his panic returning. He had been aiming for an encounter with Penny Royal all along and finally it might happen. However, he entertained the possibility that – after the debacle at

471

the Rock Pool – he should have run just as far and as fast as he could away from all known space. He reached out through Room 101, checking other sensors and clouds of disrupted data for a sign of anything dark and spiny. Instead, he detected something *snakish*. There seemed a horrible inevitability to Riss's presence here . . .

'We need to go faster,' Sverl snapped, abruptly knocking Bsorol's claw away and turning on some of the hardware embedded in his ceramal skeleton. The grav-motor worked against surrounding matter in the same way as Riss's motive power and shoved Sverl forwards. His accompanying children hurried to catch up and remain in a protective formation about him. As he travelled, he continually scanned and weaned data from his surroundings, and found himself necessarily altering the schematic in his mind.

The station had undergone many changes over the last century. Semi-sentient technology had turned large areas into those strange worm casts, and tangles of tentacles were sprouting everywhere – their pod-like fruit ready to disgorge strange insectile seeds. Wild nano- and microtech growths crusted many surfaces, and extra tunnels snaked haphazardly through the structure, lined with fused detritus as if made by some giant burrowing beetle. It was as if the AIs here had devolved into the very fauna and flora from which some of their programming and physical characteristics derived.

Soon reaching the end of the assembly tube, they came to a wide portal leading into an area tangled with strangely overgrown machinery. Sverl identified handler robots resembling steel bastardizations of the human's god Kali. Maglev routing tubes were wrapped around with those other worm tubes. Dangling on thick threads of optic and power cables Sverl noted the glittery-eyed heads of hardfield conveyors, giant hydraulic arms and spider constructors. Large masses of coagulated wreckage and unused ship components were mounded up in some spaces or were drifting to the slow tidal pull of the hypergiant. Even deep within the station, the glare of that immense sun managed to penetrate; rather than needing to illuminate his surroundings, Sverl found it necessary to filter out the light.

Through a narrow channel, Sverl could see the edge of an octagonal runcible cargo portal, which he estimated to be a quarter of a mile across. This was where they had brought in pre-manufactured components. The area had been used for some assembly work, but components were mostly routed to mini-factories spread through the station. If anything was active in here, it would probably be perilous. But the place was dead. He propelled himself in.

Drifting down the channel to the runcible portal, Sverl checked the schematic again. Had the portal been working, its meniscus would have obstructed the way, and this would not have been an ideal route. However, this runcible, like all such within this station, was dead too.

'We didn't do this,' said Bsorol, waving a claw at the surrounding devastation and snaking burrows.

No, the prador attack had not caused the damage here. It had been caused by AIs fighting inside the station, and the subsequent rebuilding by distorted minds and technology gone insane. Sverl began to note further strange anomalies: construction robots wound together in death grips, other robots half melted and stuck to the superstructure. One of the umbilici manipulators had a mummified human corpse in a space suit impaled on one limb. As they drew closer, the sights grew increasingly strange – further evidence of technology run riot. Robots lay tangled in vine-like growths sprouting from the walls. Strange crystalline growths issued from one of the big handler robots like some parasitic fungus. And another human corpse, with just the helmeted skull and one arm visible, lay embedded in solid metal. Spikes of glassy metal protruded from otherwise empty eye sockets.

They passed through the inactive runcible into the next receiving area. Here, Sverl detected a submind surviving in the runcible control mechanism. It was singing the same atonal song to itself over and over again. And it gave no response at all to Sverl's probe.

'Them bones them bones them dry bones,' it sang.

Sverl shivered and was glad to be moving away from it.

At the end of this area, a growth resembling metallic lichen blocked the route leading towards the Room 101 AI. Sverl could see movement on it and, scanning closer, observed microbots slowly and meticulously building this thing. They were working like ants but with metal rather than organic matter – slicing it from a nearby collection of bubble-metal beams and working it into interlocking puzzle pieces before bringing them over and inserting them into place. There was order here, but no reason. As far as Sverl could tell, the structure they were building served no purpose at all. He estimated it would take them about two billion years to chew up the entire station.

'Burn a way through,' he instructed his children.

Bsorol and Bsectil moved forwards and opened fire, their beams converging on the mass and spiralling outwards. Metal vapour exploded out, white-hot, then rapidly cooling as it reached them. It left threadlike metallic crystalline growths on their armour. It took them some minutes and they even had to use their impellers to hold position – the thrust from the particle beams pushing them back. Finally, they cut through and made a wide enough hole. With a brief mental command, Sverl ordered one of his war drones through first. Bsorol followed with a couple of second-children in tow.

'Clear,' he said.

Sverl went after them, feeling uncomfortable about having wrecked what was perhaps a century of work by those micro-bots. Was that human guilt at kicking over a termite mound? It certainly wasn't something a prador would feel.

On his internal map – that schematic – the tunnel was straight. But once inside it, he saw it turned sharply to the right and curved upwards. Scanning ahead, he saw the tunnel distorted into an almost perfect spiral. This was just like the work of those microbots: order and organization to seemingly no purpose. Feeling slightly baffled and rather claustrophobic in the constricted space, he followed his first-children along the winding course. Soon he began to see that more was involved than the pointless distortion of the station structure. Embedded in the walls were Golem, occasional maintenance robots and, in one case, another human corpse. Maybe this was the result of some sort of trap, so he checked his surroundings for anything still active, but all he found were near-somnolent patches of nanotech. However, those things set in the walls appeared with meticulous regularity, with any limbs arranged just so. Was this art?

Beyond the end of the tunnel, things returned to what you might expect around an assembly plant. It was as if some intelligence had managed to create an enclave of sanity. However, Sverl could detect nothing active in the vicinity. Beyond this zone, things became even more Byzantine than before. The station structure had been severely distorted, so that what lay ahead resembled a jungle of tree limbs up to a yard wide. They were all formed of compressed and twisted metals, plastics and composites. Deep inside this – seemingly the seed from which it all grew – rested a pill-shaped container a quarter of a mile across. Despite the strange protruding connections, Sverl still recognized it – the armoured abode of the Room 101 AI. With a feeling almost of dread, he advanced towards it.

Cvorn

The infection that had lost Cvorn one of his newly installed palp eyes was gone. But now his other palp eye was completely blind and beginning to sag. Diagnostics had revealed that the steady transformation of the young adult's genome in those eyes by antejects had failed because of his own immune response to those same compounds. No matter – the palp eyes weren't critical. Fortunately, a localized mutation of his own genome caused this, and did not extend to his nether regions. His body was steadily incorporating his new sexual organs. However, as he nibbled at pieces of jellied mudfish and washed them down with chasers of the foul-tasting stomach remedy, he wondered if his insides would ever return to normal.

Cvorn turned his attention back to the steadily expanding ship's schematic on his screens. Sfolk had still managed to evade the ship's security drones, so Cvorn had decided that the only remedy was a complete review of the altered schematic. To this end, his children were out with scanners. They were working their way through the ship, transmitting data directly back to him. This laborious manual method was the only reliable way of getting what he needed, as the ship's system was completely in thrall to this false schematic. But the new schematic would not be ready before he reached the coordinates where his old destroyer had been annihilated.

Cvorn again checked the data on that incident and again

found it frustratingly inconclusive. The second-child had kept the transmission open and plenty of data was available, but it still wasn't clear what had fired on the destroyer. The destroyer's sensors had detected Sverl's ship, but at some considerable distance from its own arrival point. They had then perceived objects swinging round the red dwarf, but these were cloaked in a haze of EMR, and before identification was possible an energy surge occurred and the transmission ended.

Did Sverl have allies? Cvorn could think of no being, either prador or Polity, who might assume such a role. But regardless, he had taken precautions . . .

Cvorn stared at his screens, noting a small warning scrolling in one of them. The second-children must have discovered yet another part of the ship that hadn't been there on the schematic. They'd already picked up a tunnel leading from this very sanctum to a grating two corridors away to which Sfolk must have cut the fixings. This was now blocked and the grating welded down. But it was vexing to find this so near . . . Cvorn abruptly did a double take. No, this new warning signalled something else entirely. This actually told him that some cams had gone offline towards the nose of the ship – cams in a corridor adjacent to an armoury.

'Security Drones Four and Seven head to these coordinates,' he instructed, in his excitement briefly losing control of his ability to aug them the instruction or coordinates. He waited, champing his mandibles, then inadvertently regurgitated a chunk of jellied mudfish. His ailments seemed determined to remind him of their presence. He swallowed, tried to remain calm, then sent the coordinates – simultaneously bringing up sensor feeds from the drones on two of his screens.

SD4 was the first to arrive on the scene, rounding a curve in the corridor next to where one of the cams was offline. The drone's image feed briefly showed what lay ahead. Then the perspective shot up to the ceiling, before disappearing in a bright flash. A second later Cvorn heard the distant explosion and felt the rumble through the ship.

'All drones converge on the coordinates of Drones Four and Seven!' he instructed. 'Beware mines!' Next, he ran a replay of what the drone had seen. He saw a prador in the armour of a large first-child, slicing through the door into the armoury with a green-output quantum cascade laser.

Not so smart, he thought before panicking again, and belatedly checking on the contents of that armoury. It contained hand-held particle cannons, Gatling guns, missile launchers and a wide selection of explosives. With such weaponry, an armoured prador could wreak a great deal of havoc. But still, breaking in there seemed a foolish move. No matter how much havoc Sfolk caused, he would never get away from there – the security drones were just seconds away.

Now came the feed from SD7 as it slowed before the cam black spot. It framed an object stuck to the wall just above the floor and just below the ostensibly malfunctioning cam. Before Cvorn could issue instructions, the area in sight filled with metal flinders from Gatling fire and the mine detonated, taking out one wall of the corridor and part of the floor. Though he was aware that these drones contained second-child ganglions and could therefore think for themselves, he still said, 'Get in fast and kill him.'

'Understood, Father,' replied the drone, rounding a smoke-filled corner and entering the stretch of tunnel Sfolk had previously occupied. At the far end, Cvorn glimpsed the remains of the other drone lying in burning wreckage. Sfolk must have used a planar explosive mine to cut the thing in half.

SD7 reached the doorway into the armoury – which was still

smoking around its edges, with the door lying on the floor inside. The drone entered fast, swerved left then up and to the right. Cvorn caught one glimpse of a line scoring across a wall, spilling molten metal. More feeds opened up on Cvorn's screens as the other drones started to arrive, then another of them blinked out. It was all too chaotic to absorb and would require decoding in his aug, which he wasn't capable of right then. Abruptly he backed off his saddle, turned and headed for the sanctum door, retaining enough control to signal it to open ahead of him. There he paused for a second, considering bringing his blanks with him, but knew he wouldn't have much control over them either.

'Vlox!' he called, routing that and his imperative clattering to the PA system. 'You and armed children to me now!'

Four second-children clad in armour came at a run, skidding round the curve at the end of this tunnel, brandishing Gatling guns and particle cannons. They had been on station while the others were mapping the ship, just in case they uncovered Sfolk's hideaway. Vlox came running after, unarmoured but now bearing a single-barrelled weapon. This was specifically designed to punch through prador armour and explode inside it. Cvorn liked that his new first-child was keeping on top of events and was thinking ahead. Vlox might even survive in his post for as long as Vrom.

'Come!' he said peremptorily, and set off.

Two of the second-children shot forward, tipping sideways and running along the curve of the tunnel wall to get past Cvorn's bulk and settle in ahead. They soon reached a branch in the tunnel and headed right, following its curve down – already aware of where Cvorn wanted to go. Meanwhile, Cvorn managed to control himself enough to get imagery back from the drones' cams. The armoury was now full of smoke, the green laser stabbing through it and signalling its source. The drones were targeting this with careful particle cannon shots. Cvorn felt briefly angry. Why weren't they opening up with everything they had? Then he remembered just how dangerous it would be to do so at that location. This was quickly confirmed, as a further blast knocked out two cam views – but another showed Sfolk tumbling in a cloud of fire.

Very quickly, they drew closer to the sounds of conflict. Judging by the cam feeds, Cvorn reckoned Sfolk had realized he was finished, so now fought without regard for his own safety. One of the drones that the blast had knocked down had just recovered when the young adult leapt onto it. Another explosion ensued and Cvorn lost not only the cam feed from that drone but all other feeds too. Sfolk had destroyed the drone; Cvorn reckoned he had used the methods of a particularly feared human fighter during the war and had stuck a mine on the thing. Cvorn slowed down. Perhaps his impulse to rush down here to be in at the kill hadn't been a great idea. Vlox took this opportunity to get past him and join the two second-children just as they reached the edge of the cam black spot. Together, they rounded the curve into the conflict zone.

It was getting seriously chaotic in there. Sfolk had managed to activate a particle cannon and he wasn't reluctant to hit the munitions surrounding him. He was using them, in fact – deliberately hitting explosives whenever a drone drew near. Cvorn could feel the shock waves travelling down the tunnel and a moment later saw part of the wall panel blow out, hinging down like a ramp. Sfolk couldn't last much longer now. His armour was beginning to glow and he'd lost three of his eight legs and part of one claw. Cvorn halted and decided to wait, but did not have to pause for long.

Another blast caused a cloud of flame to belch out of the

hole in the wall. Then out shot Sfolk, hitting the far wall and crashing down again. His legs were now all missing on one side – the claw gone on that side too. However, in his other claw, he still held a particle cannon. He tried to right himself to face back towards his attackers but, at that moment, he must have spotted Cvorn and began to orient himself towards him. The second-children opened fire, the streams of slugs from four Gatling cannons driving the young adult back.

The onslaught sprayed metal flingers all around, denting Sfolk's weakened armour. Vlox squatted and took careful aim, firing off five shots in quick succession, even the damped recoil of his weapon sending him skidding back each time. Three shots punched straight through the front of Sfolk's armour. One went into his visual turret and one ricocheted off his claw and punched through the ceiling. Half a second later, fire spewed from those holes, the entire upper section of Sfolk's armour lifted and hinged back on the explosions. Then he dropped like an eviscerated clam.

'Good shooting,' said Cvorn, pretending very little concern.

He headed over to the smoking remains. The grenades had spattered much of Sfolk's insides on the walls, but had curiously left the upper and lower sections of his shell intact in the relevant armoured sections. Cvorn studied these, experiencing a momentary regret over the speed of Sfolk's death. He reached out with one claw and flipped the upper section of carapace so it landed back in place, now sans Sfolk's visual turret. He eyed the dark whorl in that shell he'd used to identify Sfolk and considered having Vlox collect all the shell and glue it back together as a trophy, then dismissed the idea. He had more important concerns, and if he was going to keep trophies, his first would be Sverl – stuffed and mounted.

'Clear up this mess,' he instructed Vlox, and turned away.

Riss

In the depths of Factory Station Room 101, the construction robot closed two clamp hands around Riss's body. It tightened them like the hydraulic vices they were, applying a pressure that would have simply chopped through the prador parasite Riss aped. She didn't struggle as the robot then extended a tool head and from that extruded a collimated diamond-chip saw and set it revolving. Had that saw been operating at sea-level air pressure on Earth, it would have produced sonic shocks, since its velocity would have far exceeded the speed of sound in that medium.

The saw blade touched Riss's collar and with a puff of dust began to penetrate. The collar immediately began to issue a series of EM pulses. Riss's thoughts decohered. She lost control of her electromuscle first, then all her other systems, in an accelerating cascade. Blindness across all sense bands ensued and, as Riss descended into darkness, she knew that the same EM pulses would disable the robot's electrics too.

After an immeasurable length of time, for even Riss's internal clock had gone down, the darkness receded and her thought processes began to cohere again. This reminded her of similar spells of darkness in her past: when Penny Royal had hollowed her out and her long somnolence next to Penny Royal's planetoid. It conjured up moments of shutdown waiting, ever waiting, for a war that stubbornly refused to return. Sensors re-engaging, Riss quickly turned down light input, then felt movement – a continuous, almost seismic, shuddering. She recognized this from the previous attack on this station. These were the vibrations caused by particle beams getting through to the hull and carving it up. She had to get moving; she had to get this done.

Riss tried to wriggle free but couldn't, then eyed the two halves of her collar, floating just a few feet away. At least that had worked. Any interference with the collar would have resulted in an EM burst that would have knocked Riss out, along with any other robot nearby. Once she had full control of the construction robot, it had therefore been necessary to reprogram its hydraulic system. She'd had to simplify the collar's removal method so the robot could still get the job done, despite the EM pulses. But now Riss had another problem: her reprogramming had neglected to include the robot opening its clamp hands.

Riss strained against them and cursed. This was ridiculous. She ceased struggling, pulled back mentally and tried to analyse the problem properly. The solution arrived a moment later and she felt stupid, perhaps as stupid as any organic entity. Scanning the robot, she assessed what the EM pulses had done to it. The thing was somnolent, scrambled, but had suffered no physical damage. Now free of the collar, Riss forged a radio link with the robot and began to reprogram it – pasting together many of the blocks of code that remained. After a moment, it shook itself, released Riss, went back down on all fours and began scanning for microfractures in the floor to repair. But not for long.

The plasma blast wave, like a wall of glowing glass travelling through the vacuum in the corridor, picked up both Riss and the drone and sent them tumbling. Another weapon had hit inside the final construction bay. This was not good at all, since the protective hardfields defending that part of the station had been the best overall at one time.

Regaining her balance and adhering to the floor with her remora setting, Riss squirmed past the robot. It was now floating above the floor, moving its limbs aimlessly. Glancing back, she saw the robot spit out sticky string and drag itself back down, whereupon it began inspecting for fractures again. Riss was oddly glad – she was grateful to the thing, after all. All her systems were fully functional now and she even still had that flask inside her, containing something nasty she could inject with her ovipositor. Probing her surroundings and weaning usable data from the chaos, she began to build up a map of the surrounding area of station and soon related it to an old schematic of the station stored in her memory. Suddenly she halted. She had been here before.

Some distance ahead lay the assembly tube for a design of destroyers commissioned long after Penny Royal had departed this place. It was down this that Sverl and his children had gone – they could hardly keep their location secret in a station packed with damaged robots and AIs spilling data from their ruptured minds. Instead of heading along the most obvious route there, Riss writhed up a wall and entered a small tunnel. For a drone with her body shape, this was a quicker route. In a sense, this also took her back into her past, which might provide her with a further weapon – one she had not used in a very long time.

Riss followed two further tunnels on her schematic and the last of these brought her out into a corridor she had been in before. She writhed partway down the wall, noting that the shifts in the station had partially crushed the corridor. But the human remains of three people were still here.

Ah . . . if wishes were . . . fishes.

The woman, now a partially mummified corpse resting back against the wall, had said that – just before blowing her brains out with a pulse-gun. The two on the floor had taken curare 12 beforehand. All three had known they had no chance of escaping the station. They knew that the steady temperature rise, caused when Room 101 switched the heat-sink runcible to 'import', would kill them. Riss studied the woman. She had obviously decayed for a while. But during that process, some breach had opened this corridor to vacuum and her remains had dried out, mummifying them. Riss could see the glint of metal inside the woman's busted-open skull and the intagliation of carbon electronics on the inner faces of some pieces on the floor. Here was Riss's first experience of wartime deaths. Seeing this again somehow formed a link between her present self and the naive young drone that had found these people. She felt loss and confusion, and an expansion of some inner darkness as she moved on.

Another tunnel took her through to a chamber from which many such tunnels debarked and thence to the small tubular autofactory that had made her. It was wrapped up now, at the centre of one of those huge worm casts. She entered the factory – quietly, since she could detect skittering movement in the newer structure all around. Robots had stripped out most of the factory. However, during the heat of battle and the ensuing insanity of Room 101, they had not taken everything. A long snakish body was stuck against one curved wall by a spill of some transparent epoxy. It was all jointed spine, plaited electromuscle and flexible components. Its head consisted only of a cylindrical turret topped with an eye, faded to grey. This had to be one of the drones behind Riss on the assembly line. Had certain things occurred aboard this station only a matter of minutes earlier, this would have been Riss's fate too.

The prador . . .

It was the correct response to feel rage towards them. They had attacked the Polity, they had been responsible for the incineration of inhabited worlds and the deaths of billions. They had equally been responsible for this object before her and those pitiful remains in that corridor. Hate was the right response, yet . . . Riss found something inside her that just didn't fit. Without the prador, this station would never have existed. Without them, she, Riss, assassin drone, would not have existed either.

Certainty tottered, but Riss closed the black eye she had been using to study this nearest of her kin and turned away. She existed to kill prador – and with the end of the war the purpose of her existence, supposedly, had ended. She had waited and in some sense was still waiting for that war to begin again. She had faced lean times, but Sverl would mark the end of them. The war might be over, but she could still find reasons to kill these obnoxious creatures.

Riss moved on and into a supply area. This place seemed stripped out too and Riss felt her hopes of finding what she sought beginning to fade. Then she spotted the inset door and read the dusty writing on it. She headed over and gripped the manual handle made for human hands with her small manipulators. Bracing her body against the wall, she pulled the handle down and heaved the door open. Inside were numerous shelves and all were empty but one, and here rested three small flasks. Riss scanned them deeply, finding the contents of all three were alive, in their way, but in stasis – a biological trait of their kind. Riss writhed into the room, opening her body, and loaded all three cylinders inside her, before writhing out again.

Now she was complete. She once more contained prador parasite eggs and could inject them into her prey. Despite feeling packed and gravid, she felt no satisfaction or any anticipation of future release. Perhaps it would return to her. Perhaps Spear was right about Penny Royal taking away hope, which was something that could surely always return.

By tunnels small and large, past metal growths like fungus, Riss headed off in pursuit of Sverl.

The Brockle

With one of its units plugged into the U-space transmitter, the Brockle reached out into near space to set up a constant watch for the single-ship. Fortunately, the ships used to transport prisoners here were stripped down and unsophisticated. They did not possess the more modern U-space transmitters that were capable of sending and receiving while in U-space. This meant that the ship would receive no instructions from Earth Central until it actually surfaced in near space. The Brockle had no doubt that then Earth Central, or some other AI, would try to strong-arm the Brockle's submind aboard – forcing it to take the single-ship back under and away from there. This it could not allow, because the single-ship was a requirement for the subterfuge it was about to enact. The moment that ship surfaced, the Brockle would immediately reabsorb the submind of itself it contained and take complete control.

Leaving the unit attached to the U-space transmitter in place, the Brockle coagulated back into human form, floating amidst the shredded remains of Antonio Sveeder's corpse. This watcher had delivered Earth Central's message and the Brockle still had the opportunity to heed it. It had not yet done anything criminal for, in destroying the watcher, it had not actually killed a sentient entity. It considered all the legalities and illegalities of remaining here or heading off. But, in the end, it all came down to something quite simple. It was bored with those usually sent for interrogation here: the humans were all the same in their self-justification and their parochial mindsets, and the more interesting machine intelligences sent were increasingly rare. In fact, the Brockle had not interrogated one in decades. No, it had made its decision.

Abruptly propelling itself into motion, it headed to the back of the hibernation chamber, through the airlock and back down the length of the *Tyburn*. It was headed towards what had been its abode for over eighty years. As it travelled, it considered what other preparations it would need to make. It had no physical belongings other than itself. All it really needed was data. Although, even as it thought this, it found itself outside the room in which Ikbal and Martina lay comatose.

The Brockle had by no means gleaned everything of use from their minds, and even their bodies might contain some stray useful data – perhaps recorded to the memory of a medical nanobot or some nanofactory attached to the wall of an artery. It could take them with it and continue its interrogation, but felt reluctant to so burden itself. Or it could leave them and forgo that data, which it was also loath to do. However, an alternative existed.

It entered and gazed down at the two humans prostrate on the floor. Extracting data while keeping them intact and alive would take meticulous work and time it did not possess, for the single-ship was perhaps only days away. With a thought, it knocked out grav in the room, then began to separate. In a moment the silver worms of its body were shoaling around the two forms, which it now lifted from the floor until they were floating a couple of yards above it. It simply tore away and discarded their clothing, which it had previously carefully returned to their bodies. It had already examined every thread down to the nanoscopic level. Inserting its own nano-fibres and data drills along the entire length of their bodies, it began examining them, soon deploying meniscus blades. These cut skin and flesh away for secondary examination and full atomic recording before it discarded them. It found nanobots from the medical packages all modern humans ran and recorded their memories and physical data. Then, entering the skulls of Ikbal and Martina, it raised them out of coma, because mental examination was always better when the candidate was conscious. At this point it noticed them screaming, but that soon stopped when certain items were removed.

Where did the definition of death lie when everything could be recorded? At what point is murder committed when the victim is being converted into data? Soon shoaling amidst a spreading gory cloud, the Brockle pondered these philosophical points as it destructively recorded everything these two people were. It would take them with it, as part of itself, sure that what it was doing was not murder. However, it wasn't stupid enough to believe that Earth Central or other Polity AIs would see it that way.

19

Sverl

The armour around the housing for Room 101's central AI core was weak – so wound through with microbot incursions that it had taken on the structure of worm-eaten wood. It was also brittle: crystallized and laced all through with microfractures. The prador drone spat a single missile at the central door and the thing shattered like old glass, slinging fragments into the chamber beyond. The drone slid in there, Bsorol following.

'Clear,' he reported.

Second-children entered and spread out, and Sverl came through next. He gazed at the wreckage, then at the objects sitting in an area towards the centre. Their sad story was all too clear.

'There's nothing here for us,' he stated. 'We need a place that can be armoured and easily defended.' He reached down and picked up a chunk of the rotten door. 'We'll need deep detection all around.'

The AIs had been desperate back there near the *Lance*, using a brief burst of energy. But during their internecine war they had wasted all their internal weapons against each other and thoroughly degraded exterior station defences. Spear and the others had known they could not hold off the King's Guard, and that the only way to stop the attack was by killing Sverl. Yet in coming here, it seemed that Sverl had left them behind. Perhaps they were frightened of this place . . .

Bsorol waved a claw back the way they had come. 'That autofactory back there looks as good as anywhere. I can set up an easy perimeter, install some security . . .'

'Then that is where we shall go.'

Sverl turned, headed back to the shattered door and also gazed back the way they had come. He felt conflicted. The station AIs and their various robots didn't worry him – soon enough he could take control of or otherwise subdue them – so why did he want to build defences? Was it instinctive for a prador to install these in a sanctum? Was it the sure knowledge that the assassin drone Riss was after him? Or was it due to his doubts about Thorvald Spear? No, that parasite assassin drone might be dangerous, but, devoid of its usual weapons, it would be no real threat. As for Spear, the man might be becoming an enigma with strengths that weren't easily measurable, but his chances of getting past Bsorol and Bsectil were remote. No, Sverl knew why he wanted a new defensible sanctum – he was terrified of Penny Royal.

Sverl launched himself from the edge and began heading back, his children belatedly moving in around him. One of the two war drones forged ahead and the other stayed behind; Bsorol and Bsectil were on either side, and his eleven remaining second-children arrayed themselves all around him. All were impelled by jets of compressed air from their armour. Soon they arrived at a protruding half-circle of metal almost like a balcony and entered the tunnel at its rear, which finally debarked into the coin-shaped autofactory. Sverl reckoned this place had made some form of robot for installation in dreadnoughts – assembled in a final construction bay adjacent. However, he could not divine the robots' purpose from the scattering of wrecked machines remaining here.

He moved out to the centre, anchoring himself by a column

robot, now sans arms and sensors. Bsorol, Bsectil and the rest of his children began to see to his security. Soon they were cutting and welding metal all round, bringing in armour and other items from elsewhere. They were building a sanctum around him, so he could encyst in this station. Sverl observed them at work and issued instructions every now and then, and occasionally linked into the detectors and sensors they were installing – ironing out kinks and closing gaps. When they no longer needed his supervision, he mentally ranged out to explore his surroundings.

Soon he found that this area in the heart of the station was all but devoid of AIs – the nearest being the singer back by the runcible. Perhaps proximity to the Factory Station Room 101 AI had been fatal. It struck him that maybe, in some perverse way, the previous attacks upon him had been territorial. Since the previous one, no robots had pursued him, and he found no sign of any AI preparing to attack him now. The nearest AIs were in fact somnolent, dislocated. Those at the hull of the station were still defending it from the King's Guard's assault, but with robotic thoughtlessness, just responding and not thinking ahead. He narrowed a probe, selecting just one of these. Then, using every subterfuge he had available, he winnowed data from it. What he found was disturbing.

The AI he'd targeted did know that the King's Guard had pursued a Polity destroyer here and it did know why they were attacking. But Sverl's presence here wasn't a priority, because the solution to it was in hand. When Sverl tried to find out what that solution might be, logic descended into chaotic vagueness. The AI did not know any specifics, but did know that Sverl was no longer its concern. Nervously rubbing his mandibles together, Sverl recognized outside interference and guessed its source.

Trent

Trent steadied himself against the edge of the *Lance*'s airlock, his visor display briefly informing him his suit was running its cooling system. His visor was now as dark as a welding glass. Yet, even on this dim setting, he could see everything out here in stark clarity. This place had once efficiently turned out warships just as fast as practically possible. Now Trent couldn't help but be reminded of a long ago VR experience, of swimming over a coral reef on Earth. The construction bay was colourful and alive with strange growths. The only reminder of where he really was came from the nearby burned-out and still glowing remains of robots, 'structor pods and attached tentacles. He could also see a distant rising plume of debris from yet another explosion, composed of smoking vaporized metal. This latest weapons strike was in the same area as all of the most recent ones – deep within the bay, about five miles away. He wondered if the King's Guard out there had detected Sverl leaving the *Lance* and were now firing at the prador's present location. Then he followed Spear.

Spear propelled himself from the edge of the airlock to the wall of the bay. As he followed, Trent kept replaying the events inside the *Lance* in his mind. Spear had been in bio-espionage. However, the data Isobel had obtained on him mentioned nothing about martial training nor special uploads, beyond the standard ones at least. Yet during his fight with the robot intruder, he had moved almost as fast as a Golem. Surely, it had taken more than human strength to drive something, no matter how sharp, straight through the rear lobe on that robot's head. That had to be war drone armour. But it wasn't just that – it was his attitude. They had faced something that could have killed them all – but upon bringing it down, he had behaved as if it had been a minor hindrance. Then he proceeded to fire off the destroyer's weapons mentally, eliminating the threats all around it. And that was another skillset the man hadn't possessed before.

That was why Trent was following him, wasn't it? Spear was now their best bet for survival so the sensible thing was to stick with him, follow his lead and try to protect him. Trent felt he *should* stay to guard the *Lance* against attack, but how could he do that? The cold caskets inside it – his responsibility – would be no safer with him there. He cringed inwardly, aware that his concern was more about the one casket containing Reece; many complex feelings arose from that. He had felt her choice to go into hibernation as a kind of betrayal, and now wondered if his decision to follow Spear was a tit-for-tat disloyalty in return. He shook his head in irritation, annoyed that he apparently did not possess the mental equipment for dealing with these emotions.

'How are you going to track Sverl?' he asked Spear as they moved out from the *Lance*. He turned to take in the interior of the massive final construction bay.

The thing was miles across. It was like looking over some endless industrial cityscape. Sure, plenty of that organic-looking stuff was visible, like the tentacular writhe of 'structor pod growths. And over to his left, he could see a mountainous worm cast with umbilici protruding from the open mouths of its tunnels – just like the feeding heads of barnacles. However, larger static structures like cranes, giant grabs and resupply towers overshadowed these. Some structures had also taken on a slightly organic appearance, but only because they had been half-melted. Large areas had been torn apart or incinerated. Out in the actual space of the bay drifted wrecked ships, shattered robots and other not so easily identifiable debris. Those barnacle heads were probably feeding on this kind of thing. In places, this stuff had coagulated like piles of asteroid rubble. A slight movement was detectable overall too – probably due to the tidal forces of the hypergiant that Room 101 orbited. In other areas, because of the recent strikes, it was worryingly more than slight.

'Tracking Riss is a problem, but Sverl is no problem at all,' Spear replied over suit radio. 'There are data sources, sensors, computers and minds all around us. I can access these, and a large party of prador isn't easy to conceal.'

'And if we come across another robot, like that one inside?'

Spear turned towards him and held up the spine he carried. It had already proved to be effective in Spear's hands, but strictly on a one-to-one basis. If more than just one robot attacked, then the weapon Trent carried would be better. Upon deciding to go with Spear, he had quickly gone in search of something sufficiently effective. He'd found that the second-children hadn't taken everything they'd brought aboard. Just the installation of a manual trigger mechanism had made the small particle cannon usable, and a curved butt to go under his armpit had made it less unwieldy. He felt he carried their main defence . . . or was he just not seeing something? He remembered the spine seeming to change shape as Spear pulled it out of that robot, and shuddered.

They entered a long tunnel in the wall and propelled themselves to drift along it. Trent did not like this way of travelling in zero gravity and vacuum. You could only move as fast as your suit wrist impeller could propel you – not great if you needed to get out of something's way. But this was how Spear chose to move and if Trent had resorted to walking on gecko boots, he would not have been able to keep up. On that thought, he wondered if he actually wanted to continue. Perhaps he should go back.

Towards the end of the tunnel, at a junction, something became visible crouching on the floor. It was a construction robot and didn't appear hostile – in fact it just appeared to be doing what such robots usually did. Every now and again, it emitted arc flashes from one of its tool-head arms. It was welding cracks in the floor. Nevertheless, Trent aimed his particle cannon down at it as they drifted over. It showed no response to them at all.

'So, Riss got her collar off,' said Spear.

'What?'

Spear indicated the robot with a wave of one hand. 'Riss subverted that robot, programmed it mechanically and had it cut off her collar.'

'Right,' said Trent. He'd had an aug of his own and it had been a sophisticated one, but he'd never been able to penetrate and read the memory of a construction robot. That was usually the province of specialized technicians, who programmed the damned things. Trent considered for a moment, then looked back. He could see no sign of the collar. Had Riss taken it with her or something?

At the end of the tunnel, they reached a T-junction where they shed their momentum against the wall – then they stuck in place with their gecko boots. Even here, deeper inside, Trent's visor had only notched its filtering down a little. The light of the hypergiant flowed throughout the station like an ambient fluid.

'This way,' said Spear, and began trudging along the wall, which of course now appeared to be the floor.

'How do you intend to stop Riss, if she's set on going after Sverl?' Trent asked.

Spear paused and looked round. 'I'll try reason and I'll try pleading. However, if I get close enough, I'm pretty certain that I can now gum up that drone's workings.' Spear grinned, first tapped his hand against the spine then raised it to tap at his helmet just over his aug. He turned and moved on.

Trent was certain that neither he nor anyone else he knew of would have been able to 'gum up' the workings of an assassin drone. Spear had been a formidable character when Isobel Satomi first met him, and he was steadily becoming more dangerous.

'Then the next question I have to ask,' said Trent, 'is why?'

Spear halted, but didn't look round. 'You told me that you have been cursed with empathy, so where is it now?'

'What do you mean?'

'The fact that Riss intends to kill Sverl should be enough . . .'

Trent felt something tighten up inside him. Yes, that was wrong, but surely survival dictated—

'But perhaps I should explain to you *how* Riss intends to kill Sverl,' Spear continued. 'The enzyme acid I used to free the shell people of their grafts was a refinement of one that destroyed both prador and human tissue – and Riss has it. Can you just imagine how agonizing it would be to have your body dissolve in acid?'

Trent felt slightly queasy about that but stamped down on the feeling and tried to stick with logic. 'If Sverl lives, we all die.'

'No, we have time – the King's Guard are only, as far as I can gather, whittling down the station's defences right now. Their leader told me, secretly, that the real attack will commence in . . . ten hours.' Spear turned round. 'I have time to stop Riss and get us all back to the *Lance* and away.'

'With Sverl?'

After a pause, Spear just said, 'And then we will see how things transpire.'

This man was very confident in his abilities. However, just seconds after their exchange, it became evident his confidence might have been premature.

Trent had no time to react. Spear was walking along ahead when a section of metal under his feet seemed to drop like a trapdoor, which of course was impossible in zero gravity. Stuck by his gecko boots, Spear's lower half disappeared up to his hips.

Then a pair of skeletal Golem arms appeared, wrapped in organic tech with heavy joint motors. They reached out, silver hands clutched, and dragged him out of sight.

Blite

'What's it doing out there?' asked Greer as she threw herself down in a seat. They were all getting frustrated on the planet's surface, as they tried to make sense of activities around the distant Factory Station 101. They were also trying and failing to monitor Penny Royal.

Blite shrugged as he sat down. He'd used ship's sensors to scan Penny Royal's activities in the ruins and the data were unclear. The AI had found two objects that it had immediately destroyed. They appeared to possess roots like some weird plant, with their tendrils spreading out through the ground for miles around. But beyond these facts, he knew no more.

'It's studying the ruins I guess,' he said.

'And with no explanation offered,' said Greer flatly.

'None,' Blite agreed.

'I'm getting sick of this,' she said. 'Perhaps we should have just stayed in the Polity and submitted to whatever examinations the AIs wanted to make.'

'Perhaps.'

'You don't agree?'

'I don't, and neither do you.' Blite reached out to call up a view of the AI and noted that it had changed shape. Its spines were all pointing upwards as if, like a flower that responds to daylight, it was closing up for the night. This was now due, as the hypergiant sun was falling behind the horizon.

'No, you're right,' said Greer, staring up at the screen.

'This is unfinished business – we all felt that at Par Avion. We've allowed Penny Royal to drag us along with it, and we're seeing and experiencing wonders. We don't understand some of them and no clear explanation is offered when we demand one, but the wonders are still there.'

'And there will be a resolution,' said Brond, stepping into the bridge.

'You're sure of that . . .' said Greer, looking round.

'We're just not seeing the whole picture as yet,' he said. 'I don't understand why Penny Royal delayed the King's Guard from getting here – but is now making no effort to stop them doing what they're doing.'

'The delay was to prevent the king being involved and getting killed, apparently,' said Blite.

'Yeah.' Brond moved over to his seat and sat down. 'But it now seems we're going to see Sverl and all the rest simply being annihilated. That doesn't seem like quite the right climax to the kind of manipulation we've been seeing.'

'I agree,' Greer replied. 'But then, what do we know?'

Brond called up a large frame on the screen to display the King's Guard attack upon Factory Station Room 101.

'I was studying this earlier,' he said. 'Every now and again a shield generator blows on the station. And if you were conducting a bombardment, this would seem like the perfect opportunity to concentrate fire on the weak point. However, it's not happening. Every time one of those projectors goes, the Guard concentrates their fire on the next strongest point.'

'They could be knocking out defences ready to board,' Blite suggested.

'Maybe,' said Brond. He waved a hand at the screen helplessly. 'But why would they do that, if their aim is to eliminate Sverl as a threat?'

Cvorn

From fifty light hours out, Cvorn studied the huge Polity factory station sitting in orbit of the hypergiant, then used his aug to check historical files. He quickly absorbed everything available about Room 101, but Sverl's choice of this destination still puzzled him. Further research revealed that Sverl had been in the prador fleet that had previously attacked the thing, but that was the only connection he could find. What did it mean?

After hours of frustrated speculation, he finally abandoned further research, tuned his sensors up to maximum and waited. Within the next few minutes, he predicted, he should *see* Sverl arrive here. The other prador had already arrived in this system but of course the light from that event had yet to make its slow crawl out to his location. This was good, though, because now he would be able to see exactly what had happened there. He'd be able to see what had fired on his old destroyer. He waited, scraping his mandibles together, his stomach complaining. He trotted off to get some more stomach remedy, only to spill it on the way back when his system sounded its alert.

His gaze fixed on his screens, with recorders running and sensors ready to focus where they were directed in an instant, Cvorn saw Sverl's dreadnought arrive. Shortly after that, his own now-defunct destroyer arrived – out by the red dwarf. Sensors refocusing, he watched it begin to orient, then throw up protective hardfields between it and the suddenly revealed threat. When Cvorn saw what was coming up out of the EMR haze around that sun, his stomach complained even louder and seemed to try to escape out of his rear.

King's Guard . . .

They had been hiding close to the sun, which demonstrated

the superiority of their armour and cooling systems. Studying data, Cvorn noted numerous firings of lasers, but they weren't directed at any particular target. These were quantum-cascade refrigeration lasers to expel excess heat. His old destroyer did the best it could, but was thoroughly outmatched. The Guard just chewed it up and then U-jumped. Cvorn tracked back to Sverl's ship, because that had to be their real target. Now he saw Sverl's ship was coming apart, but surely it hadn't been hit by anything yet? Then he saw the Polity destroyer accelerating away from the ship – just as the King's Guard materialized and opened fire. The drama played out next at the factory station, now under bombardment from the Guard. Sverl had no doubt been aboard that destroyer and was now underneath those defences . . .

Cvorn champed with frustration. The king had recognized the danger Sverl posed and moved to destroy him. Cvorn could do nothing but watch this play out. And if, as seemed certain, the Guard destroyed that station, all his plans would come to nothing. His allies in the Kingdom would not move if Sverl escaped the Guard's grasp – because they knew that they would be unable to convince other prador of Polity perfidy without hard physical evidence. In fact, infighting would ensue and their new alliance would probably break up. Cvorn had no doubt that some would look for advantage by betraying the others to the king, and slaughter would follow.

New data came in: an open com message from the Guard to the station. And Cvorn listened to the ultimatum the Guard delivered to its new occupants. So, there were humans on the station with Sverl, and the Guard were trying to turn them against him. That might work, but whether it did or didn't, Cvorn had already lost. Sure, if the humans killed Sverl that would achieve the Guard's aims just as well. But, either way, Sverl was dead, and all Cvorn's plans in ruins.

Spear

Yeah, using a spine from Penny Royal, I'd brought down a hostile robot. But it had been something all but mindless and was nothing like my new aggressor. Even as I dropped down into a darker area, my visor having to reduce its filtering, and tried to wield the thing – something snatched it out of my hands. I saw Grey in glimpses, propelling me along with touches, shoves, and the occasional tight grip about one of my limbs. I was helpless, and I realized this was something I hadn't experienced in a very long time. I didn't like it at all.

He took me along a maintenance duct running parallel to the tunnel Trent and I had walked along. Then we switched through numerous changes of direction. I kept track of all this on a schematic I'd downloaded from the memory of a maintenance robot.

'Spear? What's happening?' asked Trent over suit radio.

'Seems I've been grabbed by Sverl's Golem,' I said. But I wondered. Grey was a Golem Sverl had apparently freed, so he could be taking me anywhere. I tried to contact the father-captain, but he wasn't talking. I then tried to talk to Grey, but he ignored my queries.

'What do I do?' asked Trent. 'I managed to follow you a little way but you were being moved just too fast.'

Grey was slowing, soon dragging me into a recently cut hole in a yard-wide pipe. He finally released me inside what looked like an empty fluid tank. I tumbled out into this, hit metal and bounced away, then managed to use my wrist impeller to stabilize myself. I propelled across to one curved surface, where I engaged my gecko boots. Immediately, I felt the station shaking through my feet and wondered if the King's Guard were growing impatient.

The pipe I'd entered through seemed the only way in – other connected pipes were too narrow to offer an escape route. I now turned to face Grey.

'What the hell do you think you're doing?' I asked through a channel I'd left open.

Grey crouched against the wall of the tank a few paces away from me, watching me intently, and did not reply. He was holding the spine close to his torso. I auged out and, through the sensors of a small palmbot checking superconducting cables for faults, I found Trent at a maintenance duct junction. I then used my aug to replay my chaotic memory and map my route on the schematic – while simultaneously radio-pinging Trent to get his location.

'Trent,' I said, 'turn on your suit cam and send me its feed code.'

'Gotcha,' he replied.

A moment later, on our communications channel, his feed code arrived. A moment after that, on a virtual screen in my aug, I was seeing what he was seeing.

'Head to your right,' I instructed him. 'When you reach the next junction I'll instruct you further.'

Trent headed off. Meanwhile, as I checked out his route through the sensors of various robots, I began to locate those that might be a problem. Unfortunately, some of them had now moved into the route I had taken, as if attracted by the commotion. I needed to send Trent on a different course.

'You cannot stop it,' said Grey, communicating at last.

'I can't stop what?' I asked.

'The solution,' Grey replied.

Ensuring the Golem was hearing nothing of my instructions to Trent, I said to the man, 'See that tube above your head?' Trent looked up at it. 'That's it – along that about twenty feet you'll find *a hatch. Go through that.'* Trent propelled himself up into the narrow tube and began crawling along it.

'What solution?' I asked.

'To Riss and Sverl,' the Golem replied.

'So what is Sverl doing?' I asked.

'Hiding from his fate.'

'You're not working for Sverl, are you?'

'You are the random factor.'

'It's a reactor room,' I told Trent, seeing he'd now opened the hatch. *'Go round it to the door and just wait there for a moment. Don't go through the door.'*

'Trent Sobel,' said Grey, 'is now positioned for his shot. In a moment you'll have him step through that door and fire up at the pipe junction.' Grey pointed to where a smaller tube opened above us just a few paces away. 'You hope to escape before I can react.'

I stared at Grey. He'd either penetrated our communications or was reading my mind. I realized I hadn't been thinking clearly. The thing about Golem was that they had superior senses. I had no doubt now that, like me, Grey had tracked Trent through various robot sensors. I had no doubt that the Golem was picking up his heat signature and other emissions from his suit. I could not simply bring him to me in this tank in the expectation that the weapon he carried would be enough. But something didn't add up.

'You are offering me no clear explanation of your actions,' I said to Grey. 'I understand now.' I began to walk towards him. 'You're still working for Penny Royal and what that AI intends here is plain: Sverl is a problem it wants to solve. The solution is Sverl's death.'

'Stay where you are,' said Grey, all calmness, but he rose to his feet.

I began to get some intimation of what was wrong now. Penny Royal had instructed Grey to stop me from interfering. However, he was treating me like something extremely dangerous and not simply a weak human being with mental augmentation. I considered how I had killed the robot. No, it wasn't that. I considered what had just been playing out. Grey had allowed me to think I might have a chance with Trent. Delaying tactics. Physically, Trent and I were no match for this Golem, so it had to be something else. And Grey held it.

I reached out for the spine, for that *connection*, and felt the synergy of thousands of minds working in consonance. I probed deeper into the thing, beyond storage and into its underlying function – the same function that had earlier enabled me to change its shape. I found its geometry and threw myself forwards as I changed it. The spine shattered into a hundred knives and shoaled from Grey's grasp, reforming as I came up to seize it and sweep it round. It caught one of Grey's groping hands, tugged only slightly, and sent that hand gyrating away. Now my contact was closer and the multitude of links clear to me. Grey was there too, inside the thing. It perpetually recorded him, perpetually controlled him, and I severed the link. With a snap, silent in vacuum, he folded up, foetal.

'*Trent,*' I sent, transmitting directly from my aug, '*step through the door. A coolant tank sits up to your right on your present orientation. You'll see a pipe extending from it to the left. Fire on the point where it joins the tank.*'

A second later, fire erupted from there, metal falling apart like wet paper and hot gases billowing. The beam cut through – turquoise, and violet at its heart – then shut down.

'*You will be too late,*' said Grey, slowly unfolding.

'I'm now coming out of there,' I told Trent, just in case he

505

decided to fire again. I launched myself down between the glowing edges of the hole.

'*Was it your idea to have the spine in there with us?*' I shot at Grey. It was my escape route and, to prevent my escape, Grey should have further separated me from the thing. Perhaps he had managed to subvert the black AI's control of him just a little, his intent being that I should cut his link to the spine and thereby cut Penny Royal's control of him. Or perhaps everything had played out here just as the AI had intended.

'We have to move fast,' I told Trent, as I caught hold of one of the tank's bracing struts and propelled myself towards him. 'We have to stop Riss.'

Riss

Coiled in an air vent over a corridor made for humans, Riss gazed out through the grating. She was watching the second-child guarding the end. She stayed utterly still as she used her inducer hardware to probe both the sensors positioned along the wall and the computing in the child's armour. Like a safe-cracker listening for clicks, she slowly and carefully shut down some sensors, then tuned down the sensitivity of others. Next, she worked on the second-child's armour. It had a lot more defences than the prador armour she had encountered during the war – the modifications almost certainly due to Sverl. However, Riss meticulously worked through them, cracking codes, shutting down motors, severing communications.

The second-child, which had previously been fidgeting, grew still. Riss engaged her chameleonware and flew at the grating like a released spring. It tore free on one side and she shot out to hit the opposing wall, stuck there for a moment, then slithered down to the floor and along that to face the prador. It could still move its eye palps and had seen the grating tear open. Almost certainly, it now knew that Riss was here.

Riss gazed at the thing. Though the armour was highly modified, it still possessed the vulnerabilities of the old prador armour to her. She could now dive underneath the thing and, bracing against the floor, drive her collimated diamond ovipositor straight in through one of the leg sockets' weak points. The enzyme would dissolve the thing in no time at all – fluids and gases spurting out of pressure valves. Then, after a few hours, there would be nothing left but a shell full of liquefied remains. Riss knew precisely how it went, because she'd used hydrofluoric acid before against a prador. The parasite eggs, should she choose to use them, would take longer to act, and the process would spread the parasite to many other prador in this child's vicinity. But was there any point in killing this second-child? In fact by immobilizing it, rather than just moving straight in to attack, had she already decided not to kill it?

Riss shook herself, not liking where her thoughts were taking her. Her mission objective was Sverl, so there was no point killing this creature. Anyway, her supply of the enzyme and the eggs was limited . . .

She slithered underneath the second-child and up to a corridor junction, scanning ahead all the time. At the junction, knowing what lay around the corner, she squirmed up one wall and along the ceiling. The corridor, though it did possess a ceiling and a floor – oriented by lights in the former and a stain-eater carpet over the latter – was zero gravity. Predictably, the prador in the coin-shaped monorail station at the end was oriented as if the grav-plates were on. Riss knew that all organic creatures found it difficult to shake their attraction to the ideas of up and down. The concepts were integral in both human and prador thought and language.

Riss slithered on until she was just about to enter the mono-rail station and there halted. The sensor equipment the prador had positioned here was a lot more sophisticated and Riss had been in error – grav-plates were in fact on. Here the prador had designed things precisely to trap her. If she stuck herself to any surface, remora fashion, there were vibration sensors pro-grammed to detect her particular form of locomotion. If she used her internal grav-engine, or maglev, that would be detected too. Usually she could subvert the computing attached to the grav-plates. However, the prador here, most likely Bsectil, had installed some very different hardware that wouldn't allow that. Riss could penetrate it, but its coding was changing randomly and it was perpetually reprogramming itself too. Bsectil, mean-while, was heavily armoured and difficult to scan; he had a Gatling cannon in one claw, and the tip folded down from another claw to reveal a particle cannon.

'I know you're here,' said the first-child over open com.

Something else was happening. The second-child behind had just started moving again – its armour unfreezing. Riss tried another penetration back that way, but coding changes and reprogramming were occurring there now too. Analysing signal traffic, Riss spotted her error. The vibration sensors had been set to tune out certain things, but when one of those things didn't occur, they broadcast an alert. The thing that had stopped had been the movement Riss had thought was the second-child fidg-eting. This then had been a perfectly designed trap.

'Reveal yourself and nobody has to die.' Bsectil waved a claw at something lying on the floor nearby – another collar.

Riss did nothing but continue scanning and gathering data. She could detect other prador in the area repositioning. They thought they had her now, which demonstrated a lack of dimension to their thinking also found in humans. Certainly, she had no way through here, but she was designed to navigate apparently impossible routes.

Riss stuck her spread head down against the surface she was on, hooked up and stabbed her ovipositor straight into that surface. At high speed, she moved her tail in a circle, widening the hole, then flipped round and nosed into it. On the floor above this ceiling, the prador had welded an armour shield in place, with vibration sensors scattered along it. However, they'd done nothing about the ceramo-foam insulation, sandwiched between armour and ceiling. Vibrating her head at just the right intensity, Riss nosed into that, it turned to dust ahead of her, and she burrowed at high speed. Just as she pulled her ovipositor out of sight, Gatling slugs began punching through the ceiling all around her. One hit her, full on, nearly cutting her in half. She kept moving, the smart materials of her body at that point reforming and rejoining.

Particle cannon fire hit the ceiling next, burning it away and ablating the ceramic foam. By then she was past the armour, across the corridor above and writhing up along a narrow power duct leading to the small home of a beetlebot. She moved out across a floor and along, punching another hole and heading down again. All around prador were moving towards her, because her chameleonware just wasn't good enough any more. As she slithered along one wall, it exploded just behind her and a particle beam cut forwards. She propelled herself away with maglev, engaged her grav-motor and planed forwards. An auto-laser picked her up but reflected away, as railgun missiles turned the ceiling into a colander. But Riss squirmed into a severed power duct and kept going.

It should have been exciting and it should have been

fulfilling, but it just felt like a nasty chore. As she worked her way along beside superconducting cables, she bounced attempts to communicate with her. Some of these were from the surrounding prador and from Sverl himself. Strongest, and growing stronger, were the probes from Thorvald Spear, who was rapidly drawing closer.

They'd armoured the autofactory, surrounded it with sensors and weapons and set some particularly clever traps. These showed a deep understanding of her nature and her abilities. But, as ever, there was always a hole. In this case, it lay beside this duct and just ahead. Riss stopped to use her manipulators on a series of pin rivets, punching them out from the inside and squirming out as the inspection plate dropped away. The temperature around her quickly ramped up and things began to melt and burn, but she was into the mouth of a compressed-air pipe before the beam of a particle cannon punched through. Her skin was microscaled like a butterfly's wing – and when she controlled those scales individually, they could be utterly frictionless where required. Or they could be the opposite. She shot down the pipe in a smooth series of peristaltic heaves, but then suddenly she was slowing. Sverl had just pressurized his sanctum. Vacuum began to suck Riss back, and if she didn't do something, it would draw her back into the path of that particle beam. She collapsed one side of her skeleton and stuck herself to the side of the pipe, allowing the air past. Then she inched forwards, caterpillar fashion, her skin fully in remora mode.

I'm going to die, she thought – she just wasn't moving fast enough now and the prador would soon target her. But fate intervened in the form of Gatling fire, chopping through the infrastructure all around her. One slug hit the pipe behind, pinching it shut and cutting the pressure differential. Riss expanded her skeleton and accelerated again, shooting up into Sverl's sanctum.

She hit what was debatably the ceiling, and stuck there in an invisible coil.

'The drone's in,' Bsorol clattered.

Just then, grav came on, nearly tearing Riss from the ceiling. Bsorol was close to Sverl, brandishing a particle cannon and a Gatling cannon just like his sibling. He also had anti-personnel lasers and a small hardfield generator mounted on the exterior of his armour. The laser fired, obviously tracking via vibration sensors, and hit Riss precisely. She shot away across the ceiling but the laser stayed on her, locating her for Bsorol, who opened fire with both his major weapons. Riss scribed a circle around above the first-child, a slight hint of gleeful amusement arising and then dissipating. One and a half circuits were enough, then a huge circle of ceiling – a foot's thickness of laminated bubble-metal and armour – crashed down right on top of Bsorol.

Riss flung herself clear, scribed a neat arc through the air and came down just behind Sverl. He spun round and Riss hesitated. Then she felt an intermittent vibration through the floor – the particle cannons of the King's Guard tearing into the hull of the station.

'I'm sorry,' she said, shutting down her chameleonware because it seemed so cowardly now.

This was a mistake.

20

Spear

The second-child obviously received its orders, because it lowered its bolus gun. I recognized the thing straight away. This weapon used monofilament strings in its projectiles. It was the kind of thing used in jungle fighting to clear foliage and chop up any of the enemy concealed within it. The prador had developed it during a ground conflict, to counter the human warband led by Jebel U-cap Krong and his fighters. I could understand its utility against a snakelike drone. Though it would be unlikely to chop Riss up, it would certainly delay the drone long enough for the second-child to get in close and use its other weapon: an atomic shear.

'Come on,' I said to Trent, and we threw ourselves past the prador.

'The parasite is here,' said Sverl, talking to me again at last.

A monorail station lay ahead. Weapons fire had slagged the corridor leading to it, and it was still glowing in vacuum. I bounced from a sagging wall panel into the station, caught a hand against the ceiling and propelled myself down to land beside the blade track, engaging gecko function. I then moved into a steady lope, briefly wondering if that was a train moving ahead, but then realizing it was Bsectil. The prador shortly leapt up onto a platform beside the track and progressed along it. We caught up with him as he came to stand before a newly installed armoured door.

The door opened ahead of Bsectil and the ensuing blast of escaping atmosphere threw him staggering back towards us. Trent lost his footing and disappeared somewhere behind me, swearing. I managed to bow into it and keep on my feet, Bsectil skidding to a halt just a couple of yards in front of me. As the air blast waned, he charged in. I trudged after him, and a moment later Trent caught up with me.

I took it all in quickly. Bsorol was struggling to drag himself out from under a heavy slab cut from the ceiling. Riss was facing up to Sverl and was completely visible, while Sverl's prosthetic claws folded open like nightmare Swiss army knives and bristled with hardware. Something flashed and an EM pulse passed through me, leaving my aug streaming error messages and the spine turning hot in my grip. Riss shot away, streaking up one wall with portions of her body turning invisible – as if she were attempting to activate her chameleonware and failing. Weapons spiking from Sverl's claws tracked her, and a particle beam stabbed out, bright fluorescent orange, and carved through the wall. He missed, and Riss disappeared. Sverl began firing a weapon like a pulse-gun, but each shot issued electrical discharges where it struck. The firing pattern climbed the wall and went across the ceiling. Then that particle beam began stabbing out again too.

'I only have to be successful once,' said Riss, her voice clear over every channel, despite the previous firing of some sort of EM pulse weapon.

I reached into the spine, confidently targeting its connection to Riss and inputting the code that would cause her to eject her weapons load. Something stopped me. The spine resisted me, and then it just fell to pieces in my hands, shards of black glass falling to the floor. I hit the ground next as Sverl's fusillade tracked down towards me. As I went down, I glimpsed something

513

dropping from the ceiling. Debris? No: Riss. She was a wheel-like blur moving in behind Sverl. Another pulse issued – this one causing visible ionization in the hot vapour that was dissipating in vacuum like a fast-moving wall. I saw Riss tumble out from underneath Sverl, completely out of control, black patches along portions of her body. I didn't know if she'd managed to hit him with her poisonous cargo or not. She struck a nearby pipe protruding from the floor and then slowly coiled about it.

I rose, eyeing Sverl crouching up against one wall with a steady stream of vapour issuing from his suit, which died as some sealer stopped it. Beside me, the spine reassembled, slotting together like knives going into a drawer. I reached out for it, but knew I was too late. A horrible bubbling shriek swamped every channel – it reached into me through my aug, through the spine, through data connections to surrounding robots – drowning interference. Bsectil just collapsed as if someone had cut his legs out from underneath him, while Bsorol slumped under the load he had been trying to shrug off.

'The fuck!' said Trent, sprawled nearby and holding a hand against his helmet, his expression twisted with pain. I found myself trying to claw open my suit's helmet. When I realized what I was doing, I hurriedly cut as many links as possible – even shutting down the reception in my aug – but still I could hear the scream. This, more than anything else, demonstrated just how integrally linked I was to the spine, because that's where I was getting it from.

Of course, I thought, *Sverl is recorded in there.*

But if Sverl was recorded, did that mean this wasn't murder? Did that relieve Riss of guilt? Sverl had been quite dismissive of the deaths amongst the shell people because the spine had similarly recorded them. But I guessed he didn't feel so dismissive now.

Sverl crashed back against the wall, shook himself, then ran straight across the room, bouncing off equipment on the way and finally crashing into the further wall. The inside of the film suit he wore was bulging with vapour, and black fluid was draining into its lower section. I don't know whether it was a malfunction or if he hoped to end his pain sooner, but suddenly that covering split open and sucked away into a series of holes above each of his limb sockets. An explosion of vapour followed – the fluid splashing to the floor underneath, smoking like acid burning through the metal. Sverl staggered a few paces, leaving something behind. I looked at a chunk of dissolving flesh with vertebrae and bones exposed. It looked like some half-digested animal thrown up by a predator. Sverl had just lost his tail.

He staggered a little further, then went down on his belly. His human eyes were shrivelling now and dropping out of sight. Great splits divided him, yellow pus boiling out and steaming. Then a large chunk of his body fell out like an orange segment, exposing smoking organs and the glint of metal. As I gaped in horror, he continued to fall apart. For long moments, I just lost sight of him in the fog he was generating. The screaming died to a perpetual wail that bore more resemblance to radio interference than the suffering of a sentient being. A pool spread out across the floor – a stew of dissolving tissues like chyme in a bile of immiscible black and red fluids. It was evaporating in vacuum fast; creating a crust, but not as fast as it was coming out of his body, so the crust kept breaking as another flow overran it like lava. The wail stopped and soon after I caught a glimpse of the remains. All that was left was an intricate ceramal ribcage – with prosthetic claws, legs and mandibles still attached. The items inside it bore some resemblance to candelabra and other silver antiques – I spotted a coil ring, AI crystal and a spider's web of optics. All sat on a steadily deliquescing and spreading pile of organic tissue.

I stood up, feeling sick and empty, and turned in time to see Bsorol finally freeing himself and moving leadenly over to his father's remains. Bsectil swayed for a moment, then went over and joined his brother. Meanwhile Riss unwound from that column and squirmed brokenly across the plating. Before I realized what she was doing, she had disappeared down a hole in that floor and was gone.

Cvorn

Cvorn first watched the transmission in disbelief, then watched the recording three more times with growing depressed acceptance. Sverl was dead and he had died in such a way that even his body could not be used as evidence of what had happened to him. Whatever the drone had injected had utterly destroyed him. Yes, Cvorn might be able to obtain samples of Sverl's genome from those remains, along with that ceramal skeleton, but he knew they wouldn't be enough. Certainly his allies believed the story, but the point was to use Sverl to convince others. Prador, generally, were a sceptical lot and that evidence would not convince them. The skeleton was something that Cvorn and his allies could easily have fabricated, while Sverl's strange genome was something they could have cut and pasted together too. Most other prador would only be more suspicious of its veracity upon learning of the sub-atomic processes that kept it functioning.

So that was it – all over. What should he do now? His goals had not changed. He still wanted the king usurped and he still wanted the prador to continue their war against the Polity, but now he could see no way of bringing either about. Decades of planning ruined.

As he stared at his screens, Cvorn began to feel deeply depressed. Abruptly he approached a bowl sitting on a friction-less column – designed to keep the ship lice from getting to it. Without conscious volition, he began eating the jellied mudfish he found there, only becoming conscious of what he was doing when his claw clattered against the empty bowl. He backed off, fearing what might happen to his insides. Then he realized he was still seeing the bowl despite starting to turn away. His remaining transplanted palp eye was working! He had saved his eye – using the recombinant virus his medical equipment had designed, which he'd drill-injected into his visual turret just a few hours ago. He shifted it around, revelling in the ability to look at things without having to turn his body to face them. Then, a moment later, he realized something else.

His stomach felt fine and he was hungry for something more.

'Vlox!' he clattered, 'I want a quarter reaverfish tail right now!'

'Yes, Father,' Vlox replied through the intercom.

Cvorn walked around the sanctum, shaking himself, half expecting his stomach to rebel, but it still felt fine. Of course, he would have to be careful. And perhaps later he should consider transplants of some of his internal organs. He did, after all, have those few remaining young adults aboard . . . No, on second thoughts, he had a much better option. He scuttled back to his screens, auging into his system to call up new cam views. Now he gazed into the chamber beside the hatching room. This housed about forty small male third-children, each no larger than a human head. They were swarming over some unidentifi-able meat, tearing it apart.

Eyeing all these children, Cvorn considered the option that

had occurred to him earlier. He remembered a prador legend about a creature called the Golgoloth, which preyed on the young and used their body parts to extend its own life. It was, of course, complete rubbish, but the idea of so extending one's life wasn't at all. If he harvested transplants from his own children, there would be much less likelihood of rejection problems. Now why, to his knowledge, had not other prador tried this out? He began running searches of this ship's data banks and, though he did discover examples of prador using such transplants, they weren't common. It made no sense. Was there something in the prador psyche that prevented it – which he had overcome through his previous augmentations? This was worth study, but perhaps later, because now Vlox had arrived with his food.

'Here,' he said, gesturing to the floor before him with one claw.

Vlox scuttled over and deposited the quarter reaverfish tail before quickly turning to head away.

'Remain,' said Cvorn, 'I have a task for you.'

'Yes, Father,' said Vlox meekly.

Cvorn tucked into the chunk of fish. Although he did experience a moment of nausea as he finished, it soon went away. He still took down a draft of stomach remedy, just in case.

'Now, Vlox,' he said, turning back. 'Take security drones to the quarters of Vlern's remaining children. Take some second-children too, all armed and armoured. Kill all of them and dismember them. What you do with them is up to you.'

'Yes, Father!' said Vlox eagerly, coming up out of his squat and turning away.

'Inform me at once if you have difficulties – I don't want any more problems like Sfolk.'

'You won't, Father!'

Cvorn dipped his body in acknowledgement. Vlox was a

young first-child and had not yet learned that making promises to your father about things that might not be in your full control could be unhealthy.

'Go,' he said, and Vlox went.

So what now? Cvorn's plans had come to nothing, but he felt good, had seen ways of extending his life even beyond a prador's usual long extent and he controlled an ST dreadnought. He had a growing family now too and really, anything was possible. There might be other ways to achieve his goals – other opportunities arising throughout the long years ahead. He might even outlive the king. Think of that!

He was heading to the door from his sanctum before he realized where he was going. Then he recognized that his intention to visit the females again had been forming in his mind, right from the moment his stomach started to feel better. Eagerly, he scuttled through the tunnels of his ship, his mood so good he didn't even crack the shell of a second-child who happened to get in his way, merely pushing it to one side instead. Finally, he arrived at the door into the mating pool.

The outer water lock revolved into the wall, spilling water across the floor. Cvorn eyed this and remembered how he had intended to fix the inefficiencies here. Perhaps he would do that next, now he had more time on his claws. Inside the lock he checked the environmental controls. They were still at the levels he had set last time, so it wouldn't be so cold on his prongs and clamp – which right then were feeling very sensitive indeed. Water gushed in round his feet after he closed the rear door and it was warm – felt good. He hyperventilated and packed in the oxygen for what he felt sure was going to be a marathon session.

Soon he was submerged; he surged down the ramp and dropped to the bottom of the breeding pool. The four females clustered around their feeding pillar – no strays he could corner and mount – but he didn't care. Clattering his mandibles and snipping his claws, he rushed them, slamming his full weight into the group and bowling a couple of them over. As he selected the nearest who was still down on her feet, he noted an alert in the system – Vlox trying to get in contact with him. He ignored it. Mating lasted a lot longer this time and, as if his body knew his mental intent, he was parsimonious with the seed he squirted inside her. He then grabbed another one, the remaining two not fighting so hard to get him off her. Their instinct was responding to the violence of his attack perhaps, though it was odd that they were so sluggish. Once he had finished his second mating, he paused, but only briefly – just long enough to take note of Vlox's increasingly urgent attempts to contact him, and ignore them.

Cvorn mated with the third female, and then the fourth, a hollow feeling inside and his prongs feeling sore, sucking dry. He knew he'd emptied his testicle and would have to have it refilled from his cold store. Later he would allow one of his children to develop to adulthood – in captivity – remove its testicle and use viral recombination to match it fully to his own genome. Then there would be no more need for tedious refilling.

Cvorn then moved away, feeling exhausted and hot. Reaching the edge of the breeding pool, he paused and finally responded to Vlox.

'What's the problem?'

'Father! One of Vlern's children is missing!'

What?

'Give me visuals.'

The feed came through from a recorded file, showing the quarters of one of the young adults. Just as in Sfolk's quarters, a hole had been cut in the wall. Cvorn concentrated on this, and pulled the recording back to it again. There was something odd about it . . . Concentration was difficult because he still felt exhausted and hot – perhaps it hadn't been such a good idea to increase the temperature in the pool. Then, after a moment, he saw it. The debris from the hole in the wall was lying on the floor inside. Yet when Sfolk had cut his hole, the chunk he had carved round had fallen into the space beyond. It might be nothing, but Cvorn now studied the rest of the recording intently. It took just a moment for him to confirm his suspicions. Items were scattered all about the place and storage caches broken open. Vlox and his crew could have done that, but it was unlikely they had made the dents in the walls. Then there, up on the wall, he saw a laser burn. There, on the floor: a dry puddle of prador blood. There had been a fight, and the prador who had been in here had not gone willingly. So how had that happened?

Cvorn saw it clearly now. Sfolk must have cut his way *in*, but in doing so, he'd allowed oxygenated air into the quarters and that had revived the occupant. A fight had ensued and Sfolk's brother had gone either unwillingly or in no condition to object. But why?

'Vlox, I hope you have started a search,' he said. No reply was forthcoming and the feed from Vlox had cut off. Cvorn contemplated this for a short while but found he still couldn't think straight. He looked up at his route out of the pool. He really needed to get out of here and cool down.

'Vlox?'

Still nothing. Cvorn reached out for a claw hold and steadily began to work his way up the side of the tank. Halfway up, Vlox's link into the ship's system opened again and he dumped two files. Cvorn opened the first of them, pausing to rest, even though climbing with prosthetics should be no effort.

It was another visual file. He saw Sfolk laboriously raising the inert form of one of his brothers on a hoist, lowering it into an open suit of armour, carefully inserting limbs into the required holes and getting him into place. Before closing the armour, Sfolk used a tube of black sealer foam to paint a whorl beside his brother's visual turret. Cvorn recognized it as the mark he used to identify Sfolk. Next, Sfolk closed up the armour and then turned to the cam view, pointing with one claw to a thrall unit newly attached to his carapace. As he turned back again the armour began moving, as if the prador it contained was still alive. Cvorn understood at once what that meant. And, as he approached the surface of the pool, he opened the other file.

Sfolk now stood in an airlock . . . no, it wasn't an airlock but the water lock above! Cvorn tried to move faster, but it seemed as if he was dragging himself through mud. Finally, he reached the water lock and found it firmly shut. He clung there, now feeling the need for air. The thought of that motivated him, because of course an airlock above led into the upper chamber! He dragged himself on, moving slower and slower as he neared the surface of the pool. With a gargantuan effort, he tried to heave himself out but then felt a horrible agonizing ripping down one side. The water around him turned green with his blood. He heaved again and finally crawled out onto the edge. He tried to turn his palp eye to look at the damage. The view blurred as that eye started to fail again, but he could see that the socket for one of his prosthetic legs had pulled right out; the flesh exposed there had an odd purplish red colour. Meanwhile, in the recording, Sfolk had fired up a welder and was running it round the inner door of the water lock, sealing Cvorn in. Cvorn watched as Sfolk turned to the cam view and twisted his mandibles in a prador smile. He then reached out and knocked the environmental heat control right to the top. Of course, it was old news, a recording . . .

Cvorn understood that his prosthetic leg had ripped out because things had been softening around it. He understood why his flesh was that colour – because that was the colour prador flesh turned when it was cooked. He gazed out across the breeding pool at the fog of steam above the bubbling water, but now his sight was beginning to fade. His only pain was coming from that leg socket. If you boil the water surrounding a prador, it won't even realize it is dying. He couldn't move now, which meant his nerve channels were too hot. Things were starting to get very unclear . . . he couldn't quite . . .

Blite

The King's Guard ships had stopped bombarding the station. They were now only using their weapons to take out anything the station was throwing at them. Blite switched his attention back to the screen's lower frame, but it was still blank.

'So that's it,' said Brond, sounding disappointed. 'Penny Royal lured Sverl here to be killed . . . I mean, what the fuck is that?'

'We're just toys,' said Greer.

Blite returned his attention to the larger scene displayed on the screen. Firing from the station was already waning and the ships were no longer using lasers or other anti-munitions to take out projectiles but had simply tightened up their hardfield screen. Would they leave now, he wondered? Sverl had been their greatest concern and, without him, Cvorn's rebellion was dead. But Cvorn himself was still out there and would eventually trace Sverl here. Surely the King's Guard would hang around to tidy up that loose end?

'They're still up to something,' said Brond, sending a data frame to the screen.

The blades of plasma steering thrusters stabbed vacuum, as

the fleet of thirty ships began to spread out. Only four of them were a little tardy, having sustained some damage from the factory station's defences. The data frame now showed the *Black Rose*'s sensors picking up EM reflections from the war factory. These weren't as strong as those from the weapons fire, but were substantial. The Guard ships were scanning the station. But why?

'I think I'll go and have a chat,' said Blite, standing up.

'I don't know why you bother,' said Greer. 'It never fucking tells you anything outright.'

She was obviously getting a little disillusioned with their adventure. Blite nodded to himself as he went. He too should be feeling that way, but it so happened that he wasn't. On the surface it did look as if Penny Royal had manipulated events here to result in Sverl's particularly horrific murder. But if that had been the aim, why hadn't the AI just projected itself into Sverl's sanctum and ripped his heart out, long ago? Surely, the end game couldn't be so simple and so sordid?

Blite headed towards the exit from the bridge, turning over in his mind what he intended to ask the AI. He played with the idea of running everything Penny Royal had said to him, and every event in which he had been involved with it, through some sub-AI search and translation programs to see what he could glean. The idea fled as the ship shifted underneath him.

'Leven?' he enquired.

'Our passenger is back and we're taking off,' the Golem ship mind replied.

'Destination?'

'Ooh, let me guess . . .'

Blite headed back to the bridge, where he sat down. The screen now showed just their immediate surroundings, as they rose from the landmass of this world. The horizon already showed a distinct curve as they speeded away, and he caught a glimpse of a flock of those pterodactyl things scattering from their path. He stared at the screen until he could see nothing but sky, stared longer until the sky began to darken and stars started to appear. He could hold out no more.

'Okay, Penny Royal,' he said. 'What now?'

A glassy ringing issued from behind him but he stubbornly kept his eyes on the screen. Perhaps, as the screen flicked back to a previous view from the sats he'd scattered up there, this had been the intention.

The Guard ships were now in a formation surrounding the factory station and, even as Blite watched, they began firing again. They were using particle beams this time, and more surgically too. Blite saw the station's hardfields occasionally block the beams, but most now were getting through.

'Analysis,' said Blite.

'Looks to me,' said Brond, 'like they're hitting reactors, power storage and cable runs.' Brond paused for a second. 'It's more methodical – if you had the time and you wanted to destroy Room 101 without too many losses on your own side, then this would be the best way to take out the defences.'

'So,' said Blite, 'their first attack was to drive Sverl's allies to attack and kill him, which one of them did. They've achieved their goal, so why are they attacking now?'

'Because they're prador,' said Greer. 'Do they need a reason?'

'Greer is right in the first instance but wrong in the second,' interjected Leven.

'Explain,' Blite instructed.

'We know that Cvorn could only use Sverl's physical body. This was to act as proof that the Polity had been transforming a prador into an amalgam of a hated enemy. He could not use pictures or other computer data, because the prador do not accept such as evidence. Likewise, the King's Guard cannot accept that transmission of Sverl's final moments as proof of Sverl's demise.'

'Yet they forced it.'

'Nevertheless,' said Leven. 'The complete obliteration of the station will be certain proof that Sverl is dead.'

Blite chewed at his lip as he considered this, then said, 'So, Penny Royal, you got Sverl killed and now you'll get this station destroyed. Did you come here to see the place that created you annihilated too?'

'Oh, thanks for this,' said Leven. The black AI was forcing the ship's Golem mind into the role of translator again. 'Penny Royal's focus is not necessarily on major events, apparently.'

So far, so opaque.

'We have seen that in the AI's progress towards its final goal, it can influence larger events, but this has been a side effect.'

'So what's its real aim here and what is its final goal – is it finally going to give me a clear answer?'

'The assassin drone Riss and the prador Sverl were both damaged by Penny Royal. Sometimes it is not possible to repair the damage or put the clock back, so a positive way must be found to move beyond it. For Riss . . . You what? . . . Wait a minute . . .'

'Why can't you talk to me, Penny Royal?' said Blite. 'You're not incapable of straightforward human speech.' Blite swung his chair round to gaze at the black diamond hovering on the bridge.

'Riss had to kill again to accept her own redundancy, and to realize it is possible to move on,' the AI whispered.

'All this just to change an assassin drone's mind?'

'It was important to her.'

'So in Sverl's case, the way of moving on was scrappage?'

That frame in the screen flickered and it again began showing the scene inside the station where Sverl had died. Blite stared at Sverl's remains, but couldn't see why the AI had displayed them.

'And your final goal?' he asked.

He felt that black diamond nibbling at his mind and wished, too late, that he'd kept a rein on his curiosity. He found himself floating between two endless surfaces of crystalline black and could *feel* data burrowing between them infinitely fast – because here time had no meaning. It felt as if he was there only for an instant, but for an eternity too. He perceived his mind being pushed to a limit beyond which it would surely break. He returned, gasping, to his seat, the communication ending with a sound like a thermometer breaking.

'What was *that*?' asked Greer.

Blite just shook his head and tried to concentrate on the screens and the data. He needed to shake the feeling of spiders crawling across his optic nerves.

Once beyond atmosphere, the ship U-jumped, briefly. The feeling was subliminal, and suddenly those King's Guard ships were a lot, lot closer. Blite gripped the arms of his chair, aware that the *Black Rose* was now moving very fast towards the station.

'Splinter missiles activating,' Leven warned.

Blite immediately pulled his seat straps across, noting Brond and Greer doing the same. Penny Royal did not want the Guard ships to destroy the station and was about to do something about it. Over to their right, on the screen view, he could see one of the Guard ships suddenly manoeuvring – plasma steering thrusters blading out into space.

'We can't take them all,' hissed Brond.

'Firing,' Leven stated.

'Show me,' Blite commanded.

Surprisingly, it was a view of the station that came up. Spectrally shifting lasers were stabbing down from the *Black Rose*, hitting points on its hull. These were spearing into final construction bays, carving off protruding towers and turrets. Sometimes there were explosions where they struck, sometimes no sign of any destruction at all. As Blite watched this he realized that the *Black Rose* was doing precisely what the prador had been doing, but with much more precision. Reaching out to his console, he selected filtering, and the ship's system immediately presented him with the view he wanted. Now the beam strikes were visible as simple white lines, while the station seemed shot through with glowing capillaries, veins and hot spots. This was a power map of the station gathered by induction sensors. Around where the lasers were striking the glow representing power often faded. Sometimes it faded elsewhere, and sometimes light returned as some other power supply took up the load.

'Missiles deployed,' said Leven.

Around them, the ship shrugged and, along the bottom of the screen, U-signature data briefly scrolled then sank away. On and inside the station, there were numerous explosions. Some were only visible on the induction map, while others spewed debris and fire out into space. Blite watched the results. The station was flickering like a malfunctioning light panel – areas going out and coming back on again – but the trend towards blackout was steadily downwards. Darkness coagulated in one area towards the centre – all power going down across thirty miles of station, centred on where Sverl had died.

'The fuck,' said Blite.

Why had Penny Royal attacked the station? Why had it left it open and completely vulnerable to the Guard? The obvious answer was that the AI wanted the Guard to destroy the station. Yet, if that was so, why had it intervened at all? They were doing that anyway. Blite began to summon up the nerve to ask a question, when a frame opened in his screen to show an armoured

King's Guard prador – the one that had delivered its ultimatum to Thorvald Spear. Blite decided to hold off just in case he was about to be provided with an answer.

'I am baffled,' it said, and Blite wondered at the translation.

'You have achieved your primary objective,' said Penny Royal.

'Certainty is required.'

'Physical proof is all you can have.'

Their view of the station behind this frame changed and Blite saw that it was now a straight screen view without magnification. The *Black Rose* was sitting just a few miles out from the war factory's hull – the thing looming massively behind them. And white spheres were moving out from his ship, then accelerating. He reached out to his controls and pulled up a tactical display. This showed the entire station, the position of his own ship, and the Guard ships now manoeuvring hundreds of miles out. These movements were all calculated to bring his ship into their direct line of sight and, of course, directly in line with their weapons.

'You are in no position to enforce your will,' the guard said.

'Wrong,' Penny Royal replied.

The *Black Rose* groaned and Blite transferred his gaze back to the tactical display. Here a sphere of gridlines, which was not a reality but just a mathematical construct, expanded from their ship. It enclosed both it and a chunk of the station behind. He abruptly felt cold and could see vapour on his breath in the suddenly chill air. A moment later, the gridlines disappeared to leave a translucent globe in place. Blite recognized what had happened, because he had seen and felt it happen around Carapace City – just before Cvorn's attack there. Now the air in the bridge took on an amber tint and seemed to gain solidity. Yet, when he held up his hand, he could not detect anything unusual. He waited for some attack on this massive hardfield, but the prador must have known that such an assault would be futile.

'I cannot leave,' said the admiral.

'Dock, therefore,' said Penny Royal. 'Just you.'

'You will lower the field?'

'I will, but I can put it back up in four microseconds. I can also destroy anything hostile within that boundary in even less time.'

Blite got that. Once inside the hardfield, if the admiral fired on the station, he wouldn't have time for anything more than a few beam strikes. All that would be necessary to stop him was one U-jump missile inside his ship. The frame showing the prador blanked and a long pause ensued.

'Very well,' said the admiral when he reappeared. 'The king agrees.'

The frame blinked out.

Blite wondered to himself how different the situation would have been had the king actually been here. It occurred to him that the threat to that entity's life had come directly from the black AI itself.

One of those big ships out there now began to head in towards the hardfield, which blinked out to let it through. The field acquired gridlines in a subliminal flicker in the tactical display, then reappeared behind the approaching ship. The ship came past them, settling in close to the station's hull, right over Sverl's final location.

'Our guest is leaving us,' said Leven.

The dark area was like a macula in Blite's eye, as it briefly shot across the screen view and out of sight. A red dot appeared in the tactical display and shot down towards the station, disappearing within the vast construction bay nearest to Sverl's last sanctum.

'It's a war dock,' Brond observed.

It certainly was. The Guard ship had fired anchor cables and was hoisting itself closer still to the station. Meanwhile, from a point at its midsection, it began extruding a tube. This hit the station hull fast, like a drill going into brass – and the vacuum all around filled with glittering fragments. The moment this happened, two more screen frames opened. One of them showed a view from inside the station, as the war dock bored through the hull. They caught a glimpse of armed and armoured prador clustering in the throat of the war dock, behind a hardfield. The other view was a rapidly changing one from something moving fast inside the station – Penny Royal, of course. Blite rested his elbows on his chair arms, interlaced his fingers and rested his chin on them. Considerate of the AI, he felt, to give them this view.

I am satisfied by the scraps it tosses me, he thought.

A little later, he got up and went to check on the antique space suit. He opened its visor and peered inside for a long time, then with a sigh returned to the bridge.

Spear

For maybe a full minute I was blind, in that I could see no more than my immediate surroundings. This included the column Riss had abandoned and to which I was now clinging in turn. It made sense that the Guard had attacked again. And I wondered at Riss's naivety in thinking that a transmitted recording of Sverl's death would be enough. What hit us next I didn't know – the beam strikes had been so fast and had so quickly disrupted power supplies I just didn't have much time to sort out sensor data. All I did know was that spectrally adjusting lasers had hit

531

the station all along its length. Detonations inside had occurred, taking out reactors and laminar power storage. The moving source of those destructive lasers just hadn't been clear.

A few sensors powered up again in the section of station immediately around us. And out above the hull, I could see a ship out there. It's hull metal was like that of the one that had intercepted us at Masada – a modern Polity attack ship – but its shape was wildly different. But that wasn't even my greatest concern. Now pushing myself away from the column, I tried to understand why that ship had not stopped one of the Guard ships from docking. But this became all too clear when sensors revealed the massive hardfield out there. Penny Royal was here.

'What happened?' asked Trent, releasing the skein of optics to which he had been clinging.

Through station internal cams, I watched the steady, violent progress of the business end of a war dock spearing straight towards us. I considered telling him we were about to die, but found I didn't actually believe that. I guessed that was exactly how Sverl felt – right up to the moment the enzyme acid started dissolving his body.

'King's Guard are on their way in,' I said.

Trent retrieved his weapon. It had come to rest against the pile of dried-out organic detritus sticking Sverl's ceramal skeleton to the floor. Should we run? I wondered, as I felt the vibration through the floor of that approaching war dock. I reached over and plucked the spine from where I'd stabbed it down into the floor. I'd rammed it in there when the attack on the station began throwing us about. Though separated from direct contact by my suit gloves, I felt a high-pitched, almost gleeful vibration from the thing. Meanwhile a second-child shot in through the entrance, shortly followed by another – then a whole horde of them climbing over each other in their hurry to get inside. I watched them milling about around Sverl's remains and the two first-children, who still had not moved. How the attack on the station had not thrown them about soon became evident, when Bsectil tore his armoured feet out of the floor.

'Bsorol?' I enquired.

The other first-child also pulled its feet out of the floor and turned partially in my direction. He looked utterly weary and defeated. 'Yes.'

'Perhaps we should get out of here?' I suggested.

'We have nowhere to run,' Bsorol replied. 'This is as good a place to die as any.'

I hadn't been paying attention to cam data, or to the vibration I had been feeling through my feet. The latter had stopped, while the former showed armoured prador spilling from the end of the open war dock. They were quickly moving through the disrupted volume of the station around this autofactory, to surround us. Still, there was a chance two humans could get out . . .

'What do we do?' asked Trent, looking decidedly nervous.

The vibration I felt through my hands now turned into a strange screeing in my aug. I saw Bsorol abruptly whirl round, and I turned slightly to face in the same direction. When I auged through, spreading the reach of my consciousness through the station, readings were odd. AIs that had previously been reinstating their sensors were now cutting sensor links or otherwise tuning down their output – hiding. A shadow was approaching rapidly too. The screeing in my aug ramped up, finally terminating with a shudder I felt through my feet. A black diamond threw itself into existence from an infinite distance, materializing just behind Sverl's skeleton, and I turned to face it.

'Hello Penny Royal,' I said, expecting no answer and getting none.

In a swirling pattern around this gem, matter began crystallizing out of vacuum. It was transparent at first and then darkened, each piece growing into a blade and moving into a shoal. They then began to fall into the diamond's centre point, coagulating and growing, expanding into Penny Royal's sea urchin form. Once this was complete – seemingly signalled by it growing darker and somehow more real – it began to drift. The second-children in the room again scrambled over each other in their eagerness to put Bsorol and Bsectil between themselves and this thing.

Penny Royal finally came to a halt again over Sverl's skeleton, and thereafter just held stationary. A moment later, metal vapour and dust exploded in lines – scribing circles in the surrounding walls. Then blasts ensued, throwing those chunks of wall inwards. Through these came the King's Guard. They were armoured – their armour painted in bright primary colours, highlighting the colour patterns of prador carapaces. And all were the size of first-children. They didn't hesitate – immediately opening fire with particle cannons and Gatling guns. I dived for the floor and wrapped my arms about my head, expecting this fusillade to pick me up and tear me apart. The flashing of the guns and the glare of particle cannons continued, as static bloomed over my helmet radio and in my aug. My suit threw up a power failure message in my visor, internal helmet lights faded and went out, and suddenly I started to feel cold. I thought I'd been hit, but then the flashing slowly died and power returned to my suit – its heaters immediately kicking in. Finally, I dared to raise my head.

Bsorol, Bsectil and Sverl's second-children were still huddled in a group. In a neat circle all around them lay masses of Gatling slugs – some of them still glowing – while areas of the walls and ceiling were scored with particle cannon burns. Yet Sverl's children were unharmed. On the floor closer to Trent and me were drifts of Gatling slugs too. I moved to my hands and knees and stood, just in time to witness one of the Guard open fire again. Immediately a hardfield appeared around Sverl's children, while a second smaller field encompassed Trent and me. Some slugs ricocheted off while the bulk of them, losing their energy by direct impact with the field, just dropped to the floor. After a moment that guard lowered his weapon, shrugged in a very human manner, then moved aside to allow in another much larger version of his kind.

This was the admiral – I recognized the patterning on his armour – but he was much bigger than I'd thought. He was the size of a prador adult, but who could say whether or not he actually was one? He stood there observing the scene for a long moment, then tipped up to focus completely on Penny Royal. I picked up the clattering and bubbling of prador language in my aug, quickly routed it through a translation program and set it running again from the beginning.

'You cannot kill them,' said one, who I presumed to be Penny Royal.

'I can see that,' replied the admiral.

'Take physical proof and leave.'

By the time I'd caught up, the admiral had waved one of the other prador forward. This one moved over to Sverl's skeleton and dipped down beside it, while keeping two armoured palp eyes focused on Penny Royal. With one sweep of its claw, it scraped up a pile of Sverl's organic remains. It then moved forwards over these, a hatch opening in its underside, and lowered manipulatory limbs sheathed in a monomer. In one of its hands, it held a large glassy sphere, which it separated in two. It filled this with the remains and closed it, before withdrawing it inside its armour and closing that hatch. Next, it reached out to Sverl's skeleton, closed a claw around one ceramal rib and rocked it, breaking the scab of Sverl's remains sticking it to the floor. I felt almost offended by this, and it seemed Penny Royal did too.

A silvery tentacle lashed out, almost too fast to see. The guard stumbled back, half dragging the skeleton with it, then letting go. The legs of Sverl's skeleton gave way on that side and it collapsed onto them, lying tilted now on those organic remains.

'The skeleton stays,' said Penny Royal.

'It would make my evidence complete,' said the admiral.

'Leave now,' Penny Royal replied, and then added, 'Remain here too long and your other prey will flee.'

'Cvorn – yes, we have his location,' said the admiral, 'but still . . .' There appeared to be a lot of nervous shuffling amidst these prador, but the admiral was steadfast. 'This isn't logical.'

Penny Royal had had enough by then. I saw hardfield spheres snapping into existence all about the invading prador. As this happened, my suit flashed its warning and again I felt cold – perhaps some sort of energy drain. Gatling cannons, ammunition feeds and boxes fell in neatly chopped up pieces. Particle cannons too – internal components shattering like safety glass. Chunks of armour fell next, in shiny excised flakes, as the Guard went into panicked retreat. Only the admiral held his ground, even as hardfields whittled away at his armour and threatened to expose him to vacuum. Then he ponderously turned and headed away.

'I guess *you* don't have to be logical,' was his parting shot.

Finally all the Guard were gone. I saw them returning to their war dock through various sensors, then it began to withdraw into their ship. Their next target, I assumed, would be Cvorn and his ST dreadnought. On some level I would have liked to have seen that, but other more complicated concerns were occupying my mind right then.

'Why are we still alive?' asked Trent.

'Interesting question,' I replied, and walked over towards Penny Royal. Even as I did this, the AI dropped down to one side of Sverl's skeleton and started moving towards me. Trent, who had followed me, quickly stepped aside. But I stubbornly stood facing the thing. With a small shrug, it diverted round me and slid out through the door. I turned and followed, though whether the impulse to do so was my own I had no idea. I clutched the spine tight, I don't know why.

I followed the AI through a series of corridors and out to where the structure of the station had been deformed almost into something organic. As I finally stepped out on a metal platform, on the edge of a steel jungle, I realized that none of the others was with me. I guessed that their impulse to stay had not been their own either. Penny Royal moved out into this area and I propelled myself after. At length it arrived at the pill-shaped structure that contained, or had contained, the Factory Station Room 101 AI. There Penny Royal's spines blurred and, spraying shattered metal all around, it simply bored straight through the wall to the inside. Batting aside that same debris, I followed it inside, pushed myself from a sharp edge down to the floor, and looked around.

Broken machinery was strewn round the place: Golem torn open, robots delimbed, columns of computer hardware gutted. There had been quite a fight in here. Penny Royal hovered beside the splayed ends of a crystal clamp. A skeletal metal container was secured here, in which glinted a few fragments of AI crystal. Other fragments of crystal were scattered on the floor and still others hung in vacuum – slowly drifting as they had been doing for perhaps as much as a century. I moved forwards, now noting that some robots nearby remained undamaged. From these, optic cables snaked in to disappear into a black glass dais below the clamp. I assumed these were robots once directly controlled by the Room 101 AI. The optic cable linkage must have been to prevent them being taken over by any of the attackers.

Moving closer, I looked at a single robot poised over the remains of the Room 101 AI. Even to my eyes, it didn't look normal. The thing stood on two heron legs like the others here, but the upper section – a cylinder ringed with multiple arms – was missing. A gun had been mounted in this area instead – a simple belt-fed machine gun with a single barrel, which pointed down at the AI case. I guessed the precaution of forging those optic linkages hadn't worked, and turned to look up at Penny Royal.

The black AI had now extended silvery tentacles and was stirring the floating chunks of crystal into a revolving pattern. It batted one of them towards me and, releasing my hold on the spine, I reached up and caught the thing.

'Great idea to give a factory station AI the empathy and conscience of a human mother – so it'll be sure to look after all its children.'

The mantis war drone spoke straight out of Riss's memories, but the tsunami of further memory washed it away. In the memories of Penny Royal's victims, I had experienced grief. I'd felt the loss of kin and friends, of fortunes and dreams, and I'd felt the tearing physical pain of a mother losing a child. But this was a thousand times worse. As it tore through me, I knew that had I been thoroughly and ordinarily human, it would have turned me to ash. And I found that mentally I could step back from it – even as I tore my feet from the floor and curled foetally around the pain.

The Room 101 AI was not one of the first factory stations AIs made during the war. It was a later evolution, an amalgam of survivor minds. These were harvested from war drones, Golem, ship intelligences and human memcordings – before being inserted into one package. Some of those minds had been survivors precisely because of manufacturing faults caused by the fast production of AI crystal, which would have made them unsuited to peacetime. Some had psychoses, and some thought in ways for which no description existed in human language. The overall intelligence, also incorporating a facsimile of human emotion, was supposed to be a synergistic product of these parts. It was supposed to select the best traits for its task and incorporate them. It didn't – it incorporated everything, and was unstable right from the start. Earth Central did not replace the AI because it calculated that, under wartime conditions, the drawbacks of doing so outweighed the gains. The AI did its job and did it well – so correcting that mistake could wait for another time.

The grief it felt when each of its children was destroyed motivated it to make the next ones better, more rugged, more able to survive. The hatred it felt for the prador motivated it to create weapons of increasing lethality. This was just as it should be and was the whole point of incorporating that facsimile of human emotion. Using the survivor templates in its mind, it produced some very successful AIs. And, though its failure rate in producing viable offspring was high, it was still acceptable. Then the prador attack changed things.

In response, Room 101 had to produce its children at an ever-increasing rate. It was constrained by circumstances too, so they were not the best it could make. Over a period of just a few days, it produced thousands of these and spewed them straight out into destruction. Worse than this was the fact that it had no time or resources to adjust their crystals – to wipe them of feelings. And so they died, sometimes screaming, sometimes just puzzled, all in close proximity to the AI because it was perforce commanding them. This created a feedback loop, as its children's emotions flooded through the parent mind. An amplifier whine steadily racked up into a scream. Grief began to cripple the AI and its hate turned inwards.

'Yeah,' said the mantis, mandibles grinding. '*The Room 101 AI has gone nuts, it's barking, it fell out of the silly tree and hit every branch on the way down.*'

Post-partum depression? A psychotic break? I don't know. The war factory AI escaped the prador and then turned on its children. Its logic was self-referencing and insane, as insane as the AI itself had become. If its children were dead already then they could never suffer and never die. But, during a brief change near the end – maybe a glimmer of sanity, maybe not – the AI made a decision. It had one of its most trusted robots alter one of its kind, and it turned the thing against itself. Room 101 had, in human terms, blown its own brains out.

I unfolded, my body aching in response to being so tightly locked, and the inside of my skull felt raw. A jet from my wrist impeller put my feet back on the floor and I walked over and picked up the spine. I'd flung it away as the memory hit me and it had ended up stuck point down in the floor. After a moment, I looked up at Penny Royal.

'What do you want from me?'

'I want you to understand perfectly,' the AI replied.

It took me a moment to recover from actually receiving a reply from the thing.

'You want me to understand you perfectly,' I said, 'so you manoeuvred me here so I could learn about your insane creator . . . your insane *mother*? Are you a poor abused child I must forgive?'

'The facts are plain,' Penny Royal stated.

'I still don't know what you want,' I said.

'We have returned to my beginning, and now we must return to yours.'

I can't remember what I screamed at the AI as it folded up like black origami and collapsed. Just the gem remained, briefly, before turning away like some hard insect eye and disappearing into non-existence.

The Brockle

The terms of the Brockle's confinement had been quite simple. It was to remain aboard the *Tyburn* until such a time as it was deemed fit to return to Polity AI society. Assessments to this end occurred once a decade. Meanwhile, it would provide full reports on those sent to it for interrogation, under death sentence. It could also execute that sentence as it saw fit. Otherwise, it was to obey its instructions to the letter. The Brockle had chafed under the restrictions but fully understood that its situation was not so bad, considering its past excesses. This was because, in the end, it had become very useful to the Polity. Few other forensic AIs possessed the same kind of insight it possessed and few of them knew the right questions to ask of the criminal mind, especially the human ones. Of course, Earth Central and other Polity AIs put the Brockle's greater understanding of criminality down to it being of the same kind.

They didn't understand.

And now, with the essence of Ikbal and Martina contained inside it while their remains floated in a bloody cloud in the interrogation room, it had breached its terms. In respect of these two, it had disobeyed a direct order. It had also, under Polity law, committed murder. And now it was finally about to escape confinement itself.

In the human shape of a large and obese man – a favoured form from its past existence – the Brockle smiled sadly as it strolled out onto the platform of its dock. It had prevented Earth Central taking control of the latest arriving single-ship, by quickly reabsorbing the submind that had piloted it. Now the ship was back here in the dock, with another prisoner aboard for interrogation. Somewhat impatiently, the Brockle scanned the man's record, and a microsecond later was already bored. Here was another separatist from Cheyne III, guilty of four murders in his past and recently guilty of releasing a bio-agent into a swimming pool complex and killing twenty more people. Monitors arrested him when a simple sniffer had detected the bio-agent on his clothing as he attempted to leave Cheyne III. They'd interrogated him with a cut aug for a rough outline of his associations and to confirm the extent of his crimes. A judicial sub-AI had sentenced him to death, then sent him here so the Brockle could obtain all the details before executing sentence.

But the Brockle was no longer interested. The Brockle had ceased to be interested the moment it began interrogating Trent Sobel – and began to learn of the sheer extent and intricacy of the AI Penny Royal's manipulations.

Walking over to the edge of the platform, the Brockle halted, folded its arms and gazed at the single-ship. Meanwhile, it checked its firm link to the one unit of its body it would be leaving behind. The thing was now running at full capacity, still connected to the U-space transmitter. It had also taken full control of the *Tyburn*'s twinned U-space engine. Those engines could not be more ready, and the Brockle had programmed the unit to accept and indeed relish its sacrifice.

After a moment, a door etched itself out in the side of the craft and folded down into a ramp. The convicted man, one Norris Piper, stepped onto the ramp and casually walked down.

He gave the Brockle a brief inspection, then put his hands on his hips and studied his surroundings. Obviously, he was one of those who liked admirers to describe him as a 'cool one', and shortly he would say something tough and dismissive.

'So,' he said, 'I take it you're my executioner.' He eyed the Brockle's girth and added, 'I guess the job as a restaurant critic didn't work out.'

In other circumstances, the Brockle would have immensely enjoyed the interrogation of Norris Piper. It would have toyed with the limits of his endurance, allowing him to believe he was capable of resisting. It would have revelled in his begging and crying, the terror and agony of feeling as it took his mind and body apart. It would have relished his relief when it seemed that it was coming to an end, and then his horrified disbelief when it put him back together and started again. Now the forensic AI had no time for this, because a bigger and more intricate game was afoot, and a greater threat to the Polity existed than Piper could ever be.

It paced forwards, noting Piper laughably adjusting his stance and preparing to fight. Holding one pudgy hand out flat, the forensic AI extruded one of its body units – a growing, silvery, globular mass. It tossed this ball towards Piper but, as it arced over, the man threw himself off the side of the ramp into a perfect roll, coming up onto his feet again. The unit turned at a right angle in mid-air and slapped into his chest just as he came upright. There, it broke into a dozen sub-unit worms and burrowed. Piper gaped and began shuddering, his body deforming in ways it just shouldn't, then he howled. Blood and minced flesh exploded from his mouth and ears. His eyes sucked inwards with a thwacking sound and silver worms wiggled from the sockets. He gagged and toppled, hitting the floor like a bag of jelly – everything inside his skin broken down into nothing larger than a fingertip. By that time, the Brockle had reached the top of the ramp, where it paused to look back. The dozen original worms flowed across the floor, melded into one single worm by the time they reached the ramp, squirmed up a leg and entered the Brockle's mouth.

Gone.

The Brockle turned and entered the single-ship, mentally linked to its controls and prepared it for departure. Behind, when the Brockle entire was gone, its sacrificial unit would drop the *Tyburn* into U-space and take the ship just outside the Polity. Its designated arrival point was a region scattered with Polity spy satellites – marking a route around the Graveyard that the prador might try – so they would quickly detect it. The Polity would dispatch warships and, after a brief battle, they would destroy the *Tyburn*. That, as far as Earth Central was concerned, would be the end of the Brockle. However, in reality its first port of call was the nearest: outlink station Par Avion. There it would obtain a better ship so it could hunt down that dangerous and murderous AI, Penny Royal.

Such monsters should not be allowed to exist in the Polity.